BAGHDAD HEIST

A Charlie Glass Thriller

J.J. Carson

DEDICATION

To the wee bundle at the foot of the bed.

"The most degrading of human passions is the fear of death."

- Gertrude Bell

PROLOGUE

As the clouds of war loomed over Iraq, leading scholars of archaeology, art, and history warned the authorities in Washington D.C. of the risks posed to treasured artifacts displayed in Baghdad's Iraq Museum. Despite these warnings, US troops protected the Oil Ministry instead. First estimates reported the subsequent looting of over one hundred thousand precious pieces. Locals called it the second coming of Genghis Khan. Faced with world condemnation, a small band of resolute investigators came together to track down and secure the safe return of these stolen artifacts.

CHAPTER 1

Rural Virginia, 1995

Charlie sent thoughts of killing Old Roger to the back of her mind.

For now, she concentrated on his capture.

Sixteen-year-old Charlotte Glass lay on a weathered crag, warmed by the long, sun-drenched day. A blonde, home-cut bob framed a pretty face, blossoming with bronzed freckles, indicators of time well spent in the glow of an endless summer. She was in her favorite spot, shoeless and carefree. Eyes of the deepest blue stared into the darkest recesses of the meandering waters below. There lay the plumpest brown trout in the river, Old Roger, in his usual spot, taunting and tempting her. She studiously applied her favored fly, the black butcher, then carefully cast upstream. Charlie's fidgeting fingers mended the line, centering the feathery snare on the perfect course. Tensions rose as the nymph danced around the margins of the surface. Charlie fought the urge to fidget with line, rod, and reel; preferring, for once, to allow nature to take its course. Passions ran deep as the lure slipped below the surface into the settling waters.

Moments of truth, her father called them.

She waited with baited line, nerves jittering, as the butcher drifted ever closer to the wily old trout.

Patience. Patience.

Suddenly, a stumbling hulk bludgeoned through her line of sight. Losing balance, rod, and temper, her father toppled headlong into the river before her. After much flailing, he regained his footing. A mutton-chop grin and a thunderous "Tadah!" followed immediately thereafter. Charlie sat, laughing and speechless. From the serene to the ridiculous. The merriment continued during the frenetic fumbling for rod and reel. With frothy river foam drenching her dad's bushy mustache, he gave the perfect impression of a drunken walrus scrabbling for a submerged ball. Success came slowly and noisily. Eventually, he honked and splashed his way back to the bank, his rod held high for balance and in celebration.

The performance was over.

Old Roger remained at large.

Once beached, Pop playfully chased his daughter down, his sodden frame looming large. Shrieks and growls rang through breezy leaves as his bear hug enveloped her. His cloudy gray eyes watched down from above. She was home. It had never felt so good, nor smelled so bad. They loved their place in each other's lives. She was the son her father had always wanted but never had. He was the father she'd always wanted and always had. The pair shared a soppy moment. The smell of wet tweeds ripened in the sun.

"We'll get him next time," her father promised.

Preferring the thrill of the chase more than the glory of success, Charlie smiled. "I doubt that very much, Pop." Charlie squinted. "What's that?" A glistening crevice between a nearby boulder caught her eye. She narrowed both gaze and brow but could produce no definitive answer. Her bond with her father broke when she raced to investigate. Never one to spoil her fun or curtail her adventures, Pop let her go.

Down at the rock face, almost obscured, Charlie made out the form of a mottled bauble. She flicked and picked at the object, but her fingers were too weak to pry the item from nature's grasp. When it shifted, her heart jolted. *Treasure.* She darted to her wicker tackle box and tugged its distressed leather strap through a tarnished buckle. The vintage lid opened with a dried creak.

"Scissors? Scissors? Scissors? Aha!"

In a flash, she returned to the site and started digging like a crazed Klondiker. Midway through the frenzied attack, the mystery object broke free and skittered off down the rock face. Charlie followed in hot pursuit. A desperate lunge led to its capture.

Perplexed Pop looked on. Although, soaked and shivering, his head shook more. His incredulous, admiring smile widened with every breath. Charlie pulled the trinket close and squinted in the sunlight. Mild disappointment washed over her. It looked to be an old black bauble with a buckled shank. It wasn't the magical treasure she'd hoped, but it seemed worthy of a place in her secret trinket box. She gripped it between thumb and middle finger, squatted down by the side of the stream, and washed her new totem in the fresh water. She handed over her talisman with equal amounts of pomp and pride.

"What do you think?"

Pop twisted his face to prepare for the disdain that would surely follow.

"Not much—" His face stiffened. His elbow bent and straightened, bringing the piece closer, then further away, as he sought the perfect distance to bring it into focus. A flicker of intrigue escaped the corner of Pop's eye as he fumbled under the flap of his breast pocket. As part of the inspection process, he retrieved and donned his wire-rimmed spectacles.

Charlie bounced from one foot to the other, many times over. "What is it?" she inquired.

"Old brass. It's probably nothing. Patience."

Charlie beamed, impressed that her find had induced such excitement in her reserved father. "Don't you always say patience is a card game?"

Pop rasped the button across his tousled tweeds. Even through the stubborn tarnish, the button told tales.

"What do you see?

"An eagle with spread wings and a shield on its chest. Intricate, almost imperial."

Pop turned the item over and cast his eyes around the bent shank at the back of the button. In frustration at not being able to read the lettering, he reluctantly handed Charlie the button with an accompanying humph.

"What does that say?"

It was now Pop's turn to bob from foot to foot. Charlie lifted the piece to her bright eyes and slowly twisted the angle of the button to bring the wording into focus. She vocalized each letter as they slowly came into view.

"W-A-T-E-R-B-U-R-Y."

Pop blurted. "Manufacturing? Does it say Scoville?"

"Hang on."

She lifted her head in puzzlement. "Scoville Manufacturing. Waterbury."

"Wahooooo!" With a childish yelp, Pop snatched the button back. "Do you know what this is?"

Charlie rolled a sarcastic eye. "Duh, a button?"

"A Civil War button, from a Union General. Scoville made all their buttons."

Charlie threw out a skeptical glare. "How could you possibly know all this?"

"A lifetime of studying and teaching the Civil War." Pop's time as a custodian within the Smithsonian allowed him unprecedented access to the array of artifacts held within its museums and archives.

The scrubbing intensified. "Have you seen one of these before?"

"No. But I've heard of them. Who hasn't?"

"Er, every other person in the world?"

Pop ignored the jibe, too distracted by the new find. He surveyed the scene. "It must have fallen here as they drove the ford. They skirmished around these parts for most of the war. It would have been a great place to set up camp. Easily defended, multiple escape routes and difficult to find. Grant came this way during the Battle of the Wilderness. It could be his."

"Battle of the Wilderness?"

"The first battle of the 1864 Virginia Overland Campaign. Goodness, do they not teach you anything at that school of yours?"

Even at her young age, Charlie had already inherited her father's skeptical streak. He had taught her well. "Aren't you getting carried away?

They laughed at the tenuous possibilities as Pop lifted the glinting button into view. "This deserves to be in the museum."

Charlie playfully snatched the button back. "You deserve to be in a museum." She seized a spare spool of fly line from the confines of her wicker basket. She neatly and quickly cut the dark line to the exact length. A sheet knot ensnared the shank of the button with seamless efficiency. Pop gawked in questioning disbelief when Charlie threw the fresh loop around her neck.

Under Pop's incredulous gaze, Charlie explained the rationale: "If I find out it's genuine, you will weasel me 'round to giving it away, and I'll probably never wear it. If it's not real, I will be sad. It's best that I don't know."

"The biggest lies in our lives are the ones we tell ourselves," Pop protested.

"Who said that?"

"I did."

Pop seemed transfixed by the button, but the look on Charlie's face amplified her determination. With a smirk and a shrug, she threw the trinket down the front of her shirt. Pop tossed his palms open in resignation. "Okay, you win. I am heading back up to the cabin. I am starting to stink."

"*Starting* to stink?" laughed Charlie.

Her father offered a loving nod and moved to drag her close. Charlie broke free and darted on ahead.

"Race you!"

Excited yelps clattered through the leafy enclave as Charlie made her escape. Pop trudged off through the undergrowth, well off the pace. Thorny briars snared his tangled breeches, as if reluctant to let him go. Crashes and curses accompanied his undignified retreat as he plowed an alternative furrow through the snaggy brushwood. By the time he had loosened his breeches from one overly clingy briar, Charlie had long disappeared.

Back at the log cabin, Charlie bounded into her room, slamming the latched door behind her. Dropping to her tiny knees, she pulled back the threadbare rug before tussling with a loose floorboard. After yanking the tired lumber to one side, she retrieved a dilapidated cigar box. Despite its small size, the box looked lived in. With impressive ceremony, she laid the talisman inside the box alongside all the mementos from a life yet to be lived; a faded photograph of her departed mother, letters from a friend, postcards from afar, seashells, trinkets, and findings from adventures gone by. The burnished button took its place within her memory chest.

At that moment, Charlie did not realize: one day, that little trinket would save her life.

CHAPTER 2

Paris, 2005

Charlie tied on a flame-red headscarf, drew in the belt of her charcoal raincoat, and spun for the door. Tall and athletic, she lingered before the mirror long enough to check the view but not long enough to admire it. Stooping under a crooked doorframe, she exited the bijoux garret, high in the rooftops of the Latin Quarter. Arrondissement, street, building, and studio had all seen better days—not that she cared.

The rear doorway opened directly onto a narrow backstreet with high claustrophobic walls that leaned in menacingly. She pulled the raincoat's hood over her head in defiance of the day, then ventured out into a sullen morning. As she crossed the Pont des Arts, the countless padlocks of love adorning the bridge's railings went unnoticed. Sideswiping the Louvre, she joined the throng that filled the gardens of the Tuileries. Tourists bustled as Parisians hustled. Upon entering the Place Vendome, a half-excuse for a rainbow struggled to pluck up enough courage to climb out from behind a large, lead-lined cloud. Toe tips negotiated the wet cobbles that pointed straight to the Ritz.

Swirling in through the revolving door, she lost her headscarf and raincoat in one sweeping motion. The little black dress and clutch bag said, *Trying, but not too hard. Trying, but not for you.* Spinning into an intoxicating hall of gleaming crystal, blossoming fragrant lilies, and golden mirrors, Charlie shone amongst the afternoon glitterati. Only she knew her entire ensemble was thrift-store chic.

Loud, invasive Americans prowled and preyed around the Ritz's hunting-themed Hemingway Bar. She never cared for the undertones or the overtures. Instead, opulent solitude awaited in the calm, unrushed atmosphere of the Salon Proust. She did most things by herself but only one thing for herself. Oysters at the Ritz, immersed in velvet, velour, marble, and mahogany. A legion of well-drilled attendants stood on parade; their braided uniforms as starched as the atmosphere. Gustav, the restaurant's immaculate Maître d', commandeered the greeting by cutting in front of a pretty, well-intentioned young hostess. When his head bowed in practiced reverence, his hair flounced in unison. He threw out a wafer-thin, caddish smile.

"Welcome back, mademoiselle."

With a click of his fingers, a cohort of eager attendants extravagantly rearranged a nearby table. Taking the offered seat, Charlie's face revealed trace elements of both embarrassment and enjoyment. The ceremonial handing over of the oversized menu was a mandatory precursor. Delicate, mouthwatering fragrances wafted in from neighboring booths.

In time-honored fashion, the Maître d' inquired about her health and confirmed the availability of her favored choices with unsettling accuracy.

"We have fresh Breton oysters paired with a majestically simple shallot and vinegar sauce? Arrived this morning from the Gulf of Morbihan—small, sweet, and perfectly formed."

Charlie nodded past the less than subtle double entendre. Gustav continued forward. "Let me guess. Vodka Martini, parched, Belvedere, straight up, two olives?"

Charlie beamed and handed back the menu. "Why do we even bother with this?"

With an overpowering air of self-satisfaction, Gustav presented a game face, turned on his Cuban heels, and set to work. Charlie had an uneasy admiration for the Maître d'.

How could he remember so much? Was he that professional or lecherous?

As with most things in life, she deduced that the truth lurked somewhere in the middle.

With military precision, the maneuvers continued as the vanguard delivered a crisp, clean vodka Martini, to specification. Reinforcements brought six oysters along with an arsenal of accouterments. Charlie sat back in the studded scarlet chair and brushed the grainy tactile velvet. Taking a long breath, she surveyed the scene, composed deep thoughts, and then reached for the ice-cold Martini. While savoring mouthfuls and moments, time ticked by.

The oysters arrived with aplomb Fresh, iced, succulent, cultured. She studied, dressed, and enjoyed every oyster over a protracted and contemplative period. After a few mouthfuls of blissful rumination, Charlie reached into the neckline of her fitted dress and retrieved her brightly polished talisman.

She freed the bronzed button from the necklace, examined it, then placed it in the space in front of her. As she stared at the little bauble, memories flooded back to simpler times. A loving father, a gentle stream, a summer breeze. *Were those days gone forever?* She hoped not.

After a few contemplative moments, she gripped the buckle shank, angled her wrist, and flicked the button like a spinning top. The lopsided trinket landed drunkenly on the bleached cotton tablecloth.

It sat there, taunting her. There were decisions to make, and this was designed to help. *It wasn't helping.*

After a lengthy minute, she repeated the process. This time, the button made a break for freedom, skidding off the table, and disappeared into the camouflage of the ornate floral carpeting. No sooner had panic set in than a tall stranger leered into view. He presented the retrieved button with calm poise. From his designer gelled quiff right down to his toggled moccasins, everything about the man screamed lothario. Ocean-green eyes washed over her. His facial architecture showed heavy Greek influences. The pearlescent grin would have been comical if it hadn't been so perfect.

"May I?" Before she could raise an objection, the uninvited guest had reserved himself a seat at the table. Charlie accepted the offered handshake, with a facial expression that landed well short of friendly. A silver fleur-de-lis cufflink flashed from underneath the sleeve of a well-cut suit. She didn't know the acceptable level of jewelry for a man, but this guy had exceeded his allowance. "Miroslav. My friends call me Milo. At your service."

Gratitude encouraged Charlie to welcome her guest, albeit with tepid grace. "Thank you so much. Where did you appear from, Miroslav?"

"Please, call me Milo. I was sitting at the next table. Did you not notice?" The rising intonation showed the man was not used to going unseen. Charlie could not place the accent, its sound a liquidized, multi-cultural soup. On another day, it may have been fun discovering all the ingredients, but today, such conversations were off the menu. The Manhattan cocktail placed on the table signified Miroslav's intention to stay longer. His presumptions were quickly becoming Charlie's annoyances. The interview continued.

"So, oysters? You know what they say about oysters?"

Charlie baulked at the innuendo. "If you find a bad one, it will turn your stomach?"

Milo nodded, suitably admonished. "So, what brings you to Paris?"

"I live here."

"Yes, but you weren't born here. Your accent—American?"

Charlie wasn't playing. "How astute."

"And do you like Paris?"

A cold front moved in from the west. "I love the anonymity and solitude."

The stranger pressed on, unimpeded. "What do you do here in Paris?"

"I work in the art business."

"An art gallery?

"Not quite. The Sorbonne."

"Wow."

Charlie bristled at the man's over-the-top amazement. He seemed the type to throw out a *wow*, irrespective of the answer provided. "It's not very glamorous. I help the Arabic Studies team track and trace artifacts." She didn't appreciate being goaded into disclosure. Although a proud member of the FBI Art Crimes team on secondment, protocols—and a lack of interest in the current dialogue—ensured that fact remained a secret.

"Interesting."

Charlie stiffened, in the presence of yet more fake amazement. Deeming the man to be charmless but harmless, she indulged him further. "It's far from exciting. I sit around all day, deciphering the authenticity of ancient etchings."

"Not just a pretty face."

Charlie couldn't disguise her cringe. Just as she was about to close the conversation, Milo recovered lost ground. "Cuneiforms?"

Charlie flickered and tilted towards her new tablemate. "You know about cuneiforms?"

The stranger struck a chord but could not chime in further. "Only to know they are little clay tablets thousands of years old."

Charlie's tone brightened. "Well, that's more than most."

"So, why Paris?"

"Paris auctions are crammed with looted artifacts."

"Looted from where?"

"Iraq."

"Yes, what a terrible business."

Under a cloud of contemplation, they both seemed lost for words. Libations filled the interval. Although pleased to have recovered the talisman, Charlie wanted to regain her independence. "I am thankful for your help, and I don't want to seem ungrateful. However, I am in the middle of something—"

Miroslav deployed more offensive charm. "Intriguing. What might that be?"

Charlie raised her cultivated eyebrows. "I am taking the day for myself. I have decisions to make. Well, one decision."

"If you do not mind me asking, what decision?

"Would it make a difference if I did mind?"

"Of course. But surely, a little healthy interest never hurt anyone."

Charlie minded but saw no benefit in raising the stakes. "I could be moving."

"What does your husband say?"

"Wow." Charlie added misogyny to the man's colorless list of character flaws. "There is only me, and I fully intend to keep it that way." Her declaration came without hesitation, as if she had been subconsciously practicing the phrase for years.

Miroslav's head bowed, fully censored and partially crestfallen. "I apologize."

Charlie softened her edge. “Don’t worry. I know what I am doing,” she lied.

Replying with an air of quotation, Miroslav presented a different persona. “‘Never fear quarrels; seek hazardous adventures.’”

Charlie sensed a more genuine facade. “Wise words.”

Miroslav lifted his manicured hands in defense. “Wise words, yes, but they are not mine. Alexandre Dumas, *The Three Musketeers*.”

Charlie smiled and lifted her Martini glass high between their eyeline. “Un pour tous. Tous pour un!”

Charlie emptied the glass with aplomb. Her drinking partner merely sipped his cocktail. Without seeking permission, he called to a passing server. “La meme chose, D’Artagnan!” The server’s smile and change of direction told Charlie that a second Martini would soon appear. She felt no need to change course. Never one to crave or condone companionship, she always considered herself to be two Martinis shy of a people person. A pleasant lull in conversation ensued before Miroslav ruined the moment by picking up Charlie’s talisman.

“What’s the story behind this?”

Charlie never told tales. “It’s an old friend.”

“Do you always throw your friends around the room?”

“Just the ones that annoy me by asking lots of questions.”

Miroslav scoffed too loudly for the quality of the jibe. He studied the piece with surprising reverence. “Eagles and arrows? Anything on the back?”

"It says, 'Scoville Manufacturing, Waterbury.' It's a Civil War button from the tunic of Ulysses S. Grant, himself. I found it on a fishing trip with my father up in the mountains of Virginia."

Miroslav seemed doubtful. "Has it been authenticated?"

Charlie didn't appreciate the entirely justified insinuation. "Yes, by a senior professor at the Smithsonian Institution." As she snatched back her totem, she omitted to divulge that the professor in question was her own father. The fact he had his own misgivings about the provenance also remained concealed. Miroslav's raised eyebrows did little to quantify his level of belief. Well-timed flamboyant gesturing redirected the ordered drink onto their table.

Without breaking eye contact or thanking the server, he pressed on. "What were you doing?"

"Merci." Charlie thanked the disappearing server before responding. "Deciding." The silence that followed seemed more awkward to Charlie than the unrequested interrogation. "Whenever I have a decision to make, I ask the button a question. I spin it, and if the button lands facing me, the answer is yes, it if faces away, the answer is no. I make all my big decisions that way."

"Ha! You don't look old enough to have made many life-changing decisions."

Charlie told herself not to get engaged. Only a bout of good manners elongated the conversation. "You'd be surprised" was all she could muster.

"So, how is that working out for you, miss?"

A mid-range gaze became the only response provided. The cross-examination continued. "You spun the button twice. Why?"

More strained silence ensued. The new Martini became the key feature. Charlie opened up after the intermission. She hoped that by closing off the questions, she could close down the intrusion. "I didn't like the answer, so I spun the button again."

"And if you don't mind me asking, what were your options?"

Charlie heard herself answer. "I need to decide if I should take on a new job or not."

Miroslav leaned in. "Well now, I am captivated. What is the assignment?"

Charlie leaned out. "For one so backward, you appear quite forward."

The next sips of Martini were more cordial. "They have asked me to go to Iraq."

"Baghdad?"

"You know the museum?"

Miroslav's colors kept unfurling. "Sorry, no. Baghdad's the only place I've ever heard of over there. I just guessed. What are they asking you to do?"

She kept her answer matter of fact. "To help the museum recover stolen artifacts. We will document the records; identify the lost items; and search for them through international auctions, galleries, private sales, and dealers."

Her companion tilted his head. "A hell of a move."

Charlie remained pensive. "I know. I've been nowhere. Paris was my first trip abroad. I used to think the Middle East was Ohio."

Another fake laugh followed. "How did you get the job?"

"Someone high in the organization recommended me."

"Quite the recommendation."

"Quite." Charlie sent her gaze across the restaurant. "I can't see why they recommended me."

"It's an enormous responsibility for someone so young. Of course, a gentleman would never ask a woman her age."

"How did you get here today? Time machine? I am twenty-six."

Charlie squirmed, irked by the intrusion but annoyed that she was opening up to a stranger. With only her father to confide in previously, she was unused to a dining booth-turned-psychiatrist's couch.

Miroslav was fishing, but Charlie wasn't biting, so he changed bait. "But you're going to say yes. The first throw of your button was a no, so you threw it again. That means you want to go. Am I right?"

A thoughtful silence ensued before Charlie offered a polite yet dismissive handshake. Things had gone far enough. "It was a pleasure meeting you. Thank you so much for returning my talisman."

Surprised that his rakish good looks had proved ineffectual, Miroslav resigned himself to his fate. "I am pleased to have been of service."

Charlie did her best to hide her delight at the prospect of the man's impending departure. "Enchanté." With a bow, he projected his movie star image and sidled back to his table, leaving her with a smile and a glass of ice that had once contained a Manhattan.

On reflection, Charlie realized she had been too dismissive, but that wasn't the issue. What concerned her was that he was right. Her mind was made. She cut the meditation short and called for l'addition. The server took great pride in informing her that the gentleman who had sat with her had paid the bill. Looking across to offer a nod of thanks, she found an empty table. Her mystery man had disappeared into the ether.

Gustav, the attentive Maître d', materialized and helped reassemble her ensemble. Upon her departure, he leaned his head to the side and gazed, as if they would never meet again. Cordial handshakes were exchanged. Outside, a fresh sun glinted off the wet cobbles. Charlie's aquamarine eyes squinted and blinked into the dazzling sunlight as she turned her face to the warming sky.

Things were looking up.

Next stop, D.C. via Luxemburg.

Rounding into the ornate archways on the Rue du Rivoli, Charlie bounded into the bustling, luxurious Café Angelina. She purchased two travel essentials—a Mont Blanc patisserie and a double espresso. They served her well as she meandered back across the Seine. The Jardin du Luxembourg was an oasis of refinement in the heart of Paris. She had all the time in the world, and she took it, stopping often to sip and nibble on the delights at hand. She found the quiet corner of the garden that housed a small replica of the Frédéric Bartholdi statue, Liberty Enlightening the World. In her infrequent and fleeting bouts of homesick melancholy, Charlie would turn to this lady for guidance. Today she chose the location and occasion to call her father and inform him of her decision. Under the watchful gaze of Lady Liberty, Charlie pulled her BlackBerry, then tapped her way to a connection. The phone rang out for an inordinate length of time. Calls to her father never lasted long. All the same, she found an empty garden bench, wiped away a few residual raindrops, and took her place. She needed to sit down for this one. Just as a sense of resigned anti-climax washed in, the line sprang to life.

"202-3353."

"Bonjour, Papa!"

"Charlie! How are you? I was just thinking about you."

"Glad to hear it."

They exchanged pleasantries, described circumstances, and forecasted weathers. Statuses were updated. It dawned on Charlie during the conversation that as her life continued in an upward maelstrom of achievement and challenge, the only thing that changed in Pop's life were the seasons. She didn't know if he preferred it that way or not. Eventually, she answered the questions that Pop did not have the courage to ask.

"Most of my mind is made up on the big question."

"Most of it?" Pop inquired.

"The rest of it lies a thousand miles away in D.C."

"I raised you to be the captain of your own ship. The decision is yours and yours alone."

She knew her beloved father was right, but on big decisions, she craved his approval. "You must have an opinion."

“I do, and I am keeping it to myself. Others cannot make decisions this big. It’s your life to live the way you want to live it. I told you that before you moved to Paris.”

“Baghdad isn’t Paris, Pop.” She was desperate, not for advice, permission, or approval, but for acceptance. She need not have worried.

“I understand, and so do you. When you were deciding on France, I asked you two questions, do you remember? One: what will it mean to you if you go? And two: what will it mean to you if you don’t go? The second question sealed it. Your fear of missing out was always much stronger than the fear of diving in.”

“Baghdad is one hell of a dive.”

Pop forced out a laugh.

“True, but I know you’re going in headfirst. You just don’t have the heart to tell your old man. Don’t worry; I’ll be with you every step of the way.”

Relief and anticipation washed over her in equal proportions. “Well then, you better buy yourself a flak jacket and a metal detector.” Pop’s laughter choked up the line in response to Charlie’s dark humor. Pop recomposed himself in double quick time and cut the call short, claiming he had to go to answer the front door, even though the doorbell had never rung. They exchanged love filled messages before signing off. When it came to parting words, luck never came into it.

The line clicked to a deafening silence.

They both understood.

Charlie was Iraq bound.

CHAPTER 3

Washington D.C.

The Federal Bureau of Investigation's Art Crime Team hid in one of a multitude of characterless buildings, sandwiched in and around the junction of Pennsylvania Avenue and E Street. Faceless staff, proudly displaying their photo IDs, milled in, out, and around a facade that made the building look like the world's biggest waffle iron. Charlie scanned her badge and pushed in through the heavy glass doors. Her standard issue graphite pencil suit gave little room to maneuver. Lifting her face to the CCTV, she joined the orderly line of pen pushers and trigger pullers, each one immaculately dressed for the job at hand. With all patrons fully versed in the technique of personal screening, the process passed smoothly. Exiting the security checks, she re-holstered her BlackBerry and strode to the elevator. Before she had time to read the notice detailing the floors and departments, a heavily set shadow enveloped her.

"Special Agent Glass?"

Charlie nodded.

"Senior Special Agent Mason Hancock—Hank to my friends and colleagues."

Charlie smiled.

Hank pointed to her ID and exacted a heavy handshake. "You do your photo justice."

Charlie offered a professional, polite greeting in response. She had been called beautiful her entire life, yet still she couldn't get used to it. Brindle bulldog eyes matched his bulbous jawline. It appeared that most of his mid-level FBI salary went to beard wax, tailoring, and steroids. The polished field agent look seemed alive and well in the Hancock household.

After a circuitous tour of inspection, Charlie was abandoned at the characterless cubicle that would be home for the duration of her training. Charlie sealed all thoughts of Iraq inside a mental envelope labeled, *To be opened later.* For now, she focused on the work at hand, gleaning every morsel of insight that could one day save her soul. At 1800 hours she received a march past salute from Hank. It was the closest thing to a highlight in an otherwise monotonous day. She had not been born to administer. She worked on for an hour before clicking her cubicle lamp into darkness and hoped for better days ahead.

In the weeks that followed, Hank crammed as much information on the mission as possible into the short time available. Charlie loved the highly energized itinerary. She liked Hank's company and found it easy to forgive his awkward macho posturing and boastful outbursts.

The facilities loomed large, and the training daunted her, yet she pushed on, determined to be avoid failure or embarrassment at all costs. The physical endurance classes were a breeze. History lessons covering eras all the way back to Mesopotamian times were extra-curricular. She threw her heart, soul, and mind into the work at hand.

On the last day of training, Charlie entered the office early. As usual, and right on time, Hank jogged by her cubicle, his face contorted into a half-grin, half-grimace. The unfeasibly large gym bag being lugged around looked a workout in and of itself. It seemed yet another demonstration of his exercise addiction. Charlie correctly guessed that a big gulp protein shake would make an appearance within the hour.

In the afternoons Hank cut short the high intensity briefing and dragged the class outdoors. A cloudless azure sky struggled to overpower the chilly wind, navigating its way up the Potomac. The pair walked and talked together. They lowered their shoulders and lifted their collars as they rounded onto the magnificent expanse of the National Mall. The wide boulevard that sprawled from the Capitol down to the Lincoln Memorial seemed packed with purposeful vitality. Crowds of tourists milled and spun with some place to go but no real clue how to get there. Self-important government officials crashed on from A to B with goals way too important to accommodate any form of deviation. All colors and forms of uniform provided an omnipresent air of protection. Eager students on a big day out swam in schools through the tide of humanity.

After buying hotdogs from a cart, Charlie and Hank grabbed a place amongst the haphazardly arranged bistro sets laid out around the street vendors. Hank politely pulled Charlie's chair around to his side of the little steel table. A minor incident with the mustard threatened to ruin the big moment, but swift napkin work by Charlie saved his blushes. Snorting and embarrassed,

Hank brought his broad shoulders across the gap between them. He extended his gaze straight ahead.

"Look at that."

Charlie tucked into her own mustard-smothered snack. "The Natural History Museum?" Like so many of the magnificent architectural treasures that lined the Mall, the building before them stood like a sentinel, guarding the public boulevard. Imposing and colonnaded, the building's white walls shone like a beacon in the bright afternoon glow.

"Have you ever been inside?"

Charlie's eyes rolled. "Have you read my file? My father is a professor at the Smithsonian. We didn't do movies; we did museums. I was never out of that place as a kid."

Hank was curious. "So, is that what led you to this?"

A pensive Charlie took time before answering. "Maybe. The vision had been to study in a faraway land, get functional in a foreign language. and land some classy job back in D.C. Pop always wanted a career with the FBI, and I guess there must have been a time when our visions blurred. He had a big part to play in this, but it's my story." Charlie's candidness surprised even herself.

"So, this is you striking out?"

"I wouldn't say 'striking out.' More like branching out."

"It's a big branch."

Hank's observation left a pensive Charlie speechless. He moved past her moment. "Is your father still working, still alive?"

"Just."

"Just? To which question?"

"Both. He works all the time, drinks like a Scot and smokes like a Cuban. I try to get him to stop, but he doesn't listen."

Hank seemed genuinely interested. "And what does he say about you and all this?"

"I think he likes the idea of allowing me to do my thing. He just doesn't like me being in danger. Neither do I, come to think of it. When I started out in art crimes, I was supposed to be investigating dodgy dealers flogging fake Jackson Pollocks."

"So, you just wandered into this? I don't believe you. There are two kinds of people out there. Those who were forced to come and those with something to prove. Which one are you?"

"I was duty bound to—"

"Sorry, Charlie. Respectfully, I'm calling bullshit. You could have backed out; this isn't a military operation."

Charlie knew he was right. "Well then, I guess I have something to prove."

"To whom?"

Charlie blinked through her blurted answer. "It's been me and Pop all my life—I guess I just want to make him proud."

"And what does your mother say?"

Charlie thought long and hard. "She died."

"Oh, I'm so sorry."

"Don't be. She was gone before I ever knew her."

For Charlie, the truth cut deep. She had no recollection of her mother, Molly. She was a dancer that had waltzed off long before Charlie's first birthday. As a daughter, Charlie had proved to be an inconvenience and an irrelevance. When asked about her mother's existence, Charlie would simply say she was dead. It wasn't a lie. It was an assumption. If pressed further, she would say she died in childbirth. That lie seemed less painful than the truth. After such a statement, no further details were ever sought. It seemed easier to have a loved one taken from you than to have had one decide to leave. It was her weak spot that no one knew about. The memory of her mother was seldom exhumed. If an exhumation was forced, no postmortem was ever carried out. Immediate reburials were always ordered. Pop never uttered the phrase, "Your mother would be proud." They both knew that would never be the case.

A blaring car horn brought her back to the present. "Sorry, I was miles away. I guess my Pop just worries because he's the single parent of an only child."

"Well, you're better off with a protective father than no father at all." The distant tone in Hank's voice told Charlie much more. Hank brought his thoughts back to the present. "Listen. Forget about freedom, democracy, hearts and minds, regime change. That's all just bullshit. We've screwed up over there and need to make amends." He pointed to the building ahead. "We need to build a world for Iraqis where they can take their children to places like that. They didn't have that under Saddam, but it's no better under us. Not yet anyhow. We have a job to do. You have a job to do."

Charlie stared into the distance and nodded; trepidation rippled her brow. The poignancy of the location for the alfresco snack-chat sank in along with the message. Hank placed a heavy, veiny hand on her forearm. "You won't know what has hit you until it's too late. Be vigilant."

Charlie exhaled at the unfolding revelations. "But the war is over."

"Says who—CNN? Surely, you're not that naïve. The place is a cesspit. Ideology is gone. The criminals and the extortionists have stolen it."

She chewed hard on her hotdog. She was finding it hard to follow. Hank sensed her unease. "It's not safe, but you can manage your risks."

"How?"

"Make your reports as detailed as you can, the people, the places, the timings, the facts. Remember, our guys are up to no good as well. Keep me up to speed. The more I know, the more I can help."

"There could be a lot of smoke screening over there."

"In what way?"

"People being obtuse, evasive, maybe even obstructive. You'll know it when you see it."

"And when I do?"

"Work around it."

"Go rogue?"

Hank didn't throw out the stop sign. "Trust no one."

"No One?"

"Trust only me. Do what you need to do."

"To survive?"

"To get the job done. Hopefully it won't get to more than that."

"Hopefully?"

"You know what I mean."

She didn't have a clue what he meant but didn't want to appear naive or afraid. "But you'll have my back?"

Hank smiled. "Of course. You're my number one priority."

"So, you'll be my father figure?"

"Easy! I'm not that old." The closeness Charlie felt towards Hank surprised her. Even though he would be thousands of miles and many time zones away, his words of support shored up her psyche. His heart was in the right place, even if it was boosted by too many health supplements. He was a man to be trusted. She would be grateful for his existence, if not his presence. His words ricocheted around her mind. *Trust only me.*

In the thoughtful moments that followed, Charlie fidgeted with the talisman. There were no thoughts. There was no need to spin the button. The tough decisions had been taken weeks before. Everything that needed to be said had been said. Facing a stiffening breeze, Hank called it a day.

"Let's get you out of here. These artifacts aren't going to save themselves."

As Hank cleaned up the napkins, wiped the table, and carried the trash to a nearby can, Charlie paused. *What did he mean by trust only me?*

Hank's words set a dark edge to the clouds forming around the mission.

CHAPTER 4

Dulles Airport, Virginia

Relentless, sideways rain helped push a grey minibus into a dimly lit corner of the otherwise busy airfield. Charlie stalled at the bus doorway and waited for a break in the deluge that never came. Resigned to her fate, she threw her rucksack over her head and made a break for the plane, Butch and Sundance style. The downpour only intensified as she hurtled up the stairway and through the plane's door. Regaining her composure, she clambered aboard as a deadhead on a rendition flight from Dulles to Baghdad. Even though these flights never officially existed, there she was, struggling on board with her oversized canvas kit bag. It seemed quite the carry-on. The stash of supplies being dragged into the main cabin was mere bagatelle compared to the battery of specialist equipment and survival gizmos that she had packed into hold baggage. Her bag's loose strap grappled every armrest as she jammed her way up the aisle of the plane. Judgment out the corner of the eye seemed to be the order of the day, as every passenger sized each other up.

Several curious species were on the passenger list. The nervous geek grinned and nodded at everyone as if his life depended on it. His timid fawn eyes lurked behind undersized rimless glasses. Over in their own world, a small squad of camouflaged combat junkies yacked past each other in a strange language that seemed to consist entirely of expletives and acronyms. *FUBAR*. An efficient-looking accountant sat in the back, auditing, and processing all before him. The word *shifty* sprang to her mind. A disinterested doctor and two chattering nurses sat in the middle of the plane in pristine military whites. Charlie assumed they would care for the passengers, who would reluctantly join them on the long flight back to destinations unknown.

The scariest passenger of all was the guy in a dark blue non-crushed linen suit. He sported slicked back salt and pepper hair and an expressionless granite jaw. She didn't know what his job was, but she assumed that at the end of his shift, people would be dead. He had the air of someone who loved his work and was good at it. She mused that there were two kinds of people who wear Aviator Ray-Bans indoors; pricks and guys who could kick your ass. The mystery man in 12F could almost certainly add his name to column two. To Charlie, the passengers resembled attendees of a bizarre murder mystery party. She took her allocated seat, equidistant from the other travelers on the sparsely populated, unmarked Boeing 737. Deploying all available strength and guile, she loaded her kit bag into the locker overhead. Scanning her perimeters during the process, she noticed everyone watching her struggle. No one helped. That was just the way she liked it. This would be no ordinary package holiday. As she placed her mission notes in the seat in front of her, the lustrous polish on her new all-terrain boots caught her eye. She wondered how long the shine would last.

The crew busied themselves. Manifests were triple checked, silent roll calls were completed, and clearances were given, all without the mention of a flight number. The elderly co-pilot rumbled out from the cockpit with the demeanor of someone who had been dragged kicking and screaming back out of retirement. The only thing Charlie appreciated about his disinterested safety briefing was its ending. Despite best efforts, her nerves jittered.

The waiting lasted an eternity. Tensions mounted, skies and moods darkened as the engines roared down the runway. As the plane listed up into the gunmetal gray clouds and tilted eastward, Charlie tracked the ground below. Leaving her world behind drew a flush of apprehension. She fidgeted with the underpowered, overhead ventilation. Nothing helped. As the clouds became blanked by nightfall, D.C. became a place in history.

The overnight flight passed without incident. Constant rehydration never seemed to help a dry mouth that induced bouts of nervous coughing. Her high level of anxiety meant rendered watching the in-flight movies impossible. Chasing her rubber food around a paper plate with a plastic fork seemed a welcome distraction from the doubts leaching into her thoughts. When she had signed up, it was for an office job, cataloguing missing items. Whilst the wording remained the same, the accent had thickened. She was moving into an uncertain world, with an uncertain remit, during uncertain times.

Charlie eventually fell asleep listening to some left-wing podcast decrying Bush's stunt on the USS Abraham Lincoln. That had been two years ago, and in the host's mind, a lot of today's business remained unfinished and even unfinishable. Like so many first timers to Iraq, she hoped he was wrong and that she could make a difference.

A covert refueling stage at Skopje, Macedonia, passed without incident or dialogue. After she endured a few more listless hours, the call came over the intercom, announcing the approach to Baghdad. Charlie bristled. Mr. Aviator returned from the washroom, sporting full Desert Storm regalia, sunglasses stored for landing. Uninvited, he wedged his gigantic frame into the seat right beside her. Like bottomless pools of deadly mercury, even his eyes could kill.

"Hello, Agent Glass. Special Agent Jack Dempsey."

Startled by the news, Charlie looked to close ground. "My new boss? Sir, it's a pleasure to meet you. Have you known it was me all this time?"

"Don't sweat it. The longer you spend out here, the more you crave time alone. How are you doing? Nervous?"

Rubbing her clammy hands on her thighs, Charlie rocked her head. "Something like that."

"You should be. The only people without nerves down there are the liars, the psychos, and the dead. You don't want to be in any of those camps. So, it's your first time?"

Charlie nodded.

"Brace yourself. We're nearly there. Fifteen minutes after the lights dim, we'll head down in."

Charlie sat on the edge of 16A. "Plummeting in?"

Dempsey chortled. "Like a kamikaze corkscrew."

Charlie's face failed to hide her worries.

Dempsey became deadly serious. "All the crazies are down there, howling at the moon and shooting at the stars. It's not so much an approach as it is a dive bomb. The good thing is that if we're hit by a shoulder missile, we won't be long in the air. Around seven thousand feet is their window for nailing us with the Strellas."

"And if we get past that?"

"Well then, all we have to worry about is the pilot's judgment."

"If you're trying to help, you're missing your mark, Sir."

"Down there, it pays to be prepared. Prepared, not scared. It comes to all the good operatives."

"What if I'm a slow learner?"

"I have read your file, Agent Glass. You will be fine." He leaned across her to check out the window. "We're at around thirty thousand feet." He left her with a disarming glance. "Enjoy the ride."

Despite the threat of innumerable fatal outcomes, none of her fellow passengers seemed anxious. Disappointingly, even the IT geek looked to be in control of his faculties. For inspiration, she reached into the front of her shirt and pulled out her trusted talisman. She rubbed it between thumb and forefinger in a nervous twitching motion. As soon as Dempsey had resumed his seat, the plane fell into complete, unannounced darkness. The bleak and barren unlit landscape below meant they were approaching from the west. There would be no lingering holding pattern that evening. When the dive came, it did so forcefully and without warning. The plane collapsed into a tight left spinning corkscrew that seemed destined for the center of the earth. Charlie peeled her grip from each armrest and set her forearms onto the headrest in front, supporting all her weight because of the steep angle of descent. She sensed danger but no terror.

Adrenaline flowed through a comforting calm, as Charlie fought to distance herself from the moment. The ground sped towards them in a contorted spiral. Incredibly, Charlie was enjoying the ride. Downward they plummeted. Down, deeper, down. Everything about the plane shook and shuddered, except for its passengers. Distant lights swirled below as the plane twisted towards earth. As they tumbled, Charlie noticed the eyes, mouths, and minds closing all around her. No one screamed as the roller coaster ride neared its climax. The ground flashed into view, dark and threatening. At the climax of the dive, Charlie lost the battle to keep her eyes open. She held on. At the very last second, the pilot wrenched the jet horizontally. Engines and ailerons screamed in defiance as the limited runway lights appeared with only feet to spare. The rubber kissed the concrete.

Touch down.

Charlie wanted to scream and clap like a drunk tourist landing in Cancun. The landing had been astonishingly exhilarating. She peered through the headrests to find Dempsey apparently asleep.

Only when the flaps retracted did her breathing restart. With the plane still firing down the tarmac, the Special Forces began disembarkation. No discussions took place during the taxi. This was not their first press-ganging. The jet careered down the runway, then veered left sharply towards the solitary air traffic control tower. The plane remained in darkness as it roared up to a dim, crumbling building.

It took an age for the Saddam-era bus with blacked-out windows to trundle its way across the shadowy airfield.

Dempsey arrived back at her seat. “Get your bag.” Charlie obeyed and followed in his boot strides. Her boss never looked back. “We landed on the old commercial runway. It’s longer than the military one, so they’ve had more time to dial us in. Its open tarmac out there; don't linger.” The message was dark and direct.

A bout of high-speed deplaning ensued. Once outside, the heat felt intense, despite the early hour. Everyone scurried through the arid, baked air into the waiting military bus. All sweat and jowls, the local driver swung the lever that pulled the doors closed behind them. He wrestled the enormous steering wheel in the terminal's direction and gunned an engine designed for noise more than speed.

Then it hit her. She was on the ground, in theater.

This is really happening. This is Iraq.

Once inside the refuge of the airport terminal, the small band of passengers followed on through a side door into the grandiosely signposted VIP area. Scuffed arrows glued to the concrete flooring pointed the way. On either side of the entrance to the disorganized and undersized baggage hall stood two immaculate Gurkas. Rigid and upright, impeccably turned out, fierce-eyed and vigilant, they saluted ferociously as every passenger passed. Under such security, Charlie suspected baggage theft would not be a prevalent crime in the VIP baggage hall. Kit bags of various shapes and sizes were eventually brought into the sorting area. The local baggage handlers seemed polar opposites to the Gurkas in stature, attitude, and application. Their disdain for their world hung around them like a low-pressure depression. With their kit bags collected, the new arrivals waited for the customs office to open. In the lull, Charlie sidled over to her new boss and gestured to the unmanned customs podium.

"Where is everybody?"

"Hiding."

"What are they waiting for?"

Dempsey unsheathed his sunglasses and pointed them at the emerging dawn. "They are waiting for that. Once we are out through the customs area, we are out in the wicked world. No one travels Route Irish in the dark. Letting them take pot shots at you from the darkness is tantamount to assisted suicide. Besides, we have morning prayers to accommodate."

"So, what now? We wait?"

"Yes, Agent Glass. We wait. Get used to it. You'll be doing that a lot."

"I read that's a big part of the job."

Dempsey's cynicism didn't sit well. "I am sure you've read the manuals, watched the videos, studied the briefs, and memorized your orders. Do you think that has prepared you?"

"It couldn't hurt."

His head bobbled. "Great guys get killed and idiots seem to leave with medals. Right place, wrong time, you never know. This place is a loaded game of chance. All I can do is help you shorten the odds, so listen up."

A two-person huddle ensued. "Customs will be a breeze. The contractors and grunts will get the hassle. US agents don't get any shit. They know we could help them join the ranks of the disappeared. We could smuggle anything in or out of this place right now. We're never checked. They are just glad to get us out of their country. They hate us being here."

Eventually, a tousled customs guard with depleted energy banks sauntered up to a makeshift podium. He had a magnificent mustache, in the style of Saddam Hussein, which drew attention away from a uniform that looked as if it had been slept in for several consecutive evenings. Off to the side, a hollow-cheeked local appeared beside the Customs Guard. The mystery man's gaunt face appeared jammed full of teeth and enthusiasm. His raucous smile danced beneath sunbaked muddy eyes. He wore a much larger man's uniform over what looked like the world's gaudiest Hawaiian shirt. He and Dempsey exchanged mutual nods of respect and boyish grins. The little local's arrival sparked Dempsey into life.

"Let's go. We'll walk and talk."

Charlie scampered on behind, in full wait-for-me mode. Dempsey brought her up to speed. "The guy who has just turned up beside the guard is our Terp, Tariq. He's one of the good guys. He probably dragged that lazy asshole to his post." Dempsey continued his running debrief. "This is my fourth tour, and he has been with me on every one of them. He's not just an ugly face. Unlike the rest of the money grabbing assholes, Tariq's in it for Iraq. He doesn't want a payoff or a US passport at the end."

Charlie got the picture. "So, he just wants his country back?"

Dempsey half nodded. "He wants his heritage back. He has a Master of Arts in Prehistoric Archaeology from the University of Baghdad."

Charlie took a chance. "So, he's not as dumb as he looks?"

"Ha. I'd say. He was on the excavation team at Umm al-Aqarib in 2000. Get to know him. You'll learn a lot. Oh, and don't call them Terps. They hate that."

Charlie appreciated the heads up. "Good to know."

As predicted, the customs check was both pointless and painless. The guard's heavy-set eyes barely opened to inspect her passport. "Next!" Charlie's backward glances caught sight of her fellow passengers becoming embroiled in the disinterested, disorganization that was Iraqi customs.

Welcome to Iraq.

Spilling out into the throng, she found the incredible bustle filling the terminal simply astonishing. Travelers, soldiers, guards, and greeters mingled and bustled past one another in a sloppy soup of humanity. Yelps of joy, tears of sadness, and shouted instructions filled the air. Across in a corner, an unseen child screamed the roof down. Overhead, the multitude of shadowy chrome archways covering the terminal ceiling blanketed the scene with a less than welcoming ambiance. Charlie stood in amazement at the murmuring crowd. She sensed a tugging at her kit bag. She looked around, game face on, to find Tariq by her side, offering his service as a porter. He won the very abbreviated tug of war.

Dempsey executed the introductions with military precision. "Tariq, Agent Glass. Agent Glass, let me introduce Tariq."

Tariq took the initiative and her baggage. "It is a pleasure to meet you. This is your first time in my country, yes?"

"Thank you, Tariq. Yes. You are well informed."

Tariq never broke stride. "It is my job to be informed and to inform." He skipped to the side and gestured for Charlie to pass through the juddering automatic doors of the airport terminal. When they spilled out into bright sunshine, everyone except Dempsey squinted. Charlie lowered the hand she had thrown up to shun the glare, unveiling a scene of chaos and civil carnage. The air dripped with a steamy cocktail of sweat and anxiety. People moved with panicked purpose. Irrespective of direction, everyone seemed to be "getting the hell out." Tariq dragged her oversized luggage past pillar and post. Overloaded trolleys buckled under the weight of massive bags. Tied and taped cardboard boxes laid around threateningly. Bags bursting at the seams battered holes in the crowd.

Charlie passed all forms of detritus and abandonment, each object a potential IED. A beaten, bleached gray Volvo Estate crawled past with a traditionally dressed bearded man lurking behind its steering wheel. By the time the car drew level with her, Charlie had timed her walking pace so that a massive concrete pillar blocked the space between them. The car had crawled into the distance before Charlie forced herself to draw a breath. She profiled everyone in sight until they were all suspects. Sensing her anxiety, Tariq marched to the front of the small column, throwing out a crooked yet comforting smile.

"Welcome to Baghdad."

Tariq parted the sea of travelers as Dempsey drew level with her to resume the on-the-hoof briefing. He shouted to be heard above the nearby planes. The screaming street scene only added to the mega mix of chaos. Everyone and everything had the volume set to maximum.

"It's still a kinetic roadway into the Green Zone. In several ways, it's worse now than in the war. In December last year, the State Department banned us from using Route Irish because of the casualties and attacks. Grunts in the Third Infantry now secure the road, but the locals have been playing hit and run for so long, they think themselves immune to justice. They call it IED Alley, but that only tells half the story. They can be complex attacks, mortars, grenades, RPGs, snipers, IEDs, VBIDEs—you name it. Eleven attacks for every mile of road, and at least one attack a day."

Charlie needed to pitch in. "Will we be traveling in a Bradley or a Rhino?"

Tariq remained on point. Dempsey remained on message. "A Rhino. We're not high enough up the totem pole to get the helicopter bridge. To be honest, I think we're best placed in the Rhino. You could also get a bulletproof taxi from one local, but that will cost you three thousand dollars, and it could be a one-way ticket to anywhere."

"So, they hate us?"

"For sure. Look around. They talk of hearts and minds. We broke their hearts, and they are out of their minds with anger."

"It's a smorgasbord of danger. All flavors of terrorists, thugs, and gangsters are on the menu: foreign insurgents, local gangs, and self-proclaimed warlords. Route Irish is where they all come for target practice."

Charlie dragged her clammy hands across her thighs. A low-level Blackhawk barged through the airspace directly above them. Charlie's pulse raced. Ever calm, Dempsey merely raised his voice. "So far, the number of US troops wounded by the bombs has climbed to over seven thousand seven hundred. In April alone, IEDs killed fifty-seven of us and injured another six hundred and ninety-one."

"So, this is how they fight?"

"So far. Us disbanding the police didn't help."

Charlie winced. "Who's helping us with our inquiries?"

"It's just good old Uncle Sam."

The bulky Rhino came into view, cutting short Charlie's rampaging worries. It sat out on its own, intimidating all the other vehicles in the pound. It sat, an angular, awkward beast, with lumpy, heavy armor and a lumbering gait. Charlie found climbing into the belly of the beast intimidating. She took one of the plastic trimmed seats next to a discreetly covered gun port. If this was the school bus, it was a tough school. Under the hood, the six-liter beast growled and shuddered to life. Bone-chilling air conditioning kicked in, to great effect.

Dempsey saw the look in Charlie's eye. He banged on the side panels. "NIJ Level IV composites, three-hundred-and-sixty-degree coverage. They can take Thirty-Cals all day long." His knuckles tapped the window. "One-way bullet-proof glass. They can't get to us, but we can get to them."

Charlie smiled, pleased at last to receive facts that didn't terrorize. Up front, Tariq pushed his clipboard under the nose of the petrified driver. Bald, poorly shaved, overweight, and sweating profusely despite the air conditioning, the driver seemed on the verge of a breakdown. Rivulets of sweat bubbled in the corners of his umber eyes. He wrung ornate beads through his fingers, offering prayers to and for everyone in and out of earshot. His relationship with Tariq looked to be strained to the point of breakdown, yet Charlie knew not if this was because of circumstances, histories, or personalities. Fingers pointed across a tattered map as tempers frayed. Charlie could decipher enough Farsi to understand that both parties were negotiating a preferred route. As with all negotiations in the region, the discussions were full, frank, and conducted at high volume. The pair seemed to prioritize their mouths over their ears. After a protracted bout of verbal jousting, an uneasy armistice eventually broke out. Tariq backed away with both parties mirroring the other's unhappy gestures. Taking his place beside Charlie, he took verbal potshots at the driver.

"That's Bassam. If he's not screaming, he's worrying; if he's not worrying, he's crying." Poor Bassam seemed lost and terrified.

Charlie nodded towards the driver. "Is it his first time?"

Tariq chortled. "No. He's just worried it could be his last time."

"You'd think he would get used to it."

"Like a surfer who eventually forgets about sharks? Doesn't quite work that way for people around here."

"Why would he put himself through this?" inquired Charlie.

"Money. Life-changing money."

With a fateful sigh of resignation and a prayer to Allah, Bassam released the handbrake and set the Rhino in motion. It picked up pace, as did the driver's mumbled prayers. Dempsey returned from the back of the bus and stood in the aisle with his back to the direction of travel. Occasionally, he would spin to gather his bearings and point out key sites, features, and insights. As they left the western end of the airport, Charlie craned her head from side to side, collecting as many visuals as possible. Under the watchful eye of a distant lookout tower, a winged feature stood tall. In the middle of a roundabout featuring a waterless fountain stood the gray granite tiled plinth. Atop that plinth stood the statue of an elderly, bearded man in traditional dress. Defiantly, outstretched arms readied him for a leap from a tall structure. He looked unprepared and ill-equipped for the venture. Charlie understood how he must have felt.

Dempsey noticed Charlie staring. "That's Abbas bin Firnas. The first man to attempt flight."

"Legend has it the dumbass covered himself in feathers then leaped off a cliff to prove he could fly. You'll see crazier crap than that before your tour is done. Jesus, it's fifty-fifty whether you'll see crazier than that before we reach the river! Another dreamer. The place is full of them."

"A bit like D.C." Charlie's attempt to gauge Dempsey's allegiances fell on deaf ears. The statue disappeared out of view as the Rhino took a wide, looped bend. "Don't worry, you'll be seeing him again. He'll be there to wave you home."

Charlie clung to her seat and her talisman as they raced around another sweeping bend. The Rhino lost its footing in a meteor-sized crater, jolting everyone skyward. Dempsey took the bump in his stride and kept relaying the intel from his standing position. "Route Irish is a four-lane critical supply route to and from the airport. It's jammed with diplomats, agents, contractors, journalists, news crews, and medics. A sea of foreigners, a sea of targets."

"Don't locals use it?"

"They try to avoid it. If forced, they make it damn obvious there are no foreigners in their cars. Nothing that brings attention. Nothing that draws a sniper's bead. The slightest hint of Westernization could earn them a drive-by. But even that is changing, and not for the better. All the Sunni-Shia sectarianism is boiling over. Now there's no one in power to gas them into compliance; they're all turning on each other."

Up front, Tariq and the driver had broken their verbal cease-fire. The unhappy pairing eventually forced each other to find a rhythm, each forecasting what lie ahead. The driver detailed the road and traffic. Tariq described the buildings, people, and objects in the margins and horizons. Official protocols banned conversions in Farsi. Top brass was worried about being lured into a life-threatening ambush, or—worse still—being made fun of. Dempsey had no such qualms or insecurities. Despite them having an entirely different native language, they seemed to communicate solely in US slang and acronyms. Tangos, unknowns, RPGs, IEDs all got at least one mention every mile.

Thirty-two anxious minutes after leaving the site, the Rhino trotted up to the blast-proof walling surrounding the holding area at Checkpoint One. *Nearly there.* Approaching the haven of the protected area, Charlie felt drenched by a cocktail of relief and trepidation wash over her. The bilingual signage warned of what lie ahead. It simply read: *Deadly Force Authorized.*

Charlie fought the urge to cower down even further. Somehow the sign underlined just how far from home she now was. The Green Zone resembled a dystopian gated community with its armed checkpoint and high, blast-proof, concrete T-Walls. An unfit for purpose camouflaged net did little to disguise the makeshift machine gun tower that overlooked the first section of the vehicle inspections. Liberally distributed razor-wire cloaked everything that couldn't move. A stop-go set of traffic lights sat in a position so prominent that everyone around could notice they lay disconnected. The only color came from the comically undersized red berets being sported by the Iraqi guards manning the initial checkpoint. Their maroon-colored stab jackets looked under specified for the job at hand.

Despite the blistering sun, the guards stood tall, seemingly impervious to the heat. They looked afraid, trapped in a hostile world, gatekeepers to a castle they did not build, own, or want. A large palm bursting at the leaves with the most magnificent dates garnished an otherwise miserable scene. Whilst the crew waited impatiently, the ground trembled as a massive M1 Abrams tank rumbled past, imposing and imperious. A Bradley fighting vehicle scurried after, like a little runt trying to keep up with the alpha dog. As the waiting time grew, so too did the tension.

Dempsey noticed Charlie scouring the scene. "It's not always like this. There's been a spate of suicide bombings lately. Everyone's on edge. Once we're past the front gate, we'll be fine."

When the car ahead eventually passed inspection, a lethargic guard waved the Rhino through without scrutiny. Fifty yards of channel between two incredibly high T-Walls marked the transition. At either end of the concrete funnel, .50-cal machine guns tracked and traced their progress. After yet another cursory inspection, the Rhino finally breached the inner walls. Decanting into the muster area, Bassam, the animated driver, offered a life affirming thank you to Allah. With relative safety now upon her, Charlie's jawline softened.

"Phew. Mission accomplished!"

Springing out from the truck, Tariq the interpreter sped on past, unable to stop himself.

"That's what your president said, two years ago."

CHAPTER 5

The next day, Charlie woke in her Contained Housing Unit, a glorified shipping container. Its jaundiced interior comprised industrial flooring, an unexpectedly comfortable cot bed, a canvas chair, a desk with drawers and a small vanity mirror, efficient yet noisy air conditioning, a high vent, a single window, a desk lamp, and double power outlet. Staring at the four corrugated walls, Charlie took solace because it seemed marginally larger than the bedroom in her loft apartment back in Paris. As she unpacked, she pinned to the small notice board the treasured card given by her father. *Doubt truth to be a liar, but never doubt I love. Pop.*

The words came from Shakespeare. The card came from the Smithsonian gift shop. She clambered into her khakis and new boots and tied back her shortened hair. Standing in front of the mirror, she closed out the GI Jane look by throwing her talisman around her neck and under her shirt, dog tag style. Her reflection pushed her on. *Go get 'em girl!*

She learned the routines and timetables by heart. After reading through her full briefing twice, she took a tour of the facility. Map in hand, the world's most eager combat tourist strode out into a world built on stone chippings. High concrete walls were very much a theme. Razor wire also remained a favored adornment. Every item on the base looked to have been selected just before something that would do the job properly had come available. Sandbags doubled as protection for everything in sight, including canvas tents, container units, latrines, dining facilities and a temporary armory. Massive mobile air conditioning units whirred away at the entrances to most buildings.

A barrage of F-bombs flew out as she passed a large flapping tent, dissent and dismay screaming out from the screening of a two-day-old game of baseball. The dining facility was exactly what she had imagined. When she arrived at the industrial catering unit, a night patrol arrived in for breakfast. The troops emptied and made safe their weapons before scrubbing up under a communal faucet. Overhead, a sign portraying an American eagle wrapped in Old Glory kept a watchful eye on proceedings. The scuffed and faded words on the sign read, *Operation Iraqi Freedom.* Charlie's presence seemed to stir something in their manner, but tiredness and an officious looking captain seemed to keep mischief levels to a minimum.

She passed on through the double doors providing an airlock for the air conditioning and protection against the dust. The first thing that hit her in the dining hall was the smell. If she was ever going to miss the USA—and that seemed unlikely—then the scents swirling around the dining hall would bring her back home. The amalgamated aromas of burgers, fries, ribs, skillet potatoes, and fried onions all hung tantalizingly in the air. The sheer number of diners and staff caught her by surprise. She joined a long line of uniforms, at Charlie completed her search and selection process. An assorted skillet with over-easy eggs and one of the four flavored milk alternatives accompanied Charlie to her seat within the long-benched tables.

She stabbed a disinterested fork into the skillet and began restudying her case notes. 0600 hours, breakfast in the dining facility. 0700 hours, report to her new detachment leader, Warrant Officer Jesse Kirkland. She read his bio with rising respect. His boots had been one of the first pairs to cross into Iraq at the start of the war. He had transferred from the heat of Third Infantry action into a world filled with clay pots and broken stones. Charlie wondered, *Was he interested in saving artifacts or saving his ass?*

Through the throng an even more handsome version of the man in the photograph strode across the DFAC dining facility, waving and high fiving everyone in sight. Charlie pretended not to notice him doing his rounds. He stopped along the way to steal some food, to inquire about a loved one, and to thank someone for a job well done. When he arrived at her place on the long trestle table, he could not have been more charming.

"Excuse me, are you Agent Glass?"

She hoped her humor wouldn't miss the mark. "I must be; you know everyone else in here."

"Ha, you could be right, miss. Jesse Kirkland, but everyone calls me Kirk."

Standing in his freshly laundered T-shirt and desert camouflaged pants, he looked the picture-perfect, impeccably turned out, All-American hero. Everyone and everything in the desert seemed to have gained a moon dust coating that dulled outlooks and clogged visions. Kirk seemed immune to the khaki cloud that everyone else lived under. His taut jawline stood to attention as his nickel eyes stood guard. Pristine and undaunted, he seemed the archetypal military man. His Southern accent seemed difficult to track down. It hid halfway between southern gentlemen and carpetbagger. She surmised that back in his school days, he would have been that exceedingly rare creature; the All-Star quarterback who wasn't a complete asshole. She looked forward to spending more time with him.

"May I sit down?"

Charlie gestured. "Please do."

Kirk took his seat and inquired after her accommodation and food. "So, how's the chow?"

She enjoyed her retort. "Like my unit—bland and cold." Before needing to respond, Kirk spotted a gruff looking diner shuffling his way to the most remote part of the hall. Kirk caught his eye and gesticulated for him to come over and pay a visit. Hunched over his overladen tray, he did not seem in the least bit enamored at being called for a chat. Taking his place nearby, his head only lifted when it had to, it appeared that conversations and mornings were not this guy's deal.

Kirk took the initiative. "Agent Glass, can I introduce to you Gavin MacKenzie? Mac to his friends."

Mac didn't look her way. "I have no friends."

Looking to close the gap between them, Charlie searched for common ground. "Pleased to meet you?"

No handshake accompanied his cranky reply. "Well then, you're in the minority." The curt Scot turned his attitude towards Kirk. "One of your spies, Kirkland?"

Demonstrating he had heard this kind of aggression before, Kirk addressed Charlie. "I apologize. It would seem Mr.

MacKenzie fell out the wrong side of his bed this morning. He does that most mornings; I think it's the whiskey."

A thick Scottish accent stressed his gruff manners, chiseled voice, undecipherable dialect, and fire-glow hair. His crimson beard looked to have been trimmed at home with a knife and fork, in the dark. His ruddy complexion told the tale of a life spent too long under the sun and too long in the bottle. He wore a seventies safari suit, which, like him, appeared a little frayed at the edges. Worn through hiking boots, pulled down green merino wool socks, inappropriately short moleskin shorts that were probably once gray, and an oversized shirt completed the stereotype. He looked as if he dug every day, all day, in only one set of clothes.

The air remained awkward, so the warrant officer continued the bridge building. "Mac is the liaison for the field archaeology. The new Museum Task Force includes Mac, Agent Glass."

The old man seemed to be the type who delighted in strangling any goodwill that existed in a conversation. He crumpled his soft Aussie bush hat into a roll and stuffed it under his left epaulet with ceremony. "So, lassie, are ye over here to save the day?"

"Something like that." Charlie bided her time with her cantankerous new breakfast guest. Mac seemed disappointed that she hadn't bitten. His curmudgeonly cross examination continued. "So, you see yourself as the next great Gertrude Bell?"

Kirk seemed lost in history. "Gertrude Bell?"

Charlie pushed her cause. "An inspiration, writer, archaeologist, explorer, cartographer, and political advisor."

Mac dug in. "An interfering English snob. The kind that drew the lines on the map that screwed this whole place up. Every time the English draw straight lines on a map, people die."

Charlie stood her ground. "Well, that snob founded the museum that we're all here for."

Mac became fully entrenched in his argument. "I am not here for your stupid wee museum. I'm here to stop the sites being looted. These ancient realms are dying in a festering pile of shit hidden under a blanket you people call the *War on Terror*."

Kirk held up his hand. "Thanks for the breakfast eulogy."

Mac didn't let up. His plastic fork pointed in Charlie's general direction, yet he couldn't find the gumption to make eye contact with her. "Why the hell would anyone in their right mind come to this hole if they didn't have to?"

Charlie bit back. "What does that make you then, Mac? I don't see a uniform on your back or any medals on your chest."

Mac's emerald eyes imperceptibly softened around the edges. He seemed to like her fight. He slithered as if deciding whether to hate her. "The Iraq Museum got all the headlines, but the greatest crimes are being committed out in the field."

Charlie seized the appeasement opportunity. "The plundering down south is appalling."

Mac temporarily halted his chewing and emitted a low rumble. It could have been wind or a grunt of agreement. Charlie elected to take it as the latter. Mac lifted his eyes and dropped his fork. "You might think you know things, but there's a lot more going on over here than you can ever imagine. People are vanishing every week."

Charlie's gaze flashed between the men. "Who? People on base?"

Kirk promoted himself to the justice of the peace. "Ignore him. We've heard isolated reports of skirmishes between local militia and foreign insurgents."

"Hardly isolated, and they are more than skirmishes."

Kirk held it down. "It's a war zone. People die."

"Just be careful what you say and who you say it to. Watch what you do and who you do it with."

Charlie was not one to back down. "Thanks for the threat. I will bear it in mind." A long silence ensued as all three diners worked their way through the contents on their paper plates. Too busy for pleasantries, Mac inhaled his breakfast, finished his coffee, and packed up his tray. Obviously busier than everyone else in Iraq, Mac scuttled off without exchanging words or looks. As he strode off, to Charlie and Kirk's joint amusement, he tussled to retrieve his crumpled hat from its epaulet.

"Charming," Charlie observed.

"Yeah, you can't find common ground with him. He's dug it all up." The pair shared a chuckle.

Breakfast merged into the morning briefing as Charlie and Kirk decamped to the Briefing Hut. The sessions extended into the afternoon. Tours were made and all the necessary inside tracks were laid. Ropes were shown and strings were pulled. Kirk took great care with the specifics and Charlie clung to his every word. In a world that had gone cuckoo-nest crazy, they were here to make a difference. They seemed ready, willing, and able to work together.

After night fell, Charlie returned to her CHU, exhausted and thrilled. Striding across a small square before a line of medic stations, the tat-tat of small arms fire in the distance brought the outside world back into her reality. She bumped her pace up and lengthened her stride.

Later, lying in her bed, hands clasped behind her head, Charlie stared into space. The skirmish outside the compound wall had ended as quickly as it had started. Intrigued and undaunted, her mind drifted to the dangers lying in wait outside the walls. Soon, she'd be out there.

The next few days spent sheltered behind the blast proof walls of the Green Zone passed swiftly for Charlie. Work was thrown at her, and she threw herself right back at it. It had been no surprise when she found herself the only woman on the roster. In dark moments she fought off doubts she was only there as a token female making up the quota.

In the rear office and a quiet section of the secure area, work was progressing well. Today, like most other days, she felt pioneer-like. Kirk remained patient and supportive. She responded with diligence, keen to please. Faced with short odds, they were good together. The growing catalogue of artifacts being recovered from clueless squaddies or clued-in locals gave little hope of better days to come, such was the magnitude of the thefts. For every item recovered, it seemed a hundred more were missing. The already skewed ledger worsened with every entry. They concentrated on cataloguing lost artifacts for inclusion on the global criminal databases operated by Interpol. Anything passed through reputable auctioneers was always cross-referenced against these databases. The day moved at pace, through a heady combination of history lessons and book-keeping. To break the boredom, Kirk lifted the focus from cuneiform tablets and cylinder seals. "So, Dempsey met you at the airport? That was cool of him. No one does the meet and greet at the airport. If they do, they greet you with an RPG."

Charlie snorted. "No, he was on my plane."

Kirk seemed surprised. "The sly old fox. He never said he went stateside. No one knows what he does. He disappears and reappears like a ghost."

She understood. "A friendly ghost."

Kirk's face didn't match his words. "Sure! Let's go with that."

Surprised, Charlie took the sarcastic insinuation to heart.

Kirk plowed on. "I need to chase the nerds over at systems over their late report on dark web trackers." He pulled open his reinforced laptop and crashed out a few well protected emails. Pulling the laptop closed, he announced he was heading over to Section Four to follow up in person. There seemed nothing he didn't excel at.

On departure, their respectful smiles matched.

Keen to catch up, Charlie hit the books, studying the multitude of deities that ruled and guided the worlds of Sumeria, Babylonia, and Akkadia. More files were dusted off and processed in the hours that followed. The evening closed in, so Charlie repositioned herself nearer a single table lamp and worked on diligently. When she could do no more, she pulled her fingers through her hair then patted her face.

2100 hours. Time to go.

She gathered up the files, collated them in alphabetical order, and carried them to the storage area at the back of the unit. Bending down to use her elbow to open the glass-paneled door, she spotted a flashlight flicking around the room. A wall of caution fell on her. She slipped the files down on the ground and tentatively eased the door further open. Creeping in for a closer look, she noted the back of a shadowy figure with a dark caftan and head cloth. The intruder methodically scanned the contents of a large filing cabinet. She stood transfixed as the mystery man softly shuffled his sandals across to the next cabinet. This was no random ransacking. Charlie assessed her options. She was on her own. He was more than likely armed. The wise thing to do would be to flee and call for reinforcements. Facing poor odds, Charlie reached over and flicking on the light switch. "What the hell are you doing?"

When the room burst into light, the intruder spun in panic. The longer they glared at each other, the more confident the invader became, and the less secure Charlie felt. The gatecrasher sprang forward. Charlie stalled, transfixed by onslaught. The big man lunged and crumpled Charlie into the wall. He gripped her throat, pinning her helplessly against the partition. Instantly petrified, she did nothing to protect herself. Pressed against the wall her mind raced with a hideous range of consequences. Calloused hands tightened painfully around her throat. He pushed his foul-smelling bearded face up close and in Farsi, spat a warning in her face. "One word and you will die, like the Serpent." Bolts of dark anger sparked from his anthracite eyes. Her soul folded. The firebrand attacker threw an imploding Charlie to the ground. Choking, gasping, and cowering in fear, she hid her eyes as her attacker bundled himself out the door. Tears accompanied her anger. Then came the recriminations. Despite her training, her resolve had evaporated. She stood up tentatively. *Why didn't she do something? What happened to the training kicking in?*

She vowed there and then—she would never let herself be put down in that way ever again. She was angry with the intruder, but angrier still with herself. If she ever saw him again, she would rearrange his face. She banged her head against the post of the door and angrily booted the wall.

Her boots would never be shiny again.

She gathered up her folders and tried to center thoughts. Shaking hands returned the files to their correct locations.

"Hello? Hello?" A sheepish male voice shouted through from the front. Charlie gathered her thoughts and her paperwork, straightened her gait, then treaded out to meet the inquirer. Tariq stood at the doorway, his face turning to concern. "Agent Glass. Are you alright?"

She needed more time to decide what to do. Wracked with embarrassment at having frozen under the slightest physical threat, her instinctive decision was to say nothing. "I'm fine. Just a little tired."

Tariq maintained the distance and protocols that his culture dictated but tried his best to help. His face looked disbelieving, yet his words were coated in understanding. "Make sure you do not work too hard." He took the remaining folders from her and placed them on the desk. "These can wait until the morning. It's too late for anyone to be working, especially a woman."

Just this once, she appreciated the less-than-casual sexism. She took time to tidy her workspace, collect her possessions, and—above all—gather her wits. The process took longer than expected.

As Tariq escorted Charlie back to her quarters, he dreamed out loud of the love of his country, regaling his companion with ancient tales of wonderment. Staring up at the cloudless skies, he boasted it was the Sumerians and Babylonians that devised and relayed to the Greeks the astronomical mythologies and constellations of Capricorn, Leo, and Sagittarius. Charlie hung on his every word as he proudly described how ancient astrologers observed the locations of the planets and advise the leaders of society on the reasoning and rationales behind every occurrence. The Mesopotamians thought everything happened for a reason, good and bad. He said he didn't understand the reasons for most things in his world right now, but he had faith they would become clear with the passage of time. "Inshallah."

They parted on good terms in bad times.

Later, lying in her bed, Charlie sucked her talisman in her tightening mouth. She cared not for the reasons she froze earlier that evening, but she knew one thing for certain.

It would never happen again.

CHAPTER 6

Two uneasy days had passed without incident. Today's morning routine had been electrified by the anticipation of the day ahead. This was Charlie's first visit to the museum. The Rhino stood outside the muster point, growling and raring to go. Although the streets of Baghdad were statistically much safer than Route Irish, risk levels remained high. The briefing notes had been clear on that matter. Bassam swung the bus door open. In an environment less lined with fear, a nut-brown glow had found its way onto his chubby, fuzz-filled face—though his fickle grin slid and hid when Tariq appeared on deck.

The team was on board: Dempsey, the leader; Mac the malcontent; Kirk the fixer; Charlie the grunt; and Tariq the Terp. Dempsey pulled them in for their briefing. Unsurprisingly, Mac took up a position on the periphery. The orders of the day were handed out on fact-filled clipboards.

With his sweat and prayers on the rise, Bassam tapped his trinket-adorned dashboard then set the Rhino on its way. If the purpose of the fan on the dash was to make a racket and blow dusty air around, it was functioning perfectly. The group almost enjoyed an unexpectedly easy commute up north through the Green Zone. They switched back, parallel to the Quadisiya Expressway before passing the gigantic, crossed swords of Saddam's victory memorial, a tribute to those killed in the Iran-Iraq war. They trundled past a mobile checkpoint without drama or hold up.

Once out in the open, Dempsey pulled his Desert Eagle.

Charlie squirmed at the sight. "Is that necessary?"

"Sectarian violence is on the rise."

Tariq pitched in. "Baghdad was heating up."

"So, we're tooling up," added Dempsey.

Charlie pulled a face. "And here was me thinking we were on a day out at the museum."

Agitated by circumstances with growing fears of an outside world, Charlie turned her thoughts inward. Images from the fight with the intruder flashed across her consciousness. Although her level of trust towards Kirk was on the rise, she needed time to process events, time to build her walls of trust. The decision to say nothing still made sense. People were dying every day, so some random local threatening her wouldn't make the daily news. When she knew more, she'd say more. Online research around his curious threat of dying like a serpent threw up no clues or insights. With nothing else to go on, the threat was interpreted as a poor translation. Pulling her mind to the present, she realized her tight grip on the seat in front had blanched her knuckles. She had to let it go.

Exiting the Green Zone was a relatively straightforward process, with all threats and dangers perceived to be entirely outside the walls. From very recent experience, Charlie knew that mindset was flawed, almost fatally so.

The real Iraq fell in front of her outside the wire. Tragedy littered the hostile territory. Excited to be on day release, Charlie pulled her little digital camera and started snapping like a crazed sightseer. Trees lined the boulevards, concrete lined the trees, razor wire lined the concrete, and trash littered the razor wire. Derelict buildings were potential snipers' nests. Every man with a cell phone was a potential bomber. Every traffic jam seemed an opportunity for ambush. Even the locals seemed mistrusting of each other as they strolled on, keeping their distance wherever possible. Concrete blocks steered traffic away from busy pedestrian sections. The occasional white building stood out amongst the drab weary sand and clay-colored buildings bordering the roadways. House pride appeared in short supply, even in the formerly affluent areas. Wastelands between buildings acted as magnets for the detritus of society. Kids kicked a deflated soccer ball between two burned-out cars. Every one of them sported tops from a European soccer club. How these garments made their way into war-torn Iraq was one thing, but why the locals wore the colors of their invaders seemed even more puzzling to Charlie.

Unexpectedly, they swerved to avoid the innards from a fire-ravaged home, which had been dragged out into the street. A destitute family sat on the ground, wailing at the smoldering pyre as the rest of the world galloped past, callously ignoring their plight. At the corner of a street feeding into a busy market area, four US Marines stood watch. By their side, an old lady in black screamed and cried in their faces. On her knees she wept and moaned, holding high what must have been the photo of a lost loved one.

The soldiers looked everywhere but down.

Riven with guilt, Charlie forced herself to stare at the unfolding tragedy. Her own travails were nothing compared to those of the imploding old lady, whose inconsolable wailing gave true meaning to the phrase, "A woman all alone in Iraq."

"Nice work, Dempsey." Mac's insinuation landed awkwardly.

Dempsey's silence only seemed to annoy Mac further. "Look at the place. Don't tell me you're helping."

He pointed out towards a bone-dry fountain languishing in the center of a small square. A massive concrete eagle clawing its way out from the center had lost its head and wing to bomb damage. "That's freedom, is it?"

Charlie found the stark truth difficult to comprehend. US media feeds flooded channels with stories of optimism and rebuilding, yet the reality spilling in through the bus window could not have been farther from the rhetoric.

Traveling on, a man carrying his child looked up and waved at the beast driving by. His brightly clothed daughter was encouraged to join in. "Well, someone is pleased to see us." Charlie's attempts to improve relations were soon crushed.

"It's amazing what fear can do!"

Dempsey's eye roll told Charlie he'd heard Mac's whining too many times for it to leave a mark.

After twenty minutes of awkward silence and difficult viewing, the Rhino pulled up outside the neglected architecture of the Iraq Museum. Bassam slowed and bumped the Rhino's heavy tires over washed-out yellow and white painted curbstones.

Through the vehicle's dusty window, Charlie marveled at two magnificent castellated square towers connected by an impressive bridge. A direct hit from a cannon shell had left scorched markings above the archway on the bridge. The intricately carved relief of warriors and a charioteer remained miraculously intact. The surrounding boulevards seemed blocked for no apparent reason. *Too little too late.*

Mac's grunts, groans, and sighs made up the mood music as the team exited the vehicle. Happy at last, Bassam waved them off, before impatiently closing the doors behind them. A bilingual sign stood on the mud-crusted dust bowl across from the entrance saying, *Keep off the grass.*

Viewing the front of the ravaged entrance, the magnitude of the task at hand took Charlie's breath away. She found the desecration maddening and the desolation saddening.

First to leave, Kirk and Tariq headed out to complete site security checks. The rest of the crew ambled in through the museum forecourt with varying degrees of purpose and pace. Rudimentary checks were carried out with a level of inattentiveness normally displayed by guards who hadn't been paid in weeks.

The team traversed the extensive gardens and entered by a side door obscured by an out-of-control bush. Turning away from the enormous halls, Charlie inquired about the opportunities to tour the museum. Her chances were as short as Dempsey's answer: "We're here to work."

Between the white-washed halls, the air hung heavily. At selected doorways lethargic staff struggled to muster enough energy for the tasks at hand. Two years after the looting, the cleanup operation looked to have barely started. Smashed door frames still clung to the entrances of rooms, as if the looters had left only moments before. Paper files were strewn everywhere. Rubble from damaged sculptures lay across broken display cabinets and smashed signage.

The team passed by a room filled with rack upon rack of pots and clay urns.

"So, it's not all gone," chirped Charlie.

"Too heavy to carry." Mac's additions detracted from the moment, but Charlie knew he made a good point.

Dempsey ushered them past the moment, only stopping when he reached a dingy, unlocked anteroom. He gestured for Charlie to enter. "Here you are. Home sweet home." Pulling the light switch didn't seem to add much light.

"They like to keep us in the dark." Tariq peered around the doorway. His smiling presence did more to light he room than the underpowered bulb.

"You can get online through your satellite toggle. The paperwork should hold some clues. Tariq can show you the ropes. I'll leave you two to it. Good luck. Stay hydrated." Dempsey left her with a professional nod. She found him a curious blend—charismatic yet enigmatic. She wondered why such a leader would be involved in such trivial work when the war on terror was only a grenade's throw away. His courage shone like a beacon, but there was something that jangled. For some reason the phrase *hidden in plain sight* sprang to mind. Quite what he was hiding remained a mystery.

Charlie led. "So, it's you and me, partner?"

Charlie surveyed the scene. Tariq set his small rucksack down, clearing a space on the dusty table. Along one wall stood a range of locked glass cabinets. Although apparently still locked, the glass and the contents were all gone. A layer of dusty grit threatened her laptop, so she pulled an old poster off the wall to act as a mat for her computer. On passing, Mac threw in a verbal hand grenade. "You'll be most of the morning cleaning up."

"Aren't you going to help?"

"No, that's what your lackey is for!"

Charlie cringed. She hated for someone with Tariq's education and passion to be described as a lackey. Before she could mount a retaliatory strike, the gruff Scot moved on. Shuffling off towards the bowels of the museum, he wafted the back of his hand in Charlie's general direction. "Enjoy!"

Why Westerners felt they had the right to treat the locals with such disdain remained a mystery to Charlie. It wasn't just the dusty air that left a stale taste in her mouth. A swig of water and a dark scowl in Mac's general direction helped.

"Sorry about all that."

Tariq cast her a shrug of resignation.

"Shall we?"

Tariq set his best foot forward and Charlie followed.

Every artifact on her high-tech database was cross-referenced against the limited paper records collected from around the room. With each empty box, more treasure became categorized as lost. Entries for amulets, broaches, tablets, and ornaments all graced the dusty sorting table. The absence of every artifact was noted. It didn't take long for Charlie to realize the dark truth.

"It's all gone. All of it."

Tariq's words were laced with anger. "It has been gone for almost two years. And only now you come."

"We're here now."

"To do what?"

"To help."

He cast his hand around the room. "Haven't you helped enough?"

Charlie couldn't and didn't argue.

"Why are you even here?"

"To make things better, make amends."

"No. Why are *you* here?"

"What do you mean?"

"You. Why are you here?"

"It's my job."

"That is no answer. Why take the job?"

Charlie knew she owed him an answer. She maybe even owed herself one. After thumbing through a scattered stack of listings, she found the words. "I hated what we did over here. I really want to help."

"By filling out forms."

"By finding what's missing and tracking it down. This is only the start."

"The start? Have you seen this city? This is the end."

"I can't change what's gone before. If I could, I would. But you're still fighting, and I'm here with you. Side by side."

With a distant voice Tariq said, "I stopped fighting long ago. Survival is all I hope for. When you finish, you go home. For me this will never end. You people promise to take us away from all this as compensation. Why should I leave? This is my home. The land I love."

"I understa—"

"You cannot understand." Tariq bumped the table in frustration.

It took some time before the dust settled.

"I am sorry."

"There is no need. I see what we have done."

"This is our heritage. This is what is left."

Charlie felt helpless. "I know my words are hollow, but I promise I will do all I can to find the pieces and bring these looters to justice."

Tariq appeared on the verge of an episode. "Do not talk of justice. There is no justice in Iraq."

Charlie lowered her gaze and lifted her paper stack. "Well, let's start with finding these pieces."

Tariq nodded in resignation.

Their day passed like no other, with every new piece a new story, a new love, new heartbreak. As Charlie wandered through the mists of each dark discovery, every disappointment was tinged with anger. The anger became tainted by bitterness at her own country's role in the debacle. She realized all this could have been avoided with just a modicum of empathy towards the people of Iraq and their history. She worked on, keen to make a difference. Keen to make amends. Keen to keep her word.

When the time came to leave for the day, Dempsey scoured the rooms, corralling his crew, not unlike a travel rep herding errant tourists back on a bus. The well-worked team lumbered their way to the exit. Conversations were minimal. Everyone appeared deflated by the revelations and discoveries of the day. The size of the task ahead had apparently demoralized the ensemble.

Thankfully, Mac seemed too tired to complain. Disengaged with the party, Tariq appeared to have folded in on himself.

Outside, Bassam's encouraging welcome fell on tired ears. Fully aware of the perceptions her actions would generate but with little care for them, Charlie cut short the weary caravan. With disbelief and groans, she cajoled everyone to pose for a photograph under the archway. It had been a momentous day, and she wanted the moment captured. A smiling Bassam seemed willing to lend a hand, amenable to any task that would speed up the process of evacuation. In the background, Tariq dragged the crew's bags to the bus. In true colonial fashion, no one helped him, even though it seemed more uncomfortable to watch him struggle. As he trudged back inside for the last batch of equipment, Charlie cut him off and pleaded for him to join the scene. He wore the miserable facial expression of a movie extra desperate to be sent home for the day. After a few mistimed clicks, several retakes, and a great deal of unhelpful commentary from Mac, the team abandoned the impromptu photo shoot. Shot or no shot, with fading light and disappearing patience, the crew boarded the bus. Kirk loaded the gear onto the back of the bus as the rest of the crew boarded.

Before Tariq returned, Charlie took the time to run back under the archway and take one last photograph of the museum on its own. When a sweating and struggling Tariq re-emerged with more bags, she sprang to his aid. They exchanged visual pleasantries. Charlie shared the load.

Crack! Crack! Crack!

"Get down!" Panic polluted Tariq's cry.

Tariq hit the ground instantly, dragging a stuttering Charlie with him. A fiery flurry

of bullets fizzed through the air, knocking chunks from the nearby wall. Before her mind had caught up, Tariq was kneeling and swinging his M4 carbine into action.

Bang! Bang! Bang! Bang! Bang! Bang! Bang! Bang! Bang!

Noise, smoke, and gunpowder fumes filled the air as Tariq blasted back. Fear forced his hand as the bullets clattered all around. He dipped his head and blasted blindly towards the target.

Squirming under the parapet, fear clamped Charlie to the ground. Fear strangled all reason. *Fight or flight.* Neither option seemed possible. She clung to the ground for precious life.

A near miss threw chunks of wall up into Tariq's face, forcing him to collapse behind the wall. Cement splinters flew all around. Emboldened by Tariq's rapid response and enraged at the assault, Charlie screamed into action. In one staggered motion, she pulled her Glock, knelt, and unloaded her Glock in the general direction of the attackers.

Bang! Bang! Bang! Bang! Bang! Bang! Bang! Bang! Bang!

The bullets flew. Determination gripped her trigger. Gun smoke belched and casings flew. Through the smoky fizzing air, Charlie spied the gunman. With a jungle for a beard, he fearlessly dispatched round after round, favoring quantity over quality. The driver of their battered white pickup revved, ready to flee, with or without his partner.

Suddenly Dempsey landed beside her, his Desert Eagle pistol screeching overhead.

Boom! Boom! Boom! Boom!

The noise from the .50cal handgun ripped open the Baghdad sky. Spent casing fell on Charlie, fortifying her resolve. The pair blasted away as cracks from the attacker's gun splattered the wall and splintered the air.

The pickup window shattered. Its wing mirror disintegrated. Fearlessly the attacker blazed on. Then suddenly, out of ammo and time, he jumped into the truck just before it screeched off. Bullets flew as tires squalled.

Boom! Boom!

Boom! Boom!

Tariq jumped across to Dempsey and pulled his gun skyward. Callously sending bullets into the streets of Baghdad was off limits to the Terp. Both men flicked their safeties. Charlie did not need to; she was spent. Towering overhead, Dempsey pulled her to her faltering feet. Buckling knees didn't help the process. The wave of terror only fell when the danger had subsided. Shaking uncontrollably and on the edge of tears, Charlie held on for dear life. Dempsey's broad shoulders took the strain.

Like a troop of crazed chimps, they picked over each other's bodies. No nicks. No wounds. Physically unscathed. Mentally jarred. A heavy hand steadied her arm and escorted her into the ironclad sanctuary of the Rhino.

It was then that she noticed Kirk. Sweating and out of breath, leering around the end of the Rhino. "I'm sorry; I left my gun on the bus and couldn't get to it." He pointed to the bullet pock marks on the side of the Rhino. The apology was meant for, and accepted by, everyone.

Dempsey led. "There is nothing you could have done. Let's get everyone on board."

"Did we get him? Did we?" No one knew the answer to Tariq's desperate query.

Knot-kneed Charlie staggered on board, her heart racing like a bullet train. On the verge of collapse, she poured herself into the first available seat. Quivering breaths cleared out lungs filled with gun smoke. Out of nowhere, Mac slid in beside her and put his arms around her. "You're safe now, lassie."

With everyone on board, stuttering into action, Bassam grappled the gearstick to find any forward-facing gear. Grinding and growling, the gearbox bit back. The bus jolted ahead, throwing everyone into their seats. Bassam flung the hard rubber tires over the raised curbstones, throwing everyone back up in the air. No mirrors were employed as the bus crashed its way into the five-lane highway to the right of the museum.

Against all odds, Charlie held firm. To cry would be to show weakness, to let her attacker win. Under the watchful gaze of the dour Scot, she held on. *Not today.*

Tariq couldn't be silenced and wouldn't be seated. Through a hail of adrenaline-fueled expletives, he replayed the actions, recalled the moments, and replayed his actions. It took all of Kirk's guile and support to bring him back down to earth. Eventually, he was able to convince the trembling Terp to take a set up the back of the Rhino.

Cool and collected, Dempsey brought water to each of his crew. In turn he soothed souls, one brow at a time.

As the vehicle bulldozed through the traffic, no one looked back, and no one talked back. Road signs were optional. Bassam sideswiped three pickup trucks and a street cart. No one inside the bus cared. They sped on. The redirections spilling in across the radio sent the Rhino charging back to an alternative Green Zone checkpoint. Charlie's hands shook feverishly. She grabbed the seat in front and held on for dear life. Everyone crowded around, offering support. Although grateful, she needed space, room to breathe. Time to not think. She closed her eyes to the day. Tariq seemed a little more agitated. His squabbles with Bassam regarding the best route back to the Green Zone rang around the Rhino.

Feelings ran hot all the way to the base. As the shock subsided, dialogue emerged, centering entirely on the shooting and the welfare of those involved. With so many questions but no proper answers, Charlie threw out a vacant stare to close herself off from the chattering inquisitors. The stare remained long after the questions had disappeared.

Charlie quivered from top to toe, inside and out. She recalled advice that her father had given on a trip to their mountain cabin. *"Run your world, or your world will run you."* She knew getting ahead of this thing was the only way she could stop it from crushing her.

One last time, Mac checked in. "Sure, you're okay?"

"I'm fine," Charlie lied. She felt far from fine.

She had recognized one of her attackers.

CHAPTER 7

Dempsey convinced Bassam to slow down before they came upon the guards manning the initial Green Zone checkpoint. It seemed perverse to Charlie that the bilingual warning signs were predominantly in English when the biggest threats and dangers from misunderstandings came from Farsi speakers. National guard sentries were manning the post, armed with under-car mirrors and M4s. They were assisted by the local military, still rocking the undersized red beret look. .50-cals were trained high above them. The gunner sitting on top of the lead Humvee had his jaw set for action. Once they were back through the gates, the phrase "*Mission Accomplished*" was the furthest thing from Charlie's mind. Dempsey redirected them through a bumpy side road with high blast walls closing in on either side. Temperatures spiraled upwards as the vehicle eased forward under guard in the concrete canyon.

As the Rhino slowed, Dempsey took center aisle. "This is the emergency ingress route, normally reserved for casualties. We can get you through in double quick time."

The building had been decorated with garlands of razor wire. It had been repurposed, but Charlie found both its original form and current function difficult to ascertain. When the vehicle stopped, Dempsey supported every passenger off the bus, even if, like Mac, they didn't need or want it. After alighting and hitting the intercom at a nearby entry door, the boss was buzzed inside by parties unseen.

As he held the door open, everyone decanted into a large makeshift holding area. Undersized high-level windows threw brilliant squares of light across the worn tiled floor. The large juddering fan in the center of the room blasted hot air into their faces and forced innumerable particles of dust to dance and glisten in the light beams. Unfinished plasterwork showed signs of the hurried and ill-conceived installation and removal of various doorways windows and rooms.

Before the building's front door had closed, the Rhino could be seen trotting off into the distance.

When Dempsey transferred into the adjacent room, she caught sight of faceless men chattering around a notice board crammed with photographs, maps, and information. The door closed before any meaningful information could be gleaned. *Dempsey knew more than he was letting on.* Caution was one thing; obfuscation was something different all together.

Whilst she was keeping her secrets, so too were those around her. There was more to this than artifacts. It was obvious she lay outside Dempsey's circle of trust. If she was to find out more, she needed access to that incident room.

Scanning the waiting area, she found no CCTV. The door to the incident room had no lock. The entrance door was assessed by swipe card. Before any schemes could be planned and put into action, Dempsey reappeared and courteously confirmed the well-being of everyone involved.

"The medical center is across the roadway. We can give everyone the once over."

"I'm fine. I just want to go lie down."

The bout of universal nodding indicated Mac has spoken for everyone.

"We need to follow protocols. It won't take long," countered Dempsey.

"Screw protocols. We've been shot at, but we're all okay." Kirk made a good point.

"Screw this!" Mac had endured enough. "I'm going for a whiskey and a lie down. You're the boss; you do the paperwork."

"Does anyone need to visit the doc?"

No shaky hands were raised, so Dempsey closed things out.

"Okay. Back to Quarters it is, then. Mac, do you want a driver to take you home?"

"I'm a big boy. I can manage."

"Well, okay. Let's follow protocols everyone. Take the time to rest, complete your reports, and let's try to get this behind us. Okay?"

Charlie wasn't so sure. "What's behind all this, boss?"

"Behind what?"

"The attack. No one thinks this is a random drive-by, do they?" As she looked around the room, everyone looked away.

"We work on evidence. Until we know more, it is what it is."

"Listen, it's only natural to think it's personal, but this is Iraq."

"I hear that a lot."

"We are attacked each and every day. Hell, it's their favorite pastime, isn't it, Tariq?"

Perplexed, Tariq simply shrugged.

Charlie fizzed. "So that's it?"

"Sorry. These things happen. I'll log the attack, but that's about as far as it goes."

Dempsey's words landed hard. Kirk eased his hand under her arm. "Come on. We gotta go."

Adrenaline still pumping, she yanked her arm away. "I'm not a child."

Dempsey took the last word. "Then don't act like one."

As everyone milled out, Charlie's curiosity peaked. There were too many questions. She was there to investigate, yet the obfuscation Hank had warned her about was appearing at the most crucial of times. She remembered the guidance he offered during their last meeting. On her exit, she discreetly lifted an access card sitting on the entrance desk.

Near-death experience, or not, it was going to be a long night.

It was time to go rogue.

CHAPTER 8

That night, Charlie's BlackBerry alarm buzzed at 22:30 hours; late enough to ensure there would be few people around but early enough for her not to be shot at for creeping around in the dead of night. Already awake, there was no way she was going to miss her window. She pulled on her scuffed boots. In the bathroom, she pulled dusted latex gloves from a small first aid kit and snapped them on. She cleaned the access card and placed in the knee pocket of her combats. She then placed her BlackBerry in her rear pocket. Now was not the time to erase or degrade the card's encoding by placing it near her phone. She was uncertain the card would give her access, but if it did, she could be in and out of the office in three minutes. Nothing could be traced back to her.

Outside in the shadows, hoodie pulled over, she confirmed the walkway was clear before easing out into the dark. Her unit was one of ten set in a row on the edge of a military tented village, just a mortar's throw from the nearby command center. She skirted around the poorly lit margins of the canvas alleyways before arriving at the corner of a small square. Deciding that bold was best, she straightened her back and marched across the open area, maintaining a gait and a speed designed to avoid attention. She had rehearsed an alibi that centered on newbie nerves if she was challenged. It wasn't needed.

Apprehension and the chilled night breeze ripped her skin. Breathing was proving difficult. An afternoon wasted staring at the ceiling recounting the life-threatening events of the day had only compounded her anxiety. Cleaning the gun hadn't helped. The only sliver of light appeared in a call confirming that no civilian casualties had been reported from around the museum area. Completing an incident report had only brought events back into sharp focus.

Turning a corner, she arrived at the block that housed the incident room. Looking around one last time, she produced the key card, rubbed it clean on her thigh for luck, then pulled it through the entry slot. The light turned green, and the door lock clicked. Fear quelled excitement. A three-sixty-degree scan told her she was on track and alone. A gentle push, and she slipped inside.

Her flashlight was activated and angled directly downward, sheltering its beam to keep the room as dark as possible. The key card was wiped one last time, then placed under the desk it had been stolen from. If its disappearance had been noted earlier, its reappearance under the desk would hopefully seem plausible. The late-night activation of the door would no doubt appear on the log, but that wouldn't be checked if no foul play was suspected. That was the working theory at least.

Her gloved hand tentatively turned the handle on the inner door. She had noted earlier it held no lock. Inside, the room seemed little more than a sealed off corridor. She moved to switch on the light, but quickly talked herself out of it. *There could be cameras.* Gaining a little more confidence from being in a windowless room, Charlie raised her flashlight to a wider angle and edged her way over to the info boards. They looked repurposed, hastily prepared, and confused. An array of displayed pictures and detailed attachments were haphazardly thrown up onto the sun-damaged felt board. As the flashlight beam lit the notices, it helped her scan for clues. Artifacts, smuggling, forgeries, thefts, and shipments. There were innumerable crime scenes and victims on the photo wall.

Photographs of suspects were conspicuous by their absence. A multitude of sins, but precious few sinners adorned the mottled-green boards. A hastily constructed spider's web had been scribbled on an attached dry wipe board. Nicknames, code names, and local sounding pseudonyms all hung outside of the red lined framework. The chart appeared high on intent, but low on content. In the center of the web sat one word. That word screamed out from the board.

Serpent.

Inspecting another section of the board, she recoiled in horror at photographs of nameless, sometimes faceless, and often limbless victims. Charlie swallowing hard and staggered backwards, banging hard against the main table. Neat piles of paper toppled. One pile cascaded to the floor along with the flashlight. Gripping the table edges for support, she arrested her tailspin. Suddenly, her BlackBerry beeped at what sounded to be double volume. She smothered the sound, then opened a text newly arrived from Kirk.

It simply read:

Get out now!

She hurriedly reclaimed her flashlight, made a panicked attempt at collating the disturbed papers, then broke for the door. When she stuck her head out of the unit, she noticed Kirk lurking in the murk, impatiently miming for her to hurry. She jumped across the pathway into a barrage of whispered warnings. "There's a patrol scheduled in one minute. We have to get out of here." They edged into the shadows before the promised patrol arrived. The scene descended into silence.

Unnoticed, a shadow shifted from a nearby, blackened doorway.

Charlie traveled half a stride ahead of Kirk at a pace somewhere between an ill-tempered strop and a panicked jog. They strode in silence until far enough away from the unit that their purpose had some semblance of plausibility if they were to be stopped. After a couple of unsuccessful requests for her to slow down, Kirk gently touched her arm.

"What were you doing in there?" he hissed.

Flustered and curious, she did not owe him an explanation. "Were you following me? What the hell?"

"Don't make this about me," he replied. "You broke into that office."

Undeterred, Charlie maintained a good head of steam. "Were you spying on me?"

"I wasn't spying," Kirk protested. "Looking out for you. I wanted to make sure you were okay, after all the crap you've dealt with."

Charlie's face remained unconvinced, so Kirk pressed his case. "I was staking out your place to make sure you didn't have any unwelcome visitors and when you came out—"

"I can't believe you followed me!"

Kirk did not defend himself further. "Yes. I followed you; all the way to your bout of breaking and entering. What the hell were you playing at?"

"Why didn't you stop me?"

Kirk stayed his course. "I didn't know you had a key. You were in through the door before I could say anything."

"No. Why didn't you stop me before then?"

"And say what? 'Hi Charlie, I was just over in the shadows spying on you and I noticed you were out for an evening stroll. If you don't mind me asking, what are you playing at?' How well would that have played out?"

"So, you were spying on me?"

"Not spying. Looking after."

"Why would I need looking after?"

"You've just been shot at. And Dempsey was far from helpful. Remember?"

"You were shot at too! Remember? At least I had a gun." Her hackles were up. "Is it because I'm a woman?"

"What? No! It's because you're new. This shit takes some getting used to. Believe me."

Charlie didn't believe him. "I said I was okay, and I was. I still am."

"People say anything when they've faced bullets. I was only trying to help. Stop making this about me. I'm trying to look after you."

"Ugh!"

Kirk grabbed an arm to stop her from storming off. "Jesus Christ. Calm down. You'll get yourself arrested at this rate. Or worse."

Charlie remained on the defensive. "Is that a threat?"

"Eh? Of course not. Remember, I'm one of the good guys. If I hadn't pulled you out of there, you would be in the brig right now."

Charlie continued to parry. "I don't need your help, and I didn't ask for it either. Get out of my face!"

She freed herself then stomped off defiantly. Kirk pulled up, flabbergasted. As their paths diverged, the only thing that seemed to unite them was a mental quest to figure out what the hell had just happened.

Back in her room, Charlie paced her confines. Dark, confused thoughts clattered off the walls. Lost and alone, she found it impossible to forget the photographs of the dead pinned to the board in the incident room. That almost bothered her more than the recent gun battle.

A mouthful of smuggled fiery bourbon did not help matters. The day's events ricocheted around her mind. Everything had happened in a flash. She was proud to have kept her cool and sent off some quality shots. The smell of gunpowder and the ear shattering gunfire had seemed incredible, even invigorating.

She had thrown out hot lead in a built-up area without giving it a second thought. Given the target's range and velocity, the shots were pointless. Still, she let rip. The place was lawless, and although it took her some time to admit it, she was settling right in. The bullied, weak child from the night before had not reappeared. She only saw the driver for a split second after he turned behind the museum, but she recognized him as the intruder from the evening before. He had told her she would die like a serpent and now he had aided someone in the unloading of an AK-47 in her general direction. There was no coincidence and no doubt—he wanted her dead.

She slumped into the folding canvas chair, cleared the table and her thoughts, then tapped away at her laptop. As instructed, She sent her reports to Hank. Over half of what she typed did not pass censorship. The delete button took a hell of a beating. The facts were presented without supposition or theater. To avoid panic or persecution, all unsubstantiated or inflammatory revelations did not make the final edit. Her extra-curricular activities remained off the record.

She told the truth, and nothing but the truth.

She did not tell the whole truth, for that remained a mystery, even to her.

CHAPTER 9

The next morning Charlie woke at her desk to find that she had been using her watch as a pillow. The leather cover had left a massive imprint across her high tanned cheekbone. It also took several more minutes for her hand to fully waken.

She elected to take a shower to straighten things out, though she stayed in there for longer than water saving guidelines allowed. She set the tap to cold and braced for impact, only to be disappointed by it being marginally warmer than tepid. As the water pelted down on her, she tried to compartmentalize every aspect of the hell she had landed in, but the faces, places, clues, and ideas leaped from one box to the next. She could find no peace of mind. Her thoughts were too cluttered to be of any use, so she exited the shower, loosely toweled herself dry, then threw on a t-shirt and baggy shorts—standard issue for anyone confined to quarters.

As she angled herself for another attack on her paperwork, a car horn blew. She ignored it the first few times before exasperation forced her hand. She peeked out the door to find a white Mitsubishi pickup truck. The window lowered to reveal Kirk's apologetic face. Wry wrinkles filled her face as she closed the door to throw on her combats. It only took a few moments before she bounded out the door and into the waiting pickup. Kirk opened the door in anticipation of some form of apology that never arrived. He pulled the gearshift and set the truck in motion.

"Nice wheels. Stolen or impounded?"

Kirk smirked and pondered for a half-moment. "A little of both."

"Where are you taking me? We're consigned to quarters; in case you've forgotten."

"After what you pulled last night, you're worried about breaching a daytime curfew?"

"Touché. So, why didn't you knock on my door?"

"I was scared you'd pull a knife on me. At least in the car I could drive off if you came at me. Here, put this on." Kirk handed her an open weave headscarf made from the finest slate gray cotton. Charlie donned the scarf in a well-practiced fashion. Kirk appeared impressed. Charlie bluffed her way past the moment. "Well, you know I've got form for shooting up getaway cars." The unavoidable allure of Kirk's aftershave wandered from his scarf.

Upon arrival at the exit checkpoint, the guard recognized Kirk, gave him an exaggerated salute, then signaled for the barrier to be lifted.

Charlie shook her head. "Is there no one around here you don't know?"

Kirk shrugged with false modesty. "Well, you know me."

“That’s the problem. I don’t.” Charlie’s blurted words hit the mark.

“Easy, tigress. I’m on your side, remember?”

Charlie threw him a questioning look.

“Don't worry. This baby has been redneck rigged with armor plating. It drives like shit, but we'll be safe.”

Charlie hadn’t been worried, but all the talk of armor plating brought forward fears of IEDs and snipers. She pulled the headscarf tighter and eased down a little further into the seat.

The pickup turned onto an insanely busy street. Cars hurried and harried. Unheeded horns jabbered incessantly. Adherence to lane markings and traffic signs seemed purely optional. Hijabs and havoc, clerics, and chaos—the city appeared alive.

“Where are we going?”

“You still don’t trust me?”

“Of course, I don’t!”

“Ha! Here take this.”

Charlie leaned away, startled when Kirk reached down and pulled his service weapon. Flipping the gun, he handed the weapon across, handle first. “Here.”

Charlie leaned back in and took control of the weapon. “Easy now, lady. That thing’s loaded,” chided Kirk.

Charlie held firm in the face of Kirk’s mock chauvinism. She examined the gun in great detail. “Smith and Wesson, nine-millimeter, nineteen-shot parabellum.”

“So, you have the basics. Not bad.”

"Striker-fired, Zytel polymer frame reinforced with a stainless-steel chassis, removable and interchangeable grip inserts, 180° grip angle. Need I go on?"

Kirk laughed. "Could you?"

"Melonite slide and barrel at 68 Rockwell C surface hardness rating with non-glare surface. The low slide profile holds the barrel axis at a position that reduces muzzle rise, allowing for faster aim recovery and more rapid shooting sequences."

Kirk thumped the steering wheel. "Damn! Maybe I should ask for that back."

Charlie felt part of it now and was enjoying every second. Being the only armed person in the car helped. "So where are we headed?"

"Palestine."

"Palestine?"

"You'll see."

"Don't forget, I'm armed," she half joked.

"How could I forget?"

Charlie shifted her focus. Outside felt like the real Iraq; the one she wanted to see. The one hidden behind high blast walls or one-way bulletproof glass. The anonymity brought by a headscarf and an old pickup gave Charlie a sense of security not felt since her arrival in the country. This felt quite the departure from her iron-clad trip down Route Irish.

An emaciated, flea-bitten dog who had seen too much of this life struggled past, too downtrodden to bark. The land she had left seemed light years from the world she now inhabited. As a child she had been forbidden to own a dog. Pop always said it would be cruel to leave it in house all day, alone. Now she saw firsthand the true meaning of cruelty. A dog abandoned with no home at all. A living creature abused then left to the fates. *Iraq in a microcosm.*

She needed to clear the air "About last night—"

"There's no need to apologize."

"Apologize? Me?"

Kirk bit back. "Well, you did come over a bit strong."

"Some would say, with just cause."

"Back here, are we?"

"Sounds like it. Why were you following me?"

"Look I—"

"Think before you speak. Remember, I'm the one with the gun."

A little playful brandishing helped loosen Kirk's tongue. "Look. It's simple."

"You're a newbie who got shot at."

"So, you think I was a target?"

"Hell no! It was a random attack. They happen every day."

"So then why am I so special?"

"You're not, but you see how I am with people. I care."

"Care enough to go wandering around the grounds in the middle of the night?'

"I was shot at too."

"It's not a competition."

"I don't mean it that way. I was a little shook up, so I went for a walk. Guess who I found wandering the compound?"

"That's not how you painted it last night."

"That's the scene. I thought you'd be grateful."

"Five minutes later and you would have been going home in shackles. You need to understand that."

Charlie dithered. "Can we just leave it?"

Kirk was unsure. "Leave it where you trust me or leave it where you don't."

"Leave it where I'm still deciding."

"Wow. That's the best you can do?"

"For now."

Kirk chortled and shook his head.

The truck bundled out into a busier thoroughfare. The narrow lanes running through and along the larger boulevards were filled with life and vibrancy. Ad hoc barbers, shops, and restaurants were scattered down their length. Charlie stared in awe of the chaos and confusion that swarmed the streets. Cafés were doing a roaring trade, oblivious to the stresses and strife of modern-day Iraq. Men sat outside playing dominos and backgammon, their respective levels of success and enjoyment on display for all to see. Next door at an open-sided teahouse, old friends syphoned charcoal smoke from the Nargileh water pipe. Spice-lined smoke and laughter-inducing stories floated up into the late morning air.

"It's madness out there!"

Kirk provided more color. "You're not wrong. Just before the war, Saddam released hundreds of certifiably insane criminals right out into the streets of Baghdad. They were never heard from again. They're out there raping, murdering, and profiteering without a care. Not one fully functioning brain amongst them."

Kirk slammed on the brakes as a squad of teenage boys scampered across in front of them. They shared mischief and mayhem but no malice. "Look at them. What hope do they have? You had to be a member of the Ba'ath Party if you wanted to teach in this country. Now that we disbanded and outlawed all that, who's going to teach them? And what are they going to be taught?"

The kids danced and played in the middle of the traffic, incurring wrath from all avenues. Their clothing may have fit someone at some time. But the boys were not those people, and this was not the time. The traffic stopped, and the recriminations started. Even Charlie cracked. "What the hell are they playing at?"

Kirk grinned and pointed. "Watch."

Across the lane ahead, two boys sneakily approached the back of a large stationary truck. In a slick pincer movement, they opened the cap on the side mounted fuel tank and inserted a long hose. They then climbed in under the cover of the truck's wheels. With practiced perfection, the tiniest of the terrible twins sucked eagerly at the illicit fuel source. Within seconds their plunder made its way into the dirty plastic can requisitioned specifically for the job at hand. Before the daring daytime heist could be completed, a fellow driver alerted the truck driver to the crime being perpetrated. The subsequent thump on the young lookout's back from the truck driver's baton looked a small price to pay for the newly gained commodity. The laughing cavaliers absconded into the crowd, no doubt to argue over their fuel distribution policy. It appeared a comedic tragedy.

"That's them getting their education right there," Charlie quipped. Even jammed in amongst the crowded confusion, Charlie seemed remarkably at ease. "The toughest crowds I've ever seen before this were at the Black Friday sales at Macys. This is something else." She fought the urge to wind down the window to take it all in. "Why does it feel safer in an old pickup than it does in a Rhino?"

"Because it is. We're not RPG magnets like the Coalition vehicles. It's much safer until it isn't. If we get caught, that would be a problem. But don't worry, there are reinforcements under your seat, if it comes to it." Charlie reached down and under in search of what she assumed would be ammunition. Instead, she pulled out a standard US issue hand grenade.

"Are you serious? Grenades?"

Kirk let out a startled laugh. "Be careful! Put that thing back."

A bemused and somewhat worried Charlie did as she was told. "What do you need grenades for?"

"You're not in Kansas anymore, Dorothy." Kirk smirked, brushing the question off.

Charlie squirmed in impish silence. The pickup turned into the wide thoroughfare of Yafa Street before barreling on to the Al Jumariyah Bridge. It was the first time Charlie had seen the flowing and functional Tigris. It looked far from magical and felt far from home.

Despite the bright, wide vistas, the river seemed soulless, bereft of character, resigned to its fate. Across the river, humanity flowed on. The masses slowed their progress yet again. An aging man feverishly pitched the wares from his cluttered stand underneath a faded soft drink umbrella. Nothing on his cart seemed to be of any worth or use, yet he was doing a roaring trade. Toy guns, spark plugs, jump leads, windscreen washers, fluffy towels, children's windmills, toothbrushes, and garden hoses all featured in his display.

Worthless random crap looked to be a sought-after commodity in battle-torn Iraq. Farther along, the battle of the flags raged from wall to wall. Coalition-planted Stars and Stripes motifs vied for position against two generations of Iraqi Flag—the jaded grandeur of Saddam's regime, and the new, more edgy graffiti spreading out in support of a bright new Iraq. Lurching from one traffic jam to the next, they eventually entered a busy roundabout at the end of a grid locked avenue. The edge of the roundabout crumbled into the roadway, causing multiple last-minute lane changes. Charlie gazed out beyond the windowpane towards a sight she was proud to recognize from the guidebooks. She pointed like a tourist. "Tahrir Square?"

Kirk nodded and elaborated. "Tahrir Monument. It's a beacon." Kirk drew the truck up alongside to provide a curb-crawler's view. All echelons of Iraqi society swarmed around the long, narrow, limestone mural. The homeless and downtrodden rubbed shoulders with the elbows of the affluent and eager. The diversity in direction of travel was palpable. People were going places, going nowhere, or going downhill. Every soul seemed consumed by their own story and disinterested or mistrusting of others. Charlie gawked like a tourist at the emotive bronze depictions that gilded the white stone background.

"I wouldn't say it's beautiful. It's certainly striking."

With a doleful sigh, Kirk set the pickup in motion and rejoined the chaos of the Baghdad roads. He had seen enough. "It's a crock!"

Charlie disagreed. "Well, I like it."

"It was built to celebrate the new republic in '58."

Charlie nodded. "Back when they thought they had a bright future. What does it show?"

"Iraqi tribes moving through time to a wondrous peace. From chaos comes harmony."

Charlie cut him a glance laced in disapproval. "Isn't that a good thing?"

Kirk found it difficult to hide his exasperation. "You'd think. It was designed by an Arab. The mural reads right to left, from chaos to harmony. When Westerners read it, the story goes from harmony to chaos."

Charlie understood, to a point. "So, who's right?"

"Even their memorial to peace is crammed with pictures of war." A sigh punctuated his rant. "The Sunnis, the Shiite, the Sufi, the Kurds—they all hate each other. The only thing they agree on is hating us."

A brief journey led them to a checkpoint outside a tall building. The revelation came when she read the signage, *The Palestine International Hotel.*

"So, this is Palestine?"

"In some form or another." Kirk gestured to lose the headgear before reaching security. Charlie obliged. Before exiting, Kirk pulled out a small, clanking, camouflaged rucksack from behind his seat.

"What will I do with this?" Charlie held Kirk's pistol.

"Slide it under the seat."

Charlie obliged. "What have you got under here?"

"Yeah, go easy down there."

"What the hell?" Charlie reeled at the sight of the grenade she had just pulled from beneath the seat.

"What the hell do you need these for?"

"Covering all eventualities."

"What eventualities will this cover?"

Kirk stayed cool. "You never know around here. This is Iraq. You're not in Kansas City anymore, Dorothy."

Charlie gestured towards her boots with a wry smile. "Well, I guess these ain't ruby slippers."

With no signs that Kirk was slowing down or turning back, Charlie quickly stowed the weapons.

At the checkpoint, a lowly guard threw a cursory glance across their credentials Kirk announced he had a meeting with some journalist from the *Wall Street Journal*. Backing his claim for access with a crisp fifty dollar note appeared to seal the deal. They were given a superficial inspection and ushered through into the hotel car park.

Charlie made an assumption. "There is no meeting, is there?"

Kirk checked his rearview mirror. "Of course not."

"What about the weapons?"

"Leave them. We'll be safe here."

"You're leaving a car full of grenades in downtown Baghdad?"

"What do you want me to do with them—bring them into the hotel? Come on."

The pickup door slammed shut.

Racial profiling was alive and well in the hotel lobby. The pair waltzed through security. Westerners were treated like long-lost family members, whilst anyone with a hint of exotic ethnicity was harangued and harassed with impunity. Not for the first time did the process ease because of Kirk's presence. The metal detector frame seemed an instrument of security designed for others. Whether he had something to hide or nothing to declare, Kirk brandished his badge and pushed past all the other obedient suckers.

Charlie took her place in the 1980s mock-lavish surroundings. The hotel's over-processed faux rosewood matched the ornate golden painted motifs and surroundings perfectly. The red carpeting had lost a little of its edge over time. She waited for Kirk to complete his negotiations with his long-lost friend at the front desk. He seemed friends with everyone in this town. The tall alluring manager beamed broadly and shook his hand warmly. When his hand then slipped something into his breast pocket, Charlie knew they had exchanged more than pleasantries.

On route to the elevator, Kirk offered polite introductions. "Charlie, can I introduce Kamal, an all-around fixer and good friend? He's a great guy to know in these parts. Kamal, Agent Charlie Glass. Just joined the team. I'm showing her the hotspots."

Kamal blushed warmly, raising his eyebrows to the heavens. "There are a lot of those around here, Mr. Kirk."

Mandataries completed, they moved on, leaving the smiling Manger in their wake. Passing a service trolley, Kirk picked up two teacups without breaking stride. They bounced on ahead just in time to beat the closing elevator doors. Kirk continued the tour. "So, this is the infamous Palestine International Hotel. I'm going to share the best view in town with you."

The elevator squeaked and buffeted its way to the top floor, where the heavy doors clanked opened. The couple sidled out and through a second set of heavy doors onto the hotel's large rooftop area. The entire city spread out in front of them, the cloudless panorama coated in a magnificently receding golden luster. Islands of verdant palms floated in a sea of dusty low-rise buildings. The city was a kaleidoscope of architectural styles, with beautiful, ornate minarets and gaudy palaces puncturing the city's skyline. Stale, imposing government buildings completed the mottled picture. The sounds of humanity fighting its way back to normality surged up from the city below. Iraq was everything Charlie hoped it would be. It was also everything she hoped it wouldn't be but for now, she remained in awe. Kirk produced two small thermos flasks. Shaking them, he begged the question: "Hot or cold? Either will blow your head off."

Charlie chose the hot option. Steaming Turkish tar toppled into the small teacups requisitioned earlier. Leaning over the wall, Kirk gazed out through a haze of melancholy.

"This is where all the journalists were holed up at the start of the invasion. They filmed the missiles hitting the palaces and government buildings from here. Crazy."

After a moment of silent lamentation, he continued. "Jaffar al-Mansour turned this sleepy little village called Baghdad into the capital over a thousand years ago. Mansour tried to have its name changed to Madinat as-Salaam. *The City of Peace*."

"It never came to that?"

"I doubt it ever will."

Lapsing into thoughtful silence, they drank their coffee and made their own ways around the rooftop, casting their gazes and thoughts to the four corners of the city. Paths and thoughts never crossed.

Out of nowhere, Kirk dropped the bombshell. "You really are quite beautiful."

Charlie leaned away. "Inside voice, please."

"Sorry I don't mean it that way. I-I-I mean, we're all grunts over here."

"So, it's 'What's a nice girl like you doing in a place like this?' Is that the best you can do? I thought you were better than that."

"Sorry, let me go again, please."

Charlie waved him on, desperate to leave the awkwardness behind.

"What brings you to a war zone? None of the rest of us have any real options. You could do anything."

"I want to make a difference. Make people proud."

"People?"

"My dad."

"You can do that without putting your life in danger."

"I guess I want to live the life he always wanted."

"You've lost me."

Charlie chuckled. "I lose most men."

"Seriously I'm interested."

"When I was younger, he'd have chances to travel to far-flung places as part of his work."

"Military?"

"Historian. He was called upon to support a number of archeological digs. When he left, he would leave me books to read up on so that when he returned, we could compare notes."

"Hence your love of history."

"And my thirst for travel. I would sit awake at night, waiting for his call. Sometimes it would come; often it would not."

"What did your mother say?"

"She wasn't there. I had great neighbors who would look after me when he was gone." To his credit and Charlie's relief, Kirk seemed to sense her discomfort.

"And that's where the Arabic comes from?"

She nodded. "That was Pop's doing. He visited Egypt mostly, so when we talked, we would try to carry out as much of the conversation in Arabic as possible."

"He knew it?"

"No, we learned together."

"Your Arabic is strong. He must have been gone a lot."

"He was gone, but he was always there." The words chimed in Charlie's heart. She missed her father more that she wanted to admit, even to herself.

After a few moments of reflection, Kirk broke the spell. "So, you broke into the office last night to find out more about the drive-by?"

Charlie gave nothing away. "Something like that. I thought I could unearth a lead."

"A lead? What are you now, a detective?"

"Eh, I do work for the FBI, you know. Or have you forgotten that?"

"Have you forgotten that? Breaking and entering is a crime over here, as well you know."

"I have a key card, remember? That's hardly breaking and entering."

"I didn't see any approvals for this kind of action from your boss."

"How do you know I haven't gotten one?"

"Because no boss in his right mind would sanction such a dumbass move. Why didn't you bring me in?"

"Because you'd talk me out of it by using phrases like 'dumbass move.'"

Kirk held his hands up. "Listen. Last night, I was only trying to help."

Charlie needed to offload, and Kirk was the only person she could turn to. Uncertain of her level of trust, she lay back on one of the discolored sun loungers. Feelings were not her thing, so she opened with a question.

"What do you think the attack was all about?"

"Dumb luck. They see us as invaders; every one of us shouldn't be here according to them, and this is their way of showing it."

"By killing people?"

"It sends a message."

"It's getting worse instead of better."

"For sure. Disbanding the Iraqi army sent armed, dangerous, and capable people out into the general population. Under Saddam they used to extinguish any hint of disobedience or insurgency, and now they're part of it."

"And now there's no one left to keep everyone in check?"

"You're catching on. They threw the foxes guarding the chicken coop right inside it. It's the Wild West out there. Illegal guns, vendettas, sectarian hatred, out-and-out criminality—you name it."

Charlie challenged his premise. "What if it wasn't random?"

Kirk twisted his head and slowly processed the query. He tilted his head playfully and smiled as if waiting for an explanation.

"I think I knew the driver," she elaborated.

Kirk choked on his coffee. "What?"

"Well, I met him. He assaulted me. The day before the shooting."

Kirk blinked and pulled Charlie around to face him. "Where? When?"

"I was working late, and I heard someone in the back room. When I investigated, the driver of the car was in there, rifling through the cabinets. When he saw me, he attacked me."

"Did he hurt you?"

"I'm fine. He didn't hurt me. He choked me and threatened to kill me before I got the better of him."

Pride compelled Charlie to conceal her capitulation. Kirk's brow knotted. There was no denying the concern in his eyes. "Why not report it, even to me?"

"For the same reason I didn't kick his ass; I just froze. I didn't know where to turn. I had just arrived, and there was I, allowing an intruder to escape. Pretty weak if you ask me."

"We could have gone after him. Someone could have recognized him."

"I know that now. By the time I had all that figured out, he was gone."

"And by then, you didn't want to admit your failings."

Charlie hated the word, but failings seemed apt. "Well, I'm telling you now."

"It's a little too late."

"Okay, don't rub it in. I'm knew to this, remember? We're not all perfect."

"None of us are that. This entire place is one screwup after another."

"And what would your biggest screw up be?"

Kirk smiled. "Well, I'm not proud that earlier I hid behind a bus while my crew was taking pot shots."

"We took care of business."

"Ha! Get you. You're settling in well."

Charlie reflected. "It's amazing how bold you feel with a Glock in your hand and two guns blazing by your side."

Kirk slammed his palm down. "You go, girl." Before Charlie had time to reflect on her mock bravado, Kirk brought her back to reality. "Are you sure it was the guy? There was a lot of crap flying around out there today. Heat of the battle and all that."

"It was him. The more I think of it, the more I'm convinced."

"What do you think he was after?"

"Documents. He was sifting through them like he was looking for something specific."

"Stealing paperwork?" inquired Kirk.

"Could be. Didn't you say a documented artifact is worth a thousand times more than one without documents?"

"Maybe in Paris or New York, but around here, you can pick up a cuneiform on a street corner for a hundred bucks."

Charlie was undeterred. "What if they are switching out artifacts, falsifying documents, and selling them to the highest bidders abroad?"

Kirk found it all a bit too farfetched. "How would they sell them or even get them out the country?"

"We repatriate a mountain of crap that could cover for smuggling. Selling it through the dark web would be easy."

A cynical sneer warped Kirk's face as more mad cap ideas wandered to the front of Charlie's mind. "My attacker told me I would die like a serpent. On the incident room wall there was a messy org chart and, in the center, sat the name, 'Serpent.'"

Kirk puzzled over her words. "So, either the Serpent is dead, or it was a threat against him."

"I can't remember much else."

"You didn't take any photos?" Kirk asked in disbelief.

Charlie snorted. "No, because some asshole texted me to get out, immediately."

"I was saving your ass!"

The pair let a calming silence pull them apart, and Charlie plundered Kirk's small rucksack. Before he could stop her, she had jerked open the zipper, fumbled with an old mobile phone and some keys, and pulled out the second flask.

Kirk snatched his bag back. "What are you doing?"

"It's time for the cold option." She used splashes of the clear liquid to rid each teacup of coffee sediment. Adult rations of firewater were then issued. They downed the contents and squirmed their smiling faces towards each other. Reality became temporarily contorted. A moment was shared before another mouthful was attempted. If anything, Charlie thought the second mouthful even more painful. Her face failed to hide the fact. Kirk laughed. "See? Even the local hooch is criminal."

Charlie was still certain of her theory. "What does 'die like a serpent' mean? I've been looking online, but I can't find anything."

Kirk shook his head. "No idea. Sorry. Are you sure that's what he said?"

"Dead sure. I've been running over all kinds of reasons he would want to kill me, and the only explanation is that he regrets leaving me alive in the back office. I'm unfinished business."

Kirk remained skeptical. "But there's nothing in that office worth stealing, let alone worth killing for. What was he looking for?"

"I didn't stop to ask," Charlie said, her words as dry as the Iraqi desert. "I was distracted. The files he was looking at were on shipments, nothing high end or confidential."

Kirk took another angle. "Does he just hate women who flaunt themselves in public without a hijab?

"Flaunt?"

"You know what I mean. They take chauvinism to a new level over here."

Charlie dismissed the notion. "There's more to this. He must own a pass to get onto the base. He understands English, as he was reading the files. He must have seen our schedules to know I would be at the museum on that day at that time."

"So, an inside accomplice?"

"Or he was an insider himself."

A stifling atmosphere enveloped the scene. The longer they conversed, the more their thoughts aligned. It was Kirk who summarized. "So, we're looking for a traditionally dressed bearded local, who speaks English, has access to the zone, and is connected enough to someone to find out movements and schedules. That narrows it down to only a few hundred people. Should we go door to door?"

"It's not much, but it's a start. I think I should take it upstairs to Dempsey."

Things were heating up, but Kirk tempered. "And say what? You let an intruder escape, and he came back to silence you at the museum? For your sake, I'd say wait. And anyway, I still don't understand what Dempsey's angle is."

Charlie glared in disbelief. "You don't think he's involved, do you?"

"Hell no. I just don't think you should bring in anymore unknowns. It's a case of say no more 'til you know more. It's probably just some nut job, bent on Jihad. More than likely, he'll have reloaded and set his sights on someone else before Friday prayers."

Charlie lay on the edge of retreat. "I thought it would be bad, but this is out of control. I don't know if I can do this."

"It's difficult," Kirk empathized. "I don't know you that well, but you look like you need a hug."

A grateful Charlie smiled back. "You're right. You don't know me that well."

In the heat, Kirk stripped off his collared shirt to reveal a taut t-shirt. Flexing his not inconsiderable muscles, a tattoo emerged from the line of Kirk's sleeve.

Charlie was intrigued. "Who's that guy? Impressive."

Kirk pulled down the cotton to conceal what Charlie had already noticed—an incredibly detailed tattoo of a mystical creature formed from a lion, an eagle, and a bearded man. Muscles and armor flashed. Unlike the tattoo, Kirk was low on detail. "Local superstition. My talisman."

"And does your talisman have a name?"

"He does."

Charlie closed the conscious gap that followed by pulling out her own talisman. "This is mine. I've had it from childhood. It's an old Civil War button from Grant himself."

Kirk was back on deck. "Can I see?"

She pulled the trinket over her head and passed it over. "Be careful; it's the most precious thing I own."

Kirk playfully scoffed as he inspected. "Wow, you can't own much."

Charlie took the jibe well. "It's my good luck charm, my guide."

Kirk held the button to the light and examined it, like a jeweler examining a precious diamond. "Can you prove this was actually Grant's button?"

Charlie snatched it back. "That's not the first time I've been asked that."

Kirk's inquiring grin was cut short by the announcement of a text message hitting his BlackBerry. He pulled the phone from the right leg of his combat pants and punched in the same number four times. With the phone unlocked, the message wiped the smile from his face.

Charlie sensed a change in the atmosphere. "What is it?"

"A tip-off. A deal going down tonight."

Curiosity piqued; Charlie was keen to join the fray. "What kind of deal?"

"Smugglers wanting to trade artifacts at a warehouse on the Southside."

"How do they have your number?" Charlie asked, eyeing him with skepticism.

"I put it about. We get tips, buy backs, offer bribes. You can imagine."

"I can now. Who's it from?"

"Anonymous."

"A trap?"

"More than likely, it's genuine." Kirk gathered his belongings. "Do you fancy a ride along?"

Charlie rose slowly to her feet. "More than likely genuine?"

Kirk smirked as he packed. "Come on. You're the one with the Smith and Wesson."

Charlie stalled.

"We gotta go. If you're coming, great. If not, I'll drop you back in the Green Zone."

Charlie blustered past her trepidation. "Do we take it upstairs?"

"No. Most of these are trinkets hardly worthy of comment. There have been. Too many false alarms for the bosses to be interested. I'll check it out first."

Under a mountain of mistrust, Charlie dug deep. "Okay, you got me. Let's go treasure hunting."

"Atta girl!"

"You never know—today may be our lucky day. After all, I have my talisman."

CHAPTER 10

An eerie dusk smothered the streets on the approach to the warehouse. In a dark corner, feral goats chewed away at a mountain of garbage. Burned-out cars and looted properties littered the scene. Abandoned children, too young to understand, splashed and played in the sewage-infested waters flooding part of the road, immune to the ungodly smell that enveloped them. The mayhem outside was the last thing on Charlie's mind as she fought to process the events of this spiraling chaos. By the time Kirk had traversed the anarchy, darkness had descended on the south side of the city. Much to Charlie's chagrin, limited reinforcements had been called. Kirk had been adamant; only Tariq could be trusted. Coalition troops would scare off the dealer, and the local police would more than likely steal the loot for themselves. The plan was simple. Get there early, hang in the shadows to make sure it was no trap, then move in for the trade. The location had been checked and rechecked. They were at the allotted rendezvous point, unfashionably early, on a gloomy side street.

"Where's Tariq? You said he'd be here." With one less gun on their side, Charlie's voice wavered. Her nerves jittered in the silence.

"I don't know." Kirk checked his phone. "Still nothing. Let me call him." The call rang out for an eternity. A text arrived the second the call dropped. After keying in his access code, Kirk read the text aloud.

"'Sorry, boss. Big visitor from US. No go.'"

Kirk offered Charlie one last chance to call it off. She refused, and in return, offered him the same deal. With a shake of his head and a rueful smile, Kirk exited the pickup and dragged a small rucksack out from under his seat. "I've got the cash. Got your Glock?"

A nervous smile creased her face as she tapped her sidearm. "Always."

"Okay. Keep it in the leather for now. I don't want to get shot in the ass." Charlie nodded past the insult. The hairs on the back of her neck bristled. This was what she'd trained for. This was the sharp end. She owned the moment. Butterflies churned her stomach. The pickup doors closed with a soft click. Kirk moved forward, holding his Beretta M9 pistol out in front. Their two dark figures passed without a sound through the side gate of the poorly lit compound.

Nothing stirred—even the distant traffic dimmed into the distance. An eerie silence blanketed the scene. Charlie opened the tie on her holster. She slid forward, safety in place. Her thumb itched. Her heart raced. Under the shadow of a high walkway, the pair leaned against the inside of the high walls, acclimatizing their eyes to the lighting maintained to Iraqi standards. There were no motion sensors to announce their arrival or illuminate their way. After checking the vicinity, the pair sidled around the perimeter wall to a position out of sight of the solitary CCTV camera. In the low lighting, Charlie assumed the old school surveillance equipment would be next to worthless. After one last glance left and right, the intruders snaked across the open yard. Halfway across, all hell broke loose.

Bang! Bang!

Two loud shots cracked from inside the unit. Charlie threw herself to the ground in full panic.

Bang!

Visceral fear clamped Charlie to the spot. Kirk grabbed her arm and pulled her behind a dilapidated half wall. She closed her eyes and yelped.

Bang! Bang!

Surprise morphed into fear in a split second. Gnashing her teeth, she stifled another outburst. The fresh salvo of shots from within the warehouse viciously echoed around the compound. Terror reigned. Charlie's heart raced as the outline of an Iraqi policeman exited the darkened doorway. Kirk slid Charlie's head below the wall line and cocked his handgun in preparation for the violence to come. He threw out his most officious warning.

"US Army! Stop! Wait! Na! Na! Sabr Kon!"

Shots rang out from the darkness. Kirk threw himself on Charlie's back, pinning her to the ground. She saw nothing. She felt everything. Fearlessly, Kirk took a knee and returned fire, emptying his Beretta. Before Charlie could react, Kirk was up and cantering after the fleeing policeman. Shots rang out, but by the time Charlie had rallied herself, the moment and the policeman were gone. Keen to get in on the action, she regained her footing and set off in hot pursuit. As she reached the corner of the compound, screeching tires were dragging a black car's taillights off out into the distant traffic. Charlie thought twice about sending a bullet up the street towards the fleeing gunman. Kirk didn't. *Bang!* He was incensed.

Charlie stepped in and pushed the muzzle of his gun into the air. "It's done! No one died." Charlie looked to the sky. Kirk looked to the future. The immediate future. He bolted back towards the warehouse. "Come on! We've got no time."

Charlie was staggered. "Are you crazy? We have to get out of here!"

"Not till I see what we're dealing with here. That guy won't be back. We've got at least ten minutes before the real police arrive if they arrive at all. Let's go look."

As Kirk ran on, Charlie followed, afraid of what lay ahead and behind. Once at the building, Kurt nudged open the large metal door. The pair eased into a small, well-stocked warehouse. All was quiet. Heavy-duty wooden packing crates covered the limited floor space. The remaining racks were filled with a range of military grade construction supplies. The building itself was in a poor state of repair; however, the racks looked freshly supplied by the US taxpayer. The lack of officious signage told Charlie this was no official military enclave. "Do you know anything about this?" she inquired. Kirk shook his head, never losing sight of his surroundings. The pair crept on into the silence.

In the far corner, two interconnected portable cabins were suspended on a super-sized mezzanine. Inexorably, like moths to a flame, the pair moved towards the light from the high offices.

At the foot of the stairs, Kirk reloaded and slowly crept up the treads, never losing sight of the door at the top. Charlie followed; gun trained to the rear. Back-to-back and scanning, the pair climbed the stairway. Once in position, Kirk waited for sounds of life that never came.

Tipping his head forward to see through the door's glass panel, he noticed a small white-shirted man slumped in the shadows beside a large wooden office desk. An overzealous down lighter kept the rest of the room in near darkness. "Dear God." Kirk burst through the door and onto a deadly crime scene. A small lamp lit the blood-splattered face of the dead man slumped over the desk. When the light was switched on, even Kirk stumbled. Across in the corner lay another corpse. The body of a bearded man with half his face blown open lay crumpled in a pool of blood. Peering in, Charlie recoiled at the scene before choosing to stand guard at the door.

An overpowering nausea churned her stomach, stopping her dead. *The point of no return.*

Curiosities overcame convulsions, forcing her onwards. She dared to inspect the scene, albeit from the comparative safety of the door. Kirk moved quickly, as if death was no stranger to him. He rapidly checked the dead to confirm their deaths. For the faceless man in the corner, the process was completed in the blink of an eye. With both deaths pronounced, Kirk ransacked the room.

Charlie stood guard, struggling to prevent the contents of her stomach from making an appearance. After a frantic scan, Kirk found a hessian bag inside a lidless tea chest. From the sack he pulled out a series of heavy stones wrapped in linen hand towels. When the first package rolled from its wrapping, amulets of all shapes and sizes, jewelry, small cylinder seals, and ornaments fell into view. Lured inside, Charlie abandoned her post in search of treasure. She avoided eye contact with the dead. Across the room at the table, she lifted a tiny white cylinder to the light nearest her face. A closer inspection revealed a cylinder carved from ivory, with a tiny hole through the center. The cuneiform etched into the side was barely legible, let alone decipherable. Charlie quivered in awe. The dead bodies had moved from horror show to sideshow.

"I've never seen one of these before. An amulet against fever. It could be thousands of years old. The owner would wear it to ward off disease. It's incredible. But why would the killer leave all this behind?"

Kirk eased closer then ruined her moment. "It's fake."

Charlie looked up to see him holding a handful of identical amulets. "They're making copies."

As Charlie moved to investigate further, she grabbed a desk coated in sloppy body matter. She needed to. Spinning with revulsion, her view twisted and fixed on the grotesquely disfigured second victim. Remnants of a bearded face stared back at her. Quaking on the spot, unable to avert her gaze, she held on. Kirk held it together, busily ripping through the documentation strewn across the desk. Fierce panicked eyes scanned and grabbed document after document.

"Here, take these. I'll grab the IDs." He thrust the selected files in Charlie's face to bring her back to reality—a reality she found difficult to face. Charlie glowered as each body was ransacked in turn. As Kirk pulled IDs from wallets and emptied pockets, Charlie remained in a trance. Kirk was on a roll. "Come on! Come on! Clean the switches, the door, and the frame. Leave everything else."

"We're not calling this in?"

"And get fingered for the job? This is Iraq. We want no part of this."

His angry encouragement snapped her back to half-life. Hurried attempts to wipe away any evidence of their presence were cut short when the sound of police sirens sounded in the distance. Kirk broke every bulb in the room before leaving. "That will hamper them."

He grabbed Charlie's hand and rag-dolled her out into the darkened night. Unable to find the words, unwilling to utter her thoughts, Charlie staggered on through a bewildering realization.

She knew both the dead men.

CHAPTER 11

Ever the professional, Kirk eased the pickup to a modest speed, then gently turned into the busiest traffic stream. Just as they reached the concealment of the other cars, two police cars blazed past them towards the warehouse. A casual glance in the rearview mirror confirmed their getaway.

Charlie slid her rattled body back up out of the footwell a few moments later. "What the hell just happened?"

Kirk shrugged. "Is there anything in those papers?" He switched on the internal light to help with the research. Charlie set to work, feverishly flicking through page after page of information. In the dim light, her bloody thumbprint made it impossible to read the tab on the side of the file. Nothing was going right.

"What is it? Anything?"

As Kirk leaned over to read the documents for himself, he failed to notice the pickup veering into the oncoming traffic. A blast of the horn and a last-minute swerve were not enough to save the pickup's wing mirror.

"Jesus! Just drive!" Fevers were running high.

"Okay. These are dockets, transfers, and manifests. They seem to be related to the fakes you just found."

"That's it? Where are they bound?"

"Everywhere: Egypt, Syria, Turkey. But—"

"What is it?" The tension seemed to be killing Kirk.

"They're all signed or authorized by one guy."

Kirk banged the steering wheel. "Mac?"

Charlie had grave news. "Dempsey."

Kirk seemed incredulous. "That proves nothing. Signing dockets like these is part of his job."

"So, why is he signing for fakes that are being smuggled?"

Kirk wanted a fair trial. "If the pieces are fake, the signatures are likely fake. Do they have the notarized stamp?"

Charlie pushed the paperwork into Kirk's line of sight. "They have his signature and his seal."

A gray wave of realization flooded into the now silent cabin. The thought that Dempsey was tied up in all the mendacity stunned them both into silence. Charlie collected her papers and thoughts, as Kirk drove on with steady concentration. Enough lines had been crossed. Charlie didn't yet know who to trust, but one thing was for certain: Dempsey was now a full-blown suspect.

Charlie needed to end the awkward silence. "Next time, don't throw me to the ground. I have a gun, and I can use it."

Kirk mounted his defense. "I was just—"

"Understand, but I don't need protecting. I'm here to do a job."

"So next time, I let you get shot at?"

"How about next time, you let me shoot?"

Kirk smiled wryly. "Understood. What about showing you dead bodies? You didn't seem to react well to that."

It was now Charlie's turn to throw out a wry glance. "Yeah, I kinda froze for a second."

"Kinda? A second? Have you never seen a dead body before?"

Charlie's voice crackled. "Not ones that I knew."

"What?" Kirk was on the wrong side of the road again.

"One of them was my attacker."

"The one with the beard?"

"And half a face."

Kirk juddered. "And you tell me that now?"

"I'm processing. I don't get shot at every day, and I certainly don't make trampling through murder scenes a regular habit. Cut me some slack."

Charlie's splintering tones sent Kirk backpedaling. "Okay, okay, I get it. The other one?"

"He was on my plane over from the States. He looked like an accountant—an irrelevance. I only remember him because he was so out of place."

"That doesn't make sense."

Charlie shook her head. "None of it does."

Teetering between lanes, Kirk fumbled inside his breast pockets before throwing over the stolen IDs. "Look."

The blood-caked wallets landed heavily on Charlie's paperwork.

"Thanks!" Sarcasm dripped from her words as she tugged open the first wallet, revealing some local currency, a travel document, and an Iraqi-issued government ID. Charlie wiped the plastic ID clean. An unflattering photograph of the bearded official stared back with hatred. Charlie flashed the card. "His name was Zain Abbas, from the Iraq State Board of Antiquities. Liaison Officer. Ring any bells?"

Confused, Kirk just shook his head. "He was on our side?"

"Not a chance. He tried to strangle then shoot me." Kirk was processing as Charlie moved on to victim number two. A slender leather wallet revealed no cash, one credit card, and a government-issued photo ID.

"CIA. Wayne Springer. Analyst." Kirk did not recognize the flashed ID photo.

"He was on my plane over from Washington."

"Was he there with Dempsey?"

Charlie shook her head. "He never spoke to anyone, but then again, he never spoke to me, and I was new on his team."

"Curious."

"That's one word for it. Do we confront Dempsey?"

"And say what?" Kirk countered. "It's our word against his. We still don't know how high up the organization this thing runs. We need more."

"More what?"

"More time and more info."

On the way back to base, the air swirled with permutations and prosecutions, deliberations, and defenses. Gradually, as the adrenaline levels died, so too did the conversation. Charlie threw a storm of unanswerable questions around her mind. Thoughts and fears were internalized. With information and inspiration thin on the ground, the pair agreed to sleep on it. In need of thinking time and breathing space, they negotiated a regroup for the morning. Ever the control freak, and keen to carry out more research, Charlie insisted on retaining all the documentation and both wallets. Kirk, the pragmatist, was keen to be rid of any evidence linking him to a double murder scene. The pair parted on better terms, but in worse states than the night before.

Safely back in her unit, Charlie's thoughts turned to home. She had promised to stay connected with Pop, but things had taken hold. Now more than ever, she needed to prioritize the only man she had ever loved. She needed to hear his voice. She inhaled slowly as the phone rang and rang. He answered by announcing the full phone number. It gave her the only chortle of the day. "Hi, Pop, how are you?"

When he responded, the joy in his voice made Charlie feel terrible for not calling sooner. The usual superficial chitchat was soon replaced by inquiries over safety, the local people, her boss and colleagues, accommodations, food, more safety checks, and an overall questioning around whether the Coalition was making a difference in Iraq.

Charlie's heart sang at the sound of her father's voice. Socially awkward, he found it difficult expressing his feelings, but she knew at the margins of every question lay his concerns for a daughter he loved very much. Tears formed, bending the edges of her voice.

Pop sensed it. "Is everything okay?"

"Sure thing, Pop; I'm just yawning."

"Bored, are you?" He snickered.

"Ha, far from it. I'm loving it. I'm just burning the candle at both ends. Up early with the team, then late nights studying."

"Studying?"

"You can't catalogue things you don't understand."

"Found anything interesting?"

Charlie scrambled up a memory. "An amulet against fever."

"Wow. Sounds exciting. Bring me one back—my back has been killing me."

She kept the conversation at a superficial level, fearing she would expose him to the horrors she was facing. She wanted to scream. She wanted to hear from him that everything would be all right, but things were far from all right. There was no point in worrying him, so for both their sakes, Charlie omitted a mention of the crime scene. "You've probably been spending too long in that big old chair up at the cabin."

"Going back up there this weekend. I'm heading to the store in the morning for provisions."

"Well, remember—fruit and vegetables, not whiskey and cigars."

The pair laughed at Charlie's mothering before Pop finally opened up. "Just tell me you're going to be okay. That's all I ask."

"I'm fine, Pop. It's a job cataloguing museum pieces. I promise I'm going to be okay." Fearing her father would detect the quivering intonation in her voice, Charlie moved the phone away from her mouth. A self-conscious silence fell.

"Right, lass, I better let you go. I'm sure you're busy."

His words came too early, but raising issues would only worry her father. Silence remained the chosen policy.

"You know I love you, don't you?"

"I love you too, Pop. Just promise me you won't worry."

"I won't."

"Promise me!"

"Okay, I promise."

"And the fruit and vegetables?"

"Ah, now that's not a promise I can keep. Quit while you're ahead, girlie."

"We have a deal."

"I know you can't plan in calls, but please don't forget your old dad. Gimme a call when you can."

"Remember, if you're up at the cabin, I can't reach you. No reception."

"Try on my cell, anyway. I may be out and about."

"You're never out and about."

"Well then, just leave a message. I miss your voice."

Charlie choked. "Love you, Pop."

"Love you."

As if clinging to the moment, Charlie held the phone to her ear long after the call had ended. Deep breaths were taken as she imagined her father shuffling over to get himself a large whiskey *just to settle the nerves before bedtime*. A rueful smile wrinkled her cheek.

That night, panic and fear leached into her thoughts. Plowing piece by piece through the bloody exhibits commandeered from the murder scene did little to ease her mind or boost her confidence. She was out of her depth and floundering. She only knew a handful of people in Iraq, and they were mostly dead or killing people. With her thoughts as uneasy bedfellows, Charlie made a move. After a quick cleanup, she inspected the documents further. After an hour of deliberation and frustration, nothing made sense. Even her talisman was proving useless. Spinning the button, time after time, she failed to decipher the answers provided or even the questions being posed.

The button conjured memories of happier days back in Paris. She longed for the refuge of long walks along the Seine and lazy days spent drifting through the Musee D'Orsay. A ghostly mirage placed her back in the Ritz, sipping cocktails with the mysterious Miroslav. Those distant days and gilded moments, like her innocence, were long gone. For the first time in her life, she knew what it was like to be truly lonely. She had always been comfortable with her own company, but being lonely was both alien and eerily unsettling. Pop had been a friendly voice. She longed to hear a helpful voice. She fished out, then punched in

Hank's contact number. After three rings and a requested prompt from a monotonal operator Charlie offered her access code. "Seven-three-Zulu-Delta-five."

A stern-sounding woman answered the phone. "Senior Special Agent Hancock's Office."

Charlie returned the officialdom with interest. "This is Special Agent Charlotte Glass. Can I speak with Senior Special Agent Hancock, please?"

"What is it regarding?" The misanthrope on the end of the line seemed annoyed at being asked to do her job. Charlie gave her no time.

"Confidential Bureau business. Connect me, please." The only acknowledgement she received was the ring tone of the connected call.

"Federal Bureau of Investigation. This is Hancock." Charlie was elated to hear Hank's voice, even if it had been affected by his officious telephone accent.

"Hello, boss." Her words sent Hank's voice skyward.

"Charlie! How are you doing?"

She got straight to work. "I'm fine, but I need your help."

Charlie sensed Hank leaning his voice into the phone. "Okay. What's up?"

"I can't say too much, but we have issues."

"Go on."

"Inside forces are working against us—"

Hank interjected. "Be careful. I'm not sure how secure this line is. Work with me here. First thing's first: are you safe?"

Charlie finally breathed. "I am good. No worries from my side, but—"

Hank led her away from incrimination. "Go light on the background. I trust you. What can I do for you? What do you need?"

Her coded message could not have been clearer. "We need new boots on the ground over here. The ones we have are dirty."

Hank understood completely. "All of them? Is there no other way?"

Her spluttered cry for help had been heeded. "They're not all dirty, but I can't tell. I'm not cut out for this." She was livid that her thoughts had escaped in word form.

Hank took her points to heart. "I told you to call if you needed help. It wasn't an empty promise. You're not alone. Will you be okay for the next few days?"

"For what?"

"For me to plan arrangements."

"I think so." Charlie didn't care what *arrangements* meant; she was just pleased they were being made.

"Leave it to me. If things escalate, call my personal number. Talk to no one about this."

"One hundred percent."

"Promise me you'll be safe in the meantime."

Charlie was buoyed. "I promise." She hoped she could keep that promise.

Hank was gunning and running. "Okay, now get the hell off this line. I have work to do. Stay safe. You hear me?"

"Loud and clear."

The line closed without ceremony.

She was as ecstatic as her weary soul allowed. The call had gone well. Tired, lifeless eyes stared back from the mirror on the desk. This was the oldest she had ever looked or felt. She opened her desk drawer, pulled out her Glock, and set it down in front of her. Never losing eye contact with her likeness, they both set to work. She flipped out the magazine, pulled a safety check, de-cocked it, pulled down the side pins, pulled the rail off, flipped out the spring, and pulled out the barrel. The brush, cloth, and oil were then set to work on the dismantled handgun.

At the end of her nighttime regime, Charlie gripped the sink and stared through the mirror deep into her own eyes. "Help is on the way." The two-way monologue brought a smile.

She checked the windows and doors and yanked the bulb from her desk lamp, setting it under a towel on the floor just inside her front door. She climbed into bed, double-checked the safety on the reassembled Glock, and slipped it under her pillow. Counting as she tapped the tripper guard with her index finger, she fell under the spell of sleep before double figures could be counted.

CHAPTER 12

Charlie's sun rose slowly the following morning. Tarry coffee fell from the ramshackle apparatus left behind by the unit's previous occupant. Cup in hand, she padded outside to face a reluctant dawn. It was 0600 hours as the smoldering orange orb battled its way through a thick coating of foggy morning dust. Bizarrely, the glum day did not match her mood. Although daunted by the prospect of the day ahead, she pushed on, determined to be all she could be. *One day at a time.*

The siren song of the Imam from a distant minaret called the people to Fajr, the prayers for the true dawn—Subh Saadiq. She sat down on the barren, crumbled surface and let the enchanting tones carry her away.

Frustratingly, a text from Kirk broke the spell.

Noon. Lunch, DFAC, with D

Charlie and Kirk arrived at the DFAC dining facility fifteen minutes early for their meeting with Dempsey to gain a clear two-opposite-one seating advantage. With so little to go on, their plan was basic. They were to keep Dempsey talking to find out as much as possible about his operations and opinions. Nothing more, nothing less.

Dempsey arrived ten minutes early but still had to take the single seat opposite the other members of the impromptu breakfast club. As always, he was dressed impeccably. That morning, his ironed edges seemed a little less ironed and his polish, a little less polished. When they exchanged greetings, Charlie detected a quiver of uncertainty lurking at the edges to his voice. The trio exchanged pleasantries. To Charlie, everyone's updates seemed heavily veiled and light on content. No sooner had Dempsey set plastic fork to his rubber food than the BlackBerry holstered on his camel hide belt pinged. "Can you believe this?"

To Charlie, it seemed a little too early in the day to be that annoyed by a text. When Dempsey tapped open his phone, his eyes opened wide with amazement. Kirk was curious.

"What's wrong? You look as if you've seen a ghost." Dempsey couldn't speak. Instead, he handed the BlackBerry over so Charlie and Kirk could read the text.

I have the Golden Chalice of Ur.

Interested?

Dempsey's heart double tapped. "I've been waiting for this."

Charlie was in the dark. "What's the Golden Chalice of Ur?"

Even Kirk knew. "Only one of the greatest creations in all of Mesopotamia. Looted and lost, it's one of the most valuable stolen artifacts in the world."

The number wasn't withheld; it was unknown. Dempsey called the number, but it rang out, so he switched to text.

Who is this?

No answer came, so he went again.

How do I know you have it?

The reply was immediate.

IM8272.

Kirk recognized the format. "It's the coding system from the museum of Iraq's main catalogue."

Charlie, being the newbie, had come prepared. She dragged out a pristine listing of the stolen treasures from her rucksack. Scanning the items in ID order, her index finger raced down column after column. She muttered the code relentlessly until her finger hit a stop. Her mouth dried as she read out the associated text.

'Museum No:	*IM8272*
Provenience:	*Ur (Royal Cemetery)*
Material:	*Gold, lapis lazuli*
Date: ca.	*2400 BC*
Description:	*Gold fluted chalice with two lapis lazuli handles*
Status:	*Unknown*
Value:	*Priceless"*

Dempsey was losing his customary cool. "Only a handful of people had access to these codes."

"It's not proof of ownership." Kirk was clearly skeptical.

"It's proof of knowledge, and that's a start." Dempsey needed to find out more, so his text went back.

What do you want?

Instantaneously, the mystery messenger replied.

$10k

Malwiya Minaret

1300 hrs.

Come alone!

When Dempsey tried to call the number again, it was unobtainable. He was freewheeling. "Can you believe this? I've got to go after this."

Kirk hit the brakes. "Hang on. This has trap written all over it."

Charlie agreed. "He's right; you shouldn't be going alone."

Kirk's frustrations were showing. "He shouldn't go at all!"

Dempsey stood firm. "It's the Golden Chalice. This is the big score we've been waiting for. We can't pass it up."

"He's maybe right," pitched Charlie.

Kirk hated the idea. "He's far from right. You're not the one going into the danger zone."

Suitably admonished, Charlie pulled back, allowing Kirk to consider the options. Having thought through the situation, he stood tall. "Okay. I'll go. I know the area. It's not safe up there."

Dempsey didn't budge. "It's not safe anywhere. They're expecting me. I'm going."

"At least take me with you."

"No. I'm going in alone. You'll scare them off. They said come alone. Besides, I'll have my Eagle Magnum for company."

Kirk threw his hands up in annoyed resignation, so Charlie pitched in. "Can you authenticate the bowl?"

The team lost a little momentum with the questioning of Dempsey's capabilities. Kirk had an idea.

"Charlie's right. Why don't you take Mac? It says come alone, but why don't you go in solo, check the merchandise, and make sure everything's safe. If it isn't safe, throw out some lead. If it is, pull in Mac to authenticate the piece."

Dempsey didn't hate the idea. He tapped in Mac's number. As he waited for the call to be answered, the table took a turn at being tapped. "No answer. He's probably still drunk or screening my calls."

"Or both," quipped Kirk.

A repeat performance brought about the same outcome. Dempsey cut the call. "So, what can you tell me about the Minaret?"

Charlie had pulled her case notes. She paraphrased the sourced text out loud. "Minaret al-Malwiya is a Sunni Mosque in Samarra. It was built around 800 BC. It's a fifty meter-spiral tower of sandstone and mud brick. 'Malwiya' actually translates as 'twisted.'"

Dempsey lost it. "Jesus Christ! I am not out sightseeing. What can you tell me that can help me stay alive?"

Charlie flushed at the admonishment. To spare her blushes, Kirk took over. "Well, you don't want to hear this, but anyone at the top will see an ambush coming for miles. It's close enough to the city of Samarra for them to make a quick getaway into the land of the Sunni insurgents. Chances are, the Chalice will be close by, ready to be called in. The mosque has a rectangular compound that sits on the edges of a built-up area. The compound is big—say, ten acres—but there's also an extended area around with no cover for anyone approaching. It has a ten-meter wall and archways all around the edges. The mosque tower sits at one end. How are you with heights?"

"They don't bother me."

"Good, because the staircase is on the outside, and it gets high. It's the tallest building for hundreds of miles. The tower's a sniper's nest. Literally. The US used it for that very purpose."

Dempsey didn't like the sound of that. "Great. I should have stuck to the history lessons."

Kirk tried to help. "The outer walls are intact, so the archways will provide cover right up to the Minaret steps. That shouldn't be a problem, but you're heading into a snake pit. Samarra saw a lot of fighting. Your credentials will get you past the guards, but there's always Uncle Sam. Our troops won't want you up there, so you'll have to haggle at the checkpoints. You can't stay long either. If word gets out that you're there, there could be a departure committee ready to send you off."

"That's if there isn't a reception committee waiting for you already." The men both stared at Charlie. Her commentary wasn't really helping. She had a question for Kirk. "How come you know so much about the mosque?"

"I spent a few weeks up there, setting up the communications for the sniper nest we built at the top of the tower."

Charlie threw him a withering look. "In a three-thousand-year-old tower?"

"All is fair in love and war. Anyway, after the locals protested, we evacuated the post."

Dempsey weighed in. "Yeah, then the locals bombed it, anyway. This place is a madhouse." He looked forward. "It's too good a lead not to follow it up."

After another failed attempt to contact Mac, Dempsey appeared to fray just a little. "He's hopeless."

It was obvious, despite the risks, Dempsey desperately wanted to get his hands on the Chalice. Charlie thought it strange he would bring the revelation out into the open if he intended to steal the item for himself. She looked at Kirk just as he stepped further into the decision-making process. "Go get the cash and get organized. We'll cover for you."

In his excitement, Dempsey blurted his demands. "Contact Mac and make sure he's on board. Get him ready to be picked up at Checkpoint Six in an hour's time. If there's a problem, text me."

Out of character fist bumps and nods were offered and exchanged. Dempsey made for the exit, leaving behind a cold, untouched breakfast.

"Call us!" Kirk's plea passed unheard. The pair exchanged looks of disbelief. Their plan had fallen apart and reformed into something totally different. Kirk pulled up and called Mac's number. He blinked in surprise when the call was answered after only a couple of rings. With one finger in his other ear, Kirk struggled to hear the call over the clatter of the dining hall.

"Hello, Mac, it's Kirk."

Charlie grinned when Kirk jokingly pulled the phone away from his ear to protect his hearing from the abuse no doubt being hurtled down the line by Mac. Through a veil of indignation, the message was finally received, understood, and agreed to. By the sounds of Kirk's responses, Mac was unhappy with almost every element of the plan. Eventually it sounded as if a barely amicable agreement had been reached. After abruptly ending the call, Kirk sent off a text to Dempsey. He showed Charlie the screen before hitting send.

Mac's in. Get that Chalice.

CHAPTER 13

The next morning, Charlie rose from a nervy sleep with a cramped hand clamped to the handle of her gun. She pulled the piece from under the pillow and set it down carefully beside her. Extending her hand, she massaged her trigger finger. Turkish coffee helped, and a stiff shower closed out proceedings. She was dressed, ready for action, and in position way before the allotted start time of the briefing set up by Kirk of 0700 hours. The start time came and went before anyone appeared. An hour later, Kirk burst through the door at full speed, arms filled with beige folders. Getting straight into it, he sat down opposite Charlie.

"And good morning to you too." Game-face on, Kirk ignored her.

"Dempsey's dead."

"What?"

"I know. I don't know what to-"

"How? Where?"

"It's all in here.' Kirk faltered. "It's difficult viewing." Kirk passed her over a copy of a file. Charlie winced as she turned the file open. "Yeah, sorry, but murder is murder." Kirk's half-assed apology related to a series of photographs showing Dempsey's crumpled body lying in a dried-up pool of splattered and crusted blood. The nearby sand was stained black by the coagulated body matter that had seeped from his misshapen corpse. "He was thrown off the Minaret at Samarra."

Charlie was summoning up all her powers to not look up or throw up. "Where did you get these photos?"

"The local police. They're calling it an accident and moving on. They don't want to hear about Westerners being murdered."

Charlie was unconvinced. "How did they get the photos so quickly?"

"A local police patrol found the body fifteen minutes after the rendezvous time."

Charlie pulled a face. "And you believe that?"

"The police may have lied, but the camera didn't. He's gone."

"He could have fallen."

Kirk didn't miss a stride in dismissing the assumption. "No chance. His gun was out of its holster. The only way that would happen would be if he felt threatened."

"Could the gun have fallen out on impact?"

"It's a Desert Eagle."

"And?"

"It's a ridiculously big gun. The holster needs a leather strap to keep the gun in place."

"So, he had pulled the gun?"

Kirk nodded. "It gets worse. Mac is gone, nowhere to be seen."

"Have you called him?"

Kirk answered. "Multiple times. No answer. It's not even ringing out."

Charlie continued to look for evidence, pouring over the photos. "Were there any witnesses?"

"None living. There was a guard, but he was found behind his shack with a couple of slugs in him. Next photo."

Charlie flipped over the photograph. "Double tap? Heart and head?"

Kirk nodded. "Just like the other bodies. The same signature moves?"

Charlie stared in horror at the poor guard. "Signed in blood."

"Let's go."

"Where to?"

Kirk was a man on a mission. "Mac's place."

"To do what?"

"Do you have a better idea?" Kirk snapped.

Charlie bowed a shaking head. "Okay. Let's get after this."

They gathered their belongings and ran for the door.

Back on the road, Kirk issued orders from behind the wheel. "Pull the file from my case notes in the back seat. His address will be listed in there. He lives not too far from here; he took me there once. He usually rides in to steal the free breakfast."

"Why doesn't he live in the Green Zone?"

"He's a freelancer. He's been coming here for years, so he knows his way around. If he pushed the point, he'd get a berth, but he likes to do his own thing."

The insane atmosphere of Iraq during conflict had been normalized by the events unfolding around Charlie. She gave the world outside no thought. Charlie matched the address to the map yanked from the dash. Kirk was almost impressed. "Can you get us there?"

Charlie raised her eyebrows at the veiled sexism. Before she could react, the truck swerved violently to avoid two young, mud-crusted boys who had run out to retrieve their makeshift football.

"I'll get us there; you just try not to kill anybody before we arrive."

Kirk smirked. "And after we get there?"

Charlie didn't appreciate the grave humor.

With checkpoints and side streets negotiated, Kirk was directed straight to the low block of neglected apartments where Mac lived. When the destination was announced, Kirk nodded, impressed with Charlie's map reading skills. The pickup didn't stop. He rolled it slowly around the back of the property. Communication wires littered the airspace around the rear of the buildings. Scattered pallets at various stages of disintegration littered the driveway. The heights of most of the walls had been extended by the addition of corrugated sheeting, barbed wire, or wooden boards. Broken bottles had been cemented onto the tops of some lower walls to welcome any unwelcome guests. All the apartments looked unloved, but Mac's seemed to have been selected for special neglect. The apartment showed no signs of life or hope.

Kirk tried to take the worry off his partner's face. "Pretty rough, eh? Around here, 'Bang goes the neighborhood' means something completely different."

His efforts didn't work. After another unanswered last-minute call to Mac, the pair braced themselves for a home invasion. The pair checked their Glocks in unison before Kirk gestured to his accomplice to hold position. He slid quietly out into the shadows, intent on subterfuge. The pickup rocked as Kirk climbed up onto its roof then vaulted across the top of the craggy wall.

Charlie sat still, surprised at how comfortable she was with the options being selected. She knew her actions breached several FBI codes and practices; but the times, the people, and the place were all desperate. She wasn't playing this by the book. She was adding a few pages of her own. A light in Mac's apartment flicked on and off twice to signal all clear. Under cover of the inadequate rear lighting, Charlie scuffed her boots, scrambling over the high wall. Pulling herself up through the rear window was easier than she had envisaged. Her landing on the beautifully ornate tiling felt much harder. The already tiny property was made even smaller by the sheer volume of books laid out like a ransacked public library. Everything you'd ever, and never, want to know about archaeology cluttered each surface. An oversized ripped and stained leather sofa took center stage. Kirk was already hard at work, carefully sifting through desk papers. Charlie began her very own literature review. Every book location had been categorized by theme, then by period, and alphabetized by author. Amongst the books three larger volumes stuck out, literally. She read the intricately printed titles with puzzlement. *Robert Burns: The complete works in three volumes.* It seemed strange that books of Scottish poetry would corrupt his filing system.

As she picked up the first volume, the weight of its contents shifted in her hand. Perplexed, Charlie opened the book to find a small, almost empty bottle of Scotch.

"Look here, the sly old fox," she called over to Kirk, brandishing the bottle. The observations barely registered. His disapproving look told her they had more important things to do. Charlie returned the fake book and checked Volume Two. It contained his passport, personal photographs, and a small stash of US dollars. She lifted Volume Three. It was a much heavier tome. She flipped open the book. To her astonishment it contained what looked like a series of war medals and an old Webley revolver. A picture of what could be his father in Eighth Army Desert Rats regalia took pride of place. Some faded letters sat at the bottom of the book. She saw a different side to Mac in that box. Kirk didn't share her love of literature. "Quit it. We don't have time. Check the bathroom. I'll get the kitchen."

Charlie slapped the fake cover back into place and rehoused the book in its allocated space. Kirk's guidance rang in her ears. "Be careful. Leave everything as you found it."

She set to work in the bathroom, carefully pulling out everything that may or may not have been of interest. The depressing little room smelled of drain with a side order of old socks. Charlie suspected excessive cleaning was not the reason that the shower curtain had been half pulled from the bent rail overhead. Toiletries were in short supply, but the laundry basket had taken many recent deliveries. In the bottom right-hand corner of the peeling bathroom mirror, she noticed a small black-and-white photo booth photograph wedged into the frame. Leaning in close, she recognized a young girl sitting on the knee of a much younger Mac. She wondered what had become of the young girl and the older man. The plundering continued at a pace. With time, optimism, and options running out, she stepped back and scanned the room once more. Her eyes popped at the sight of a small Ziploc bag protruding from behind the sink's pedestal.

"Kirk? In here."

Her partner resurfaced. "What you got?"

She opened the bag. "Burner phone." As she switched it on, Kirk moved forward to grab the phone. Her palm told him this would not be an option. Her eyes popped. "It's not locked."

Kirk leaned in. Charlie provided a running commentary, as she scanned the contents. "The call history is empty."

"Any messages?"

"There's only one chain of texts, sent just after eleven this morning."

She read the chain aloud:

"'Outgoing text: I have the Golden Chalice of Ur - Interested?

"'Reply: Who is this? How do I know you have it?

"'Outgoing text: IM8272

"'Reply: What do you want?

"'Outgoing Text: $10k, Malwiya Minaret, 1300 hrs. Come alone.'"

"Mac set this up," Kirk stated the obvious.

"Why would he do it?"

Kirk spat venom. "Why does anyone do it? Greed."

"For a ten-thousand-dollar chalice?"

"You're not getting it."

"Iraq street value isn't Paris street value. I thought you'd know that."

Charlie fought to regain credibility. "Maybe it was his way of getting out?" Charlie checked the phone's contacts and almost dropped it. There was only one listing. When she showed the screen to Kirk, he almost exploded. The screen simply read 'Serpent."

Charlie couldn't process the revelation. "Dempsey's the Serpent? What does that even mean?"

Kirk's expression made it clear he had no clue. He pushed the cell phone away. "Put this back exactly how you found it. Exactly." Charlie followed the instructions to the letter as Kirk beat a retreat towards the rear window. "Let's shift; come on! We don't know who could be watching this place."

The pair bundled out and down the back of the apartment at full speed. Taking the lead, Kirk climbed the frame of the back gate. As he leaned down to pull his partner to safety, Charlie vaulted the low wall. As she leaped over, a shard of glass cemented onto the wall sliced her palm. Pride and adrenaline muffled her yelp as she clambered back into the pickup. Blood splattered in every direction. Once inside, Charlie pinched her sliced flesh tightly in a vain attempt to stem the blood. Her pulse raced. Kirk had the pickup off and running before he noticed her injury.

"Are you okay?"

"I'm fine. It's just a scratch," Charlie lied.

"Dumb luck."

Charlie inspected her wound, annoyed at her lack of focus. "More dumb than luck."

"Try these. Compliment of the dining facility." Kirk pulled some paper towels from behind his seat. Charlie only managed to stem the flow, after plastering everything in a two-foot radius with blood. Emotions rose.

"I'm sorry."

Kirk needed to move Charlie past the moment. "Do you think Mac's running?"

"I don't think so. I found his passport at his apartment. If he wanted to murder then flee, he would have taken it with him."

"True. That only proves he didn't plan the murder. He could still have done it."

Charlie didn't want the obvious to be assumed as the truth. "They could have been kidnapped by insurgents."

Kirk countered. "Why kill one and let the other live?"

"Ransom?"

Kirk shook his head. "We haven't seen any video or posting relating to a kidnap."

"It's early yet."

"Not really. As soon as they have a victim, they get the word out. We need to face facts."

"Which are?"

"He's in the wind, with a stash of cash from smuggling fake treasures."

Charlie was at a loss. "So, what next? Stake this place out?"

Kirk shook his head. "He wouldn't be dumb enough to come back here."

"He could come back for his passport."

"He'd have done that by now. He's probably got himself a fake. Maybe the one you saw was a fake. They're easy to come by."

Charlie exhaled hard.

"What's up?"

"This thing is on fire."

"Meaning?"

"I came to catalogue artifacts. Half my team is dead or MIA."

"Look, when Dempsey died, I was put in charge. You're following orders."

"Orders that are now way out of scope."

"Out of original scope yes, but things change. Iraq is kinetic. What does your boss back in the US say?"

"Hank?"

Kirk nodded. "When I mentioned Dempsey, he seemed shocked, but he'd heard of you and of your reputation."

"So, he was only too willing to leave you on the hook?"

"It wasn't like that."

"So, your underplaying things."

"Not at all."

"Yeah right. You're telling me you're going to mention tonight and your injury?"

"When I meet him."

"And when will that be?"

"When circumstances permit."

"And let me guess—that won't be for a while?"

A smiling Charlie lifted her damaged hand. "Well, I can't type or work a phone with this, can I?"

Kirk couldn't help but laugh in the face of Charlie's independent spirit. "Your hand's a mess. We need to get you cleaned up."

"So where to?"

"I'll drop you off at the military hospital at Ibn Sina. They will look after you."

"And then?"

"In the morning we catch a killer."

CHAPTER 14

After one jab, six stitches, and a fistful of painkillers, Charlie exited the 10th Combat Support unit at Ibn Sina Hospital. Outside, Kirk was there to meet her, illegally parked and sitting on the hood of his pickup.

"I'd shake your hand but—" He motioned towards Charlie's bandaged right hand.

She raised it in return and smiled. "I'd slap you, but—"

Kirk sniggered. "Jump in. Let's go grab some breakfast. My treat."

Back at the busy DFAC dining facility, inspiration was in short supply. Kirk sighed and shook his head. "We've sent out alerts to all guard posts, military and local police."

"Anything back?"

Kirk shook his head. "Tariq's coming over. He staked out Mac's place all night."

Charlie read Kirk's face. "Nothing?"

Another shake of the head followed. Both bowed as they chewed over the limited options. Charlie and Kirk endured their late breakfast. The fork in Charlie's wrong hand chased unappetizing food around a sorry-looking paper plate. The clattering chatter of a fully operational Army camp was drowned out by noises ricocheting around Charlie's mind. Unable to focus, unable to hear herself think, she closed her eyes to the moment and tried to close off the noise. Kirk reached out and cradled her throbbing, damaged hand.

That didn't help in the slightest.

Suddenly, flushed and in full flight, Tariq appeared across the hall. Spurred on by panic, he jostled through the crowd. Squaddies squinted and belched as he elbowed his way through the queueing throng. As he fought to gather his breath, Kirk rose to offer him a seat. The offer was declined. He proffered Charlie the humblest of bows, as if surprised to see her there. He was uncertain about proceeding with his proclamations, but Kirk gave him the nod that told him Charlie could be trusted.

"We've found Dempsey's SUV."

Kirk was first to react. "Where?"

"In a back street, on the south side." As Tariq flattened out a map on the table, the news unfolded.

"Is Mac there?" Charlie interjected.

Tariq shrugged, before he gathered up his map. "If we are going, we need to go now."

Charlie held them in the blocks. "Is this it? Us?"

"For now. Yesterday a supply convoy was ambushed as it left our air base at Al Asad. They threw everything in the mix: IEDs,

RPGs, MGs. We lost twenty security contractors from all over the world. Everyone is too busy blaming and deflecting. It's a cluster. We're all there is. Are you in?"

Charlie's inner renegade answered. "I can see no other choice."

Their transport, a battered old Toyota, was parked nearby. Tariq pulled an old rug from the cluttered trunk of his car, and Charlie caught sight of a black uniform. The find puzzled her. Tariq quickly threw the rug into the back seat. "Once we're past the checkpoint, cover yourself and keep down. We don't want a Western woman in the car."

Charlie understood the implications. Trepidation on the rise, she climbed compliantly into the rear. The engine spluttered into pitiful existence before they headed off in search of Mac. Post checkpoint, Charlie eased out of sight. When she pulled the old rug over her frame, a well-used AK-47 slid into view. Up close and personal, the gun smelled of oil and gunpowder. This latest discovery concentrated her thoughts.

What the hell am I getting into? Who the hell keeps a recently fired AK-47 on his back seat?

From her prone position, she found it impossible to keep her eyes or her hands off the rifle.

What troubled her most was that when Tariq had defended her outside the museum with a US-issued M4 Carbine. "Where's your gun?"

She didn't understand or appreciate Kirk's explanation. "We're off the reservation."

"Head down! Police checkpoint." Tariq's raised voice seemed to redirect proceedings.

Charlie laid dead still as the car slowed then edged forward. A cursory ID check passed before the car moved on at pace. Doubts and fears swirled around Charlie's cluttered mind as she fought to make sense of events.

Is Mac even alive? Is he being held captive or fleeing?

Will we get there in time?

Her last thought seemed to be Kirk's first as he pushed on through the traffic. Up front, a frantic debate, amped by excitement, raged between passenger and driver. The jostling and jolting intensified as they drove around the convoluted maze. It felt and sounded like Kirk became lost a few times. The route seemed littered with countless twists, turns, lumps, and bumps. Charlie's stitched hand throbbed as she rubbed her talisman for good luck. Whether worried for Mac's safety or her own sanity, she prayed for the journey to end soon.

Almost on cue, the car slowed. Tariq confirmed their arrival. "This is it." Charlie edged her head above the door line. They stealthily pulled up at the rear of the premises. Fender to fender, they eased behind Dempsey's Land Cruiser. The signs of a desperate society in free fall lay strewn across the restricted thoroughfare. Errant trash, unidentifiable burned-out materials, and damaged boarding littered the narrow passage. Charlie felt an eerie quiet not experienced before in Iraq, nor anywhere else. The lack of a human presence gave the harrowing scene a haunting, almost post-apocalyptic aura. Charlie checked her Glock, its magazine, chamber, action, and safety. The scene had ambush written all over it.

"Okay. Game faces. I need to turn the car. We're boxed in. Tariq, take Charlie—back exit."

"Where are you going?"

Kirk was on a mission. "'Round the front. I will go in the main entrance. If anyone flees, hold them up."

Tariq's twisted face contorted further. "And if they don't?"

Grit formed at the edges of Kirk's words. "Stop them or drop them. Dealer's choice."

Charlie found herself nodding alongside Tariq like some performing dog. She had never once considered shooting a man in an ambush. Kirk completed his weapons check and gave Charlie one last beam. "Take care, and don't go in without me. Be careful."

After they exited, Kirk gently reversed the car back down into a side alley. Tariq swung his AK-47 into firing position and crept forward. Charlie held back, covering the rear angles. Adrenaline pumped through her veins, her heart battering her rib cage. *Time to step up.*

Against Kirk's explicit instructions, Tariq sneaked on ahead, gesturing for Charlie to follow him. He lost eye contact before Charlie could show her disapproval. Fearful that her shouting would alert any prospective guard, Charlie held her cries of complaint. From his crouched position fifteen yards into the compound, Tariq moved his grip from his gun to the door handle. *Unlocked.* It opened with more noise than any old neglected wooden door could ever muster. Tariq took a firing angle and waited to see if anyone had been alerted. They had not.

He waved again for Charlie to follow him before sneaking on into the warehouse. Charlie shook her head, unnoticed. Following him in seemed less dangerous to her than being left behind in the alley. Not for the first time since landing in Iraq, she disobeyed orders. With a look to the skies and a series of quick breaths, she crept forward with purpose. Gun trained and with safety released, she crept forward, eye fixed on the open doorway. The lack of gunfire gave her hope. She stood, composed herself, and leaned in through the doorway. Charlie cast the Glock across the scene.

A greasy, dank atmosphere hung inside the dark, abandoned garage. The first room seemed to have served previously as a mechanic's kitchen and store. A series of small steel-framed windows were cut into the side wall. Two panes were missing, four or five were cracked, and all the rest were filthy. She caught Tariq as he stalled at the edge of the main internal entrance. It was in units like these that most of the IEDs destined for Route Irish were produced. In places like this, the battle for hearts and minds had been lost long ago, and no one was taking prisoners. The sound of water dripping from a tap into a nearby sink marked time. Charlie stalled, transfixed by the moment, unable to go back, unwilling to go forward. She hoped this was as far as it would go before Kirk made an appearance. Inexplicably, Tariq stood without warning and moved on into the main area. Before Charlie could grab his shirt, the Terp was out of reach.

She jumped on after him, suddenly afraid to be left behind. Whatever she was facing, she didn't want to face it alone. The pair slipped out into an oil-soaked workshop so typical of the local "chop shop" area. Charlie winced at the tragic scene. Like some macabre cabaret, a dead body sat tied to a chair, staring up into a low-hanging lampshade. It only took a second for her heart rate to plummet to an all-time low. The bloody and tousled safari suit gave the first clue. Even from this distance, she knew the poor soul under the deathly spotlight was Mac.

Shadows fell across the scene. Charlie flinched at the sight of another dead body. A queasiness rippled the lining of her stomach. The solitary underpowered light bulb cast shadows across his gaunt, lifeless face. Cold, dead eyes stared longingly to the heavens. Tariq completed the scan and stood up. "All clear." He advanced, and Charlie cautiously followed on.

Checking the corners of the workspace, the pair carefully encroached. Charlie stopped Tariq as he reached for the body. Her FBI training kicked in. "He could be wired."

Cautioned and embarrassed, Tariq lifted his hands out of the danger zone. Charlie moved to the foreground, studying the scene, and relaying her findings. "Four gunshot wounds; two to the heart, two to the head."

Tariq circled the body. Charlie threw him a puzzled look. "Strange."

The Terp stepped back. "What?"

"No orange jumpsuit. No video. No ransom demands." Things were not adding up. "There's very little blood."

Charlie kneeled behind Mac. "His hands are tied, but there are no ligature marks, bleeding or bruising." Charlie rose in panic. "He didn't die here. This is a set—"

She turned to find Tariq pointing his AK-47 straight into her face.

CHAPTER 15

Tariq's voice seemed clearer. "Why could you just not believe it?

Charlie trembled in disbelief.

"One filed report and all this would have gone away." His accent had vanished. He pulled the safety lever on his AK.

Charlie pleaded. "Please, we can work this out. Kirk will be here at any minute."

"Exactly. That's the last thing we need."

When Tariq pulled the trigger, his machine gun clicked. Charlie reached for her gun, but before she could react, Tariq's chest puffed, splashing blood across the scene. The gun went flying as he dropped to his knees. Terrified and spluttering, he lifted a contorted hand and spat out what sounded like "Nergal?"

Convulsions from two more shots threw his lifeless face into the oil-hardened dirt floor. From the shadows, Kirk materialized, clutching a smoking pistol. Charlie stood there; gun still cocked. Kirk holstered his, then pushed Charlie's quaking hand downward, forcing her to lower her weapon. He grabbed her other hand and dragged her forcibly from the murder scene, barking questions as they moved.

"What the hell just happened?"

Charlie didn't break eye contact with the floor. Kirk continued the mobile interrogation. "I told you not to go in without me! What were you thinking?"

The specter of death numbed all dialogue. Only after reaching the safety of the car could Charlie break the spell. "It was a trap. Tariq staged the whole thing. He was bringing us here to clean house. You didn't need to kill him."

Kirk disagreed. "You're welcome. He was about to unload his AK into you,"

"No. He wasn't."

"I heard the gun click."

Charlie reached into the side pocket of her combats and threw a handful of 39mm shells on the dashboard.

Kirk was stupefied. "What the hell? Are they from his gun?"

Charlie threw out a stuttering nod. "I emptied his gun as we drove over."

"What?"

"I knew it was an ambush." Charlie held her ground.

"How?"

"I saw a black police uniform in the car's trunk. That's what set me off. He found the car within a day in the middle of the chop shop. Really?"

Kirk's mouth dropped open in disbelief. "You couldn't have known. You could only have suspected."

"And how did those suspicions turn out?"

"They turned out with me shooting dead one of my closest friends."

Charlie held her line. "Shooting him was your choice. I had it covered. I was going to bring him in."

"Bring him in? This isn't *Law and Order*!" Kirk banged the steering wheel. He was panicking and processing in equal measures. "How did you know?"

Charlie was conscious of the time they were wasting. "Look, we can get to that. We need to get out of here. Someone would have heard the shots."

Kirk dismissed her hypothesis. "If everybody rushed to the sound of gunfire in this town, every day would be a stampede. No one will have noticed or cared. I just shot my friend. How did you know?"

Charlie scoffed. "That he just tried to ice me should be proof enough."

Kirk remained in denial. "It's still one hell of a leap to strip him of his ammo."

Charlie shook her head. "Tariq owned a US-issued M4 Carbine. He used it at the museum shoot out. So why did he bring a terrorist's gun to a stakeout?"

"He may not have wanted to have had his gun traced."

"Why? When I thought Tariq could be bad, it made me think about the attack at the Iraq Museum."

"Why?"

"It's obvious now. The bearded guy wasn't trying to kill me. He must have been trying to kill Tariq."

"Is it? Amazingly, the bearded man's found days later in a warehouse with his face blown off. Coincidence?"

"So where does the other dead guy, IT geek, come in?"

"I don't know. He wasn't the one looking to kill me—Tariq was."

Kirk shook his head with the slightest hint of admiration at her deductions and held his hands up in surrender. "So, what next?"

"We've done nothing wrong. He was a murderer pulling a gun on an agent. We can explain everything."

Kirk voiced a plan. "My contacts in the Army couldn't give a rat's ass about trinkets or a Terp. They have a war to fight. If I put it through them, they'll clean this place out and allow me to draft the report."

Charlie didn't hate the idea. All she could muster was a rocking motion that resembled a nod.

The weight of recent events flattened all emotions as Kirk set the SUV in motion.

CHAPTER 16

Charlie gained great insight into her current state of mind when she realized she had taken her Glock into the shower with her. She reached a personal compromise. The gun was left on a towel beside the sink. With a head full of panic and hair full of shampoo, she scolded herself.

What the hell use is a gun sitting out there?

She swiftly rinsed before the gun was rehoused in its locker. It had been three days since Tariq's death. On their virtually wordless drive home, Charlie had disassembled Kirk's Glock, wiped each section down, and thrown the pieces out the pickup window as they crossed back across the Tigris. The unmarked AK-47 was handed into the Armory as one of the many random arms finds from the city. The body count was rising, as was the mountain of lies.

Mac's death was called in anonymously. Local police investigations threw a jaundiced eye over the scene and reported back their findings. Mac's death was a kidnap gone wrong at the hands of Tariq. Officially, his death remained unsolved.

Unofficially, the investigation had already been shelved. Sometimes a little corruption went a long way.

Charlie had called an unavailable Hank but left no message. The scattering of dead bodies had totally derailed the mission, yet no one seemed to care. All eyes seemed to be focused on the rise of insurgent activities. Recent bombings, emboldened attacks, and foreign incursions had drained the resource pool. A dictate from Hank temporarily ceded command from Dempsey to Kirk. When the orders eventually came through, they could be summed up in two words: "sit tight."

The mission was decomposing before them as the body count increased, yet no one seemed to care. Charlie found it enraging. Kirk's more philosophical views were yet to rub off on her.

The days passed without incident, purpose, or direction. When the time came to draw up the official reports, Charlie omitted all sidebar conversations, assignations, and investigations. Paperwork processing by the FBI only took place when staffers were forced into it. It would be weeks before anyone cared enough to read them. D.C. staffers always had bigger things to deal with, irrespective of the subject at hand. The official communique with the joint project team contained even less information, limiting itself to the logging, tracking, and posting of artifacts. It was an account that would even bore a librarian. It served its purpose; the team back at Paris had fallen asleep on the reply. As far as they were concerned, things were tough out in Iraq, but slow progress was being made. They were high on trust but low on verification. No one volunteered for the opportunity to fact check the report in person.

There was still no word from Hank, but Charlie knew he would be on her case. The utterances from official channels were dismal. To Charlie it seemed a soulless, uncaring world where fellow mortals were being wiped out and discarded from memory almost simultaneously. Dempsey, Mac, the Springer, the IT geek, and the local agent Abbas—all lost without trace or recognition. To her dismay, there was no collective mourning for these departed souls, good or bad. No one wanted to know them. No one seemed to care.

Kirk had classed the response as being an integral part of life and death in a war zone. Charlie wasn't so sure. She was relieved that the threats and dangers were now behind her. Until any formal investigation had begun, she would leave her days as an amateur sleuth behind her. She had consigned her findings and notes on the recent horrors to one large box file and was now trying hard to focus on completing the mission ahead. With the reports finished and no fieldwork in play, she had set herself in a holding pattern that comprised research, cataloguing, and fitness. Mundane research was a tonic. Her talisman remained out of sight, on its string. For the first time in a long time, she had no decisions to make.

A vociferous bang on the unit door startled her. On opening it, she was amazed to find Hank standing with two large coffees.

"The full Turkish, Agent Glass?"

Charlie yelped like a newbie.

"Brought you some coffee."

The drinks were set down to allow decorum to take hold. Hank looked born to serve with his immaculately ironed FBI attire, dust-proof hair, clean-shaven jaw, and freshly polished Oakley wraparounds. He seemed to have been working on his tan.

"When did you get here?"

Hank seemed pleased and embarrassed by the welcome. "An hour ago. Special clearances, and all that. How are you?"

Charlie toned everything down. "Well, you dropped me in the middle of a deadly smuggling ring, but apart from that, everything is fine."

The smile fell from Hank's face. "Really?"

"I am honestly fine. Kirk pulled me through, and we are on the other side. It is so good to see you. Sorry to have dragged you into all of this. I'm such a wimp."

Hank threw up his hand to close her down. He grabbed a chair and motioned for Charlie to take a seat on the bed. "I was due a visit, anyway. This thing has been turning nasty for some time. We knew the situation was getting out of control, but we didn't know who we could trust. Kirk had proven himself, but we don't know who was in and who was out. That's why we pulled you in as an outsider."

"Well, I've definitely felt on the outside of something."

"Yeah, the alarm bells were clattering when people on our own team started dying. That's a game changer."

"We can lose an army of rag heads, but when one of our own dies, we need to act."

Charlie pushed on past a term she hated. "A heads up would have been helpful. It might have avoided me being strangled half to death and shot at. Twice!"

Hank held up a defensive posture. "What?"

"It's fine." Her face told a different tale.

"We couldn't risk you showing your hand. It was your first assignment, and these guys are sneaky. Tough times, tough measures."

"Tell me about it."

"I'm sorry I couldn't bring you inside the ropes. But you're on the inside now. I promise I will do everything I can to keep you there. You've earned that much."

Charlie wasn't going to argue with him.

"Listen, I owe you more than a drive-by chat and a cup of cold tar. An incident room has been set up near Checkpoint Six. It's here, on the map."

Charlie mulled over the map. With Hank's verbal guidance, she tracked her finger to the exact location. She hoped she had been convincing, for she knew the room's exact location.

Hank closed things out. "Go get some grub, then meet me at the briefing room at 1400 hours."

Charlie beamed. Things were turning her way. "1400 hours it is boss. See you there."

After Hank left, Charlie punched the air.

She was inside the ropes and swinging.

CHAPTER 17

The door buzzed, allowing Charlie to enter the holding area of the building housing the incident room. The receptionist appeared far from receptive. Charlie had her number. *Forty-something, female and frosty*. Returning to the scene of her crime, she took her usual seat. She appreciated the fact Kirk hadn't told Hank about her brief bout of breaking and entering. Like a doctor calling a patient into surgery, Hank pushed his head into view.

"Agent Glass?" Courteous exchanges were made with the indolent receptionist as Charlie tentatively entered the room.

"That's all, guys. I'll call you if I need you." Hank dismissed the two minders as she entered. The contractors nodded and exited without acknowledging Charlie's existence. They were quite the sight; as broad as they were tall, they looked as if they used bullets more than words. Even their haircuts and outfits looked coordinated. The black boots, combat gear, and graphite armor were set off by a selection of weaponry and barely necessary equipment. The taller man stood around six foot, four inches. For the shorter man, five foot nine would have been a stretch. Only the disparity in height and their facial scars differentiated them. Charlie couldn't fathom the dynamic. After they left, Hank noticed the wrinkles in her questioning brow. "With so many rotten apples, I needed to look in a different barrel. We go way back. I needed people I could trust. If it goes dark, these guys will throw lead."

For Charlie, the bent penny dropped. "And if they need to cross a few lines to get a result, they are on their own."

Hank smiled. "It's not a US mission. We can deny all involvement."

"The FBI hires mercenaries?"

"Contractors," Hank corrected her.

"Who are they?"

"The Kevlar Twins." Hank chattered on past Charlie's questioning look. "They are brothers, but they're not twins. The Kwiatkowski brothers. They came out of the shipyard town of Gdansk in Poland. Hard as nails. I hired the big guy first for some work out of the Balkans. The crew couldn't pronounce his surname, so he was christened K. After a nasty mission, the crew renamed him K9 because he fought like a dog. The name stuck; now everyone calls him K9. His little brother was brought on a couple of years later, and within days, the guys could see he was a meaner, angrier version of his big brother; so, he was called K2."

"K2, like the mountain?"

"Yep, smaller but much deadlier."

"You can't be serious. They answer to that?"

"Deadly serious. I think they like it."

Charlie was still perplexed. "But why wouldn't you just bring in the locals if you were short of muscle? They know the lay of the land."

Hank flinched at the suggestion. "The place is a powder keg. Saddam loaded the police with Shiites. They persecuted the Sunnis. Now the police have been disbanded, it's open season for the Sunnis, and they are out there loaded for bear. So now Shiite militia are infiltrating the Iraq police force, exacting revenge. Bodies are turning up everywhere—rivers, garbage dumps, sewage plants, sewers, out in the desert—you name it. These people can't be trusted."

Charlie bristled at the use of the term "these people." Pretending to only notice things for the first time, she pulled up a chair in front of the crammed notice boards. On second impression, the board appeared to have lost names and masked profiles, but she couldn't be sure. It was not in her nature, but Charlie played dumb.

"Okay, boss, amaze me."

Hank kicked it on. "It's a smuggling ring led by a mystery man. A guy they call the Serpent. He showed up in the online chatter and local intel as soon as the invasion started. He became a bit of a legend, a myth. No one knows if he really exists or not."

Charlie stood and pointed to a fresh picture of Dempsey. "But now we know?"

Hank nodded. "It's ironic that the guy leading the investigation was the mastermind. Rumors have been surfacing that some players sent to prevent the looting were getting themselves in on the act."

Charlie felt the need to comment. "And not in a good way."

Hank worked on past her banal comment. "Dempsey had been here since the start and came highly recommended. Over time, the rumors became realities. When traps were laid, the bait went stale. That's why we embedded you, but things collapsed before we could get you up to operational speed."

Charlie's comprehension lagged. "What was Dempsey doing on my plane?"

"Returning from leave."

"Who's this guy?" Charlie pointed to the murdered IT operative, from the warehouse attack.

"Wayne Springer, CIA communications," Hank explained. "All around eavesdropper, dark web specialist, and loner. You wouldn't want to see his browser history. Our guess is that he was a good guy who was turned."

Charlie nodded as if all this was news to her. "He was on my plane as well."

"Yeah, as far as we know, they had the same leave patterns as Dempsey. Probably aided the smuggling or masking of information transfer."

"Makes sense." Charlie pressed on, keen to learn, keen to stop making trite comments. "So, what set all this off?"

Hank pointed to another photo. "You know this guy, Zain Abbas?"

Charlie stuttered silently.

"Don't worry. Kirk told me all about both incidents. It's okay; I wouldn't have wanted to tell my boss I'd let a killer escape. That must have been tough on you."

Charlie didn't need sympathy. "Did he also tell you I went after him at the museum?"

"The attack at the museum set the whole thing ablaze. Tariq turned nuclear."

"His only way out was if everyone involved was wiped out."

"Exactly, once he knew he was a marked man, he lashed out."

"First to go were Springer and Abbas. Simple plan: lure them into a trap, kill them, and blame insurgents."

Charlie opened up a new front. "Mac and Dempsey were next."

"Our guess is that he killed Dempsey up in Samarra. Pushed him off the Minaret. We think he killed Mac there too and brought him back to Baghdad to use as a decoy."

"Ballsy play."

"He was desperate. Fighting for his life."

Something didn't gel with Charlie. "Why kill me, and why Kirk?"

Hank shrugged. "You weren't supposed to die. You were supposed to be some newbie who saw an insurgent murder and reported it."

"You think that's why he didn't wait on Kirk to go in there?"

Hank nodded. "When you smelled a rat, the game changed."

"He panicked and pulled his weapon."

"Kirk got to him before he could pull the trigger."

Charlie resisted the temptation to mention emptying Tariq's AK-47. She deflected by studying the board. Amongst all the photographs and lines, words seemed in short supply. "What a mess. Kill or be killed?"

Hank nodded sorrowfully. "Dishonor amongst thieves." He clasped his hands behind his head, leaned back and sighed in resignation. "They operated in a world where you could easily cover your tracks."

"Even if those tracks were deep and bloody."

"When things went south, the world they operated in was the perfect cover. It's an absolute cluster."

Charlie was relieved the truth had eventually come out. "So, where do we take this from here?"

"Upstairs, although they won't give a shit about it."

"What? Why?"

"It's low priority, and it's contained. It can be easily blamed on the locals. My job is to make sure it doesn't stay that way. You and I will work the angles. You'll handle Paris, and I'll sort out D.C."

"And after that?"

Hank sighed. "You'll probably be reassigned to France until the heat dissipates."

Charlie made no effort to disguise her groan of disapproval. She had unfinished business in Iraq.

"Sorry, that's likely to be nonnegotiable. It's just the US doing what the US does best."

Charlie didn't like it. "Covering up for criminals?"

Hank censored the speculation. "Taking care of our own."

"Even if our own kill and steal?"

Hank shrugged. "War's a filthy business." He rested his big hand on her shoulder and set his staring eyes across her lowered field of vision. "Look at me. You've acquitted yourself well. We'll have you back out in the field in no time. Right now, we have more shit than we have shovelers."

Resigned to her fate, Charlie knew he was right. "I'll have a report back to you by the end of the week."

Hank straightened. "That's the spirit. I'll meet Kirk, close out his debrief, then we can triangulate our reports." Sliding his big hand on her arm, he turned up the intensity of his glare. "Never underestimate the work done here."

"What work?"

"You uncovered an entire smuggling cell."

"I was sent to recover artifacts, not uncover cells. People died."

"They knew the risks. Jesus, they caused the risks. Without you, countless more would have gone the same way. It may not feel like it, but you leave here, job done."

"Come on. I'm on the edge of this. We need to keep pushing."

"You've pushed enough. As you say, people died. The bosses have deemed the risks far greater than the rewards."

Charlie was one part proud, two parts annoyed. A knock on the door cut her argument short. Hank seemed relieved. "Yes!"

The receptionist brought in tea for one on a tray. Hank distanced himself. "Well done, Agent Glass. We're done here. Can you get the report to me by Friday?"

Charlie joined the formalities. "Yes, sir."

"Excellent. Please see yourself out."

Charlie smiled inwardly at the sight and sound of her boss pretending not to care. "Sir, yes, sir."

For the first time in days, she followed orders.

CHAPTER 18

The days raced past as the prospect of leaving the magical, murderous land of Iraq loomed large. Charlie hadn't been there long enough to discover the real country or its people. She wasn't ready to leave. She loved it and loathed it in equal quantities. The mythical marvels of the ancient land continued to be blighted by the mists of corruption and the fogs of war. The overwhelming desperation that gripped the flawed nation felt palpable. Sadly, the innocents were the ones suffering the greatest agonies. For all Hank's rhetoric, she knew deep down, she hadn't made any real difference. That thought saddened and annoyed her.

Her immediate future entailed passage back to D.C. for a full debrief, a little R&R, and then a return to Paris. For Kirk, the road ahead looked to be more uncertain, with the threat of a transfer to Fallujah looming large. Charlie had spent a morning of their waiting-in-limbo time with him. It proved to be time well spent as they mapped their respective reports and agreed upon the details and timings of the principal events. Assumptions were aligned, facts were checked, and protagonists were characterized. Although the bullet points for their outlined reports were agreed,

Charlie doubted there would be a seamless alignment. She had completed copious finely penned notes on countless reams of agency paper. Kirk, in contrast, used a blunt stubby pencil and a moleskin notebook. They differed in so many ways. She was meticulous. He made it up on the spot. She cross-referenced. He guessed.

By the time her reports entered the final stages of their fourth rewrite back in her quarters, Charlie was reading more and writing less. She felt wretched about leaving Iraq. She hadn't followed in the footsteps of the gods and the greats, hadn't experienced the sites from the cradle of civilization. With longing, she pulled out her history books and artifact catalogues. Ancient tales of heroes, villains, gods, and lost treasures soared from the pages. The term "unfinished business" had never felt more apt. Her brain blasted out pangs of self-pity, as she recalled the less fortunate, the innocents, no longer walking the face of the earth. Disturbed that she could not continue her love affair in Iraq, Charlie abandoned her books and padded over to the desk. After brewing up some of her addictive thixotropic coffee, she revisited some old friends online. In her time studying at the Sorbonne, she had spent endless days touring the Near Eastern Antiquities and Islamic Treasures in the Louvre. Visiting these treasures online would be the closest she would get to the real thing for some time. Her housing unit had received the Intelligence Services upgrade. This delivered internet access—horrendously slow satellite internet access—was internet access all the same. She fired up her laptop.

The sluggish internet gave her enough time and annoyance that she opened her media player. To fill the time, she opened a previously downloaded podcast on the history of Mesopotamian deities. The monotone droning of an expert from the University of Chicago quickly stifled her interest, reducing the program to background noise, at best. *Worse than useless.*

She decided to let the man drone on, glad of his company, however tedious.

Eventually the internet caught up, gradually unveiling the images to support the research. Charlie studied the Louvre website intently, unveiling several treasures. Minutes morphed into hours. The endless entries, artifacts, drawings, and guides were surfed and studied. Marveling at the magnificence of history, she reviewed each piece. One fact was gleaned from each item and consigned to her memory banks. Patterns were developed, timelines were mapped. Mini quizzes were enacted. The hard-core studying bolstered her battered confidence.

Over time, page after page loaded as her anticipation lowered and avarice waned. The night closed in.

Almost imperceptibly a word floated in from the monotonous podcast.

Am I hearing things?

Through a veil of tiredness, she clicked the podcast back a few minutes. Alerted by the moment, she focused on every syllable. The expert recounted tales of the Mesopotamian underworld god of death. Bored by a lack of war, he had infamously murdered everyone in Babylon. Charlie sat, fixated on his name: *Nergal.*

She stumbled through the jumbled corridors of her subconscious.

Have I heard that name before?

Was it on the notice board of the incident room?

Uncertain, she slammed the name into the search function on the Louvre website. Tapping in frustration, she slowly learned the tragic truth.

A stunning carving of the god was brought forth digitally. With each downloaded pixel, her heart sank to a new low. The mysterious underworld god of death wore a snake headdress and rode a chariot. The image matched the tattoo she had noticed on Kirk's arm. It then hit her: Nergal was the name Tariq had shouted when Kirk shot him.

The dawning was pitch dark.

Nergal was Kirk, and he was in it up to his eyes.

CHAPTER 19

Betrayal. Deceit. Murder.

Desperate words contaminated her mind with every heavy footfall as Charlie panted and sweated her way down the space between housing units. Dressed in full gear, and with every conceivable and portable item from her unit either in her kit bag or on her person, Charlie decided on that the exercise run would help her achieve clarity. The deal she had made with her conscience was that she would not stop until a plan had been hatched. Then, and only then, could she lay body, mind, and soul to temporary rest. So far, success had eluded her.

As she traversed the compound, the heckles and encouragements thrown at her by the less restrained squaddies temporarily distracted her from her desperately confused thoughts. She pounded the rubble pathways, around and around and up and down. Sweat saturated her clothes; her knees were on the verge of buckling. Her ill-fitting helmet had eventually worn a blister on her temple. She drove herself on. Plans were incubating, not hatching.

Mind outpaced body as she reached a set of rudimentary mortar shelters. Her feet kicked up large stone chippings as she dug in for the slight climb. Dust flew as her thoughts raced ahead. Unless some twisted miracle of fate occurred, Kirk was involved. The tattoo, the snake, the lies, they could all be brought into the open, but ultimately the evidence remained circumstantial. It could just have been a nickname. In a world where cover-ups seemed actively encouraged, she needed more. It would be her word against that of a decorated veteran with years of experience. She knew her evidence wouldn't stand up to any form of cross-examination. There were way too many unanswered questions. She needed more details before she blew the bugle. Machinations swirled around her mind. Nothing made sense. If Kirk and Tariq were in cahoots, why were they shooting at each other at the warehouse murders?

Hope sparked. *Kirk could be innocent.*

Not knowing her destination, Charlie set Kirk's housing unit as a waypoint and kicked on through clouds of wet sweat and dry dust. Another grueling thirty minutes of self-induced pain carried her past Kirk's unit.

The discreetly armored pickup parked near**by** meant Kirk could be close. She kept her prying eyes downcast as she struggled past, sneaking looks out of the edge of her peripheral vision. The back of the pickup was, as usual, loaded with items hidden by a desert camouflage tarp. She fought the urge to look underneath and trudged on. After rounding the corner, she slid back into a blind spot. She pulled the crammed kit bag off her shredded shoulders and dumped it on the ground. Bent over double, she disguised her stalling with much needed gasps of air and wearisome calf extensions. From here, she could see the pickup clearly.

Charlie filled her lungs, elongated her muscles, and considered her options. Her suspicions against Kirk were clear and present. The facts to prove his guilt were not. Just as she turned to head for home, Kirk appeared from his unit. After bobbing his head around somewhat suspiciously, he climbed into his truck and drove off. Ever vigilant, he kept the pickup just below the speed limit. Charlie turned her back subtly as he drove away. She knew that if he was taking the pickup, he would not be staying close by. There would be time. She pulled the leather back on her outdoorsman watch and waited five minutes in case he returned, having forgotten something.

When the allotted waiting time had expired, she made her move. Needing access to his unit, she chose a full-frontal advance. After a double knock on the unit door went unanswered, Charlie casually wandered around the back of the unit, surveyed the scene, and stowed her kit bag. The solitary top window on the unit had been left wedged open. Like every other window in the complex, it was too narrow for a grown man to climb through. Charlie was no grown man. She hauled a nearby trashcan underneath the window and pulled down a few of the sandbags that covered the walls. She looked around twice before climbing up onto the can, then cast her left knee up onto the ledge of sandbags.

There she paused, checked once more that nobody had seen her, then flung her right foot in through the long narrow opening. With little energy to spare, she scraped her torso in through the inviting aperture. The latch ripped her shirt and scraped her skin as she fell into the unit. Landing half on the bed and half on the side table, she watched as her ripped shirt buttons skittered across the floor. She wiped the blood clear then scrabbled around the floor until her button had been retrieved. Nothing was left to chance. The blood leaching through the bandage on her stitched hand would need to be looked at later. The room was scanned, and drawers were gently plundered. Great care was taken to avoid disturbing any items. If they needed to be moved, their location was noted beforehand. Their replacement was precise. Nothing was left out of the previous order. At the back of the standard-issue steel cabinet, Kirk's rucksack fell into view. With the canvas prize in hand, she sat on the corner of his bed, unzipped the sack, and tipped its contents onto the bed. Fresh sportswear, a map, a compass, a phone charger, keys, and loose change fell into view. Encouragingly, she found nothing incriminating.

The sound of an approaching vehicle stopped her heart. Only when it passed did her blood flow restart.

When replacing the items, she touched the side pocket. Inside, she found the cell phone she remembered from earlier on the rooftop of the Palestine Hotel. Her heart sank. She had not noticed nor remembered the similarities. It looked identical to the cell phone she'd found in Mac's apartment. Her mood darkened at the discovery.

She tried to open the cell phone, but frustratingly, unlike Mac's handset, it was locked. She threw the handset on the bed in despair. She retraced the time on the roof in her mind and remembered that Kirk had used the same four digits to open his BlackBerry. Unsure of which number was used, the keystroke beeps had definitely come from the one button. She knew that people in the service, including herself, often used the same single digit access codes on their equipment for ease of access in an emergency. Uncertain of how many attempts she had, she still had to try it. She drew a breath and typed 1111. An incorrect pin error message popped up. Take two. She sighed and typed in 2222. Another incorrect pin error message popped up alongside a warning that one more failure and the phone would be blocked.

"Shit!"

She had been hoping to follow the number sequence, but that additional security measure had derailed her plan. There was no time to wait for a lapse on the code entry, nor could she steal the phone. Panic gripped her stuttering fingers. Kirk could return any minute. Her hands and eyes scurried around the desk area in search of inspiration or clues. She checked papers, notes, and a calendar with no joy. When she picked up and read Kirk's ID card her face flushed with exhilaration. *Date of birth: July 7th, 1977.*

That could mean only one thing. She snatched the phone and typed in 7777. The phone opened with a heart-racing buzz.

A frenetic interrogation of the phone's contents ensued. There was only one text message in the history. *"Execute."*

Kirk had sent it on the morning that Dempsey and Mac were killed. Charlie's worst fears were realized. *Kirk had sent Tariq to kill both men.*

Charlie rehoused the phone and refilled the rucksack, then continued to scan for clues. Cupboards were checked, boxes were hauled out and drawers were pulled. Care was taken not to disrupt the scene. Every hiding spot imaginable was inspected. Frustratingly, when the time came to leave, she had yet to find evidence that wasn't circumstantial. Everything disturbed was reset and rechecked. Giving the room one last check, she noticed the bedding looked a little tousled from her rucksack search. It needed to be reset to Army specification. When she flicked the blanket into the air, a glinting item appeared to flip out across the floor. Charlie fell to the ground like a magpie chasing down a shiny object. Her eyeline dropped as the palms of her hand brushed the flooring. Suddenly her unbandaged hand rasped against a piece of metal. Between forefinger and thumb, Charlie lifted the item into view. It was a blank 9mm cartridge. Iraq was awash with live cartridges and spent shells, but no-one carried blanks. Charlie now knew the truth.

That night at the warehouse, when they'd found the two dead bodies, Kirk and Tariq must have staged the gunfight using blanks.

The gavel fell on Kirk's guilty verdict.

Angry for allowing her fears during the gunfight to cloud her judgment, Charlie couldn't remember any bullet landing. Her mind raced to dark places.

Kirk set up the whole warehouse scene.

He pushed me behind a wall not to protect me, but to fool me.

She pocketed the blank and made for the door. Equal amounts of anger flowed. She was angry at him for the deceit. She was as angry at herself for the stupidity. After peering out to check her exit path was clear, she rolled out confidently before the door automatically locked behind her. She strode back behind the unit to return the sandbags, rehouse the trashcan, and recover her kit bag. As she threw on her oversized backpack, the straps rasped her tenderized skin. She pulled the straps tighter than before. She took a long breath and checked her exit route one last time. Striding out into the narrow aisle with counterfeit nonchalance, she turned homeward, weighed down by a heart filled with unwelcome answers. Anger tainted her thoughts. Fear and naivety had again blinded her. It was time to grow up.

It was time to get even.

CHAPTER 20

The first action of the day became freeing up the time and space to work. A call into Hank asking for an extension on the report helped set the scene. If he had been surprised or disappointed to receive the request, he hadn't shown it. He remained as courteous and understanding as ever. His closing words focused on making sure she was engaged in laying down hard facts. That had always been her intention. Hank would get the truth—not some half-baked work of fiction—and for that, she needed evidence. She resolved to take all necessary action to deliver that very evidence.

Kirk had sent her a text requesting a catch up at the dining facility. She didn't consider it a trap, given that there would be fifty witnesses in the hall and all weapons had to be emptied and checked before entry. She replied by asking him what his movements and availability were. He said he could make an early dinner, but after 1700 hours, he had things to do. She agreed to meet him at 1630 hours.

Charlie formulated alternative plans. In the intervening moments, she prepared for all eventualities, ranging from silent observation to pitched gun battle. She didn't want it to turn vicious, but if it did, she hoped she would step up when it mattered most. All her life she had found challenging herself to be not particularly challenging. In these moments she felt alive yet afraid. This was a truly electrifying ordeal. When the time came, she felt ready.

Kitted out for action, she checked her mirror. As a last-minute addition, she stuffed a city map inside her flak jacket. The gesture seemed futile. She felt pretty lost already.

Charlie marched through the compound with purpose. She took up a position at the margins of a crosswalk within sight of the DFAC, but out of sight of the thoroughfare. The same soldiers who'd heckled her earlier in the day were scrubbing away at the wash station. Blasting the afternoon sky with obscenities and insults, they recalled the events of the day's patrol.

From an acute angle, she watched Kirk stride up imperiously. The soldiers stood to attention when he arrived on deck. He greeted them with the presence of a general and the closeness of a grunt. The men responded with bucket loads of reverence. The group washed up and walked in together. A born leader, Kirk held the door open as they all trooped in under the wooden canopy that acted as an air lock.

She waited. *1640 hours. Time to fly.*

She turned and strode purposely past the hall towards Kirk's pickup truck. The bitter truth remained; Charlie needed to discover evidence of his weapons grade criminality. That lay outside the Green Zone. To find it required wheels. Even if she could wrangle transport, she wouldn't negotiate her way past security in time to keep up with Kirk if he left the safety of the compound. Before she could flash her badge, Kirk would be long gone and hidden in the humanitarian quagmire of Baghdad. She knew every checkpoint was a direct line of intel back to Kirk. If she moved, he'd find out.

She arrived at his pickup, then feigned fatigue. Leaning back on the tailgate, she surveyed her surroundings. With time running out, she needed to act. Backing away was not an option. *It's now or never.*

At the point of no return, she conjured up all the courage available, clambered into the back of the pickup and slid under the desert-camouflaged tarpaulin. She crawled in between the boxes she had noticed on her earlier jog past. Her vain efforts to get comfortable did not succeed. Even through the tarpaulin, the searing sun had taken the bare floor of the pickup to a burn inducing temperature. She bundled up a small pile of the sackcloth used to make sandbags and stuffed them in under her shoulders. Whether for cushioning or heat protection, it didn't matter. Neither goal was achieved. With her head dangling outside the tarpaulin, she checked her watch: 16:45. She sent the text to Kirk.

Sorry, can't make it. Surprise party!

However tenuous, the text was an attempt at an excuse if Kirk found her in the back of his truck. She would say the surprise was on him. It was a shoddy plan, but she forced herself to roll with it. She hoped it would cover her if she were found inside the Green Zone. After that point she would be truly on her own. She waited for the reply. Her hand buzzed, and the message came through, short and sweet.

? Enjoy!

Under her shroud, Charlie's waiting game intensified as the minutes passed. Her compulsion to wriggle and adjust grew as the need for total stillness drew nearer. She carefully timed everything so that Kirk was now pushed to be mobile in time for his previously announced seventeen-hundred-hours deadline. He would be back soon. Listening intently for any activity proved fruitless. Gunfire peppered the distant air. She speculated: a wedding? A murder? Both? Suddenly, she felt and heard the vehicle alarm unlock. Footsteps raced up to and inside the truck. Sandwiched in the airless gap between fabric and metal, she lay motionless, afraid to breathe. The engine fired up, yet still she lay in a stifling, breathless cocoon. Only as the pickup rumbled into action did she feel safe enough to exhale. She eased her face to the edge of the tarpaulin, gasping for oxygen. The rattling ride on the compound's crushed roadway hammered her head against sackcloth and metal. Her weight was distributed more to the flak jacket to help stave off the heat from the truck bed. In her mind, she traced the path of the vehicle with the directions being taken. She took extra breaths, realizing the security gate would arrive soon. One last big gulp of air was relished as the vehicle slowed. It would be inexplicable for the guards to search the vehicle. Check-outs were far less rigorous than check-ins, and Kirk seemed immune to both doubt and regulation. As predicted, the checkpoints were routine; they passed without incident. The side of her head received relief when they hit the smooth tarmac. With the pickup gathering pace, she pushed her face back out into the airless afternoon. The sky appeared as brilliant as she had ever seen; an incredible bright blue blanket enveloped her. Marking the sun's location, she deduced they were heading south. *Bandit territory.*

A massive pothole brought her back to reality, thumping the side of her head against the floor of the truck. Her head shook and bounced. She saw stars on a sunny day. The sounds of another two less-than-strict security checks passed. Two bridges were crossed on the next phase of the journey. The car took a last second swipe to the right, back onto what felt like a furrowed back street. Ruts, hollows, bumps, and bangs made it difficult for Charlie to read her watch, but she eventually discovered she was thirty-three minutes into the journey south. She guessed they had just entered Dora, a district home to all bad manner of life. Snipers, bomb makers, looters, chop-shoppers, carjackers, kidnappers, and a multitude of terrified, gentle, honest souls. As she peered out the side of the sheeting, the pickup banged and bounced its way downside streets with ever decreasing road quality. She deduced that all this excessive circumnavigation had more to do with losing tails than losing direction. The vehicle unexpectedly stopped. Charlie's breathing followed suit.

The driver's door opened and closed. Only then did Charlie consider it might not be Kirk driving. Before panic set in about what she had climbed into, she shook herself back to the job at hand. It was too late to turn back.

It was too late for surprises.

Over the puttering engine noise came the sound of a clanking, unraveling heavy chain. A gate screeched to the side just before the driver returned to the vehicle and drove on through. Charlie eased her gun into position as the vehicle slowed. It felt like the truck was being repositioned for a quick exit. It sounded as if the driver then exited and cantered off at some pace. No voices came, so Charlie eased her head over the edge of the pickup truck. Wild-eyed and curious, she quickly scanned the scene. A rapid risk assessment ensued. The gate was left open, so either this was a flying visit or reinforcements were arriving. Others could come soon to unload the truck. She needed out but didn't know where to go. Regrets on setting off with a crappy plan flooded her thoughts.

The compound offered limited cover. Decision made, she checked her gun, crept over the wall of the pickup, then crawled underneath the vehicle. She looked for grip locations in case the truck was moved. Nothing held. If the truck moved, she was dead. She needed options.

From her snake-level-view, the locale was immaculately clean, bereft of the detritus that marred the entire city. For that reason alone, the compound stood out. A freshly painted roller shutter door sat beside a reinforced pedestrian doorway. Everything about this place screamed military. From her disadvantaged position, she could not spot CCTV cameras. That didn't make her feel she was in the clear. Far from it.

The plans came fast.

In one corner sat a well-ordered stack of pallets, offering the only potential cover. She decided to hide there until everyone had left. She would then break in, uncover the crimes, find the location, and call in Hank. *Simple.*

Suddenly, the roller shutter door cranked into life before she could make her move. Still under the vehicle, she crabbed away from the sound of the door. Two sets of sandals shuffled up to the side of the pickup. Sandals as cracked and dirty as the feet they housed shuffled around to the tailgate. The sound of the tarpaulin being untied preceded the clatter of the large boxes being dragged across the bed of the truck. The groans and the deflection of the truck told Charlie the box was heavy. The hapless porters wandered back into the building, straining with every sidestep. Their unhappy mutterings translated into every language. Charlie waited: one box down, one to go. Judging from the raised voices that accompanied its transfer, the second box was even heavier. A single pair of sandals then returned and closed the compound gate, the pickup tailgate, and the roller door.

Alone again, Charlie crawled out, keeping the vehicle between her and the door. She confirmed the lack of CCTV, then worked her way across to the stacked pallets, never losing sight of the doorway. Overhead, she noticed a small four-pane frosted window with one pane smashed out. Lifting her chin towards the missing pane, she heard gurgling and running water. Watch and sun were checked. Peering through the broken pane, careful not to cast a shadow, she saw the two chattering porters carrying out Wudhu, the act of washing before prayer. Back against the wall, she stood tall to see the top of a magnificently ornate minaret. She checked the sun, then waited. Within minutes, the minaret speakers came to life with the melodic and hypnotic call to Maghrib prayer. She now had around twenty minutes where the henchmen would be otherwise engaged. *Call it ten for safe measure.* All she had to worry about was the mystery driver. Her mind sparked. *Perhaps one of the locals is the driver?*

She checked her vital signs—panicked, on the verge of collapse. Callously crushing her fears, she convinced herself that there was an opportunity get in and get out without confrontation. No sound came from behind the broken window. *It's now or never.*

In a heated frenzy, Charlie ran to the door then checked the handle. It eased open. With her head through the gap, the sound of prayer floated out from the small room, connecting the corridor to the washroom. With glacial speed, her eyes rounded the door stand. Two sets of sandals rested at the doorway. Further in, two men were bent over in prayer, chanting, and moving in convicted unison. When the men bowed low, she skated past the doorway and on into the main workspace, undetected. She took up a position behind a stack of uniformly wrapped and stacked pallets and scanned the space. She sucked her quivering bottom lip between her teeth and breathed through her nose. Slowly, she refilled her lungs. Sweat ran into the corner of her left eye, causing her to blink and twitch.

At one end, a mezzanine office hung overhead. It seemed the perfect location for an overbearing supervisor. In what looked to be the rear of a large retail space, one wall housed several stacked sofas, all in some state of unwrap. They had been pushed to the side, as if making way for some kind of underground house party. Each sofa was a diversely colored variant of the standard Iraqi design; oversized, gaudy, and frilled, with outlandishly large armrests. Whatever was being smuggled out of Iraq, Charlie knew it wasn't last season's Saddam sofas.

Across at the loading station, the prayer appeared to have disturbed the packing of a consignment of .50-cal magazine tins. Boxes lay in order across the floor of a defined section in the warehouse. A brand-new forklift truck with a military paint job and decals sat with its forks under a box made from roughly sawn timber. The crates told a different story. They were military grade, stacked uniformly in high rows. In that unguarded moment, she requisitioned one of the shipping documents attached to a stand-alone crate. The paperwork appeared thorough and officious. All calibers of ordinance, ammunition, weapons, and guidance systems had made the manifest. The munitions were marketable, yet unremarkable. Armed with fresh answers but even more questions, she dug deeper. It contained the entire shipping documentation for formal US administrative transfers of Excess Defense Articles. The articles cited numbered, government-negotiated, Foreign Military Sales agreements that were cross-referenced to export licenses for Direct Commercial Sales. It was all there. Everything about the paperwork looked legit. Everything about the operation did not. She needed to shift gears. She had seen enough. Suddenly, the prayers died. Short on time and long on panic, she turned and ran across the warehouse. Voices approached. Cursing her decisions, she lurched to evade the encroaching goons. Racing for the other doorway twenty paces away, she risked no backward glances. She sped up as the voices closed in from the rear. As Charlie reached for the door handle, it turned. To her horror, Kirk appeared through the doorway.

The startled pair stared in silence. When Kirk bent to retrieve his falling clipboard, Charlie raised her gun. Painful disbelief wrenched them both. In their own panicked and tortured way, each of them surveyed the scene, assessed the situation, and planned their next moves. Despite holding the weapon, Charlie was clearly the most terrified.

Kirk deflected. "So, this is your surprise? Are you here to check the shipments?"

Before she could answer the two locals approached her from behind. She hurriedly repositioned herself to a wider position where she could threaten everyone. "I won't get all three of you, but I can take down two. Don't try me." The strong words didn't match her weak and quivering gun hand. She stiffened her gaze and her grip. "Back off!"

The locals raised their hands, yammered, and backed away. Charlie's confidence grew with every backward step. Faced with the options of flight or fight, the thugs were clearly leaning towards option one. At three against one, she needed to even the odds. She pointed to the door.

"Yalla! Yalla!"

The men got the message. Needing no second invitation, they turned and fled in full every-man-for-himself fashion. Charlie hoped they wouldn't be back with reinforcements. Turning her weapon and attention back to Kirk, she chose her range, moving close enough not to miss but far enough away to avoid being pounced upon. She gestured with her gun.

"Turn around." Kirk obeyed. Noting he was unarmed, she corralled him across to the packing area. Amid the various packing materials, she spied some large cable ties. "Put one of those ties on your wrists."

Kirk tried to reason with her. "Listen I don't know what—"

"Shut it. We talk when your hands are tied, not before." Kirk took the cable tie, made a circle, and pushed his hands forward. "Do you think I'm a complete fool? It didn't click. Close it and let me hear the ratchet."

Kirk sweated. He ratcheted the cable tie into a wide loop then pushed his hands through. He gestured to Charlie to pull the plastic wire closed. She was having none of it.

"Use your teeth!" Kirk obeyed. "Tighter!" Kirk obeyed again. Charlie pushed Kirk's face down on the peeling concrete floor then darted a look, in and out of the nearby showroom to confirm they were alone.

Kirk grasped the most effective angle of attack. "Listen, this is a legitimate arms shipment."

Charlie wasn't buying it. "So that's why you're using local goons to guard it?" As she unsuccessfully ransacked the neat piles of correspondence on a standard-issue US Army desk, her frustration mounted. None of the addresses on the shipments related to their location. She found the answer in a discarded pile of unopened envelopes addressed to the adjacent furniture shop. Her language skills were enough to make out the business name, street and building number.

"My guys will be back any minute now," Kirk pressed on. "You'd better get out."

"I don't think so. My guess is they are off at home for a change of underwear. They will be back tomorrow to offer their services to the people they find running the show. We both know it. You're on your own."

"For now, but you need to get out of here. The guys who are picking up this shipment are coming soon. They will be tooled up. Please, I'm begging you. You need to get out." Kirk almost sounded sincere and convincing. Charlie built her own stone wall.

"These shipments are nowhere near ready. They won't be picked up for days. I think we'll be fine for now."

"Well, you can't stay here. Good luck getting back across town. A Western woman can't drive alone around here, and you can't take me with you. I own the checkpoints in this town. I own everything and everyone around here."

Charlie tried to stay focused and confident in response to Kirk raising the ante. "That may be the case, but not everyone is from around here."

She reached in her pocket and switched on her BlackBerry. She called the only friend she knew in Iraq. "Hello, Hank?"

Hank was delighted to hear from her. "Charlie! How goes it? How are those reports coming along?"

Her reply reset the tone. "Not well, boss. I need your help."

Kirk squirmed, forcing Charlie to rattle her firearm in his face. She followed up. "I'm holed up in a warehouse in Dora. They have been smuggling out of here."

"They? Who's they?"

Charlie wouldn't be drawn. "I have one suspect in custody. Two insurgents have fled. I need reinforcements."

Hank's voice reached DEFCON 1. Charlie sensed he was already running. "Where are you?"

Charlie translated the address on the furniture shop letter. "Five-five-seven Abu Salam Street. Around the back."

"Hang on. Five-five-seven Abu Salam Street." His staccato reply indicated he was noting the address on the run. "How far?"

Charlie's lip quivered in anticipation. "Thirty minutes."

"I'll get my guys over ASAP. Call Kirk and get him to bring a crew."

Charlie needed help more than questions. "There's a small entrance at the back. The back door's open. I'm in on the left side."

"Okay. I'll get to you. If anyone else comes through the door, blast them. Don't take any chances. If things change, I will call you. You do the same."

"Roger that." The line closed. Charlie bristled. Kirk kept pace with proceedings.

"That's it? That's your cavalry? The oversized gym jockey and his two brain-dead buddies? You're bringing them to their deaths. My guys are coming, I swear. Get going before they get here. You can't defend yourself with that peashooter, and your extraction team couldn't pull baby teeth."

"You may be right." Charlie found one of the many crowbars then sought reinforcements. One-handedly, she pulled open a box labeled *M4 Carbines*. The inside wrapping was lifted, a brand-new oiled up rifle retrieved. She split one of the ammunition boxes. Her eyes and handgun stayed trained on Kirk. Gun and ammunition were quickly united. Charlie took up a position covering both doors with a prone Kirk in the middle. "If this kicks off, you're the first to go."

She inspected her surroundings as she paced the temporary battlement. Kirk kept up the conciliatory rhetoric. "Look, you're not going to shoot me if I don't threaten you. Can I…?" Kirk invited himself to regather his footing then sat on some nearby .50-cal ammunition cans. "Can I explain?"

Charlie remained vigilant. "Can you?"

"What we are doing here is legal."

Kirk's explanation got no airtime. "I swear. Stop talking or stop lying."

The curious glances Kirk threw towards the ammunition boxes piqued Charlie's curiosity.

With one eye on the prize and one on her captive, she returned to the newly opened box cartridges. Pulling out the pack on the top layer, she was amazed to find sackcloth.

"Careful!"

Kirk's yelp made her almost drop the package. She set her gun down close enough to her for it to remain a deterrent and pulled the sack from the ammunition case with tentative ceremony. When she unraveled the small heavy package, a delicate cuneiform tumbled out of the bottom.

"Go easy. That's worth a small fortune."

Charlie held on as the penny dropped. "So that's the game."

"Sorry, I don't understand."

"Really? You're still denying it?"

The angle of Kirk's sneer became more obtuse. "Denying what?"

"Setting up government-sponsored arms sales as a front to steal antiquities."

Kirk seemed almost relieved that Charlie had figured it out. "Well done. I would clap, but—" He presented his bound hands. He mounted his defense. "A lot of what we ship is fake."

Charlie's disbelieving tone cut through the storyline. "So, you're telling me you're offering a public service: one that kills to protect genuine treasures?"

"Exactly. We fake the pieces and the documentation. The most valuable thing we have is the route out. Authorities are so paranoid about illegal arms that they're relieved to see honest brokers like us follow the rules. They don't give us a second thought, and if they do, we pay them to go back and remember their first thought."

"And that it's coming through a disreputable channel gives no one heartburn?"

Kirk shrugged. "People tell themselves what they want to believe." Charlie shook her head, so Kirk tried again. "I'm not saying we're saints. We started shipping arms, graduated to looted items."

"Then relegated yourselves to high-class fakes and murder?"

"Things just spiraled."

"I'll say they did." All the while Charlie struggled to avoid staring at the magnificent little cuneiform.

Kirk changed tack. "When did you know?"

"About you?" Charlie clarified. He nodded. "When you walked through that door."

"You must have known before then."

"Maybe I knew, but I didn't believe it. I had suspicions long before I ever realized."

"How so?"

Charlie pointed. "Over there on the desk is the same paperwork that you planted to incriminate Dempsey. Identical."

"So?"

"I stared at the files from the murder scene across at the warehouse for hours knowing that they held a clue."

In the absence of a response from her captive, Charlie continued. "It wasn't what was on the files—it was what wasn't."

"Which was?"

"Nothing. No blood splattering, no body matter. Everything in the murder scene was caked in blood. Tariq planted the files after he shot them, didn't he?"

Kirk was running low on options, so Charlie piled on the pressure. "When I cut my hand, the blood gushed for ages. That reminded me. All the blood at the warehouse was dry. He must have shot them hours before."

"Remember the shootout? I protected you!"

"With blanks?" Kirk stalled. "I found the blanks you used for your fake gun battle."

"Where?"

"In your housing unit."

Kirk sounded almost impressed. "You have been busy."

Charlie laid down the cuneiform and lifted her gun. She then pointed it at Kirk's tattoo. "The ink was the final give away. Nergal himself."

Kirk played dumb. "Nergal."

"The mystery name Tariq called you when you put a bullet through him. I recall seeing it on the wall of the incident room. Remember, the one you dragged me out of?"

"It was for your own good."

"Just like killing Tariq was for your own good. Your own friend."

Kirk squirmed under the interrogation. "He was no friend, and he was going to kill you."

"It was a brilliant move, getting lost on the way to Tariq's ambush. You knew exactly where you were going. You were just buying time. Building your backstory. Did you leave him to finish me off?"

"No. He was freelancing. I saved your life."

Charlie didn't quite understand. "Why didn't you just let him shoot me?"

For once, it sounded as if Kirk was selecting honesty as his preferred policy. "Self-preservation. If you shoot a white woman in Baghdad, it makes CNN Headline News. Terps go missing every day."

"So, the gig was, get me to write a report that fit your narrative, but when I saw through the scam?"

Kirk lifted his palms skyward. "You left him with no choice. And he left me with no choice."

"There were plenty of choices."

"He had fewer options after you emptied his AK-47."

Charlie felt in no mood to deal in flattery. "Save it. Innocent people died because of you."

"It was Tariq," Kirk leaned in. "We had a great gig running until Dempsey interfered. That's when Tariq cleaned house. He lost it. I knew nothing about it until it was too late. It was his idea to send the texts about the Golden Chalice to trap Dempsey."

Charlie wasn't letting up. "That show with you making a call to Mac and him being spotted heading out of town with Dempsey. Just bullshit. Was Mac already dead?"

Kirk didn't answer.

"Damn it! Wasn't it convenient that the phone you planted at Mac's had no code, and only one number linked Dempsey?"

"It's not like that."

"It never is."

Kirk was rattled. "What would you know about anything?"

"Enough to have you at gunpoint."

"There's a big difference between holding a gun and shooting someone."

"And you'd know all about that."

"I had no choice."

"So, you fought with Dempsey and Mac over who could steal the Chalice?"

Kirk squinted at her misapprehension. "Way off. They wanted to recover the Chalice for the museum, not to steal it. They were a pair of do-gooders. Unimpeachable, unrelenting, pain-in-the-ass, do-gooders."

"Unlike you? An out-an-out thief?"

"You don't know me. You can't judge."

"And yet here I am."

Charlie felt ashamed and disheartened to have been so wrong about the dead innocents. The roll of dishonor listing her innumerable misjudgments lengthened with every new revelation. Her heart went out to the two misunderstood victims. Anger would come, but for now disbelief was in the ascendency.

"Why would they fall for such an obvious trap? Everyone knows the Chalice is long gone."

Kirk's smug grin could not have been wider, and his words more dumbfounding.

"If it's long gone, why are you standing right beside it?"

CHAPTER 21

Charlie looked back in disbelief before Kirk pointed at the ammunition she was leaning on.

"Look! US .50-cal cans. One hundred cartridges, four-ball M-thirty-three, one tracer M-seventeen. Hardly standard issue, though. The code on the bottom tells a different story. Find the one with the code ending in I-M-eight-two-seven-two. I just set it in there ten minutes ago."

"Nice try," Charlie scoffed. "I'm not Dempsey."

Kirk tried again. "Consider it my cooperating with the authorities."

"That won't wash. Murder is murder."

"They won't want any publicity. I'll blame it on Tariq and be out of a military jail in no time. Or you may be persuaded by what you find in the ammo box, and a different route could be taken."

"Not gonna happen."

"Listen, I'm over here tied up, you've got the gun—humor me. But hurry, we have little time."

Charlie's curiosity got the better of her. She scanned the boxes as Kirk recited the code to her. "I-M-eight-two-seven-two."

With her wrong hand, she used the top straps to drag the ammunition boxes to one side. Her Glock and her gaze remained firmly focused on Kirk. Fleeting glances landed on each box. To her astonishment, the number appeared on the third box along the line. *IM8272.* Her eyes raked over a grinning Kirk. The end catch of the box was yanked over and the top cover lifted. She pulled out a very heavy belt filled with bullet after bullet. Her gun hand helped carry the load.

Kirk ducked as the Glock swung his way. "Easy! Make sure that safety is on!"

"That's a chance you have to take."

Deliberately, line after line of bullets were laid across the nearby cases. Only two layers of bullets had been dispensed before the belt emptied out the top. Her eyes flashed before a smug looking Kirk.

"Go on!" he cried.

Gently, she lifted makeshift polystyrene packaging from the container then peered expectantly into the can to find a sackcloth package. She laid her gun down with a look that told Kirk, *One move towards me and you die.* He, in return, set his hands in prayer to show that he understood. Pulling the sackcloth package from the container, she grasped the package inside. Her soul lit up when a gleaming golden chalice appeared before her eyes. She recognized it immediately as the lost Golden Chalice of Ur. It looked much smaller than she imagined, but it was even more precious for it. She held it to the light. The magically ornate chalice, thousands of years old, still gleamed. The golden flecks in the two lapis lazuli handles still danced like delighted sprites. There was no doubting the quality and authenticity of the craftsmanship. *This is it.*

"Where did you get this?" she gasped.

Kirk worked the angles. "Well, there are two answers. If you join me, I can tell you where it comes from, where it's going, and how it gets there."

"And?"

"And if you want to stay out of the game, I have never seen it before in my life."

Charlie was incredulous. "Come on! You just told me where to find it!"

"Only to show you what we're missing. Join me. Let's call this one in together—our joint collar."

Charlie stared and slithered. Her stomach churned. "You were the only one."

Kirk's hopeful eyes blinked.

"The only one I trusted. And yet it's come to this."

"You can still trust me. We can do this, together."

Charlie welled up. "There is no *we*." Thoughts ran back to earlier moments. "Those times are dead. You killed them."

Kirk clasped his hands in desperation. "Please, we can do this. Together. We blame Tariq and the locals. We can be rich, split everything fifty-fifty. Come on, before the cavalry arrive! Think about it. Christ, you can even have the Chalice."

Her resolve weakened at the very mention of the Chalice. Her astounded gaze edged across to the enchanting piece. Intoxicated by its beauty, intrigued by the stories it held, she faltered.

Beep, Beep, Beep.

Hank had arrived. The sound of the car horn snapped Charlie to her senses but sent Kirk into a spin.

"Please, for God's sake, join me. We can do this! Even if we just hand it all in, I will stop. Please."

Hank's welcome shout worked its way through the doorway. "Agent Glass, are you okay?"

"In here. All clear." Charlie did not show her decision when she called for Hank and his team to enter.

"We're coming in."

Kirk neared the point of implosion. "Please. Please. You don't know what they are capable—"

Suddenly, K2 and K9 barged into the room in sequence, all in black with guns at the ready. "Easy, boys." Hank followed in fearlessly. Holstering his gun, he sprinted over to Charlie. There were no hugs this time. "What's going on?"

Kirk pitched in first. "Thank God you've arrived. We've just fought off the gang; Charlie just saved my ass. They were going to kill me."

Hank set his guys to work. "You check all exits. You cut him loose."

When K9 motioned to free Kirk, Charlie screamed. "Stop! He's one of them."

All three men froze. Hank's face demanded an explanation. Kirk exhaled in disappointed disapproval.

"He's your smuggler. He was in it with Tariq."

Kirk protested. "Bullshit!"

"I don't care if you don't believe me, just don't trust him. Bring us both in. You can question us back at the base. Just don't untie him. Look around."

Hank gestured for his guards to check the merchandise. He looked stunned as he addressed Kirk. "You're the Serpent?"

Kirk switched swiftly into self-preservation mode. "No. Tariq was the Serpent."

Hank's training kicked in. He swiveled his gaze back to Charlie. "Was he working alone here?"

"No. There were two locals, but I scared them off just before I called you. They could be back any time. We need to get out of here."

Hank's voice sharpened. "If they think it's only you, they'll be bringing back lead. This guy must have many friends outside the Green Zone. We can't hold out here; we've got to get moving. You two, load what evidence you can into the pickup, and let's get him back to justice."

The men busied themselves as Hank frog-marched Kirk outside to the waiting SUV. Angrily, he pinned his captive to the car's front door, as he fumbled for the key fob. The men loaded the pickup as Hank threw Kirk into the passenger seat more roughly than protocol permitted.

Hank opened the back door and pulled a couple of bottles of iced water from a giant cooler. He threw the first at a grateful Charlie. Breathing threats into Kirk's ear, Hank's cool demeanor deserted him.

"Charlie, please don't—" An angry Hank silenced Kirk with a punch laced with testosterone and precision. Sensing he may have gone too far; he grappled the cap off the second water bottle and drenched Kirk back to semi-consciousness. As Kirk wallowed in the front seat, punch-drunk and blood-soaked, Hank strengthened his bonds. K2 brought over a handful of spare cable ties to secure Kirk's hands to the grip handle above the vehicle door. Hank's guards stood tall and wide, bristling with armor, muscle, and equipment. Despite their awe-inspiring bulk, they still knew that Hank was the boss. They were ordered to close shop and drive Kirk back to base in the SUV.

He pointed to K9 and K2 in order. "You drive. You sit behind him. Don't listen to his crap. If he twitches or even speaks, put a bullet in him. Lock this place up, then head to Checkpoint Five. I'll go on ahead with Charlie and arrange a reception committee. He's not weaseling his way out of this one. Remember: one word, one bullet." The K-twins appeared to both understand and appreciate the premise. K2 trotted to the open gate. He pulled his IR night vision goggles over his eyes and kneeled. He slowly peered around into the street, carbine at the ready. The *all clear* was signaled. Hank courteously opened the passenger door. "Jump in. We will see those guys back inside the wire."

Charlie obeyed orders but struggled to buckle her seat belt because of the Glock in her hand. As he set Kirk's pickup truck into motion, Hank smirked.

"I don't know if that's still necessary."

Charlie's face didn't change. Looking dead ahead, she clenched her weapon.

"Neither do I."

CHAPTER 22

By the time Kirk's pickup turned out of the guarded gate, night—and all that came with it—had descended upon the city. After a few backstreets spent on high alert, Charlie finally plucked up the courage to release her breath and lower the gun. Switching gears, she snatched a headscarf and placed her blonde hair and Western features under wraps. The stunned silence inside the pickup seemed an oasis of calm compared to the manic street life outside.

Arguments amongst friends continued over pipes of peace. Fruit sellers screamed to be heard over kebab salesmen. The yapping grandmothers pointing fingers at protesting vendors demonstrated it was never too late to haggle in Iraq. Kids jumped around the shell of a burned-out old Mercedes bereft of wheels and seats. Overhead streetlights cast darker shadows over cloaks, headscarves, and veils. Sirens screamed and alarms rang as lights and signals flashed. With the nightly disorder flashing past them, Hank broke the extended silence.

"Why didn't you call me before?"

A blurted half confession was all she could muster. "You told me never to trust anyone, remember? I had to see for myself."

"Didn't you trust me?"

She bristled. "It wasn't like that. I thought Kirk was up to something, but I didn't know what. Things just spiraled. It was me or him, so I acted."

"I'm glad you did. That took some balls. This whole thing is unbelievable."

Charlie sped past the compliment. "I've been wrong so many times on this deployment. I needed to get this right.

Hank's eyes conveyed his pride. "Well done. This is great work."

"How deep do you think this runs?"

"I'm not sure—deep, and wide. This is big."

"We can find out once Kirk starts squealing."

Hank nodded. "We need to watch him. He seems slippery."

"As an eel."

Not for the first time, Hank pushed the conversation on. "That was great work, Charlie. What did you find in there?"

"Damn it!" Charlie fizzed. "I left the Chalice behind! Argh!"

"Chalice?" asked Hank.

"The Golden Chalice of Ur."

"Never heard of it."

You wouldn't have, thought Charlie. "It's priceless."

"Priceless and you left it behind?"

"Argh! Idiot!" She looked in the mirror and pointed behind. "Can we go back?"

"Don't worry; the guys will have picked it up," Hank reassured her. "Besides, back there is the last place we'd want to go. It could be crawling with Hajis by now. If they can't get in, they will be lying in wait, burner phones and AKs at the ready. We'll go back tomorrow in force."

In frustration, Charlie yanked off her flak jacket. After unfastening her straps, she pulled the heavy vest over her head. As she lifted the panels, some Velcro hooks caught her t-shirt. The higher she lifted the jacket, the more skin she exposed. In this almost comedic strip, her bra became visible, and her talisman gamboled into view. In a vain attempt to cover her blushes, Charlie's gun hand grappled with the garment.

"Careful."

Setting down the weapon, she scrambled to recover her dignity. Hank jumped into action, taking a hand off the wheel, pulling down her t-shirt.

"Classy." Charlie uttered the only word between them on the subject.

Hank provided the much needed segue from their recent state of undress. "Did your Grant button protect you?" Charlie looked askance, so he grinned, gestured, and elaborated. "Your charm. Did it protect you?"

She felt a little self-conscious, given the mocking tone in her boss's questioning. "No, it's just a thing I do for fun—one of my superstitions. And anyway, who told you it was from Grant?"

"You did, back in D.C."

Charlie couldn't recall. "I didn't mention him by name."

"Yeah. I think you mentioned it in passing."

She still wasn't convinced. "When?"

Hank dithered. "It must have been on one of the debrief sessions. I can't remember. Anyway, I'm glad you're safe. That's all that really matters."

Charlie stalled. Her senses jangled. Something felt off. She couldn't remember mentioning much about her charm to Hank. Then it hit her. *Kirk knew. When were Hank and Kirk chatting about me in that much detail and why?*

Charlie scanned the scene. Although dark, nothing seemed familiar. Questions morphed into doubts as they headed over a never-seen-before expressway. A crushing wave of realization pinned her into the seat. Hank was going south, directly away from the safety of the Green Zone. Silence fell as Charlie surveyed the street names.

Eventually, as the thoughtful silence elongated, Hank sensed things were going astray. "Damn it! I think I'm lost. I need to get turned around." Charlie failed to make her sigh of relief go unnoticed. The truck slowed. Hank then pulled over into a side street to make a U-turn. "Reach into the glove box, I think there's a map. I'm lost."

The truck slowed further. Charlie's spine shuddered. Her fingers twitched with terror as she edged her hands towards her Glock resting between the seats.

"Oh, I wouldn't do that." Hank's ice-cold words chilled her to the bone.

Charlie spun to see the barrel of Hank's pistol protruding from underneath his left arm. "One move and I will plaster the dash with your brains."

Charlie froze.

"Keep your hands where they are." Hank adopted a sinister tone as he thrust the barrel further into her head. "Understand?"

Terrified, Charlie nodded her compliance.

Hank pulled the gun out further and lifted it to her face. "Easy now." He pulled the pickup into a grimly lit back alley then coasted to a dead darkened stop. Charlie whimpered as abject horror overtook her soul. Tears flowed. "Please. Not like this."

"You're like a dog with a bone." Hank growled. "How many chances do you need before you walk away?" His eyes glared and his nostrils flared.

Speechless, Charlie swallowed hard.

Hank snatched her gun and threw it behind her seat. "Now the phone."

Charlie nodded and pulled her BlackBerry from its holster. With his right hand still jamming the gun barrel into Charlie's skull, Hank seized the phone with his left. One-handedly, he fumbled the back open, stripped out the SIM card, bent it, and bit it in two. Then he threw it out the window. The phone was broken over the steering wheel and discarded out the same window. The realization of the consequences of her naïve actions flooded her thoughts.

She feigned defiance. "You can't get away with this."

"Oh really? No one cares about another carjacking gone wrong, especially if a senior FBI agent calls it in."

Charlie drowned in her fears as Hanks ominous tone deepened. "You should have listened to Kirk. He knew if you didn't take the deal, you'd have this coming to you."

An attempt by Charlie to raise her head and reason with Hank was met by a callous pistol whipping. Petrified, she pleaded. "Please. What are you going to do?"

"Probably introduce you to people who'd love to get to know you better. You want to be famous? You will be. CNN, Mujahidin, Al Qaeda, rape, torture, beheading. The full orange jumpsuit."

Charlie did everything in her power to hide the fact that she was at her breaking point. She bit the back of her hand in fear and frustration. Hank was enjoying the one-sided power struggle.

"They will pay a hefty price for your sweet little American ass."

Charlie had nothing to lose but no means of escape. She screamed to the heavens in desperation. Blood splattered the dash as Hank smashed the pistol across her left eye. Recoiling in pain, she was set back against the door by another blow. Her banshee screams were cut short by the barrel of a gun jamming into her vocal cords.

"Shut the hell up."

Charlie railed on the brink of collapse. "Why? You're going to kill me, anyway."

What came next strangled her resistance. "If you die on your terms, your father dies too. Professor Douglas Glass, head of

American History at the Smithsonian Institute. One word from me and he dies. Who lives and who dies is your choice."

Charlie rocked forward; her head bowed. Eyes closed, her fear and loathing were gradually replaced by anger. Hank pulled another cable tie from an inside pocket.

"Get this on. Pull it tight."

Following instructions, she fought to shore up her shattered defenses. *Think! Think!* She retraced her steps, looked for angles, searched for rescue. Memories flooded back. "I'm not in Kansas anymore." She bent herself double, an emotional mumbling wreck.

Hank was triumphant in his intimidation.

"That a girl. I'll ask that they make it swift, but I can't make any promises."

Suddenly, Charlie yanked her head back with force to throw her hair off her face. Hank froze, staring in disbelief at the round pin jammed between her teeth. Holding the grenade with its handle depressed, she spat the ring pull into his horrified face. "I said, I'm not in Kansas anymore."

Steroid-soaked blood bulged the vein in Hank's neck. "You wouldn't dare!"

Charlie glared in fiery defiance. "Try me. Right now, my only choice is to get my head blown off or sawn off. Option one looks favorable. Shoot, and we both go up. Switch off the engine." Hank snatched at the key and the truck fell silent. "Drop the gun." Hank obeyed but kept it in his grasp. Charlie held out her hands. "Cut my ties."

"Screw you!"

She pressed again. "Give me my gun."

"What, so you shoot me stone dead? No chance."

"Get out!"

"And leave you with the car, a handful of grenades and my gun? Pure suicide."

A standoff ensued. Charlie needed out of there before fear froze her psyche. She opened the door, giving Hank her deadliest glare.

"If you go for that gun, I will blow you straight to paradise. There are six more grenades under this seat. Understand?" Hank nodded. Now she was asking the questions. Charlie flashed her gaze around the street. Apart from fluttering rubbish and a posse of feral dogs, the place looked deserted. The overhead bulb trickled a jaundiced light across their faces as she turned and cast Hank her best Dirty Harry face. "Don't doubt me on this. I have nothing to lose." She kept eye contact as she exited. Leaving the car door open, she eased out of the passenger seat. Her grenade was the last to leave. Eye contact lasted until the last split second.

Quickly, she ducked behind the pickup.

Crack!

When she turned to run, a bullet snapped past her head.

Crack! Crack!

Another two in quick succession fizzed past within inches. Instinctively, she buckled, throwing the grenade behind her.

Crack! Crack!

Two more desperate shots cracked a wall behind her. She sprinted as fast as she could before diving face-first into the caked mud.

Boom!

The night screamed. Flashes and shards splintered the air. Flaming debris scattered. Prone, she cowered around to see the pickup ablaze. To her desperate astonishment, Hank staggered out of the vehicle. Flames billowed from his jacket and hair as he flapped and yelped. Kirk's makeshift armor had done its job.

The high-pitched whining pinned her to the ground for longer than she could afford. She stumbled in the race to regain her senses. Eventually, her staggering inertia gained momentum. Reaching the refuge of a fatigued alley wall, she threw her shoulder against its jagged corner. Hank was lost, the yelling had stopped, and the pickup was now fully ablaze. She kicked the wall to spark her senses. She was on the run and on her own. Lurching down the darkest alleyway in sight, she scoured her tumbling mind for options. She stumbled on, as fast as her shell-shocked legs could carry her. There was now only one goal: get as far away from here as possible. The destination didn't matter. The cable ties cut uncomfortably into her wrists as she ran, preventing her from picking up speed. She ran on, blood pumping, pulse racing.

Careening forward, she suddenly noticed an SUV crossing the alleyway two blocks up. She threw herself into the wall, uncertain if she had been seen. She chastised herself for running up the middle of the alley. It was the only section in which she could have cast a silhouette. Pinned against the wall, her chin sank into her chest—the SUV screeched to a halt. The high-pitched whining of a car reversing at full speed was her signal to change lanes.

She sped off in a panicked scramble. She yanked at every closed gate with both hands. Each one was locked. In desperation she, jumped up, and threw her hands over a high gatepost. Grabbing the post with both hands, she clambered up then straddled a leg up and over. The SUV's gearbox whined ever closer. Her scrambling intensified; her ties dug deeper under the strain of clambering on top of the wall. With freedom in sight, a bullet shattered the gatepost, throwing splinters into her face. She recoiled from the impact. Both balance and post gave way, sending her crashing over the wall into a pile of rusty scrap metal. Winded and writhing behind a pile of scrap metal, Charlie searched for a new exit. Screeching chickens in a nearby plastic pen added more alarm. The light at the rear of the building came on, and the back door burst open. A gigantic man with a distorted T-shirt blocked the doorway. A growling, fearsome guard dog snapped by his side. With perfect timing, the door to the alley was kicked open, and one of Hank's bodyguards piled into the conflict zone. Inaudible, Arabic expletives were hurled as the dog was sent in search of blood. Snarling across the small yard, K2 was hit before he could react. The dog's frothy jaw ripped at his arm. The homeowner bounded over to join the fray, carrying a baseball bat along for the ride. K2 retreated as both bat and dog forced him back into the alley. With the screaming bedlam spilling out into the street, Charlie sprinted across the cluttered courtyard and behind a washing line adorned with multicolored Hashimi dresses. On her way past, she clutched the last dress in the lineup, before jumping inside what she hoped would be an empty house.

After bursting in, she noticed two freshly poured cups of steaming tea sitting on a metallic draining board. A nearby gas burner remained lit. She clutched the one and only knife visible and hurdled into the next room. A panic-stricken family had pinned themselves into a corner of the sparse, bleak room. Pink gloss had made it halfway up the walls, furniture was in short supply, and floor cushions were omnipresent. Petrified, the family gawked in shock at the intrusive vision before them. A Western woman, tied up, brandishing a knife. The mother cowered in black, shrouding her screeching toddler. The son, about seven years of age, stood out on his own, smiling in bemusement, pointing out the design on his new sweatshirt with great pride.

Charlie apologized as she stumbled past. In her haste, she tripped on the rucked-up, mismatched rugs and toppled on and out through the front doorway. The sound of the dog getting the better of the guard was brought swiftly to an end by two cracks from a handgun. The raging screams of anger from the homeowner told Charlie the war was not over yet. She stuffed as much of the stolen dress as she could into the waistband of her combats. She flew on, knowing she would not be alone for long.

Closer to the main drag, narrow alleyways running between houses fell into view. At the first opportunity, she took a narrow artery at full flow. She barged on between walls, pin-balling around blind bends and twisted passages. Desperate to outrun what lay behind her and terrified of what could lie ahead, fear poisoned her every step. Disorientated by the twists and turns, she soon lost her bearings.

The sound of the arrival of an emergency service told her that the scene of her grenade attack remained close by, to the west. She reset her course away from the now static sirens. Burning every ounce of available energy, she distanced herself from the sound of the crime scene. Boot heels dug up the crumbling mud in time to stop her before the next big corner. Exhausted, she crouched down so that her head edged around the corner at an unpredictable height. Two refuse skips lay in a black alcove. Checking her sightlines, she slid across the lane and into the nook behind the trash bins.

The ungodly smell that overpowered her when she lifted the lid of the first skip almost made her throw up. The smell from the second skip sent her back to the first. Climbing in, she wished she had kept one more grenade. Fighting every instinct, she dug herself under the surface of the rubbish in case the bins were checked. It seemed that rotten food, human waste, drain sweepings, and dead animals had been left there to bake in the searing sun for days, if not weeks. The deeper she dug, the worse the smell. The rotten juices soaked her skin as she lay lifeless at the bottom of her filthy cesspit. Her stitched hand, bandage long gone, was already weeping. She pulled her talisman close and bit down hard, resigned to a fate where either her pursuers or cholera would carry her off.

With time, she pulled out the stolen knife, then turned the serrated blade upside down. Dropping it in between her hands, she set about cutting her cable tie. The first attempt ended with the knife falling into the grimy sediment. After she sifted feverishly through the sludgy excrement, she retrieved the knife. The next few frenetic minutes were spent sawing and jabbing both cable tie and forearm before the plastic clasp eventually gave way. With her hands freed, she fought every nerve in her body not to rub her bleeding, seeping wounds. The knife was rehoused inside her right boot. It had served her well. She lay trembling in the filth of the skip, head bowed. As she rocked imperceptibly, she felt her talisman buffet against her chest. In the darkness, she clutched it close.

If Hank had not mentioned the talisman, she would not have suspected his collusion with Kirk. She took a moment to kiss the amulet that had just saved her life. Filthy air filled her lungs as she took the time to regroup. As time passed, she regained her breath but lost her nerve. It didn't take long for her to retrieve her knife. It would be hopeless in a gunfight, but with the element of surprise it could just save her life. Callously calculating taking someone else's life made her realize survival mode had kicked in.

Low-toned voices arrived from afar. She reset the knife into a fighting position as she strained to decipher the dialogue between the two voices. The eerie silence of a city in lockdown meant that the voices carried well in the dry night air. One voice came from a man standing in the vicinity, the other from a man on the other end of a walkie-talkie. The conversation continued in English, although the voice nearby carried a heavy Eastern European accent.

"Nothing, boss."

"Sweep the alleys back to the bridge and we'll pick you up there. We'll get her at the gates." The voice jumping from the walkie-talkie unquestionably belonged to Hank.

"Roger." With that, heavy boot steps thudded off into the darkness. Relieved to be alive, Overwhelmed by exhaustion, dismay, and asphyxiation, Charlie set her head into the grime and almost passed out. Eyes closed, she faded into a deep haunted trance.

Panic dragged her back to life.

Pop was in mortal danger. She needed to get to a phone. Her heartstrings snapped, knowing she had brought death to his door. Why hadn't she told him? Why had she left so many things unsaid?

She needed to move. He was the priority, not her.

Clambering to the top of the pile, she peered out of the skip. With no one in sight, she climbed out before falling back into the dark shadows at the rear. Keen to get out of uniform, she threw on the dress dangling from the front of her combats. It enveloped her frame even after being wrapped and tightened to the max. The built-in hood afforded her much needed concealment. She waited in the darkness as two older men shuffled past, bemoaning married life and everything it refused to offer. They were out of sight but not earshot when she turned towards the flickering neon sign lighting a nearby street corner. A small line of restaurants—some empty, some closed—lay beyond the dimly lit junction. The light gave her the opportunity to check her wounds. They were superficial, yet open to infection. She scanned the scene for landmarks, street signs, and any other clues to her location. Her previously useless map was pulled into play. She deduced that she stood a couple of streets back from Tuma a' Street, near the Mechanics Bridge. That placed her on the south side, near the Expressway. She tapped the map in relief. Knowing her location was a start, but her destination remained a mystery. No matter how hard she tried, she could not convince herself to make a break for the Green Zone. She knew salvation lay back inside the wire, but to get there, she would have to run the gauntlet of forces, both legitimate and illicit. Every checkpoint lay just one radio message away from betrayal and almost certain death. Instead, she set off north in search of a busier road that could provide her access to a phone. Her step quickened as she thought of the threat to Pop's life.

Edging along the margins of each street, she noticed that the local dress didn't seem to help her much. If anything, it attracted attention. It was no time for a woman to be out alone, and this was no town to be out in. A passing van driver shouted abuse, accompanied by an aggressive horn and disapproving gesticulation. Getting help was not going to be easy, so she switched back onto a darker street. She needed to move north, so the forced march transitioned into a jog. Two streets into her route, she ducked back into an alley as the sound of a car encroached from a nearby street. It passed without incident or recognition. With the car gone, she drifted out and recommenced her run. Her head lowered upon hearing the high-pitched whine of an approaching scooter.

The scooter wobbled past drunkenly. Charlie held her breath. The two giggling, gabbling youths sandwiched on board swigged from a shared bottle. With a frantic yelp, the riders slithered and spun back towards her. She exhaled at the prospect of returning trouble.

After passing her, they slewed around and brought themselves level. The scooter matched her pace, wheel for stride. The boys were around twenty years old and enjoying the new illegalities that were easy to come by since Saddam's toppling. Inebriation and dialect made their words hard to catch, but their meaning was universally understood. Charlie hiked on, head down, face turned away, in hopes that they would grow bored and ride off. The front rider's mood descended and darkened with every unanswered question. Pushed on by his pillion partner, he mounted the scooter up onto the sidewalk, pinning Charlie against the wall. He dismounted as his accomplice struggled to keep the bike upright. One-way laughter filled the void.

Charlie turned away in fear as a handgun appeared. She leaned against the wall for steadying support. Her mind raced to make sense of events. She knew that local rapes and hijackings were on the rise, and it would be little runts like this who were to blame. The front rider was the boss. He stood there more terrified than Charlie—cut-off jeans, soccer top, and oversized plastic sandals. He bounced from side to side, brandishing his gun, spitting out incoherent threats and ultimatums. His apprentice giggled and ogled through a drunken haze. Charlie's frame buckled as the gun-toting youth pressed in further. High on crime, he thrust the gun into her hood, and belched out more insults and threats. As the gun boy boasted back to his partner in crime, Charlie stood tall and pulled off her hood. Her attacker gawked open-mouthed at the Western beauty before him. Before he could react, Charlie's fist crashed into his larynx. He fell to the floor in a gargling puddle. Before the distraught second youth could kick-start the bike on the run, Charlie drop-kicked him into the road. A set of knuckles between the eyes settled him right down. A second helping obliterated his senses. When she motioned to hit him again, the blubbering mess skittered off into the shadows, probably in search of his mother. Charlie snatched the gun lying beside the floundering criminal.

"Are you kidding me? A fake?"

Anger and frustration boiled over as she bounced the bogus firearm off the head of the floundering wannabe gangster. She grabbed his headscarf before heading over and lifting the scooter. To the sound of whimpering, she sparked the scooter into life. Without looking back, she hauled at the throttle and sped off into the darkness. The choking wails behind her gave her no concern. She was on a mission.

The chilling night air blew life into her face. She ventured on with unimagined freedom. Head down, stopping for no one, she left the boys behind at the scene of their crime. A couple of streets later, she pulled over into the dim slot between two underpowered streetlights. The attention-gaining dress was first to go. She wrapped the scarf around her head, pushing every strand of blonde hair out of view. She checked her look in the scooter's solitary cracked mirror. She looked like a boy under siege. *That will have to do.*

She weaved the scooter northwards and onwards in search of a phone. The world flew past, oblivious to her flight. Covering the miles quickly, the route led her into a more residential area. She slowed to match the sparse evening traffic. After a few eventless streets, she noticed activity ahead in the distance and sped on to discover more. When the shapes in the distance became more visible, she noticed one road at a crossroads had been barricaded. She twisted the scooter's throttle down to a gentle crawl, and eased to the side, far enough away to avoid raising suspicion. The barrier looked paramilitary grade. Razor wire hung in extended coils across a framework of crossed poles. Even the oil drums that burned to give the sentries warmth appeared US Army-issue. The guards looked to have been sourced locally. The ramshackle crew were clearly militia, imposing their own version of martial law in their district. Their clothes were as casual as their attitudes as they huddled around the makeshift fires shooting tall stories up into the night sky. A human spindle in sandals held Charlie's attention. The AK-47 that hung nonchalantly like a sidewinder did not concern her; she was more interested in the cell phone he was holding. She knew not if the guards were friends or foes. She waited for proof one way or another, but it never came. Wrapping her headscarf tight, she killed the light on the scooter. She could see the checkpoint well enough, and approaching lights tended to spook checkpoint gunners. Traveling at a pace she hoped looked normal for the situation, she pressed on, unnoticed but conflicted. *The phone is vital, but what good will it do to get killed in the process?*

Her heart raced past the moment. Sweaty palms slithered on the scooter handles. Holding a straight line was proving difficult. Thirty yards from the checkpoint, a forward sentry spotted her. He looked worryingly confused by her arrival. The sign he stood next to had been hand-painted in Arabic. It proclaimed an Islamic enclave. That was enough. She rode on, no one there would loan an American their cell phone. If they were using cell phones around Americans, it would be to set off IEDs. Split-second decision made and at the point of no return, she bailed. Head down, she veered right at the crossroads. Giving the militia lots of space but no eye contact, she rode on. Pointlessly, she braced herself in horrific anticipation of a deadly hail of bullets that never came. She rode on stiffened by fear. Tears formed, making it impossible to check her mirrors. Gasping for air, she wobbled on the edge of implosion. No sounds of disturbance followed her. Chastising herself for going into a dangerous situation with no plan, she felt her anger turn inward. She remembered that Dempsey had called this place *a loaded game of chance.* Right now, her actions were skewing the odds. She fought the urge to scream into the night. She lost that battle.

A US night patrol suddenly turned into the street, running at full pelt away from her. *Redemption at twelve o'clock. Up-armored M1114 Humvees.*

Charlie knew they could get her back in through the gates of the Green Zone. She gunned the throttle. Fully focused, she raced to catch the high speed four-vehicle convoy as it sandblasted the neighborhood. After kicking her lights into full beam, Charlie rode on through clouds of dust, screaming at the top of her voice.

Up ahead in the Humvee, a set of standard-issue goggles peered over the armor, protecting the .50-cal machine gun. Charlie took the gunner's appearance as a positive. She beeped her horn and waved in hopeful filled celebration. The gunner eventually stood, like a beacon of hope, but to her dismay, he pushed his shoulder forward, then yanked back the spring to cock the gun. The limited visibility and high-speed maneuvers didn't help, but he seemed in no mood to take heed or chances.

"Ead 'iilayh!" Over the loudspeaker the squaddie's voice boomed through the dark dust. "Ead 'iilayh! Ead 'iilayh!"

Charlie grappled the throttle in defiance of the crude translation thrown out by the young gunner. She rode closer. "I'm American! I'm American!" *He had to hear.* She rode closer still, grit and dust flying in her face. Without warning, the Humvee's searchlight sent splintering beams into the back of Charlie's eyes, causing her to weave and falter through the blinding light. The turret gunner twitched and slid the searchlight in all directions. Charlie rode ever nearer, but the closer she rode, the more animated the turret gunner appeared. She screamed for help in her loudest American accent. "American! Help! Stop!"

Salvation sped on only a few yards away. Shafts of dusty light swirled as the shouting from both sides missed the mark. Speeding on, the patrol, in line with protocols, careened straight through a busy junction throwing the local traffic into disarray. More desperate than dauntless, Charlie sideswiped a car and narrowly missed a head-on collision with a speeding truck. Desperate, she rode on. Through the dust and mayhem, the near-miss junction only served to accelerate and animate the screaming and waving. The gunner yelled louder, as Charlie moved to reveal herself. Around fifteen dusty yards from the Humvee, Charlie made one last desperate play. As she yanked the headscarf from her head, all hell broke loose.

Bang! Bang!

An earth-shattering explosion disintegrated the bike's engine block, sending Charlie careening sideways. Skidding off the road, bike first, she tumbled headlong in flailing turmoil. The bone-shattering power of the .50-cal ripped shards of fiery metal through the air. Flames burst across the scene. Chunks of flesh flew. Numbed by the trauma, Charlie collapsed into a rag-doll cartwheel that pitched her headlong through splintering wood and slashed canvas. Her dark world spun with a heady cocktail of fear, uncertainty, and pain. The agony racking her body helped stave off unconsciousness. Unable to process the moment, she writhed in agony, spitting and coughing up blood. Nearby flames from the blackening wreckage of her exploded scooter licked the debris from an obliterated market stall. She pulled air painfully into her wounded torso. Miraculously, she had survived the bout of demolition and landed in a heap. The festering garbage had cushioned her fall.

She clung on.

Lights flicked on and dogs barked as, crushed, and scuffed, Charlie lifted herself up onto a wavering knee. A painful panic set in as she checked her wounds. With disbelieving relief, severe gravel rash, painful winding, a jarred shoulder, and a few splinters seemed her only injuries. Blood belched from knees and elbows. The splitting headache arrived with full force. Still, she clung on.

By the time she had regathered her courage, the Humvees were gone and with them, her last chance to enter the Green Zone under guard. Relief turned to self-loathing, at the realization, she had blown her shot at rescue. Cars and trucks slowed.

Rubberneckers stared. Horns blew. Around her, a posse of prying eyes emerged from the shadows. Trembling with shock and worried at the response her landing could generate, she rose to her stumbling feet. No one helped. Everyone stared. Five became ten. The mood of the forming crowd darkened with every new arrival.

Sympathy seemed in short supply. Suspicion infested the swelling crowd. Ten became twenty. All men. All local. Anger simmered to boiling point. The damage done by the westerner seemed the source of the angst. Irate shouts corrupted the whining in her ears. The mob encroached while she remained dazed and confused. She checked her boot. Her knife was gone. Threatened and vulnerable, Charlie grabbed a nearby splintered baton. "Ead 'iilayh!" Flailing wildly, it was now her turn to scream, *Get back.*

She dragged herself out into the now-congested roadway. Desperate to evade any irate locals, she pushed ahead through the traffic. She staggered on, too afraid to look back. Thankfully, the cries from the curious onlookers did not follow her flight path. Relieved and recovering, she raised her gaze. Cracked joints ached and bled, and she broke out into a full canter. Favoring distance over direction, she ran on. Pumping adrenaline carried her through the pain barrier off into the unwelcoming night.

Only after a couple of streets did she have the courage and resolve to look back. To her relief, no one had followed. Crushed ribs ached as she filled her lungs. It was unavoidable; an evil she had caused. The sensible thing to have done would have been to follow the patrol discreetly then approach them once they stopped. She could have even followed them back into the Green Zone. A distant police siren sent her scurrying into the shadows.

When the siren echoed off into the distance, Charlie lingered in the gloom. Dark times, indeed.

Driven on by fears for her father, she overpowered the temptation to curl up and die in the corner. She needed wheels. A glow in the night sky a few streets over gave her hope. She hobbled on, fearful that some local have-a-go-hero would be plucking up the courage to hunt her down. Ducking down a series of darkened alleys brought sanctuary, not fear. The dim glow from a series of backstreet lights led the way. With every step the fear ebbed, the blood flowed. She needed help. Street after street, the distance from the crash site grew. Drawn like a wounded moth, she flapped her way over to the cluster of streetlights. Around another corner, a string of cafes lay on three sides of a small square. Businesses appeared slow. Incredibly, a universally understood green sign burned brightly in the corner of the square: *Pharmacy*.

With no money and no time to lose, she barged on. Charlie burst into the store without breaking stride. Spying the bloody pillager sent the frail old pharmacist into spasms. His greying beard quivered as his frail hands flapped in submission. "Yalla! Yalla" Charlie's bloody screams pushed the old man, who cowered and retreated in fear. Charlie screamed as she rattled her way around the tiny cabin. Barely ten feet square, the little unit held everything needed. She grabbed bandages, pain killers, and mouthwash, on a first-found, first-stolen basis. Item after item was stuffed down her shirt. As she turned for the exit, Charlie read the signs. A crowd was gathering outside. She spun towards the rear of the cabin. It was easy to corner the old man cowering in the corner. Charlie spat. "Mafatih? Mafatih?"

The pharmacist fumbled in his pocket before dragging out a small set of keys. She needed more. "Ayn? Ayn?"

When the old man pointed to the exit, Charlie dragged him across to the exit. Bundling him out the rear door she asked again, "Ayn? Ayn?"

The man stumbled to the side before pointing a quaking finger in the direction of a nearby scooter. "You're kidding me?"

The poor old man looked in fear of his life, but sympathy had not yet formed in her psyche. The only man that mattered to her was Pop, and he was in danger. When she turned to run for the scooter, the old man slipped from her grip and jumped back in the cabin. The door slammed with a bang, as did the locking mechanism.

Her busted, jittery hand seemed incapable of fitting the key in the scooter ignition. Eventually, success came. The engine started the first time, much to her relief. A painful shoulder made pushing the scooter off its stand a painful pursuit. As she threw her leg over, the warped gyroscope in her brain buckled her sense of balance. It took an eternity before she established a manageable equilibrium. After a number of failed launches, Charlie set the scooter into motion. Woozy and fearful, she needed every ounce of effort and concentration to get back and stay on track. The bike wobbled and slewed as both machine and rider got back up to speed. There was no looking back.

Warped vision and a busted light made the next stage of her flight difficult. Speeding ever northward, she took stock. *No money, no phone.* She'd been right to leave the fake gun behind; it would only have attracted danger. She mentally inventoried her possessions: *FBI badge, a watch, medical supplies, and a map*. Item by item, she worked through how each of them could help her. The watch was easy. She knew the time—so what? Her badge couldn't be used to impress or intimidate locals. It had no jurisdiction, and like a fake gun, it would only bring trouble.

Her thoughts fled to petrified locations as they imagined how a captured FBI agent would be treated in front of an Al Qaeda camera. Corralling those black thoughts, she pulled her mind back to the terror at hand. She could flash the badge at the US Embassy complex, but to get there she needed to pass through the Green Zone checkpoints—the very ones Kirk would have covered. That left the map.

With an almighty yank she pulled the scooter across to the first working lamppost. Circling to a dimly lit alcove near the lamp, she pulled the medical supplies. Mouthwash was swilled in and around every wound. She crunched and guzzled down a mouthful of painkillers with more mouthwash. Wipes swabbed her gashes. She abandoned the effort to bandage her wounds after the first two attempts quickly unraveled. Running repairs completed, she checked her angles. Nearer the streetlight, she snatched the map open, flattened it across the handlebars, and scanned it anxiously. For the second time that day the map was tapped. Charlie knew exactly where she was going and exactly what needed to be done. With a quick glance back into the non-existent traffic, she grabbed the scooter's throttle and made it wail.

She had a plan.

Nothing held her back. She made no eye contact, obeyed no lights, and crossed all lines. Charlie blasted on through a nation deserted, speeding past closed business after closed business. Every one of them looked destined to never reopen. All humanity had faded into the eerie darkness that enveloped Baghdad's disorienting web of backstreets. The chop shops had closed. No hookah pipes were being shared amongst friends. No tea was being dispensed. No old men argued over a rigged game of dominos. Dying flames in an old oilcan were the only signs that life had previously existed. She was a creature of the night. Concern for the old man and guilt over how she had treated him corrupted her thoughts. She screamed inside and forced herself to focus on the threat to life. Feelings were for another day; for a time long gone. As she rode on, the painkillers kicked in, nulling her pain and her guilt. She gathered pace and regained focus.

Nearing her destination, she took a more cautious approach. One last pit stop allowed for the reexamination the map and the fine-tuning of her bearings. She traversed two more streets before reaching her destination—Mac's squalid little apartment.

Approaching with stealth, she cut the scooter's light and engine early, arriving safe and soundless at the back of the building. She checked her sightlines and crossed to the rear entrance, hugging the darkest shadows possible. She chose the threat of a fall from height over the possibility of another lacerated hand. Thankfully, on that higher section, no glass had been cemented into the surface. The scooter was pinned to the wall to act as a climbing frame. An all-or-nothing leap landed perfectly. Both hands gripped the top of the wall. Boots, knees, chin, and elbows scraped their way up the rough wall as she hauled her weary body up the wall. Her struggles intensified. Not even the flea-bitten alley cats stirred as she struggled over. Dropping on the hard concrete and buckling her ankle almost felt like a relief. She stumbled on, perturbed but not broken, cracking the barless window before slithering inside. She landed clumsily, producing a horrifyingly loud series of clatters. If someone was there, her game was up. She plowed on regardless, straight towards the bathroom.

After pulling the light cord, she pillaged the pedestal. She yelped when her hand hit the Ziploc bag. In a frantic panic, she ripped apart the bag and pulled out the phone. Switching it on, she begged for power.

"Please! Please!" The old phone took an eternity to load up. "Come on! Come on!" When it finally mustered enough energy to switch itself on, the unlocked phone had only one bar of battery lit, and there was no signal.

"No! No!"

She revisited the living area in search of a charger and a signal. She recalled Pop's number. Thankfully, he grew up in an era where those receiving a call would inform the caller what his number was. Charlie always teased him that she knew his number; she had just dialed it. But right there and then, she had never been more appreciative of her father's eccentricities.

After punching in the number, a sliver of signal popped up in the corner of the screen. Only the burners used by criminals had international dialing capabilities, so she had hope. She tried her luck with the green button and waited. Her heart leaped as the connection was eventually made. The phone rang and rang and rang.

No answer.

Fearful that her battery would give out, she darted around the darkened room, vainly seeking a battery charger. The phone buzzed to show an even lower battery level. Screaming through the phone at her absent father, she threw caution out the window and switched on the living room light. The search for a charger commenced at a panicked rate.

"202-3353."

She exploded down the line. "Pop, Pop. It's me."

"How are you, girlie? You're lucky to have caught me, I was just—"

"Pop, I'm sorry. Listen!" She had neither the time nor the battery power to allay any fears or listen to inane drivel.

"What's wrong?" Pop sounded flustered.

"Just listen. I'm fine, but you are in danger. Some bad people across there want you dead. Do you understand?"

"What? Why?"

"Forget the whys. Just trust me. Okay?"

"Okay, but—"

"No buts! Listen! I don't have any battery. Some bad people are coming for you. They're probably already on their way. Get out of the house. Now! Don't say its name over the phone but go to where I found the button. Call no one. Tell no one. Take provisions and go. Go full Unabomber on this. I will make contact when it's safe. Say you'll do it."

Pop reeled on the other end of the call. "Charlotte, you're scaring me. Are you okay? How can I help?"

"I'm fine," Charlie barked over his concerns. "It's you who's in danger. Get out now; it's not safe. Protect yourself. Say you'll do it and do it now. Do what you need to do to survive."

"But—"

An ear-chilling monotone broke the connection. The phone had died. "Argh!"

Charlie's plundering amplified as she ripped the house apart looking for a charger. She continued to shout at herself in monosyllabic braces. "Come on! Come on! Think! Think!"

She remembered the fake book with the cash. That could buy her a connection or a charger somewhere, somehow. She sprinted over the carnage to the bookcase, pulling out book after book, engrossed in their contents. Only when she opened one of the books, did she notice a shadow in the doorway.

She looked up in horror to see Kirk standing over her, Glock in hand.

CHAPTER 23

Kirk looked resigned to the dark task at hand. "You did well to get this far, but you should never have switched on the light." He brandished his gun towards the cluttered sofa. "Take a seat." Charlie used the book box to knock all the crap out of the way then dutifully took her seat on the sofa. Her former friend faltered, despite their relative positions, Kirk appeared to be the one falling apart.

"Why didn't you take the deal? I would have protected you."

"I can protect myself. I can even protect you."

"Impossible."

"There's still time; please turn yourself in. You're not Hank. You're a good man."

Kirk seemed unwavering in his conviction. "I can convince Hank."

"He's alive?" Charlie couldn't believe it.

Kirk sounded disappointed. "Somehow." He scoffed. "He's a little charred around the edges. Those were some badass moves you pulled. He told me all about it."

Charlie almost blushed. "How is he even alive?"

"The truck was rigged with redneck armor, remember?"

It dawned on Charlie. "Lucky man." She remained resilient. "He's never going to forgive me. We both know that. Even if I wanted to, which I don't, it would never work. Our only option is for you to come in. You've done some smuggling. The blood is on other people's hands. Take a plea."

"It's too late for that." Kirk remained adamant. "Hank's put a warrant out for your arrest."

"On what charges?"

"His attempted murder and the murder of Tariq, Dempsey, and Mac."

"That's bullshit!" Charlie railed.

Kirk stood steadfast. "You did lob a grenade at him. He's off the rails."

Stunned into silence, Charlie reeled at the news.

"What if I finish off the job you started?"

"Kill him?"

He nodded. "Then we let the dust settle?"

Charlie knew Kirk was dreaming. "And we all live happily ever after?"

"Not happily, but we live."

"That's not living."

"Lady, get off your pedestal."

"I'll take my chance in court."

"You won't make it to court. Have you heard the phrase 'resisting arrest'?"

Charlie held her ground. "It won't work."

"Why not?"

"Because you'd never trust me. Christ, I'd never trust me. We both know it."

Kirk's realization pained every muscle in his face as he mulled over his options. "So that's it? Either I surrender or you die?"

Charlie appealed to him. "You still have options."

Kirk steeled himself. "Not from where I'm standing. If I give myself up, I die in jail before I even get to trial."

"We have witness protection."

"You mean, witness elimination. The guys doing the protecting are the ones who would be doing the killing."

"It wouldn't be like that."

"It's always like that. I can't hand myself in. It would be a death sentence. Please, I can get rid of Hank. Join me. I will trust you."

Standing to face her fate, Charlie welled up at the finality of the situation. "And if I don't join you, I die right here, right now?"

Kirk appeared at the point of collapse. "I am so, so sorry."

Charlie begged. "Please! There has to be a way."

Kirk looked lost. "If there is, I can't think of it. Can you?"

Charlie searched for a way out for both of them. "How did it come to this? You're a good man."

Kirk's gun hand quaked. "I thought I was. It's not that easy."

"It is. We can ride it out."

Kirk swallowed hard, tears welling up. "If you get out of this alive. I won't."

"Please, you're not a killer." The look in Kirk's eyes told Charlie she was wrong. In a blinding terror, she stumbled forward. "The same road that brought you here can take you back."

"I brought this on. No one else, only me."

"You can still make it right."

"That ship sailed long ago."

"There's always a way. Transfers, new commissions, hell—even witness protection."

Charlie dragged herself onto her knees and screamed through her choking tears. "Don't do this."

In the tortured moments that followed, she came to realize there could be only one outcome.

Kirk wilted, bereft of hope. "I am sorry." When he glanced down to cock his gun, Charlie heaved the Webley revolver from the book box and shot Kirk straight through the throat.

He crumpled in a heap, his spinal cord shattered. A second bullet seemed unnecessary, but Kirk got one all the same.

Charlie toppled forward and wept like she had never wept before. With two hands still on the Webley, she jammed its barrel into the rug to prevent her total collapse. "So am I."

The consequences of her actions crushed Charlie.

Swaying on the spot, the survivalist in her soul screamed for her to get up. *Kirk's guys could be coming upstairs right now.* Still, she sobbed. Scuffing her knees, she crossed to the living room doorway to take up a firing position in sight of the front door.

With no sound outside, her fumbling fingers checked the gun. She broke the revolver and counted. Five shots left. *Thank God it was loaded.* She rolled the chamber to make sure there would be no misfires and took a bead on the door. If it opened up, she would open up. Shoot now and don't ask questions later. Blood poured over the floor, caking the rug with blackening sludge. As she lay in wait for intruders, Charlie noticed Kirk's blood kissing the soles of her once shiny boots. She never flinched. Checking her watch, she gave herself three minutes—enough time for any gang members to come in search of their partner, but way before any authorities would arrive if they ever came at all. A dog barking in the apartment next door put Charlie on high alert, but as the time passed, so did the fears of a home invasion. Warm black blood oozed between the fingers. She recoiled in panic, flapping her hand frantically across the filthy old rug.

She retrieved the whisky from the book box and swallowed hard, twice. After checking her wounds, she withdrew to the bathroom. Her gashes screamed as she scrubbed soap deep into them. She almost passed out when the final contents of the whisky bottle hit her lesions. After guzzling a handful of painkillers, she used the heel of a filthy glass to crush more tablets into powder form. The powders were then poured into her cuts before Charlie swiped the remaining contents of the entire bathroom cabinet into the plastic bag. A ripped-up towel served as a wraparound bandage.

Charlie fought to dam the adrenaline pumping through her body. "Process. Process. Think. Think."

None of it seemed to help. The chattering continued, all the way back into the living room. She recovered the small rucksack found on her recent bout of ransacking. She set to work filling it, starting with the plastic bag from the toilet. The money and the spare Webley ammo from the book box were next to be requisitioned. She couldn't bear to look at Kirk as she picked over his blood-soaked lifeless corpse. She took everything that could cover her old tracks and anything that could help her make new ones. His silenced Glock and three spare magazines, phone, SUV keys, money, and ID all made it into the bag. She pulled a blackened congealed pile of soggy red papers from an inside pocket and stuffed them into the bag. Kneeling beside Kirk's blood-spattered face, she felt compelled to look at him. Gaunt and haunted, the true horror of her actions lay before her. She touched him gently on the forehead. "I am so sorry."

She knew with Kirk's killing she had crossed her very own Rubicon.

Her world would never turn the same again.

At that second, she readjusted. *Time to go.*

CHAPTER 24

A glance at the closed front door gave her time to raid the kitchen. She pulled a bottle of fresh water from the fridge and guzzled. The remaining two bottles found their way into the rucksack. On one last sweep of the room, she picked up a flashlight, a compass, superglue, and an old tourist guide to Baghdad. The Glock returned to its home in her waistband at the small of her back before Charlie threw the rucksack over her shoulders. The spy hole in the door showed an empty hallway. Afraid of what lay ahead, she nipped back through the apartment and climbed out the rear window. This time no mistakes were made as she scaled the wall. The lessons were tough, but she was learning.

With her scarf retied, she pushed the scooter up the alley, keeping her lights off until reaching the side road. From there, she opened the throttle and switched on the beam. One more left turn before she cruised past the front of the house. Not a soul stirred. She noticed Kirk's empty SUV parked across the street. At the next junction, she threw a U-turn and repeated the drive-by, only this time with less speed. She jammed the scooter in behind the SUV at the very last moment. In a matter of seconds, she had beeped open the alarm, climbed inside, and set the vehicle in motion. Three last-minute directional switches ensured no one followed. A northern bearing was followed until a suitable landing zone was found. Once clear and safe, the SUV was positioned on a gas station forecourt with multiple exit options.

The enormity of the situation and the ramifications of her deeds finally crushed her resilience. Inside her metallic shroud, she allowed herself to wail and scream at the world. She sobbed and flailed until she had nothing left to give. The process didn't take long. At the end of her meltdown, Charlie drew in three long breaths, blinked her eyes, and set her chin down on her chest before emptying one of the water bottles over her matted mop. When her head rose again, it rose with purpose. She fumbled Kirk's phone from the nearby backpack, glanced skyward to the heavens, then punched in what she remembered, and hoped, was his access code: 7777. The phone opened. She dialed Pop's number and waited. The car's décor abuse had reduced to a rapid tapping of the steering wheel. With every additional beep of the dial tone, fear transitioned into hope. *No answer.*

She chose to believe that Pop had fled, as every other conclusion seemed unthinkable.

Somber recollections of her last moments with Pop drifted through her psyche.

When her Iraq deployment date closed in, her preparations had been painstakingly completed. With such few ties, loose ends were minimal. The fishing trip up to her father's mountain cabin had been the last item on her agenda. It had passed without drama, celebrations, speeches, or ceremony. At the time, she knew they shared unequal quantities of the same emotions: fear, pride, trepidation, and exhilaration. Sadly, those days ended no differently to many others that had gone before; emotions were neither vocalized nor recognized. She vowed to change all that the split second they met again. Thoughts of that brighter future drove her on. *We will meet again.*

Over time, thought overrode panic. Bouts of eustress had replaced her complete distress. Thoughts of Pop were a tonic. With time to breathe and think, plans formed. After rechecking her surroundings, she called into base, on the emergency access number. The crisis protocols that Hank had convinced her to avoid were now the ones she needed most. With caution to the fore, she withheld her number before she dialed. The fewer people who knew she had Kirk's phone, the better. The answering service kicked in: "Thank you for calling. Name and access code please."

"Special Agent Charlotte Glass, seven-three-Zulu-Delta-five."

"One moment please."

Charlie thumped her door in triumph when the dispatcher's voice kick-started the conversation.

"Good evening, Special Agent Glass. What is your status and position?"

Charlie set off. "You have to help me. I'm in trouble. I need to come in, but I can't trust anyone."

"State your current location please, Special Agent Glass," the handler reiterated.

"Baghdad. That's all you need. I need you to work a safe passage for me back to the US Embassy. The Green Zone checkpoints have been compromised."

The handler maintained a monotonous calm. "Special Agent Glass, I cannot help you unless I know your location."

Charlie steamed down the phone. "Yes, you can. You don't need to know where I am. You just need to get me through to someone who can help. I need to get to the US Embassy now, or I die."

The handler remained indifferent. "I apologize, Special Agent Glass, but protocols—"

"Do you want me to die?" Charlie snapped. "Because that's what's going to happen. Do you work for them? Is that it?" The thought was enough to send her into a reactionary panic that forced her to cut the call. Hank once told her that it was better to be cautious than dead. She didn't know if it was obstinacy or corruption blocking her rescue. Either way, she couldn't take the chance of finding out. She had to find new routes. *Think! Think!* Her eyes took it upon themselves to close despite all her efforts. Kirk's phone then buzzed with a message from Hank. The message was, like its sender, short and direct. Any sign?

After considering all options, Charlie decided to reply. Not yet, will give it an hour.

She was eventually proven right in her assumption that no reply would come. She checked her watch. *A little past 2300*. The endless night rumbled on. Sleeping in the car was not an option. That model sat high on every carjacker's hit list, and the prize of a woman inside would be way too tempting for any criminal. Selecting which checkpoints to use at the Green Zone would be a deadly lottery. Kirk or Hank could have easily set an alert up against her. She had to lie low for now and take time to produce a solid plan. With a new angle in sight, she dragged the guidebook from her backpack and scanned for a suitable hotel. Betrayal and danger awaited her in every hotel used by locals. She knew of only one place outside the Green Zone where westerners wouldn't stand out. She flicked through the guidebook, seized the phone, punched in Kirk's access code, and dialed the number. When the receptionist answered, she rolled the die.

"Hello. Can I speak to Kamal?"

CHAPTER 25

Propelled by a renewed purpose, Charlie sped to the Palestine Hotel. Any actions to save herself were set on hold. Her wounds needed cleaning. She felt dead on her feet. She needed to get off the street, get some rest, get cleaned up. Battering on through the gloom, she struggled to quell her fears and center her scampering thoughts. Kirk's killing had been forced out of view of her mind's eye. Keen to get to her destination, she had moved on, foot down and chin up. The timid little girl who'd hunkered in the back of the airport bus was growing up.

On arrival, she parked the SUV in the dimmest section of a street, two blocks away from the hotel. She choked down another bottle of water, then gathered all her worldly belongings into her rucksack. She clambered into an oversized black bomber jacket and a Texas A&M baseball cap found in the back seat. Head down and collar up, she climbed out of the vehicle. To avoid the flashing lights that went off in tandem with the key fob's alarm, she locked the car by key. Her gaze and general profile were kept low as she strode to the hotel's security checkpoint. It felt safer to approach on foot, as she needed to avoid the SUV's vehicle registration making its way onto any list. Upon approach, two mismatched local guards sidled out of a glass-sided hut. Bemused and concerned, they stood behind the barrier, a Kalashnikov between them. The lateness of the evening seemed to have them on edge.

"Stop!"

Charlie knew the homemade survival kit she was lugging around would not pass inspection, so she sauntered on, confident the guards were likely more afraid than she was. At the last minute, she pulled off the baseball cap, cast back her head, and pitched the hapless guards her most glamorous pout. Jaws and defenses dropped as she glided past the astonished sentries.

"Evening, boys. I'm looking for the reception."

The competition to come to her aid was both frantic and endearing. Directions were thrown and fingers were pointed. If anything, too much information was offered. Charlie thanked the young men and left them with a smile. Moving swiftly onwards, she brightened at the sound of the two guards behind her. Arguments raged over what they'd just seen, what had just happened, and who should have done what. *Sometimes being pretty helps.* The nattering behind her back widened her grin.

Once through the lobby door, she noticed the vertical pillars of the metal detector had been paired with a horizontal guard who seemed actively disengaged in mapping the hotel's not insignificant ceiling cracks. Approaching the detector, she gauged her pace to perfection: fast enough to catch the sleepy guard unawares, slow enough not to startle him into action. Neither guard nor Charlie looked as if they wanted anything to do with the metal detector, or any process associated with it. She never broke stride or eye contact as she flashed her FBI badge across his startled face. With the detector unused and the guard unmoved, Charlie strode on, unencumbered. *So far, so good.* The alerted receptionist had seen everything. He had picked up the phone well before Charlie could speak. When Kamal, the manager, emerged from a rear door, the receptionist threw his receiver down then dissolved into some non-existent paperwork.

"Agent Glass. Thank you for thinking of the Palestine International. Officer Kirkland—will he be joining you?"

Charlie remained alert. "You know he will, Kamal. You texted him, and he replied."

Background check complete, a softly chastised Kamal opened up. "Yes, of course, my mistake. You need two rooms for two nights?"

Charlie stopped him mid-keystroke. "No records please, Kamal. Kirk wants this one off the books. Cash only." Reaching into her backpack, she pulled some of Mac's emergency stash and discreetly placed it onto the counter. Kamal remained cool under bribery.

"I need copies of your photo IDs. It's the law. I am so sorry."

Charlie revisited her bag of tricks. She produced her ID, Kirk's ID, and yet more cash. "This should do it. Kirk is parking the car out the back."

When Kamal inspected her ID, she caught sight of dried blood across Kirk's ID card. She splashed more cash to gather time to wipe the blood onto her thigh. The look on Kamal's face as he read Kirk's details told Charlie success had been achieved. To Charlie's horror, her turned to the photocopy and started the process of replication.

"I said off the books!"

It was Kamal's turn to be disarming, as he continued the process. "I need these in case I get challenged. It's one thing to misplace a booking, but it's another thing to allow total strangers to roam the hotel." He handed back the ID cards. "Don't worry, I will wipe the entry once you leave." Looking around, Kamal nodded and pulled the cash out of sight. "If you need to come and go with discretion, the rear entry code is three-four-five-three. The same code works to gain access to each floor from the stairwell." Kamal searched for the rooms on his system. "Two rooms opposite each other?" Lesser hotel managers would have felt the urge to raise a suggestive eyebrow at the sleeping arrangements, but Kamal seemed above that—professional to the core.

Charlie nodded. "On the first floor, near the back stairs." Kamal neither approved nor disapproved. He was not being bribed for his opinions or his judgments. He worked on expressionlessly until producing two key cards.

"I have you in room 109. Officer Kirkland is across the hall in 111."

Charlie wanted to make a point. "Which is the one with the best view?"

"That would be your room, Agent Glass. 109."

"Excellent, 109 it is then." Kamal nodded his understanding. They shared a look: Charlie had given him much more cash than the going rate, and Kamal had not insulted her by counting it. They both knew what they were doing. Charlie threw her bag over her shoulder and strode out toward the elevator. Turning to bid Kamal goodnight, she saw the back of a man with money to count deserting his post. The elevator doors pinged open, and Charlie followed the signal.

Pacing the first-floor corridor, Charlie checked all exits and alcoves. She measured the short run to the fire escape on the way to her room. She closed the jammed-open fire door in the corridor. Reassuringly, it squealed and clunked. She stalled outside her allocated room. Checking for onlookers, she skipped across the corridor and pulled the other key card through the lock for 111. Once through the door, she confirmed a lack of witnesses through the spyglass of "Kirk's" room, which was now hers. Inside, Charlie immediately set to work. It started with running a scalding shower at full blast. She peeled off every item of rancid, sweaty, blood-splattered clothing then threw it in the tub. The stolen dress was also sent to laundry. While the shower boiled, she tossed the entire contents of her trusted rucksack out onto the second bed. All pockets were emptied into a singular heap before acts of separation and organization were dutifully completed. The blood-crusted paperwork from Kirk's dead body promised much in the way of insights and info, so each page was chiseled apart carefully and laid out for future inspection.

A wave of panic sent her back to the eyeglass in the room door. The view of an empty corridor helped ease her mind. After regulating the piping hot shower Charlie slid in, armed with her Glock and a mental inventory of everything that lay on the spare bed. A simple shower had never been so needed, nor so appreciated. Scrubbing Kirk's blood from her hands was the hardest part. She dispensed all the complementary toiletries and trampled every item of clothing into submission. After scrubbing and sterilizing her cuts and bruises past the point of inflammation, she exited the shower with everything, but her sins washed away. Wrapped in her towel, she set out the sodden clothing on the balcony to dry. A shiver of reality hit her when she noticed Kirk's phone had a missed call, and a text, both from Hank. No answer had been left, but the follow-up text left a clear message.

Where R U?

Kirk needed to be kept alive for as long as possible, so ignoring the text was not the sensible option. She thought hard and fast about the response. Checking the style of previous texts to Hank helped shape her response. Vague and questioning were the selected nuances. As she typed, she questioned every button strike.

Sorry taking a leak.

Nothing doing here.

Any orders?

Hank fired back abruptly.

Gates covered

K Twins on the hunt

Heading home

All night stake out?

Charlie's relief could not be gleaned from her response.

Roger that!

Hank's sign off put the texting to bed for the night.

Any changes we let each other know.

Job done. Charlie worked through her options. All she had to worry about was Kirk being found, and they wouldn't search for him if she kept the deceitful texts flowing. The chances of them noticing the SUV missing were reasonable, but they wouldn't think to check this side of town. The charge on Kirk's phone had diminished. *No charger.* She should have plugged it into the charger on the way over in the SUV. Charlie cursed her lack of awareness. The advantage of staying in contact with Hank outweighed the benefits of a battery-saving power down. Her nighttime routine was completed with more rigor and intensity than normal. She jammed a chair under the handle of the balcony's patio door. She set one of her boots precariously on the patio door handle, ready to fall at the slightest movement. After hauling the mattress across the tiled floor, she crammed it into the vestibule, hard against the front door. Pillows and blankets were cast into the den before the other boot was placed on the adjacent front door handle. With her early warning systems in place, Charlie settled into her nest, silencing the Glock on one side and the fading phone on the other. She checked the gun safety before finally taking a breath.

Lurching between bouts of uneasy dozing, Charlie tossed and flailed on the mattress. Time dragged. A disturbingly inordinate amount of time later, she startled. A squeal from the clunky fire door had cut through her sleepy haze. Pressing an ear hard against the door, she listened to the dull thudding of approaching footsteps. Straining her eyes through the spyglass, she stared towards the oncoming noise. She pressed the Glock against the door at torso height and prepared for her last stand. Anxiously gripping the handle of the gun, she waited.

The tension snapped when two drunken lovers spilled into her narrow field of vision. The state of their undress and levels of alcohol told Charlie they were likely Western journalists out to improve international relations. The war-drunk couple stumbled noisily past her lowering Glock. The man shushed more loudly than the woman giggled. The well-oiled woman checked back up the corridor to make sure that they weren't being followed. Charlie stood for five minutes longer to do the same. The corridor fell silent once more. She leaned her back to the wall and allowed her body to slide down to the mattress. It was going to be a long night. She took the time to make running repairs. Where the wound on her hand looked to be splitting, she applied super glue. She shunned painkillers in an attempt to stay awake. She shredded a pillowcase into a new bandage on her cut hand. The glue stitches still held.

Having time to think, she pushed her thoughts to the back of her mind, polluting her stream of consciousness. *Pop could still be in danger. I put him in danger.*

Those thoughts sickened her to the core. Both body and soul churned long into the night before tiredness eventually put her out of her misery.

Hours later, Charlie became half roused by the sound of Kirk's phone chiming with a text. Peeking past her protesting eyelashes, a dagger of light stabbed through the curtain gap. Morning had arrived too quickly. Painfully setting straight her crumpled bones and creased muscles, she eventually mustered the energy to go view the text, it sent her flailing through her morning mist.

Kamal here

Two men going to 109

Get out!

With cramps, pins, needles, and fatigue deforming disobedient limbs, she staggered around the room. Her face smacked into the door as she attempted to make eye contact with the spyglass. Bouncing on a mattress, phone in one hand and gun in the other, she knew what was coming next. Before the phone in her room had hit its fourth ring, she snatched the cable of the room phone out from the wall. From down the corridor, she heard the fire door that she had closed the night before open at an unnaturally slow rate. *This is it.* From her left, the twins arrived at the scene of their imminent crime. A cold wave washed over her flushed body. The Glock was manhandled once more. K9 slipped past the door as K2 stayed on the left. Their customary Kevlar jackets, boots, and combats remained in vogue. K9 pulled a silenced automatic from inside his cut-off jacket. In response, Charlie breathlessly unlocked her Glock and aimed it through the door, at a height and angle that she hoped would find K9's chest. She purposefully pushed the gun hard against the door. She made her decision. If they turned towards her door, she would be the first to pull the trigger. Her pulse raced as time stood still. K2 placed a crudely bandaged hand over the spyglass on the opposite door then rapped twice. *The old guard dog had left its mark*. The twins nodded their heads as if counting in silent unison.

When their count reached five, a salvo of suppressed bullets was dispatched into the door opposite. K9 then held the smoking nozzle against the door lock and blew it to pieces. In a coordinated routine, his brother barged through the doorway, gun in hand. In a split second, K9 followed. The door closed, and the corridor returned to an apparent calm. Charlie kicked her footing clear and rechecked her stance. *This wasn't over.* Suddenly the door opposite casually opened. K2 sauntered out, alone, as if on the way down for breakfast. He discreetly looked both ways and strolled off after tapping the room door. Three seconds after his departure, K9 repeated the process. Lobbing the *Do Not Disturb* sign over the recently shattered door handle was his final act. A temporary ceasefire returned to the corridor. The bouncing mattress underfoot did nothing to alleviate the uncontrollable shaking in Charlie's legs. In search of firmer ground, she stepped off and texted Kamal.

Got her

We're safe

Let me know if they've gone.

She waited in turmoil, gun strapped to her hand, eye re-glued to the spyglass. When Kamal's text arrived, she buckled into a bundle on the mattress beneath her.

Clear

Get out!

Still in her underwear, Charlie rampaged from room to balcony and back. Climbing into her clothes, all the preparations from the previous night were heading out the door with her. She pulled every possession laid out the night before into her bag or on her person. A spare dry towel, pen, and paper were added to the list of things she might need. With the bedding cast back into the room, one last check was completed. The room looked like it had been visited by an RPG. She stuffed the Glock down the back of her waistband. The spyglass confirmed an empty corridor. Taking a leaf from K9's book of dirty tricks, she casually strolled out, leaving her own *Do Not Disturb* sign in her wake. Once to the back stairwell, she careered down the stairs, taking them three at a time. When she reached the rear entrance, a battered and bruised Kamal stood holding the door. On seeing Charlie, his bloodshot blackened eyes quaked with apology.

"I am so sorry. They searched every Westerner hotel, looking for you. They made me tell them. They didn't know Kirk was here. They only came for you."

A tear escaped from his swollen left eye.

Charlie's cautionary actions had paid off. She eased out. "Thank you! Thank you! Kirk went out the front to find you. You haven't seen us."

Kamal beamed with relief.

Tenderly, she glided past him. "I owe you my life. Thank you."

Kamal lowered his head in shame and modesty, allowing Charlie to leave without ceremony. One last piece of advice came her way. "There is a hole in the fence, across on the right." A tangential change of direction sent her back on course. She scuttled through the busted fence then squeezed between the closely parked cars. Shading her eyes, she hid her face from the relentless Iraqi sky. She never looked up or back. Two sharp turns, one back track, and three last-minute street crossings, and she was back at Kirk's SUV. She only made her decision to open it and slip inside after giving the street two full sweeps. Engine, air-con, and phone charger were engaged in that sequence. Her head bobbed and twisted like a sparrow-fearing a hawk. The skies were clear that morning. With her options narrowing and her pursuers closing in, she knew she had to take a risk. There was a chance that Hank had blown his cover.

But to find that out, she needed to put her life on the line.

Kirk's phone was on its last legs. With his access code inputted and his number withheld, she called the crisis line for the second time. The automated answering service kicked in yet again. "Name and access code please."

"Special Agent Charlotte Glass, seven-three-Zulu-Delta-five."

"One moment please."

A lengthy pause ensued.

"Good evening, Special Agent Glass. What is your status and position?"

Charlie chose another path. "Baghdad, West of the Tigris across from the Green Zone. I have been compromised. I need an evac as soon as possible. Tahrir Monument in thirty minutes. I will be wearing a black hoodie and maroon baseball cap. Please hurry. This is life and death." Before the handler could respond, Charlie dropped the call. She didn't need to repeat herself. She knew all calls were recorded. After donning or carrying all the necessary clothing, she set off, unaware of the fates that awaited her at Tahrir Monument.

Doubling back from her SUV, Charlie strode out with purpose onto the verdant strip she had noticed running along the banks of the Tigris. Dedicated to the spirit of the ancient poet Abu Nuwas, the park served as a sliver of hope in an otherwise desperate urban desert. Concrete paths away from prying eyes were afforded additional shelter by the plethora of exotic trees and bushes that flanked its perimeters and passageways. Gaudily painted playground equipment lay under layers of dust and rust. A neglected merry-go-round spun in the breeze, alone and lifeless. Passing an empty set of swings, Charlie heard the creaking of its chains calling out to the children of yesteryear. Despite the sounds of the city, daunting and ominous in the near distance, the park was an eerie biosphere of abandonment. The only sign of life came in the form of a plastic bag that danced and dipped in the vortex of a windswept waterless fountain. Quick backward glances and a last minute 360-degree scan confirmed no one was following. At the exit to the park, she braced herself to re-enter the tortured civilization that was modern-day Baghdad. The cough-inducing congestion clamped her lungs as she crossed the road towards the square. Car horns blasted out a blanket of noise, occasionally pierced by the fervent shouting. Overwrought drivers dripped out the sides of their cars, screaming obscenities and instructions to the invisible and ambivalent souls ahead. A company of children ran amok, baying for blood with crudely fashioned wooden guns. Like half the grownups in the town, they were playing at war without fear of the consequences. Charlie had them pegged. *Toy soldiers, the lot of them.*

Man-sized sinkholes and a gushing sewage main did not make the journey any more pleasant. Nearing the circus of life that was Tahrir Square, Charlie noticed that the crowds intensified. A dark wave of weariness flooded everything before her. The pace seemed faster, yet her progress slowed under the sheer volume of people. She counted more heads but saw fewer faces. She heard more voices but fewer conversations. Across in the distance, the Tahrir Monument stood like a proud sentinel. Remembering Kirk's tainted condemnations, she found herself tilting towards his memory with heightened sympathy and regret. With every step nearer to the famous War Memorial, her heart raised its game. Arriving with only a handful of minutes to spare, she made her preparations. She looked around for sources of inspiration and support, before hatching a plan.

Uncertain of what lay ahead, Charlie gripped her seat and waited anxiously for the arrival of friend or foe. Questions swirled around her mind.

Who will come, if anyone?

Will the government be smart enough to send a separate rescue team?

Will they inadvertently send Hank?

Will they knowingly send Hank?

What if Hank sends someone I don't know?

Lopsided dark answers skewed her thoughts. Anxiety leached through into her right knee. It tapped ferociously underneath her garments. Her hidden hand clamped the Glock on top of her thigh. Being armed settled the nerves, even in a crowd. If Hank was coming, he'd be coming at speed. Charlie conjured visions of him barging his way through static traffic, screaming torrents of steroid-laced abuse. Far from still, she waited and waited. Her sweaty hand slithered around the handle of the Glock. Both gun and knee were now tapping in double time. All angles and approaches were continuously scanned. The occasional stand and stretch gave confirmation no one was following on. No unfriendly faces filled the crowd. Her senses suddenly twitched when a bulky Westerner in a black leather jacket flashed in and out of view. She quickly lowered her head and heightened her senses. The crowd scanning intensified. Her grip on the Glock intensified when she caught another glimpse of the Westerner. The sight of K2 told her all she needed.

Betrayal. This is it.

Head bowed; Charlie checked her periphery. She spied Hank striding through from the opposite side, intent on capturing her in a claw-like movement. From a distance she noticed the two thugs exchange less-than-subtle hand signals. The body snatchers rolled through in unison.

Charlie set herself—dejected, exhausted but ready. Never risking direct eye contact, the two felons slithered in on either side of their quarry. Hank pounced, jabbing his concealed weapon into a bony ribcage. Hank looked around to confirm an exit route, the maroon baseball cap removed, the hoodie pulled down. An unfamiliar, filthy, boyish face trembled into view. K2 exploded, gripped the boy by the hoodie and dragged him to his feet. "Where is she?"

The petrified looking youth spoke no English. Charlie waited within earshot of the escalating incident. The teenager kept his nerve, despite the attention-grabbing rag dolling.

The boy eventually spoke. "Dollars?"

K2's fist reacted poorly to the attempted extortion. Hank, aware of a turning in the surrounding tide of onlookers, thrust a one hundred-dollar note under the kid's bloodied nose. In perfect Farsi he asked. "Don't point. She is looking. Where is she?" The wilting urchin snared the bank note, leaned in, and replied. Hank translated the mumblings for K2's benefit. "Across the square. Restaurant roof." Hank completed a frantic 360 of his surroundings, before his gaze hit the mark. His quick point and jabbering orders showed the way. Charlie stared through the veil on her stolen dress. The street decoy was dispatched as disdainfully as circumstances would permit before Hank and K2 strode back towards their waiting driver. Once inside, the car sped off at a screeching pace. The bloody-faced young entrepreneur retook his seat, regained his dignity, and, under the protection of his new hoodie, recounted his money. Across from him, Charlie lifted her tired frame from the raised flowerbed and shuffled across, under the monument. Unlike the rest of the world, she felt concerned for the well-being of the blood-splattered child across the pathway. When she bent over to offer him a rag to wipe his face, he gingerly held out his baseball cap. A pair of cunning dark eyes rose meekly before he regained the strength to speak. "Dollars?"

Looking down, Charlie reached in under her dress and retrieved another fifty dollars. "Half now, half later."

She tousled the young conman's hair as he glowed eagerly at the magnificence of it all. With a wink of approval and a glance all around, Charlie turned herself back into the crowd. In the blinking of two sets of eyes, both Charlie and her co-conspirator vanished into the milling throng.

As she retraced her route towards the park, Charlie took stock. Kirk's contacts had closed off the Green Zone. Hank and his crew were baying for blood. The local police were even less trustworthy. Her little stunt proved that random calls to the embassy would be handed back to Hank's crew. Any calls to the media would be deemed crank, and if she went public, she'd probably be framed for it all. Too many people were involved, all of them too high up for Charlie to knock down.

It was her against the world. She hated the odds.

If it must be, it must be me. Charlie drilled her father's old pep talk deep into her psyche as she marched back to the SUV. Her pace quickened as she ignored the safer, more circuitous route through the park. Time, along with everything else in this far-from-godforsaken land, was against her. She barged past an old man cooking the most delicious smelling bread on the corner of a sidewalk. Olive oil and cigarettes confused the air around his eager purchasers. Her pace lifted as she passed a young man preparing an open flame stir fry beside a cage filled with gas canisters of all shapes and sizes. *Health and safety gone mad.* Striding on, she tripped over two small children fighting valiantly over their rightful shares of a freshly split pomegranate. Their mother turned from provider to referee as Charlie thundered past. Whole roast chickens and succulent dates were next on the stride-by menu. The sights, sounds, and smells of the busy marketplace propelled her on.

As she arrived back at the vehicle, Charlie had only one target—the warehouse. She was already well behind Hank's schedule. In the relative seclusion of the back seat, she replaced the headdress with her headscarf before she climbed between the two front seats and sparked the engine. Armed with Kirk's keys, she would hit the warehouse, snatch the documentation and whatever proof of the crime she could find, and then get the hell out. With one more frantic look in the rearview mirror, she skidded the SUV into the face of the oncoming vehicles and let fly. Loaded with vague ideas and bad intentions, she barged the SUV out into the traffic, leaving a trail of rubber in its wake. The chase was on.

Weaving in and out of the traffic with inhibitions thrown to the desert winds, she made good time. After re-plugging Kirk's phone into the charging jack, a message notification rang through the car's speakers. When she pressed play, Hank's voice exploded around the cabin.

"Where are you? We need you. Call me back. Now!" Hank unraveled before her ears, but Charlie had no clue whether that was a good or a bad thing. She understood the less time he had to make decisions, the worse those decisions would be. She reached for Kirk's phone again and sent another text.

Found Her!

Checkpt 6

Need a bigger badge

Can't talk

Come quik

She almost broke out a snigger at the false panic conveyed by her deliberately misspelled words. When the call from Hank came in, it was enjoyably ignored. A jumped red light and a near head-on collision brought her back to reality. Charlie drove on, clipping a wing mirror as she switched lanes. Around here no one stopped for fender benders, so she pressed on. Slewing into a new thoroughfare, she almost rear-ended a cart and donkey as they crossed the median in search of less brown pastures. Another screaming halt. Another screaming match. After the ranting eventually subsided, she sent another text to chase down Hank.

Where R U?

ETA?

Help

When Hank's call came through the car's intercom, it was killed instantly this time. A crack in the wall of traffic ahead allowed her to lean the car across into the oncoming lane. She caught sight of the reason for the stoppage: a US Marine Corps checkpoint. Up ahead, every car was being stopped well in front of the checkpoint and ushered through four Humvees set in a crisscross pattern. Atop two of the Humvees sat gunners with .50-cals trained on everything that didn't move. Each car seemed to be getting the full cavity search, with under car mirrors and "everybody out" up close and personal frisking. Charlie was smart enough to realize that barging her way into U-turn would only earn her a couple of .50-cal salvos, but she needed to shift. Her idea of telling the troops of her predicament was shot down. *They may know Kirk, and they certainly wouldn't go haring off across town.*

Her give-a-damn snapped. She exited the vehicle and charged towards the lead soldier, FBI badge in one hand, recently doffed headscarf in the other. The lead squaddie stared as the stunningly beautiful blonde vision that appeared before him. Straight out of a movie, traveling at pace, Charlie flew into the guard's face before he could raise his voice or his weapon.

"Special Agent Charlotte Glass, FBI. What's the hold up?"

Carved from the blackest marble, the statuesque guard filled every inch of his 6' 4" frame. His eyes of polished onyx were sheltered beneath an oversized helmet, tightly strapped to his firm jawline. The jerry-rigged addition of a Go-Pro camera on his large helmet topped off his look. Canvas webbings and ammunition could not hold the trooper down as much as the stare from an angry woman.

"Lady, you can't be out here." The enormity and absurdity of the situation seeped into his challenge. Marching up, she scanned the soldier's name tag and his stripes. "I am no lady, Sergeant Thomas. I am an FBI Special Agent, and the only reason I am out here is because of you and your dumbass crew. I have a satellite call with Cheney scheduled at the Oil Ministry in fifteen minutes. If I miss it, we're both screwed!"

"Agent Glass, I am sorry, but I just can't—"

Charlie sliced through procedure. "What's your first name, Sergeant Thomas?"

"Tyrone, ma'am."

"And where are you from, Sergeant Tyrone Thomas?"

"Greenville, North Carolina."

"Well, Sergeant Tyrone Thomas from Greenville, North Carolina, if you don't want to end up riding shotgun with me up and down Route Irish for your next four tours of duty, knock me a hole in this goddamn traffic."

The badge, the veiled threat, and the name drop did the trick. Charlie yelled her version of a thank you as the sergeant turned and gave the signal to clear the way. "And tell those guys on the fiddies to stand down!"

Every pair of eyes within a fifty-yard radius bore through her disapprovingly as the bewildered recon team helped cut a path through the lines of dumbfounded drivers. As she negotiated her way past every guard, they acknowledged her passing in their own unique way, from stares to salutes, from waves to whoops. With the last few bollards negotiated, she sped on, struggling to contain a smile only worn by women who just got their way. On a beeline generally reserved for suicide bombers, Charlie's SUV sped on, parting the sea of terror-stricken drivers before her. The risks were high, but the stakes were higher. When Hank's next message barked out into the SUV, it gave her location, a time, a bearing, and an indication of his state of mind. *Apoplectic.*

"Where are you? You've never been to Checkpoint Six. If I find out you've been lying to me..." He stopped short of issuing open threats. "Call me."

Charlie carried out some high-speed processing.

Hank now knew Kirk had never been at the checkpoint. He'd been lying.

He'd likely think she and Kirk were in cahoots and the shipment was the target.

She calculated that her deception had bought her at least twenty minutes at the warehouse. Her one-woman car chase continued as she bobbed, weaved, slew, and skidded her way through the crazed streets of Baghdad. After innumerable near misses, three bumps, and one crash, she finally hit the warehouse.

The first order of business became a measured drive-by, starting around the back. In the gaps between the railings on the over specified gate, she noticed two armed guards taking strain from the overhead sun. She didn't slow on the way around to the front of the shop. She parked within sight of the building's peeling hand painted sign. It seemed to refer in some way to Alibaba. The irony wasn't lost on her as she gathered up her essentials. She stowed her FBI badge in her breast pocket, Kirk's now silenced mobile phone and keys in the back, flashlight on her belt, and Glock down the back of her waistband. Another unanswered call to Pop neither eased nor heightened her anxiety, although she felt relieved, he hadn't answered.

Logic dictated that he would have listened to her and would have been well on the way to the sanctuary of the mountain cabin. That was the only narrative that allowed her to breathe, allowed her to function. The thought of any other outcome or circumstance traumatized her to the point of paralysis. She needed to believe he was safe. She needed to move.

Time to go.

Charlie selected an indirect route and approached the front door casually. With no guards at the front, she peered through the abandoned shop window. Away from prying eyes, she scrambled through a series of trial-and-error attempts to find the correct key from the set lifted from Kirk's dead body. With options running out, she eventually deployed the right key. A sigh of relief followed her through the doorway. Once inside, she checked behind for any tail she may have just grown. *So far, so good.* The front door was immediately re-locked. The long-abandoned retail foyer was empty, apart from a very lonely desk and a mismatched chair. Silent echoes of long-lost livelihoods filled the shop's stifling, hopeless air. When she cracked the metal door slightly, the light from outside slithered into the cavernous storage space. She squeezed through swiftly, returning the warehouse to darkness. With the belt flashlight discreetly deployed, Charlie checked her watch. *Fifteen minutes.* Acclimatizing her eyes to the light, she completed a perimeter search. After pulling the shade on the table lamp within a few inches of the desktop, Charlie felt confident enough to flick its switch. A corrupt world of paper lay before her, just begging to be explored. In the growing visibility, she scoured the paperwork. She examined the same shipping documents from before, this time with a greater understanding of the crimes they masked. Laying out the documents geographically helped her map out the smuggling route.

The historically sounding Ottoman Ordinance looked to be the front established to orchestrate the official export and import of excess munitions and weaponry. A Moldovan intermediary by the name of Skeyetranz based out of Tiraspol, Transnistria, seemed to misplace the deliveries through dark web brokers and freight firms. The inclusion of additional humanitarian aid within the shipments added hints of credibility and lashings of irony. Every new document straightened out the particularly crooked jigsaw. Legitimate arms disposals were being laced with a cocktail of illegal weaponry and stolen artifacts. It seemed overkill though. The low street value of small arms deals hardly justified the wholesale murder and betrayal that had descended upon this less-than-merry band of thieves. There seemed to be only one conclusion.

It has to be about the artifacts.

Charlie dug deeper. Over at the munitions section, she started to pull the numbered boxes aside in a valiant yet fruitless search for the artifacts that had so intoxicated her. A check of the relabeling station at the side of the table yielded only freshly painted stencils and dried-up paints. No codes of references seemed to make sense. The adjacent museum catalogue, with stencil ink splattered over its oily well-thumbed pages, held no obvious clues. The book back had been broken in the vain attempts to hold certain pages open. Turned down ears gave indications of what may lie in store. It told tales of what treasures could be found but gave no clues as to their location. In her frustration, Charlie thumped the book to the warehouse floor. She was going to have to do this the hard way. She yanked box after box through a screening process. The workout proved tough going, but her determination and fitness levels pulled her through.

When she hauled one cartridge aside, its contents rattled slightly. Intrigued by its different sound, she tugged the lid open. Underneath the top layer of bullets lay more sackcloth that hid a collection of magnificent cylinder seals, each more intricate and enchanting than the next.

Her fist landed in triumph.

Ancient scenes and deities graced the mystical stories told on each individual scroll. She uncovered similar treasure in the next ammunition box. They were using ammunition boxes to smuggle artifacts.

Setting her frantic hands to work she checked the stenciling on the side and cross-referenced the pallet number with the overall list of pallet numbers. Her pallet was numbered fifteen. There were around twenty or so more, but the numbering continued into the thirties. After uncovering nothing but bullets on her next two openings, Charlie reconsidered her approach. Her paperwork inspection became more frenetic than forensic.

Ottoman Ordinance. She knew little of the failed empire, other than that it existed for hundreds of years before the Turks lost it after the First World War. She rattled off the limited facts that she could muster up in her mind.

Ottoman Empire

Named after Osman I.

Thirty-four million subjects

Predominantly Sunni.

Istanbul used to be called Constantinople.

Ran from 1534 to 1918.

She scribbled down the numbers to find any semblance of pattern. *Fifteen, thirty-four, nineteen, eighteen.* Things clicked. The pallet number that held the seals was fifteen. She frantically sought out the pallet marked thirty-four and pulled open one of its cartridge boxes. After digging out the top layer of bullets, the contents of the box blew her backwards across the forks of a nearby truck. Startled to the point of disbelief, she staggered back to the fate-filled box. Even in the half-light of the warehouse, it glowed with an alluring, bewitching, even magical charm. Deep inside the sackcloth lining gleamed a bar of solid gold. Carefully, Charlie lifted the heavy bar with the care and delicacy normally reserved for an IED. It shone wondrously as she transported it to the nearby weigh scale. It read just over twenty-six pounds. She cross-checked the box weight with a standard .50-cal ammunition box. They matched perfectly. Other than the pallet number, no one would recognize the difference between the two. She scribbled the numbers down in her brain. Twenty-five pounds at sixteen ounces equaled four hundred ounces per bar at five hundred dollars per ounce, which meant every bar was worth two hundred thousand, give or take. Charlie struggled to ground herself on a pallet of good old-fashioned ammo. One opened box had turned this small arms shipment into a murder worthy, multi-million-dollar haul of guns, gold, and looted treasure.

As she leaned motionless against the full weight of the contraband, a voice spilled into the shop front next door. Blind panic forced her back towards the wall. She outpaced the voice, scrambling behind a stack of pallets underneath the mezzanine. She pinned herself to the darkness, trying to keep her breathing shallow enough not to be heard. Hank and the K-twins had made much better time than she'd predicted. She scanned the scene. All exists were blocked. There was no way out. Back to the wall, she clung to life.

Hank arrived in full flow, barking orders for someone to hit the lights. A flicked switch bathed every inch of the warehouse in a yellow tint. In several blinks of her eyes, Charlie's only protective shading had disappeared. With Charlie straining to hear more sounds of life, Hank continued the high intensity monologue.

"The Moldovans are here in two days to sample the goods. We can't afford any more slip-ups. Check with the rag heads at the back to see if Kirkland's been around." From her disadvantaged point, Charlie caught sight of one of the twins opening the back door. To her horror, Hank and K9 burst around the corner side by side, right beside her, taking the mezzanine stairs two at a time. If they turned around, they couldn't fail to see her. Charlie pulled her Glock and aimed. If they turned, she was going out in style. Perverse thoughts of getting the first shots in when their backs were turned were instantly discounted. Caution chimed as they climbed.

"I don't trust any of those goons. Change the locks and double the guards, front and back. No one gets in except me. Understood?"

K9 remained loyal. "I'll sort it tomorrow afternoon. My best guys."

The light in the mezzanine office turned on as the pair moved inside. Knowing even a cursory glance from above would reveal her location, she kept her Glock trained on the overhead windows. Fortunately, no heads appeared at the window, so she eventually put the Glock down. The sound of K2 industriously clanking and yanking contraband boxes behind her told Charlie the exit route was blocked. She had to think fast. Killing K2 and making a run for it seemed her only option.

Stiffening her shivering spine, she edged forward to neutralize K2. Gingerly, she eased towards an unthinkable conflict. Suddenly, her boot trod on a steel panel. *It moved.* The drain cover rocked beneath her boot. It could be an improbable way out, a hiding spot, or the pit she would die in, but Charlie needed to find out. Across the narrow passageway, she spied a small crowbar resting on the top of a freshly opened wooden crate. Peering around the corner of the pallets, K2 had his back turned. Above her, Hank and K9 could be heard chuckling at someone else's expense. Two swift well-timed dashes secured the crowbar and her safe arrival back at the drain cover. Down on her knees, Charlie frantically wedged the narrowest tip of the crowbar into a slightly deformed corner. As she lifted, the waft of putrid air choked her. She recoiled, lost her purchase, and dropped the cover. Mercifully, the dust and debris around the panel edges dulled the sound of its fall. No harm, some foul. Drawing a quick breath, she tried again. The undeniable, horrific stench of raw sewage enveloped her as the pit cover lifted open.

The prospect of entering the foul labyrinth below terrified her. The alternative was almost certain death. She could not see how deep the pit was, nor what lay at the bottom. Afraid of using her flashlight and short on time, she took the dark plunge. When the edge of the manhole reached her shoulder, her boots found sludgy ground. Overcome with relief and fumes, she pulled the metal panel in on top of herself and kneeled into the tiny chamber. Indescribable slurry soaked her combats. She kept her flashlight unlit, still afraid of what it could find. Decades of spiderwebs snatched at her face as a rancid claustrophobia gnawed away at her resolve. An acrid smell clawed at the lining of her lungs. *What if the lid can't be opened from my side? What if they put a pallet over the cover, even by accident? Are these fumes poisonous?*

A three-against-one gun battle suddenly seemed the more desirable option. She pulled out Kirk's phone for one last throw of some desperate dice.

At Mac's

Glass broken

Need Cleaner

Miraculously the text managed to find its way onto the network. Seconds after the sent text, heavy boots thundered down the metallic staircase. Hank took the lead, as always, his voice partially muffled by the drain cover.

"Get the car. She'd better be dead. He needs to eat a bullet too. I don't trust a thing he's done or said since she arrived. Let's get out of this place; it stinks."

After a bout of boot shuffling, the place fell into an eerie but welcome silence. Within seconds Charlie stood her shoulders up against the metal plate and pushed with all her might. The panel opened with relative ease and negligible noise. She dragged her convulsing torso up onto the concrete floor, spitting as much foul air as possible from her putrefied lungs. She pulled out her flashlight and set it to work.

Looking back into the brick-lined pit, she watched an industrial sized rat scurrying down what looked to be a servicing tunnel. After quickly dragging the cover back across the nauseating pit, she climbed the office stairs to complete her surveillance. Inside, she found a small workshop.

A dirty bottle of tequila sat beside two dirtier glasses in the middle of the workshop table. In one corner two workbenches had been set up to house various small power tools, engraving punches, and routers. Sandstone cuneiforms in various stages of reproduction lay strewn across each bench. In the other corner a small sand blasting unit had been set up to impart just the right level of aging on each counterfeit part. Nothing had been overlooked.

At the finishing station the master cuneiform took pride of place in a central stand. Facsimiles lay piled on the left-hand side. Charlie lifted the master cuneiform and studied its beauty. The misshapen clay tablet felt warm to the touch, its edges long lost to the winds and touches of time. Compartmentalized into boxes, each miniature section told a story from a land and time long forgotten artistry and imagination hid in every well-worn niche.

She gazed in awe at the ancient workmanship before sliding the original into the knee pocket of her combats. She needed new routes. *Hank said he was changing the locks.*

With one last look around, she spied an accessible, albeit well barred, roof light. After standing up on the table, Charlie set the crowbar to good use again, bursting open the roof window. After clearing away the busted lock and wooden splinters she left the room in darkness.

With the flashlight aimed at the metal grating, Charlie safely exited the mezzanine. Back at the desk she reignited the table lamp and set the crowbar back in place. After laying out the most incriminating paperwork under the lamplight, she scribbled the headline details onto the back of the most insignificant piece of paper she could find before setting the documents back in order. Flashlight replaced lamplight before Charlie made her measured exit. Through into the shop front, the dismal street lighting stumbling through the weathered windows rendered the flashlight surplus to requirements. With the relative safety of the outside world just a few steps away, her pace quickened. After a cautionary glance outside, she exited. Unimpeded, she crossed the street, with the thrill of a minor victory pulsing through her veins. Back at the SUV she threw her belongings in the back seat. Suddenly, a bulky figure emerged from a nearby shadow.

"Agent Glass?" Astonishingly, the affable driver from the Rhino stood before her. Charlie had never been so pleased or confused to see a friendly face.

"Bassam? What are you doing here?"

The look on Bassam's face and the gun wobbling in his quaking hand told her that this was no happy coincidence.

Before she could react, a blow across the back of her head sent her into darkness.

CHAPTER 26

Charlie came to, her head thumping and her hands tied tightly behind her back. The strain from being knotted in an unnatural position ripped at her shoulders. A crude bandage attached to the back of her head marked the source of the splitting headache that blurred both vision and thought. Peering through the pain, her troubles became apparent. The wooden chair she sat on had been centered in a pale cell under a single underpowered bulb. The windowless room held heavy, wet, and stale air. If she weren't in such pain, she would have been in panic. She roused, clueless about how long she had been unconscious. The only sliver of knowledge remained that Bassam lay at the heart of her abduction. She had no clue how to get herself out of the ties, the room, or the building. To stop herself from imploding with fear, she concentrated on planning her actions once outside.

After what felt like hours of piercing pain, the sound of faint steps crept in under the door. As a key turned in the lock, Charlie took the biggest breath of her life and slumped her head to the side. A panicked argument in high-speed Farsi made its way into the room. Tied lifelessly to her chair, Charlie struggled with the translation. Even with their heightened levels of dialect and distress, enough keywords came through for her to understand. She assumed the first man to shriek was Bassam.

"You've killed her! What were you thinking? Why did you have to hit her? I am no murderer!"

A grizzled, harsh hand gripped her chin, pulled her face to the side, and then slapped her hard. Killing every nerve ending in her body, she remained stone cold. The person she assumed was Bassam couldn't steady his wavering voice.

"What are we going to do?"

The same grizzly hand placed two fingers strategically on her neck. "She's alive. Be quiet."

"You've kidnapped an American! We don't even know if she's one of them."

"Why was she there? Wait here." It sounded to Charlie as if the heavy-handed captor had left the room. In his absence Bassam softly tapped Charlie's cheeks. This time he jabbered in panic-stricken English.

"I am sorry. I am sorry. Please wake up. Please."

Charlie gave him no signs of life.

When the second man arrived, the good-cop interrogator was brushed away, and Charlie imperceptibly braced herself for heightened levels of physical abuse.

Without warning, a wall of water knocked her out of her pseudo-coma. What sounded like a metal bucket bounced off into a corner as Charlie coughed and spluttered back into half-life. A yank of the hair pulled her head back with a gargling jolt. A gigantic untrimmed beard entered her groggy vision, up close and impersonal. Crazy raven eyes circled overhead. Over her attacker's shoulder, Bassam stared, looking more afraid than anyone else in the room. When the hairy abuser spoke, both his words and his eloquence were surprising.

"We meet again, Agent Glass." Charlie peered through a veil of fear, at a loss for recognition. "The last time we met you gave me this." The bearded bully before her twisted his bushy head to reveal a slightly weeping bandage across his right ear. Charlie felt incredulous. The intruder who threatened her then tried to shoot her and Tariq at the museum wandered from her memory back into clear view.

She built her wall. "I was defending myself! You fired first, remember?"

An angry scream cut her short. "Abbas was a good man."

Bassam jumped into the witness stand. "Your people lured him to a warehouse and killed him."

"They are not my people. They tried to do the same to me." Charlie fought on. "I am no criminal. I am a US Federal Agent sworn to defend the—"

"So are all the other snakes in the pit. Why are you any different?"

Charlie took her chance. "Because I have already killed one of them."

A stunned silence filled the void as the two men exchanged glances laced with intrigue. Charlie seized the moment. "I can tell you more in the next fifteen minutes than you've learned in the last fifteen months."

The bad cop bit back. "I doubt that."

"I know where everything is, where it's going, and who's involved."

Again, the men stared blankly at each other. Charlie moved to fill in the blank. "Get me out of this chair before I shoot your other ear off." Bassam's chortle was cut short as the bearded attacker dragged him gruffly out of the cell. Both door and lock slammed shut, leaving Charlie alone with her embattled thoughts.

After five more excruciating minutes, the two abductors returned. The bearded warrior owned the moment. "Tell me what you know."

Charlie strengthened her position. "Show me you can untie knots."

Bassam broke up the staring competition when he started to untie Charlie's hands. In disgust, the bearded oaf lumbered off to brood in the corner. Charlie inspected her reopened wrist wounds and rubbed her recolored bruises. It was the beard that broke the Iraqi standoff.

"Who did you kill?"

Charlie shook her head. "You first. Who are you, and where am I?"

"You are in no position to ask questions," the beard countered.

"So, I confess details of a murder to a total stranger in a strange land?"

"This land is only strange to invaders like you. You have already-"

"You are in the basement of the Iraq Museum. We both work here. You know me. Bassam. I am a janitor and driver. This is Rashad; he is our head of security."

An unimpressed Rashad cut his partner a withering look then spat at Charlie through his unkempt beard. "Who did you kill?"

"Kirkland."

Her captors exchanged an excited glance.

"Prove it."

"I have his phone. Or rather, you have his phone. You took it off me when you beat me unconscious."

Bassam stepped in again. "Oh, yes. As I said before, we are both very sorry that—"

Rashad restarted the lopsided interrogation. "Your phone is conveniently dead."

"The charger is in my car. We need to get it. There's also a rucksack. It's filled with evidence that will prove we're on the same side. The car is close to where you beat me up."

The two Arab heads brought themselves in close and shared an undecipherable dialogue. With their joint decision made, they gave the verdict to Charlie. "We will get your so-called evidence. You will stay here."

Charlie hesitated before offering more advice. "They don't know I'm here, but they may be watching. They have eyes everywhere. Be careful you're not spotted. Bring back everything but leave the car there. Better still, set it on fire in some bad neighborhood. That will throw them off the scent."

For the first time, a restrained grin seemed to peek out from behind Rashad's beard. "We are blessed with any number of bad neighborhoods to choose from. I will go. Bassam will look after you. Do I have your word you will not leave?"

Charlie didn't give him any such assurance. "Where else would I go?"

With a gruff shrug, Rashad nodded to Bassam then left. Not long after, like some demented concierge, Bassam escorted her out of her cell into an equally dismal corridor. "Please. Come with me please." Nervous sweat poured off his balding head down into the fuzzy creases of his swollen face. Gesturing again he reiterated the request. "This way, please."

He showed her into a small shower area with broken tiles, rusting chrome, and grimy grout. Charlie doubted the shower had ever been graced with a privacy curtain or a cleaning brush. An almost finished bar of soap was presented to her on an unfolded second-hand towel. Before he left, Bassam made a big show of the fact that he had helped her and that the shower room door could lock from the inside. Like everything else in Iraq, the bolt mechanism had more than one loose screw. Sliding the dilapidated latch across gave her time to think and plot potential escape routes. The open window above would be easily accessed if she stood on the wooden stool hiding in the shower. Dragging the stool from the shower, she succumbed to the overpowering urge to take its place. There would be time enough in the future to mount an escape. She set the water to a near scalding temperature then fell into its grasp. Sewage-infested gunk caked and soaked her clothing. Her heart bumped when she found in her knee pocket, the little clay tablet stolen from the warehouse. She felt grateful for the Iraqi-level stop and search. She peeled her few layers of clothing off and trampled them into the chipped tile floor. With the remnants of the soap long gone, she scrubbed her talisman with the most decrepit nailbrush in existence. With the amulet back safe and shined around her neck, Charlie exited the shower and attempted to dry herself with the world's smallest towel. She laid the now sodden cloth out over the wooden stool and flopped down, aching, and exhausted, staring blankly at the pile of filthy sodden clothes that wallowed in the filth at the bottom of her shower. She was the very definition of a woman with nothing to wear. Bassam, having listened for the eventual shower stoppage, rapped quietly on the door. "I have brought you some fresh clothes. I will leave them outside the door."

After listening to confirm his departure, Charlie nipped her head out into the corridor and retrieved her new clothes. The blue overalls looked more roadway than runway. Black sandals and a sky-blue hijab completed the ensemble. Her cuneiform was secreted inside the pocket of her trousers. The search for a non-existent mirror was called off before a deep breath was taken and the rickety door latch pulled to one side. "I'm coming out!"

As she entered the empty corridor, a sense of imprisonment filled her soul. She padded on down the narrow blue corridor in search of her new best friend, Bassam. Negotiating the museum's cool, dark maze, she ambled past a myriad of open doors and closed off passages. She edged forward, drawn to the sound of a blaring TV in the distance. Upon approach, she noted that the channel had been set to a station only the locals could understand, and its volume set to a level they could certainly all hear.

Charlie craned around the open doorway. An overdressed, overexcited, news presenter barked propaganda from the TV set in the corner. Both presenter and TV looked as if they belonged in a museum. The small anteroom must have been the museum canteen. Bassam wobbled eagerly between an open fridge and a small wooden table. He appeared hard at work, cramming plate after plate of Mezze onto the table. Her captor ensured care and delight were given and taken in equal measures. He placed beautifully prepared dishes in a spice infused collage across the table. Two posters advertising exhibitions long gone filled one wall. On the wall in the alcove hung a long-forgotten calendar. The faded photograph of an unmolested museum and a date untouched since March 2003 spoke volumes. When Bassam saw her, he let out a little shriek of joy before running over and reaching up to shut the news report off. Taking the offered seat, Charlie felt a wall of questions fall upon her.

"Please. Please. How was the shower? How are the clothes? Do they fit? How is your head? Do you need a new bandage?"

He seemed to be the perfect blend of a friendly soul with genuine empathy and an ingratiating remorseful ass kisser. Charlie felt grateful the hideous partner wasn't in charge of proceedings.

"I need to use a phone."

Bassam shook. "Oh no, that is not possible."

"Please, I need to call my father; he is in danger."

"Not possible. All our lines are down. Nothing has worked since the invasion."

"Really—two years later?"

"Take a look around."

"Do you own a cell phone?"

"So, you bring in the army to attack me? Sorry. We wait for Rashad."

Charlie motioned to leave. "Please, that is not possible. We are both locked in. Please, help yourself. Do you like Mezze?" It was now her turn to play the role of the friendly, ingratiating ass kisser.

"This looks lovely. Sorry. I am an ignorant American. What is all this?"

Bassam proudly introduced the dishes held within each little stainless-steel container, one by one.

"Mesopotamian cuisine at its finest. My wife prepared these for you when she heard we were entertaining a guest."

Charlie was incredulous. "Entertaining?"

Only Bassam's head wobbled this time. To move things on, each dish was introduced with pride. "Muhammara. Peppers, walnuts, and pomegranate. Tourshi, made from picked beet and turnip. A salad of cauliflowers, shaved almonds, golden raisins. Presented with my wife's own pita bread and washed down with some Turkish red wine."

Charlie's incredulity was morphing into genuine intrigue. She avoided the subject of alcohol at the table and bent in for a closer look. The intoxicating smells lured her closer. Bassam picked up each dish in sequence and offered her first helpings. "Please, please."

Bread was broken, wine was shared, and stories were exchanged. The flavors possessed a majesty like nothing she'd ever tasted before. A ravenous appetite, exotic spices, friendly company, and a renewed sense of security all served to leverage her love for the delicious food laid out before her. For a few blissful minutes, the terrible world she inhabited evaporated from her consciousness.

Over time, Bassam grew more nervous about his colleague's return. No questions were asked, and no explanations were given as the now empty half-bottle of red wine was disposed of, and the dirty glasses cleaned and set away. The Palestinian fresh sage tea proved equally intoxicating. Charlie savored a quiet moment as she considered what lay ahead. The moments of bliss became tainted with trepidation as the minutes wore on. By the time Rashad arrived back with the rucksack, most of the precious moments from the meal were distant, fond memories.

The mellow couple leaped up in unison the moment Rashad barged back through the door. Her rucksack was thumped down with unnecessary angst amongst the empty steel dishes. He tossed Kirk's phone over for Charlie to catch. The entire process was heated and bereft of ceremony.

"I charged it on the way over. I can't get into it. Where's your proof?"

The phone activated when she punched in the magical number: 7777.

That just seemed to annoy Rashad further. "If it's his phone, why do you know the code?"

"The same way I know that they are smuggling millions of dollars of stolen loot, and you are helping them get away with it," Charlie snapped back, tired of defending herself. When the phone opened, it announced a text. Charlie opened it and turned the phone to display the message from Hank to both men.

I am coming for you

You're dead!

The two locals lifted their eyebrows. Her bearded interrogator remained on high alert. Charlie helped to close the circle. "They are both dead. Kirk killed Tariq to save me, and I killed Kirk to save myself."

"Dead?" The two men made no effort to disguise their joy. "So, there are only the two bodyguards and this Hank person left?"

"It's not that easy. They have many people on their payroll," Charlie cautioned. Her captors hung on to her every word. She paused temporarily. The two men across the table had beaten her unconscious, kidnapped, and interrogated her. One of them had helped empty a machine gun in her general direction. But right there and then, they were the nearest things to friends she had in the world. She took her chance.

"Ammunition, guns, cuneiform tablets, cylinder seals, and gold. Lots of gold." Charlie took the risk, building the list from the bottom up. With every item recited, excitement infected her captors' eyes.

"Gold?" The childish yelping that met her last item of inventory ceased when she placed one more article onto the list.

"Oh, and the Golden Chalice of Ur."

Silence ricocheted around the basement. The men sat themselves down, too astounded to emit any sound. The excitable Bassam broke first. "Have you seen it?"

"I held it in my hands." Her questioner almost fainted, so Rashad took over.

"Describe it."

"Beautifully intricate rolled gold, two miniature ornate handles made from golden-flecked, lapis lazuli. Floral etchings on the base. Simply the most precious thing I have ever seen."

"It's inside that building?"

Charlie had their attention.

"It's there. Along with a truck load of gold bars." The mention of the gold bars went unheard, as they had lost control of their senses at the first mention of the chalice.

"We must get it! Bassam's chubby cheeks wobbled at the prospect of a hunt for both treasure and glory. "We would be heroes if we could return the chalice. Heroes!"

Astonishingly, Rashad asked for advice. "What can we do?"

With the mention of one small artifact, Charlie had apparently been elected de facto leader of this newly formed confederacy. "What did you see at the warehouse?"

Rashad provided the intel. "I took a drive around. Two guards outside both entrances. They don't look like much."

Charlie had a hunch. "Locals?"

"Yes, but they will be able to call in reinforcements."

"And if we try to buy them off?

"They will turn on us and steal everything. They cannot help us, but they can call on people who can hurt us."

Charlie tried to stay positive. "Hank won't trust them enough to allow them inside the building."

"They can't know what's inside, or they would have broken in and stolen everything already."

Bassam remained true to form. "Or they are too scared and too sensible to do anything?"

"The local police are worse than anyone," Rashad cut him off, talking over his friend's timidity. "When Saddam's regime collapsed, we lost the entire police force."

"Culled from society?"

Rashad nodded solemnly. "I was Ba'athist. I lost my career, my home, my savings, my identity, and my standing in the community. Everything was taken from me."

Bassam had some sympathy. "In the last year they have recruited over sixty thousand people. Over a thousand a week, so how well could they be vetted? Most of them are trustworthy, but none of them can be trusted."

Rashad's mood darkened. "We couldn't take back the treasure with force. We'd need a small army."

Charlie was catching on. "And by the time we've managed to recruit one, someone will have tipped them off or stolen it for themselves?"

"That's how it probably got there in the first place," added Bassam.

The only things they seemed to agree upon were the various methods of failure.

"So that's it? We give up?"

Charlie didn't know from Bassam's accent whether his question was a suggestion or a challenge. She hoped it was the latter but feared it was the former.

"Never. For as long as I draw breath, I will not rest until this evil has been driven from my country. I will die before those thieves steal our history from under us. I believe it with all my soul, as did Abbas." When Rashad's response came through, she was appreciative of his commitment and raised an invisible glass as a toast to her fledgling ally. "I'll drink to that."

For the first time her new partners smiled as one. "We can celebrate with cake." Bassam dove into the fridge as if he had been waiting for that moment all day. "Harissa. Semolina filled with shaved almonds, soaked in a cinnamon syrup, and three spoons."

Whilst Bassam performed his head waiter duties Rashad bent down and fumbled at the back of a nearby cupboard. He produced a label-free glass bottle, along with three mismatched mugs. "We can drink to our new partnership, but only with water."

After the glasses were filled, eye contact and toasts followed. When the local water hit the back of her throat, fiery convulsions choked Charlie's eyes. The resulting coughing and spluttering caused great hilarity between her new partners. When she slammed down her glass and motioned for a refill, the deal was sealed. Glasses were refilled, raised, clinked, and emptied in unison.

Charlie turned to Rashad. "About the day at the museum. Can we just say that you were shooting at Tariq, and I was just defending myself?"

Rashad's hard edges softened. "If we can agree that I only hit you because you shot my ear off."

Glasses clinked, and not for the last time. "Agreed!"

"In that case, I apologize for shooting off your ear."

Rashad's deep-set eyes loomed back at her. "Let's hear no more of the past. Let us speak only of the future. A bright and prosperous future." Sharing one more toast, Charlie doubted that anyone around that table believed in a fairy-tale of a bright and prosperous future—but she knew she would do all she could to play her part. Mistrust ebbed and stories flowed as the trio questioned, explained, and debated long into the night. As they babbled and bubbled, Charlie remembered her toast back at the Ritz Hotel in Paris. *All for one and one for all.*

She had come a long way since then. With pressures easing, she made her request. "Can I please use your phone?"

"Why?"

Bassam couldn't help himself. "She wants to call her father."

"It's important. He could be in danger," added Charlie.

Rashad nodded to the phone in the corner.

"The lines are down." Offered Charlie.

"Says who?"

Charlie motioned across. "Bassam. They've been down since the start of the war. I thought you'd know that."

Rashad roared with laughter. "You old goat."

Bassam almost blushed. "I am very sorry." He handed her the phone.

Desperate for an update, she called again. Tapping the handset as it rang out didn't make a blind bit of difference. After a full minute's ringing, she hung up.

"No answer?" inquired Bassam.

Charlie shook her head.

"Well, that must be good, yes?"

She hoped Bassam was right. She allowed herself to follow a new path of logic. If her enemies had tracked and captured her father, they would be lying in wait to answer his phone and issue their threats. More than ever, she hoped no contact was good news.

She needed air. "Would it be possible to go for a walk?"

Bassam was appalled at the prospect. "Out there?"

She gestured towards the museum above. "No. Up there."

Rashad offered his services. "It will be my pleasure to act as your guide. You must be tired. Bassam will make up a small bed for you in the staff quarters whilst we are away."

Charlie moved to clear the table as a gesture of gratitude. "Please, no. You are our guest. Bassam will see to that."

On cue, a beamingly obliging Bassam, jumped into subservient action. When Rashad stood to lead the tour, Charlie placed her palms together. "Could I make this journey on my own? Please?"

Even Rashad understood the moment. "Of course. I will set the lighting and leave you to roam in the path of kings. Please follow me." He courteously brought her up to the top of a series of wide, minimalist stairways. At the end of an unlit hall, Rashad bent over and clasped her shoulders. He gestured down the length of the pitch-black hall.

"Wait here," he whispered. "The museum is yours." He completed his exit with a playful request. "Don't steal anything!" After soft sandals had shuffled off into the resounding silence, Charlie trembled in anticipation of the voyage that lay ahead in the darkness.

In sequence the recessed lights that peppered the ceiling dawned across a vast hall adorned with carved stone friezes. Above each section, lights on extended stalks burst into action, casting shadows and tonal tints across the marble scenes. Deities, creatures, warriors, chariots, and lions were etched across sweeping landscapes. In the mid-distance, two winged creatures struck a pose underneath either side of a lit archway. The guardians were a hybrid of a bearded human with the body of a bull and wings of an eagle. Charlie recognized the famous Lamassu from the Palace of Sargon. She faltered at their feet, in awe of their power.

Against all protocols and belief systems, she reached out and placed her palm on one of the eagle's wings. The wondrous sculpture felt warm to the touch and alive with stories spanning three thousand years. She trod in the footsteps of the pioneering women who had made all this possible: the great Gertrude Bell, who helped found the museum, and the mysterious Agatha Christie, who helped recover the Lammasu. She hoped that whatever lay ahead, she would have the courage and conviction to emulate her heroines.

Under a brightly colored dome, she spun, eyes wide with wonder. Scattered bulbs lit the beautiful fresco that showcased the magnificent history, artifacts, and architecture that had been gifted to the world by the cradle of civilization. With unbounded astonishment she perused the hall and anterooms that quietly revealed humanity through the ages. As the rooms diminished in size, so did the exhibits and the optimism. A saddening trail of devastation and forlorn abandonment strained her despondent eyes. A ghost town of long-lost treasures lay before her. The smashed artifacts, the broken display cases and the obvious signs of looting cluttered every corner. With each new discovery, a little more hope was lost. She found it difficult to have faith in any future after viewing the devastation from a recent past. Returning to the middle of the vast Assyrian Room, she took a seat on the unpolished concrete. The Mesopotamian cycle had been laid bare before her: civilization and culture, glory and magnificence, invasion and conquest, destruction, and devastation. She doubted the days ahead would be any different. Sitting with her knees under her chin, she imagined a daunting future. Not for the first time, Iraq seemed almost too much to bear. She felt trapped, unable to trust anyone and likely on the run for Kirk's murder. All entries to the safety of the Green Zone were barred. Having gained rogue agent status in the eyes of the US agencies, she hung her head just for a moment.

Sometime later, she stirred to find a gentle arm swinging a large woolen blanket over her sleepy shoulders. Through a drowsy haze, she spied Bassam's hulky frame shuffling off into the ancient backdrop. Although the prospect of a freshly prepared bed lay close by, she pulled her shroud close and buried her face. She felt safe in the cocoon of the museum walls, but more than ever, she longed for home.

CHAPTER 27

The morning call to prayer woke Charlie from the deepest of sleeps. Throwing back her woolen blanket, she peeled herself off the marble floor and stretched her drowsy limbs. Sunlight crept in from the small, square windows high above. After she released a few angry cats and downward facing dogs from her body, she stood to finish her yoga routines under the watchful eyes of the Lammasu statues. Despite her night on the tiles and her painful abduction, her body was faring well. Under the torrid onslaught, she almost managed to convince herself that a slashed hand, shredded wrists, a colossal lump on the back of her head, and a few facial cuts and bruises were superficial. Her mind, on the other hand, remained on the at-risk register. To her delight and surprise, her freshly laundered combats were folded neatly beside her. Only Bassam could have made that happen. She smiled at the thought of her friend's kind gesture. The switch of outfits helped ease her back into routine. A stroll outside in the air represented the first step to a full recovery. Charlie was surprised by the lack of an alarm system, but with the museum now under guard and most of its moveable treasures long gone, she understood the reasoning. She pulled across a pair of gigantic bolts, allowing one of the main side doors to the museum to creak open.

A run helped clear the minefield in her mind. Jasmine and rose bushes garlanded her starting line. The melodic minaret nearby laid down a backdrop of encouragement as she broke her bare feet out into a gradually increasing jog. The museum compound was deceptively cavernous, given its mid-town location. Laid out perfectly around an L-shaped building complex, the gardens epitomized the faded grandeur that threatened to overpower the great institute. The topiary had fallen into disarray, along with everything else in the vicinity. Neglect was, as ever, the dominating feature. Charlie switched from a jog to a canter. With the bright morning sky splashing her face, she soaked in glints of optimism. Pace, pulse, and thoughts all quickened as the compound transitioned into a personalized running track. Faster and faster, harder, and harder, she tested her limits.

Head down, she had failed to notice the activity up ahead. Upon rounding the final corner of her latest lap, a squad of newly appeared GIs piled out of two dusty Humvees and a shiny white utility truck.

On approach, she saw Bassam standing patiently, towel outstretched and ready to welcome his new friend back in from the madness that had caught hold of her. Tearing past for a second lap, her sweaty, lopsided grimace showed she had unfinished business. However implausible, it appeared Bassam's sweat levels had risen. As she ran past the group of squaddies, she rolled her eyes—they proved it was never too early to start with the sexist chanting and innuendos. When her withering look of disapproval hit its mark, the heckling ceased immediately. She pushed on unencumbered and unaccompanied.

At the next lap point, the soldiers hollered and yelled out encouragement, holding opened water bottles at the ready. The support was appreciated, but she shunned the offer of hydration. The third and final lap was completed at full speed. Burning legs carried her bursting lungs home over the finishing line. Her unwanted reception committee seemed much more impressed by her efforts than she was. Bent over double and more embarrassed than grateful, she waved across to the cheering grunts. After regaining a sizeable percentage of her breath, Charlie stood tall, and extended her fit-to-pop muscles and tendons. Leaning against the wall to extend her calves, she noticed Rashad in the middle of the group of soldiers loitering around the back of the utility truck. Intrigued by their activity, she felt compelled to complete her very own investigation. Nearing the soldiers, Charlie recognized them as infantry. A fresh out of college captain, very aware that his crew had been verbally undressing this woman, put steel in their backs and called them to attention. Immediately, the squad stood as one. Charlie felt discomfited by the unwarranted military machismo, but it was not her place to stand the men at ease. The soldiers and the orders were let stand. Drawing closer, she read the captain's Velcro nametag and insignia.

"Good morning, Captain Bartlett. Quite the crew you have there. Special Agent Charlotte Glass, Federal Bureau of Investigation."

The young captain blushed. His pockmarks and pimples had taken quite a beating from the scorching Iraqi sun. His overly tight chinstrap did not help the situation in the slightest. Disarmed, he shook her hand.

"Captain Daniel Bartlett, Third Infantry." The pair exchanged nods before the soldiers were set at ease then dismissed back to duties.

"What brings you to Iraq, Agent Glass?"

She pointed. "I'm working with the task force on the recovery of the looted items from the museum."

The young officer sparked a connection. "You must know Warrant Officer Kirkland?"

An instant fear of discovery jarred the edges of her reply. "Indeed, I do. He's quite the character."

The boyish captain seemed set to cry. "Yeah. A great guy. I'm kind of lost without him, to be honest. How's he doing? We don't see much of him these days."

Charlie felt desperate to distance herself from the subject. "He's been out on a field trip examining the site lootings down south, I think. I haven't seen much of him either."

"Yeah, this place has gone to shit since we arrived." From his manner, Charlie deduced that the good captain would see no cause-and-effect relationship between the invasion and everything turning bad. Relieved that Kirk's death hadn't yet been reported, she dragged the conversation as far from him as possible. "So can I ask what you are up to?"

The young captain stood tall. "We have a US State Department VIP in a few days' time. I have my suspicions as to who it might be, but we were not told."

"Top secret?"

"You know how that goes. We are here to complete a sweep of the area and buildings to check for IEDs." Listening in from the sidelines, Rashad's nod corroborated the captain's story. Charlie questioned Rashad. "You know about this?"

He shrugged. "No one does."

The captain chortled. "We don't know who it is. We just got told to come out and do the sweep. They want to do some hearts and minds BS photo op in front of the statues. We're getting hammered in the press for not protecting their heritage, whatever that means. A bunch of old busted jars if you ask me."

Internally, Charlie bit back. *I didn't ask you.*

Two large German Shepherds bounded into view, dragging two larger and angrier handlers behind them. Charlie moved in to pat the first dog.

"Ma'am, step away."

She recoiled from both bark and bite. Sabre and Sultan were introduced from a distance then released under explicit instructions. They set to work, sniffing and scratching around the compound with their tails held high and their noses grounded. Liberal lashings of urine helped mark their tracks as the minesweeping continued all around the surrounding gardens. Their two female handlers seemed intent on out-screaming each other in their quest to control their formidable charges. In the background, a couple of soldiers pulled what looked like a large-wheeled electrical snake out from the back of the utility truck and set it down on the pathway.

"And what does this do?" Charlie asked, intrigued.

The captain took pains to demonstrate his vital involvement. "The very latest technology. It's an Underground Detection Device. Basically, it's a camera train. It was designed for inspecting telecom ducts. We use it to check for IEDs. The sneaky Hajis plant them in culverts and drains and then wait and wait. When the time arrives, *boom*!"

Charlie hated the slur, Haji. "So, you're testing it here?"

"The museum is a key target because it ticks all their boxes: frequent VIPs, gods that defy Allah, Westerners, and a global audience. For good measure, there's always the chance that the US will run some dumbass pointless photo-op on the site. We have two teams: above ground and underground. This crew works the underground robot. The dogs work above ground. This is day one of a two-day mission."

Charlie watched attentively as the little remote-controlled robot was put through its paces. A large single, blue-tinged light adorned the front end of the flat-topped stainless-steel gizmo. The tiny camera unit sat proudly on the footplate of the little train. Eight oversized rubber wheels gripped the ground. The body articulated to accommodate changes in elevation and direction. Power and control were provided by a cable dispensed from a large yellow steel drum. The GI working the electric train joined the small team of players wanting to impress Charlie. "It's all connected to a camera; have a look."

Charlie found a TV camera on a lightweight tubular stand. "The camera sees everything. You work the unit like a remote-control car; back to front with the joystick." The dual control stick propelled the unit back and forward. A separate joystick swiveled the camera and sent the images back to the linked screen. "We have ones for bigger ducts and ones for smaller-sized drains. If we find something, we detonate it. If we don't, we put a security seal on the drain to show that it's been inspected."

The cogs in Charlie's mind meshed and turned with every new revelation. She appeared impressed. "May I?"

The impressionable young GI seemed keen to share. "Hell yeah. It's pretty cool."

Within a second, she was playing the role of bomb seeker. The wheeled snake sallied back and forth across the pathway, much to everyone's amusement. Charlie maneuvered the snake's head and sent it scuttling off down the longest path. No one seemed brave enough to tell her to stop. "How far can it go?"

Captain Bartlett placed his hand across her sightline. "Farther than we have runway, Agent Glass."

Conscious of the censorship, Charlie reversed the unit. "I'll bring it back."

By the look on every face, it was a tie for who hated the idea the most. Captain Bartlett may have sneaked it. Only when lashings of terror-stricken advice from the trained operator were applied was some level of control achieved. The unit slithered back up the pathway like a rattler with heat stroke. When it had completed its journey back home, the handler threw Charlie a high five, dripping with relief. It was evident that high fives were not her thing.

"We best get back to work." When the captain ordered a return to duties, unmentionables were mentioned on the edge of earshot. The scorching sun bounced ferociously off the utility truck, piercing Charlie's straining eyelids. Turning to shelter her gaze, an impromptu inspection was carried out on the high-tech vehicle. The over-the-top chrome grill glowed white hot. Its crisp new paintwork had not yet succumbed to the hardships of the Iraqi desert.

Charlie was quite taken by the truck. She turned to Bassam and whispered out of the corner of her mouth, "Don't get caught, but make sure that truck doesn't leave this site today."

She waited impatiently until the message had sunk in. Bassam nodded, certain of the instruction but lost to its reasoning. Before any questions could be asked, she beckoned him on his way before turning to Rashad. "Come on, we have work to do."

He lumbered behind. "What's going on?"

She strode on. "You'll see!"

Charlie burst through the door of the staff quarters. Rashad scuttled in behind. "Something to write on?"

Without questioning his new orders, Rashad set about plundering an old set of drawers. He retrieved a few tinged sheets of paper. A well-chewed pen made up her makeshift writing set.

Charlie set to work, scribbling and scheming with voracity. Rashad busied himself with three glasses, tea leaves, a kettle and questionable tap water. He added copious amounts of sugar then lifted the boiling water across from the stove. He set the ornate tray between them.

Bassam filled the bottom half of the doorway, grinning from chin to chin. A distributor cap and unclipped cabling mischievously appeared from behind his back. *At least now he has a reason for the stains on his t-shirt.*

Tea was shared as the new top dog barked out new tricks. The men were lost for words. Charlie's list of items for immediate requisition was short, specific, and pre-allocated to her prospective bounty hunters.

“I need the following items back here by 2100 hours tonight. Bassam, we need a boiler suit for each of us, two small tents, a large crowbar, and some bollards. Rashad, we need a spotlight, two gas masks, a bulletproof vest, two walkie-talkies and a street map.”

The men gawked at Charlie, then each other.

“Oh, and can you get a detailed map of the city utilities?”

Rashad pulled his bearded face. “Why?”

Her gaze ensnared the fledgling gang members. “We’re stealing it back.”

Rashad sounded utterly lost. “Stealing what back?”

Charlie stared. “All of it!”

CHAPTER 28

By the time 2100 hours arrived, Charlie was in full flow. She paced the floor, wondering if her plan would work, uncertain whether she could carry it off or if her fellow gangsters would even show. As usual, Bassam was almost on time. Rashad arrived unfashionably late. It was not the start she was hoping for. Their outfits were more janitorial than sartorial. Sleeves and hems were rolled up to accommodate Bassam's width, whilst Rashad's lack of height made his suit look as if it would benefit from excessive boil wash. They made quite the sight, lugging their instruments of criminality into the back of the utility truck.

Charlie quizzed Bassam. "How did the captain take to his truck being vandalized?"

"Not well. I told him that he could trust no one around here—except me, of course! He said he'd send over new parts and an engineer tomorrow afternoon. I told him that the truck would never leave my sight until the morning. He left me the keys for safe keeping."

Charlie's plan to make herself scarce during all the vehicular turmoil proved a masterstroke. She wondered how long it would be before the plans went awry.

Rashad inspected the multitude of steel cabinets that stretched the length of the vehicle. He rechecked the housing and controls for the man-sized bucket that sat atop the pristine cantilevered boom. Bassam scrimmaged away under the hood of the truck before reappearing, covered in yet more oil. With everyone on board, a twist of the key and a weapons check set them on their way. Rashad jumped out to open the compound gate and waved Bassam through before the massive gateway closed. Somewhere nearby, a disgruntled dog made its annoyance known to the entire neighborhood. Rashad clambered back on board. They were off, eyes fastened on the road ahead. Charlie was determined. Tonight, they would cast shadows—not chase them.

The equipment's rudimentary functions took a little time to understand. The process of trial and error consisted of more error than trial, but eventually, Rashad declared himself the man for the job. Bassam could not have been more pleased. Charlie set the timeline with input from Rashad. At the point where Charlie's over-eagerness bordered on lecturing, Rashad lifted his hand. His gentle words taught the would-be lecturer a lesson: "I am Iraqi. I am not a fool."

Suitably admonished, Charlie set her hand on his shoulder. "I am sorry. I know. I am new to this too."

Bassam felt the need to pitch in. "We all are."

Rashad had moved on. "Are we ready?"

No one seemed to know the answer, but Charlie felt they were as ready as their window of opportunity allowed.

Charlie relayed the plans, and the team rehearsed their roles, before the truck rumbled its way out into the darkness. Charlie tried to convince herself that determination would outweigh their lack of preparation and inabilities. The nightly traffic was sufficient to avoid attention yet limited enough to avoid the dreaded stop-start traffic jams that drew curious side glances. No one liked the fact that the truck looked all-American.

They followed a predetermined route before sneaking up one of the side streets near the warehouse. Bassam killed the lights and coasted the truck to Charlie's designated drop-off point, several buildings down from the warehouse itself. Charlie fitted an earpiece into her ear. Walkie-talkie volumes were set, and channels were matched. With a nod of encouragement and a final pep talk, she bounded from the truck's cabin. Boiler suit tied in place and ball cap pulled down low, she looked every bit the diminutive utility contractor.

She turned to find Rashad emerging from the gloom cloaking the rear of the truck.

To her horror, he appeared flanked by two Iraqi policemen wielding AK-47s.

CHAPTER 29

Rashad was first to react. "Easy. We are friends. Friends."

"Who are these guys?" Charlie became incensed. They hadn't even crossed the first hurdle, and Rashad was already dragging them off track.

Rashad stuck to his hired guns. "They are like brothers. We can trust them."

"What do they know?"

"They know they will each get five hundred dollars cash to protect a new IED testing device. Five hundred dollars for a twelve-hour shift."

"And they believe that?" Charlie scoffed.

"Of course not. But the threat of their old chief inspector hunting them down will be enough to keep them in line." Rashad proudly pointed at his own pigeon chest and pulled back his overalls to reveal a full Iraqi police uniform. "Don't worry. They love money, but they fear me."

It was too late to pull them out now. Rashad set them to work. Charlie didn't have time to argue about the lack of consultation or the heightened risk. "Remind me to shoot your other ear off when all of this is over."

Rashad laughed a little too loud for the moment. Kirk's phone and Charlie's Glock were both silenced. The handgun assumed its normal position down in the small of her back, inside the combats, beneath the hem of the overalls. The phone slid into the knee pocket of her suit. Her flashlight, paperwork and communications were rechecked, and the gas mask was clipped to the belt loop. Her stolen police issue bullet-proof vest almost fitted her. Combat ready, she tapped the side of the truck. "Right, get me up there."

Bassam fled into the sanctuary of the truck cabin, switched on the engine, and engaged the controls for the exterior hoist. The two policemen kept watch as Rashad smiled like an executioner about to switch on the chair. He was soon mishandling the bucket hoist, yanking away at the stubby joystick controls. He seemed incapable of learning on the job. Charlie's exasperation reached new heights as the bucket dipped and bucked like a snorting mustang. It took all her remaining courage to climb up the frame and leap into the bucket. Her bullet-proof vest came in handy when she took a heavy knock from the jolting pail. Her last words spoken without the aid of the radio were not a request. "Be careful!"

Charlie wedged herself into the bucket to avoid being thrown overboard. Every jar seemed less controlled than the last. With an almost comical air, he missed the target height again and again. Charlie yelped for the bucket to stop. The gap from the bucket to the roof below could have been lessened, but the threat of yet more sloppy work from Rashad persuaded her that the drop was preferable—even survivable.

She clambered tentatively out of the bucket and braced herself. Gripping tightly, she took time to muster the nerve to leap onto the nearby roof. The prospect of the bucket lurching and tossing her off was all the incentive she needed. In the end she let go before landing heavily on the nearby flat roof, rolling safely on impact. A half-finished wall helped arrest her tumble. Down below, she heard the bucket hit two buildings three times on its way back down to the truck. Suddenly, she was pleased to be stranded on a strange roof in a strange land. As she peered over the wall, sporadic house lights snapped on. Curtains twitched and shutters clicked. The crew stowed the bucket as if maximum noise was part of the plan. As they packed up and motored off the scene, the cops remained well undercover. Their clattering departure told the neighbors what they needed to know: the strangers had left. One by one, curtains and shutters resumed their normal positions and the overseeing lights eventually closed down. *Rashad knew what he was doing.*

After taking her full five-minute allocation, Charlie negotiated the flat concrete roof, keeping her silhouette below the level of the wall. Across the rooftops, a dusty moonlight enveloped the scene. The soft aftermath of an earlier sandstorm hung precariously above, bouncing the ardent hue from the streetlights down into the streets. Bars and shutters protected every window, skylight, and doorway. After registering every sight and sound she set to work leaping across the rooftop residences. In the hot night, Charlie dove behind any cover available. Fresh laundry, unfinished concrete pillars, and oversized pot plants were all employed as shields. Climbing walls and making drop, she negotiated the multiple roof heights on her high-level crossing.

Voices and sounds escaped from each lit window before disappearing off into the night air. Charlie pressed on. She slipped carefully onto a low-pitched roof and cautiously scrabbled across its clay tiling, making sure she had a firm grasp of the situation before each tentative step.

After jumping onto the safety of the next roof, she cowered in horror at the biggest, blackest mongrel of a dog snoozing gruffly on a well-chewed wicker chair. When she motioned past, the drowsy hound lifted its massive head, elongated its back, then lethargically wandered over to assess the situation. Seizing the initiative, Charlie stepped forward and rubbed his ears. Petrified, she kissed his slobbery face, and squeezed his massive head. As boisterously as safety allowed, she praised and welcomed her new friend. To her relief, a rising paw flapped playfully in front of her face. His giant tail wagged blearily. It was all too much for the dozy pup. With a shudder of his shoulders, he wandered back to the comfort of his own sofa. Charlie took a final moment to kiss the dog's fat chops goodnight before heading on her way.

Kneeling under windows, she made her way across the skyline. Only when there were no alternative routes did she bounce past open doorways.

Commotions of all form and function leaked from home after home. In an open-sided loft, a posse of off-duty police officers watched soccer on an undersized TV. They were taking on beer and off-loading insults. She had no clear way past. With no alternative she resigned herself to a life on the edge. She clambered over the nearby railing and dangled herself over the ledge, high above the street. Unable to look down, gripping hard, slinging herself hand-over-hand, she grappled her way across and under the ledge of the balcony. She fought hard not to look down.

With each hand movement, her grip involuntarily weakened, and her pace quickened. Dreading the appearance of an unfriendly face over the ledge, she strung herself along. With the far wall in reach, her efforts doubled, and her grip tightened. A dusty section helped loosen her grip. Grit fell into her eyes, yet still she clung on. One final heave brought her up and over the balcony railing and across onto the nearby roof. To her relief, all nearby lights were down, and all shutters were up. She lay there for longer than she could afford to regain her strength. The gash on her hand wept again in protest.

She peered towards the night sky and found the broken skylight that would give her access to the smuggler's warehouse. The sizeable gap across the alley proved daunting. It looked too big to jump, especially at night and in combat boots. She leaned out just far enough to visualize the distance, only for her head to jerk back behind the wall. Hank's untrustworthy guards were directly below, patrolling their own exclusion zone. Charlie spent the next few minutes timing and tracking the guards' routine. They had none. *Amateurs.*

A sadly familiar SUV suddenly rolled into view down below. The two guards mustered all their reserves of energy when they noticed it approaching. An improvised Q&A session took place through the open passenger window. Charlie convinced herself that the passenger's muffled voice belonged to Hank. With reports and instructions exchanged, the SUV's passengers rumbled off into the Baghdad night. No sooner had it disappeared than the two guards retook their seats in time for a well-earned smoke break.

Returning to the challenge at hand, Charlie noted that the gap between the buildings had increased. None of the options passed the risk and reward stress test. But it was too late to go back; she couldn't get back across under the balcony ledge. She had no choice. The "screw-it" option had to be taken. Charlie launched a treasure hunt for useful tools. Uncertain salvation came in the form of a heavy, rotten panel door. It took a lot of effort to drag it across the rooftop. With depleted energy reserves, Charlie clumsily heaved the door onto the top of the low wall. After checking it could take her weight, she paced out the necessary wide steps before mentally marking her long jump-starting point. With her eyes fixed on the edge of the door, she pulled her talisman from under her shirt and kissed it for luck. With a deep breath, she filled her lungs and emptied her mind before hurtling herself down the unconventional runway. She hit the last panel at full tilt, throwing body, heart, and soul into the wind. Her airtime lasted an eternity. When a trailing boot thumped the roof wall, she toppled, head over buckled heel. Twisting on impact, her shoulders took the brunt of the impact of the ragged concrete. Scraped and scuffed elbows and knees carried her off into the darkest corner of the terrace. She took her bearings in double quick time. Safe and intact, she was almost enjoying herself. Making up time, she climbed underneath the skylight that sat above the warehouse. She was relieved to find that her previous vandalism had remained undiscovered. The window swung freely open. It didn't take long for her to clamber up a ridge to reach her target. After leaping in through the skylight, she landed hard. A bolt of pain jolted her already twisted ankle. She let out an involuntary yelp, unconcerned by the sound she made. She was on her own.

She called in reinforcements over the airwaves. "M-Two calling M-One. M-Two calling M-One. Do you copy? Over."

"M-One calling M-Two. M-One calling M-Two. We hear you clear. Over." Bassam's voice wavered, a clear sign of his fear, but his enthusiasm showed he was trying his absolute best to be professional.

"Entry made. Are you in position? Over."

"Nearly. We are in alley, but do not find cover. Hang on." After three or four agonizing minutes, Bassam's excited voice refilled the airwaves. "Found it. We don't know if it is right. We found one!"

"Okay. Okay. Radio silence until you hear from me. Over and out."

Charlie waited for an acknowledgement that never came and flicked on her belt flashlight. She kept the beam low and scanned the office under window height. No changes since her last visit. No unwelcoming committee. She momentarily considered stuffing her combat pants with cuneiform tablets before snapping herself back to the present. She had bigger plans. Only time would tell if Bassam and Rashad had found the right location. All she could do was deliver her part of the thieves' bargain. With the currency of the cuneiforms discounted, she crossed to the office door, killing her flashlight before cracking open the door. After hearing only silence for a minute, she stuck her head around the door stand. No life existed in the warehouse. The flashlight beam was relit and thrown around with far less caution. After moving swiftly back to the office desk, the table lamp was snatched up for future use. Creeping down the unlit steel stairway, her eyes darted between the sections of the warehouse that housed the doorways. Down across at the busy desk, the additional lamp became part of the new lighting regime. The two lamps were pulled to the maximum of their length and pointed downwards, back in on each other. The flashlight was then set up on a pallet and triangulated in to provide her with the best view of the pallets possible. She grabbed her radio.

"At my station. Status, please. Over." She waited an eternity. "At my station. Status, please. Over."

Eventually Bassam's flustered tones crackled through the radio. "Sorry we were setting up the tent and lighting. We've got the truck all lined up and—"

"Fewer words, M-One. Tell me when the light is on. Over."

"Oh, okay, sorry. Over."

Charlie's simmering blue eyes searched for salvation high above. She found it impossible not to like Bassam, despite his best efforts. Whilst waiting for the signal, she pulled out a listing from her breast pocket and flattened it under the barely useful lamplight. An old stapler, a calculator, some pens, a small stack of Marlboro cigarette boxes, and an old Zippo lighter made way for the inspection. She had her previously calculated shopping list of canisters to search through. With each ammunition box weighing the same as a gold bar, she knew it would be some workout. A plan to conserve her energies was vital. Recalling the Ottoman Empire reference, pallets fifteen, thirty-four, nineteen, and eighteen were her prime suspects. A selection of codes relating to the missing catalogue items stolen from the museum also made the cut list. The top of them all was IM8272: The Golden Chalice of Ur. The stolen forklift truck stood in the corner of the warehouse. Given the close nature of the pallets and the noise they would generate, she reluctantly chose the quieter, manual option. Moving swiftly into action, the pallets were selected by hand, and the ammunition boxes pulled.

Her code deciphering was on the mark.

From the top layer of boxes came her first gold bar. With the stash confirmed, she scampered across to the drain cover. After unclipping the gas mask from her belt, she set it to her face. Having confirmed the mask's functionality, she sent her trusted old crowbar in to open the chamber. Sticking her head into the gloomy pit, she found only darkness. She clicked her radio open and shouted through her mask.

"M-One. Switch on the light. Over."

In the lengthy silence that followed, she imagined Bassam waddling around frantically, searching for his misplaced radio. "Hello, hello. Sorry. It's on. The light is on. Over."

Charlie lowered her head. "Is it in the space? Over."

"Yes."

Her soul sank. She detected no change in the tunnel's luminosity. *They've missed the mark.* She slumped down, uncertain of what to do next. Inspiration came from an unlikely source.

"M-One to M-Two, we will flash the light. See if you can see the changes…Oh, over."

Charlie killed the lights, ripped off her mask, took a deep breath, then sank her face down into the pit. The stench in the chamber burned her eyes. Through the stinging nausea, she blinked at the distance in blind hope. She stared through the darkness and waited and waited and waited.

Amazingly, the faintest of flashes tinted the darkness. *On. Off. On. Off.* She ripped her head from the pit and screamed a whisper down the radio. "I see it!" In the mayhem, it had been her turn to break protocol. "Send it!"

The heist was well and truly on.

With the dismal lighting back up to an almost bearable level, her system developed, safe in the knowledge that the guards outside were barred from entry and the real bad guys were off to the airport. The plan was a simple smash and grab raid with no cover up. Opening each in sequence, she pulled back every top layer of bullets and checked for plunder. When contraband was found, Charlie cast the bullets to the floor and shut the ammo boxes tight for easier and safer transportation of the treasure. She had considered a cover up and replacing the bullets, but time was not on her side. She would take the treasure and leave the devastation.

With a box in each hand, she carried them over by the handles, perfectly balanced. She made good progress preparing for the mechanical train. Halfway across, it dawned on her that the reason for the lack of light penetration could be a ninety-degree bend in the drain line. If that, or any other combination of ducting was in play, they were up shit creek. Literally.

She worked through the worry. With no alternative, it was too late to turn back now. The smell from the sewer was not one that any living soul would ever get acclimatized to, so Charlie pulled her gas mask on again before she jumped in to complete her inspection.

Miraculously, the stolen detection device trundled up the slight incline towards her. She struggled to contain the emotions that coursed into the radio. "I can see it. It's coming. Ten yards. I will count you down. Five, four, three, two, one—stop."

For no plausible reason, the unit sped past before lurching to a stop.

"Damn it! Backwards two yards." The unit spluttered back, almost twisting itself into a jammed coil. Charlie climbed into the wreckage and realigned the unit's wheels. The ducting seemed bigger in the light. There was more than enough space to fit one or two ammunition boxes in at one time. Any mishap would jam the line for certain, so her decision remained set: one box at a time. *No time to get greedy.*

Claustrophobia and crap aside, the worst the sewer could offer was negated by the genius masterstroke that was the gas mask. Charlie jumped as a gigantic rat scurried past. Its big brother scampered on behind. It was a three-way tie as to who was the most terrified. Charlie leaped from the pit in search of gloves and composure. She found neither. The plan had been to use the wrapping tape to secure each box to the train. In her search to find some much-needed hand protection, she found two bungee cords, the ones used to attach goods to pickups and roof racks. It was a definite upgrade.

She scuttled back to the pit and pulled in an ammunition box. With one last check of the contents, she primed the first box for evacuation. The inspection camera had been detached from the unit to make the surface of the bed flat. After misjudging its weight, the first golden box thumped down hard onto the unit, sliding off to one side. It took a good deal of strength to set the box back into the middle of the unit. After wrapping the bungee cord twice around she tucked the hook in behind the box's leather handle. Charlie jumped out the pit to avoid being struck by an overzealous carriage. She held her breath, dragged off her gas mask, and awaited another decisive moment. "Go! Go! Over."

After a stuttering start, the unit chased the muddy rats back up the drainpipe. *It is working.* With the unit returning to base,

Charlie donned the gas mask and reentered the pit. The flashlight followed the unit valiantly before wattage and distance changed her view. Staring ominously into a black pipe with an underpowered flashlight didn't seem a good use of energy, so she cut the exercise short. It was never repeated. Instead, more boxes were inspected, discounted, or selected, and transported towards the pit.

After only a few boxes, the strain across Charlie's neck and shoulder muscles began to take its toll. She calculated that by now, the box would have reached its destination and would be on its way back to her. She pulled out her radio once more.

"Send it back. We're behind schedule. Over." Charlie knew not whether they were on schedule or not, she just wanted to cut short the party that was no doubt in full swing at the other end of the ducting. She threw herself back into the work at hand. Progress was much slower than predicted, the physical effort much more demanding, but the stakes were high enough to justify such extreme exertion. After only a few trips to the golden well, her hands were starting to crack. The fact that over one million dollars of gold stood at the edge of the pit helped eased her pain. She wasn't after the money; she was after the evidence. She rested at ground level and peered down, giving up on the added hassle of the mask all together.

After the unit careened past the entrance, she shouted for it to be stopped and reversed. She held her breath and hopped back into the pit. "Where's the bungee cord?" Without a single word of response, the unit disappeared back from where it came. "Unbelievable!" Although annoyed, she was glad for the rest. "We need to go back. Put the cord back on. Over." The unit crept back.

After grabbing a few more panicked breaths, she jumped back in and loaded up her next box. After tightening the rubber cord, she gave the command to haul away. Every time the process was completed, improvements in both efficiency and efficacy were born. With every delivery that sidled down the pipe, Charlie started to turn her thoughts to her quest for the real prize: The Golden Chalice of Ur.

The agonizingly long periods of downtime between deliveries started to play with her mind. A stock of gold-filled boxes now lay at the pit. Charlie's methodical process that had controlled the project rapidly disappeared down the drain. Ignoring her pre-planned lists, the patterns in packaging methodology went unnoticed. Clues and indicators of what may lie where went unheeded. With inspections less planned and more hurried., she cast yet another unsatisfactory box to one side. It clanked into a previously discarded box that was perched precariously on the edge of a pallet. A new kind of panic set in when the teetering box fell off the pallet and crashed headlong across the concrete flooring. To add to her idiocy, in trying to retrieve the first box, Charlie managed to push another one in on top of it, producing an even greater clatter. She held on to the pallet to prevent the entire warehouse from spinning.

Fear took over. She rushed to the back door and listened for the sounds of newly alerted guards. She didn't quite know what that would sound like, but she knew she would recognize it if she heard it.

Silence.

She decided not to check the front, as the external guards were further away, and she didn't want to expose herself in the street lighting that bled into the showroom area. She scraped the handle of her Glock across the scar on the side of her forehead in self-admonishment. "Idiot!"

As far away from the pit as possible Charlie took a breather, before circling around the table with all the shipping documentation. She leaped across to the pit just in time to see the next train hurtle by. The call back and loading procedures were completed in double quick time as the conversion to a gold train was promptly completed. She brought the paperwork back to the pit and sat on the edge to peruse the patterns in the documents and cross-reference the results from her scattered recollections of recent findings. She had lost track of the number of boxes that had been shipped by the time she heard the morning call to prayer. She checked her watch. Depending upon airport traffic and local interference, she calculated that they could have time enough for another ten or so runs. The gold was there for the taking, so she ramped up her efforts and carried box after box across to the pit. The two-at-a-time lifting method was downgraded to a one-at-a-time drag race. Her legs withstood the strain that her shoulders could no longer hold.

The makeshift train was loaded and dispatched on a tight timetable. The painful progress stalled. The train did not arrive on schedule. Charlie grabbed the radio. "M-Two to M-One. Are you receiving me? Come in. Over."

Her dark world had fallen silent.

After two more unheeded calls, uncertainty transitioned into blind fear. Had she been screwed over? She had stolen US property, given it to un-vetted locals, and there she was—trapped inside a guarded warehouse with nowhere to go.

Fears that she had been abandoned to the fates corrupted her psyche. To fend off the growing paranoia, she rifled through new boxes to find the batch of M4 rifles that were on the manifest. Ammunition was united with her new weapon, and backup magazines were added to her arsenal. Somehow that didn't feel like enough protection from what lay ahead. If she was going out, she'd go out fighting. From the back of the area, she pulled out a box of grenades and spilled them across the desk. She checked then rehoused her Glock before tightening her flak jacket to the point of discomfort. She took one last shot with the radio. "M-Two to M-One. Are you receiving me? Come in. Over."

The silence that followed broke her heart.

The original plan had been for her team to lift her from a nearby roof. Because they were long gone, she eliminated the roof from the list of escape routes. The plan in the short-term was to go out tooled up. The rest would follow.

Preparations made, the only decision left was the front door or the roof. She pulled her talisman and stared. The pathetic little girl who made every decision on the pitch and toss of a bauble had left this world. The woman she had become would make her own decisions and live or die by them.

Daylight from the skylight had started to peak through into the overhead office, but the heavy grime covering the undersized windows kept the main warehouse wallowing in the murk. Resigned to an uncertain fate, she started her slow walk to the rear exit. She knew the size of the enemy: two lazy guards out the back, lightly armed, poorly prepared. She eased forward to meet her fate. As she reached for the handle, she heard her radio snap into life.

"Hello? Over."

Her knees gave way, forcing her to grab a crate. She had never been so pleased to hear another person's voice in her life. She ignored her own protocols. "I'm here. Where have you been?"

Bassam's voice made her want to scream in every way possible. "Sorry, praying. Train is on its way. Hurry."

The M4 was left on the stair as she bounded back down the flight of stairs. Joyous at the lack of betrayal, she threw everything into finishing the job. Dropping her weaponry, losing patience and time, she threw the handset on the desk.

The promised tram trundled back into place. On the following trips, the boxes were doubled up. The cutoff point was set at the number of boxes now sitting at the pit. Any more than that, and greed would be their downfall. With the carriage on its way back down the tunnel and no more boxes to be dragged into the loading bay, there was time for one last treasure hunt. Another foul-smelling fresh start.

Scattered papers, cluttered worktops, and continually reloading the gold train hampered the search for clues. A crude drawing of a bronze bust fell from the corner of a pile of papers. On inspection the note came from the shipping company, Sargon Distribution. *Sargon?* Charlie half recognized the name. At a frightening pace, the search for the discarded museum book took off. High-speed, low-level sweeps amongst the discarded boxes and bullet belts brought immediate success. She thumbed and scanned the index cards until reaching the letter "S." Her rampaging bout of research eventually bore fruit. Saragon, the King of Akkadia. The first Empire to rule all of Mesopotamia. Born 2334 BC.

Charlie wondered if this would follow the same pattern, with the dates marking the pallets containing hidden treasures. Pallet thirty-four had already been ransacked because of its association with the Ottoman Empire. Perhaps twenty-three was the final clue? The idea sent her scurrying around the remaining unbroken pallets. She found twenty-three jammed in near the back. Without the time or the energy to transfer tons of bullets by hand, she inspected the previously discounted forklift truck. Charlie thumped the seat in anger. It was an electric truck. Charlie pulled the charging cable. After pistol-whipping safety beacon into darkness, she kindled the silent motor and whipped the truck around into position. The same treatment quietened the reversing alarm. Swinging the pallets around produced the minimal scraping of wood on concrete.

Charlie fought the urge to ask herself why she hadn't used the unit earlier in the night, given its silent running. Seg cut the elusive pallet twenty-three from the herd and brought it over to the inspection area. Before she could pull open any ammunition boxes, her open mic walkie talkie crackled with a demand for more gold. She hung back over the pit and called in the train's reversal. Although her eyes were acclimatizing to the darkness, they couldn't see past the pit's blackness. She took her trusted flashlight and shined it directly into the pit. The final two boxes were stacked on top of each other, and the bungee cord wrapped in place before she made the call for extraction. With the doubled-up cargo, Charlie had bought herself time for one more trip, even two. Without her headset, she lifted and clicked open the radio. "Take her away." The underground train remained in its station. She tried again. "M-Two to M-One. Take her away, do you read? Over."

The sound of Bassam's voice crackling out into the warehouse was welcoming. His words were not. "We have a problem."

"What is it?"

"American soldiers."

Charlie moved to calm both ends of the walkie-talkie conversation. She was flying in a blind panic. "Okay, have they seen you?"

"Yes. Yes and no. They are talking to Rashad. They do not see me."

"Okay. Hide. Tell me what you see."

Seconds of silence turned into agonizing minutes as Charlie waited in the darkness. She fought the urge to click the walkie-talkie for updates.

"Two trucks. Big guns. Four soldiers. Rashad talking."

Charlie kept her voice low. "What are they saying?"

"Not good. Checking IDs."

With no escape route, no options, and no influence, anxiety closed in. "Give the handset to the American leader?"

"That is not wise."

Charlie pressed the order. "We have no option. Hand it over."

At the edge of the pit, she waited, wondering what the hell was going on. She had suffered through her first bout of doubt, and the fact that the guys had alerted her to a problem dispelled any fears that this was a pending act of desertion. That still left other unpalatable recipes for disaster. After the radio cracked open, her relief quickly turned to bemusement.

"Desert Fox One, to Desert Fox Two. Do you read? Over."

With immediate relief, she recognized Rashad's voice. He had improvised US sounding call signs, so she played along. "Desert Two receiving. What the hell is going on? Why the delay? Over."

A deep Southern US voice told Charlie that Rashad had handed over the handset.

"Excuse me, ma'am, this is Sergeant Thomas from the Third Infantry. We are completing a sweep of—"

"Sergeant Tyrone Thomas from Greenville, North Carolina?" a joyous Charlie bust back through the airwaves.

An astonished deep voice cried back. "Yes, ma'am."

"It's Agent Glass, FBI. Are you holding me up again? Unbelievable!"

The sergeant laughed. "I believe I am, ma'am."

Charlie punched the air at what felt like her first stroke of fortune. The sergeant's playful disbelief washed over the coincidence. She pushed her luck. "Remember that call I had to take at the Oil Ministry?"

"Yes, ma'am."

"We are part of a sweep team scanning for IEDs, trying out a new technology. We are in final testing. There's a VIP coming over from the US in a couple of days. We are completing a final sweep."

"At this time of night?"

"Fewer prying eyes. You can check your base if you don't believe me."

The sergeant needed far more convincing. "They won't know that, and they wouldn't tell me even if they did. What the hell are you doing in this hole? Ain't no VIPs coming 'round here."

Charlie pulled out a pre-rehearsed cover story. "We have two sites. The museum and here. We cleared up the museum yesterday. We're doing this area for some press event."

"Why pick this location, Agent? There is nothing here."

Charlie banged the handset off her head in a growing rage. She could hear the panic filtering through her explanations. She made a concerted effort to sound bolder. "Well, I can't say too much, but what we're doing here relates to that call from the Oil Ministry. The same outcomes exist if we don't get this sorted ASAP. You've no doubt checked our IDs, and you know me on a one-to-one basis."

"Yes, ma'am."

She thought of dropping Kirk's name in, but felt the risk outweighed the reward—besides, she knew she had won their last skirmish. "We're using the local guys for low profile, and the longer you guys are hanging around, the bigger the target on our back is getting. My guys have it covered. We'll be gone in twenty minutes, tops. Why don't I come over to Third HQ soon? I'll bring beers!"

The sergeant had heard more than enough. "That won't be necessary, agent. I'll settle for you just getting the hell out of here. The sooner you're gone, the better off we'll all be."

Charlie sent her warmest GI Jane accent over the airwaves. "Roger that, Sergeant."

Moments later, Rashad's voice returned. "They have left."

Charlie sensed their luck was turning. She inhaled a deep breath of hope. When the breathing restarted, so did the train. Charlie checked her watch. They were past the point in time she had given herself. She was now in the red zone. Anyone in their right mind would leave right there and then—but anyone in their right mind would never leave the Golden Chalice of Ur behind. *It has to be here.* She cursed the time she had spent waiting for an answer from the last delay. She went full out in her search of crooked stenciling on the side of any ammo box in pallet twenty-three.

Rashad's call possessed an edge. "We must go. Now!"

Charlie kept on, pummeling boxes to the side with the truck to check their numbers. Now, she even ignored the boxes with the doctored stenciling. It sounded like Rashad was losing his mind. "We're out of time; get out!"

As he spoke, Charlie flipped a single box onto its side. Even at this awkward angle, the magical serial number for the Golden Chalice was clear. *IM8272.*

Charlie yelped, as she split the ammunition can. After pulling back a layer of foam padding, the Chalice fell into view. It was more beautiful, more beguiling than Charlie could ever have imagined. Rashad's voice boomed from the handset. Charlie had one care, and that wasn't it. She snatched the walkie-talkie. "We have time. It's at least an hour for them to get here from the airport."

"It takes half that time on a Friday."

The air turned sour. Charlie glanced at her watch. Her rapid recalculations told her that Hank and his cronies should already be here. The blood drained to her boots. As she reached for the walkie-talkie to call for the truck, the world turned. Suddenly, the metal chains on the large warehouse door cracked together, announcing its opening. Alarmed but determined, she clamped the Chalice in one hand and bolted for the stairs.

The lights menacingly flickered above as voices swarmed in from under the opening shutter door. *Too late!* Charlie knew she wouldn't make it. She leaped to one side and ducked behind the nearest stack of pallets. In a thoughtless flash of panic, she doubled back and made a break for the darker side of the warehouse. With no obvious options, she jumped towards the stacks of old furniture. Dusty cellophane crackled and creased as she clambered over and behind the heap of sofas. She trembled in the darkness as the footsteps and voices loomed closer. Fear was the last thing on her mind. The tiny chalice resting in her hands shone through the horror. Despite being a breath away from death, she lay there, bewildered, and enchanted.

CHAPTER 30

With the switches pulled and the large shutter door now opened to the world, the warehouse became flooded in light. Against her better judgment, Charlie peeked out to find Hank and his two minders walking ahead of two mystery guests. Keen, hawkish eyes darted around the warehouse. Hank seemed to be sporting items stolen from Dempsey's wardrobe—slicked back hair, Ray-Ban Aviators, immaculately ironed, white cotton shirt, black suit, and patent leather shoes. As usual, everything bulged as if it was a size too small, even the sunglasses. The K-twins, in comparison, wore the national dress for every modern-day mercenary: black combat gear set off with splashes of off-the-shoulder Kevlar.

Their two guests could not have looked more different. The swaggering lead sported a black suit, black shirt, black tie, and black brogues. A poorly concealed weapon distorted the outline of his made-to-measure suit. With nervous and shifty tawny eyes, the mouse-like creature scurrying up behind him seemed a different species entirely. Meek, beige, and unassuming, his tired little suit fit where it touched, but it hardly touched anywhere. Clutching a shiny new briefcase like his life depended on it, the little man scampered to keep up. the whole time he scanned for predators. From her distant position, Charlie felt secure and concealed.

"Come forward gentlemen, let me show you the merchandise. You will not be disappointed." Hank played host as he strode towards the central desk. The group sped to keep up with him.

Hank broke first. "What the hell?" His scream carried all the way to where Charlie hid in the partially lit section of the warehouse. It was the little accountant who scuttled forward to lead the challenge. His devious little voice was thickened by French stock. "What is going on?"

Hank unraveled before everyone's eyes. Lashing out, he kicked the table, sending the boxes flying. Fire and brimstone rained down. The place had been ransacked, and Hank was only adding to the chaos. If this was a setup, he was doing a good job of hiding it. The little man shifted front and center.

"I asked you a question. What is going on?"

Hank threw his head back to the gods. "It's gone!"

The little man fizzed. "Gone?"

"Someone's stolen it!" Hank kicked a half-opened pallet and imploded. The little accountant handed his briefcase to his business partner then surveyed the devastation. Coldly and methodically, he audited the scene and calculated the outcomes. He wandered over to Hank and pressed his little round glasses right under his nose before summing up his findings.

"If you are saying the goods are no longer here, then our deposit needs to be back in our account by close of play today. That is a minimum. My employer will decide your fate after that."

Hank reeled. "I can't. I will get you your goods."

The accountant pressed his case. "Forgetting the fact that you have stolen one million dollars of our money, we have people relying on these goods. We have made promises that you seem incapable of keeping."

"I can fix this."

"You need to. The money today, or the consequences tomorrow."

Resigned to any number of gruesome fates, Hank slithered and paced around the scene of the crime. Charlie tightened her flak jacket and pulled her Glock into position. Desperate for angles, she pulled Kirk's phone out and switched it on, safe in the knowledge that it had been silenced earlier. The phone had no service signal. She scanned the texts and numbers in search of salvation. If a signal came, she needed quick access, so disabling the access code seemed all she could do. She stuffed the phone back into her knee pocket and prayed for a miracle.

Across the warehouse, Hank pled. "I don't have the money. It went on bribes and organization. I had the goods, I swear. They have been stolen. You have to believe me."

"What you have to believe is that if we don't get our money back today, you will not live past tomorrow." When the accountant responded, his partner edged by his side. In response, the K-twins repositioned themselves behind Hank in support. The makings of a standoff formed between the two groups. Charlie jittered at the prospect of an escalation that could lead to her enemies' demise.

"There has to be a way," Hank floundered. "Every door was bolted and padlocked, and I had the only set of keys. Check the front door and the office." His gesture sent K2 lumbering out towards the shop front and K9 towards the stairs. In the intervening moments, Hank ran his oversized forearm across his withering brow.

K2 returned with a vacant expression. "It's all locked up, boss."

"Boss!" K9 strode down the stairs, brandishing the M4 Charlie had left behind.

Charlie screamed inside and braced for impact. The sight of K9 standing above them with an M4 set the accountant and his minder on high alert. Their hands immediately reached for their pistols. Hank sped to the bottom of the stairs between the two groups.

"Easy! Easy!"

For what must have been the first time in his life, K9 was innocent of any wrongdoing. The fact that the two visitors had taken up threatening stances made it impossible for him to keep the M4 pointing away from the would-be assailants. K2 came late to the illegal weapons party. Hank triangulated his glare between the protagonists, acting as go between.

"Relax. Relax. We're on the same side here." No one's expression seemed to agree with him.

The radio cracked. "Is everything okay? Where are you? Over."

Bassam's anxious tones crackled out of the handset that Charlie had left on the desk. She silently screamed at her own stupidity. The acrimonious standoff was broken. Curiosity reunited the gang. Hank took the lead and sent out the search party, shouting clear instructions for the group to find the thieves. The remaining lights were powered up across the entire warehouse. The sound of the gang frantically searching the space sent her mind racing with panic.

“Boss. Over here.” The excited yelp from the other side of the warehouse made it apparent that the open sewer had been discovered. She waited impatiently for the inspection to be carried out. Of course, Hank had all the answers.

“It’s too small. It's a decoy. Keep looking.” One by one, the potential hiding spots were checked and discounted. Close by, the sofas rustled and scuffed as they were pushed and pulled to the side. The fracas ceased and a quiet, rational voice carried across the warehouse.

“Boss?”

Charlie didn't know which of the K-twins was beckoning over his leader. What she did know was that she had been spotted. The curious group approaching her location confirmed her worst fears.

This is it.

Hank’s voice told her the game was up. “Come out before we blast you out.”

For now, Charlie was all out of options. “Don't shoot.” Her dirty hands and slashed wrists trembled into view. A matted bob of blonde hair followed. When her face and form rose into view, everyone except Hank threw out a look of surprise. She slowly climbed out from behind the sofa, Hank dragging her into full view by the hair. Charlie fought every urge to scream at the pain. A kick in the back of the knee brought her back down to earth. Despite the agony, she held her defiant silence. Not content with giving her one welcome, Hank lifted her head and punched her square in the face. Blood flew as he dragged Charlie across to the desk chair. Coughing blood, she choked down her tears and swallowed hard. Another blow hit its mark, sending her sprawling in pain.

The accountant observed, appalled at the violence but intrigued by the storyline. With measured menace, Hank stripped off his suit jacket and threw it on the table. The sick look in his eyes told Charlie that he was going to enjoy this. Painful blow after painful blow rained down on her. Every blow hit its mark. Fearing a loss of consciousness, Charlie held on. Before a final blow could take her off, the accountant motioned for his enforcer to stop the one-way contest. "Don't kill her. Yet."

Through a blur of tears and blood, Charlie peered out defiantly at her punisher. The emerging pain clamping her body to the chair made it impossible for her to focus on events.

Suddenly her world steadied. "Stop that! What is going on? Release that woman." The voice moving in from the open shutter door belonged to Rashad. Charlie's vision straightened, as did her back. Her friends in the police had clearly sent the guards outside the back door on permanent break.

Hank remained defiant. "Who are you?"

Rashad and his two guards marched in front of Charlie through a misty red haze. Their guns looked trained. "I am Chief Inspector Rashad of the Iraqi police. I demand you release that woman."

Hank directed his guns on the uninvited guests. "Back off. Walk away or die."

Before he could spit out so much as another syllable of threads, the accountant switched roles. "Well, Chief Inspector Rashad. Thank you for the introduction. That will make it easier for us to find you later. We will be delivering you and your entire family presents later today. You get to choose them right here, right now. Go backwards for silver, or step forwards for lead."

Charlie thought hard and fast, scrambled to her feet, and ran towards the already stalled Rashad. A back hander from Hank sent her sprawling. Scrabbling across the table, she floundered her way onto the chair. Only K2 helped her to her seat. Everyone else focused on the standoff with the dithering locals.

In the melee, K9 had shouldered his M4. The accountant provided one last statement. "Let me be truly clear, Inspector. If you do not leave now, we will come for you and your family. If you return at any stage, we will come for the families of everyone you return with. If we never see you again, we will hunt you down and make a significant donation to your favorite charity. Trust me, we will find you, and we will be grateful. As I said before, it's your choice."

Charlie fought the urge to beg for help, the odds were so stacked against them. A tiny part of her was even relieved when Rashad and his men lowered their weapons, held their gaze, and retreated from the field. On his unavoidable departure, Rashad fired her a visual apology. She caught it right between the eyes. He could do no more, and she knew it. Every other move would mean suicide.

After they left, Hank screamed for the back door to be closed. The quiet accountant's whispered tones carried more weight. "Just what kind of show are you running Hancock? Where did those guards go? More to the point, where did our gold go?"

Before Hank could answer, Charlie threw out her own blood-splattered accusations. "He stole it."

That earned her a forceful punch to the gut. "Shut it, bitch."

The accountant raised a delicate well-manicured hand. He had seen enough violence and was intrigued to find out more from the mystery woman. "Let her speak."

Charlie went for it before Hank could object. "I worked with Kirk. He was the brains of the operation. He was your main contact, correct?" The accountant's only response was to stop Hank from objecting. Charlie pressed on. "Kirk and I got too close. Hank got jealous and greedy and killed him."

Another smack in the face made the accountant move in more forcibly. "It seems you don't want her story to be told, Agent Hancock. I hope that's not the case. Let her speak."

Charlie dialed it up a notch. "He killed Kirk, stole the gold and—"

"Why would I do that?" Hank reeled.

The accountant lost his patience, raising his voice for the first time. "Let her finish!"

"He was worried that Kirk and I were going to cut him out, and he'd be left with nothing."

"And were you?"

Charlie gave a tired, bloody nod. "Yeah. He's an asshole."

Hank hit her again with enough force to send her head spinning and her eyes rolling back. This time the accountant smiled. "You asked for that one. I'd have hit you myself. What proof do you have?"

Her gargled drowsy response was barely audible. "None. That's why I'm here."

"How did you get in?"

She raised her chin and pointed it towards the overhead office. "I climbed in through the window."

"Go check!"

The accountant countermanded Hank's order to K9. "No. You go." In response, his colleague in black raced up the stairway, handgun now drawn. The accountant's interrogation continued as the search started overhead. "Is that your M4?"

"What's an M4?" quizzed Charlie.

Unlike Hank, the accountant remained cool under pressure. "Very good, but if you treat me like an idiot one more time, I will stick that very same M4 up your ass and empty the magazine. And for the avoidance of doubt, please understand that I do not have time for metaphors. Is that your M4?"

"No. It was here when I arrived. The place is full of them."

Above, the accountant's partner exited the office door. "The window's been busted open. There's nothing up here."

In a desperate attempt to get everyone back on message, Hank butted in. "This is bullshit. She's behind it all. She killed Kirk."

The accountant interjected. "You're saying Kirk is dead, yet on the way here, you said he'd been called away on special duties. That's why you had to step in."

Spitting blood, Charlie laid it on. "I'm confused. Are you lying now, or were you lying then?"

The testosterone was bulging out of Hank's temple at the prospect of the tables being turned on him. He ignored the taunt. "I'm not saying he's dead; she is!"

With every word, Hank's scales of injustice tipped Charlie's way. "I was there when Kirk got a text from Hank threatening to kill him."

Hank turned a very bruised shade of purple. "No way."

Now it was Charlie's turn to keep pummeling. "So, you're saying he's alive, and away on tour?"

"I don't answer to you!" Hank sputtered, murderous rage building in his eyes.

Things began to add up for the accountant. "True. You answer to me. Is he alive and on tour?"

"No, I'm saying I don't know where he is. What is this? Call him and we'll see what he has to say for himself." Hank knew Kirk's phone would condemn Charlie. "Call him."

The accountant liked the plan and pulled out his phone. "I have tried to call him, but his phone is dead." After tapping its buttons, he gave a positive glance that told the group of a dial tone.

Instantaneously, the desk vibrated as Hank's jacket started to buzz and ring. Before Hank could reach it, the accountant's minder reached across and retrieved the ringing mobile from the suit jacket. He flashed its screen to his partner. It simply read, *Agent.*

Hank was in trouble, and he knew it. "I've not seen that. That bitch had his phone!"

Before Charlie could react, she took another beating from Hank. As the punches flew, the distracted accountant casually examined Kirk's phone.

"Enough! There's a message here from you, Hancock:" 'I am coming for you. You're dead!'"

As the accountant spoke, an old Luger pistol made its way out from under his jacket. "Why would you send my partner a message like that?"

Everyone in possession of iron now set it out on display. The accountant's assistant aimed directly on the biggest threat, K9.

"To take my money for the shipment and lose it is one thing, but to murder a dear friend of mine and try to steal everything? You know the people I work for. You know this simply cannot end well."

Hank was ready to blow. "She did it—not me."

The accountant ensnared Hank's vision but pointed the gun at Charlie. "Quite possibly, but I am very much past the point of caring. Either I get my gold or my money back right here and now, or you both die." His voice and his Luger swung deliberately towards Hank. "She's not armed, so you'll be the first to get it."

"This is crazy!" screamed a quivering Hank.

The accountant gave him no credit. "I need to bring back the gold. It's your choice; our money or your head. For the last time, where's my gold?"

Hank was cornered. He pulled his gun across to point at Charlie. "I don't know, she knows. If you want to find out—" The accountant had heard enough.

Bang!

Bang!

His first shot had hit Hank in the chest. Hank's reactionary bullet smashed into Charlie's stomach.

Screaming in agony, she dropped like a stone. Wheezing, she fought for breath. Terrified, she clutched her side to stem the blood.

Bang!

The assistant nailed K9 in the head before he had the chance to bring the M4 into play.

Bang! Bang! Bang!

K2 evened the score by sending a hail of bullets through his brother's assassin.

The accountant and K2 leapt for separate cover.

Bang! Bang! Bang!

Overhead bullets flew in every direction.

Charlie writhed in a heap. Miraculously, her flak jacket had saved her for now, but death lurked nearby. Clutching her wrenching gut, heaving, and belching, she clawed her way to safety. K2 crawled to his brother's corpse. The accountant switched across to his dead partner to double up on his weaponry. Hank floundered on his back, blood, and bone splintering from his chest. He wheezed and gargled his way behind cover, digging his leather heels in for extra purchase. In his desperation, a scuffed shoe skidded across the concrete.

K2 let out an ungodly scream upon reaching his dead brother. One half of his brother's face was perfectly intact, but the other half had been scattered across the warehouse. Snatching the M4 and a couple of grenades, K2 took the nuclear option. With a bone-shattering yell, the grenade went flying, quickly followed by a barrage of bullets.

Boom !

Smoke and fiery fragments crashed the scene. Diving to the side, the accountant took a chunk of shrapnel to his back and shoulder. Oblivious to emotion or pain, he rose onto one knee and double fisted the content of both handguns into K2. The Kevlar took the strain until a single bullet sliced a neck vein, sending him crashing to the ground. The accountant limped across, bent over, and stuck a Luger in his face. With a snap of the hammer, the gun declared itself empty.

Noticing his victim's wounds, the accountant stood as tall as both stature and shrapnel would allow before jamming his heel firmly in K2's gushing and gurgling neck wound. With his victim drowning in his own blood, the accountant casually threw his Luger to one side and switched his partner's pistol into his gun-hand. He was enjoying the show. He drew out the process of checking his ammo for his own sick satisfaction. His heel squashed yet more bubbling blood from K2's wounded throat. The accountant grinned into K2's contorted, glinting stare of death. In a horrific twist of fate, a live grenade tumbled from K2's withered hand.

Boom!

The detonation blazed flesh and thundered through the air, sending fiery fragments into the adjacent ammunition. The chain reaction was cataclysmic. Sparks and shards screamed from the explosives, triggering a twisted pyrotechnic inferno. Explosions shredded the warehouse, ripping rafters and bending beams. Death ricocheted around in multiple guises. Charlie clung to the concrete floor as the air spun and spat around her. Under a hail of flames and phosphorous, she emptied her soul, crawling for her life towards some unseen sanctuary. After eventually righting herself, a flying knee crashed viciously into her face. She flapped and flailed in a tortuous bid to regain her senses. Hank's massive hands were on her throat, squeezing tight. She punched and wailed. Two punches to the bullet hole in his chest forced Hank to wince and stall, but his grip remained. All around, the fire raged, threatening to swallow the warehouse whole.

As the life drained from her, each landed blow lost efficacy and gained desperation. On the edge of succumbing to the suffocation, she grasped and stabbed the air in one last desperate attack.

"I'm nobody's bitch!"

Charlie jabbed the key from the forklift through his protruding jaw. The stubby key burst his neck, spraying blood in every direction. With a blood-curdling howl, Hank clawed at his neck and slumped to the floor, gargling and groaning. Flames and sparks crackled overhead. Under the searing heat, Charlie tried to regain her footing, only for another nearby explosion to send her reeling. Walls of flames blocked her exits and drove her backwards. Her only escape was the mezzanine. She stumbled and zigzagged through the explosions until a bitter and vicious blast threw debris and destruction across her path, knocking her sideways. The remnants from the last explosion now blocked the stairway. Fighting for breath, more flaming roof parts crashed into the stairway in front of her. Flames licked and spat all around.

Smoke and fear clawed at her lungs. More ammunition went up. There was no way out.

In frantic desperation, she lurched across to the desk and seized the radio before throwing herself headlong into the sanctuary of the open pit. Coughing and heaving, she righted herself in the well as smoke licked and billowed overhead. She cowered under the intense heat, smoldering in pain and panic. Ordinance cracked and whizzed overhead. The foul air being drawn through the underground network temporarily staved off her suffocation as the building blazed above.

She flicked the radio switch. "I'm trapped. Help! Please help!" The call went unheeded. She clambered down into the sewer in hopes of escape. Clawing at the walls of the tunnel, she scraped down into the pipe. Asphyxiation threatened her every move as she inched forward. Only two feet into the black duct, any hope of escape was abandoned. She could go no further. The lack of leverage, claustrophobia, suffocating stench, and enormity of the distances involved drove her back. Alone and abandoned, she screamed for help, knowing that no one could hear. The threat of suffocation was now her greatest fear. Down in the pit, the heat intensified. She fought to rehouse the steel cover, but the searing heat pushed her back under ground. In desperation, she screamed through her radio.

"It's Charlie, I'm in the sewer. You have time. Bring help. Keep pushing. I'm in the sewer!"

Still, no answer came.

She floundered in the filth and retrieved the previously discarded gas mask. The smoke belched and puked overhead as she grappled the smeared mask into position. The breathing eased, but the claustrophobia intensified to the point of implosion. The gas mask that clamped her face smothered her screams.

"Is there anyone there? Help! Help! Don't give up on me." The truth was, she was giving up on herself. The sparks and glimmers spat at her combats with increasing venom. Portents of a slow agonizing death raced through her smoldering mind. For the first time, she contemplated the misuse of her Glock. Her hand slid towards the weapon as each, and every alternative went up in smoke. *There is no way out.* With all hope gone, she lowered herself into a position of submission and pulled her gun. Memories flooded her fears as her life flashed before her. Fears for Pop turned to hope of his survival. Her helpless screaming intensified.

Suddenly, the little gold train crashed into the pit, painfully cracking her shins. Whilst untangling herself from the wreckage, the cinders set her hair alight. She dropped her Glock and flapped the flames from her hair. Gripping the unit with what strength she had left; she clicked the radio on and coughed through the desperation.

"Go! Go!" Both hands back on the unit, she stalled as her message went unheard. She knew the gas mask had to go if she was to be heard. After one last gasp of filtered filthy air, she ripped off the mask. At the top of her smoky lungs, she screamed as if her life depended on it. "Go! Go!"

The unit lurched forward, forcing her skull off the splattered bricks. The heat threatened to burst her combats as the skin on her legs rippled and twisted in agonizing defiance. She kicked out as the flames flashed into the pit beside her. Another lurch, and the unit took off. Whining and grinding, it took the strain of her small frame. With each jarring jolt her shoulders, hips, and elbows ripped the tunnel wall. The jagged rustic bricks and concrete gnawed away as she bowed and scraped down the drain. With the immediate threat of incineration now feet away, progress was dreadfully slow but less painful. The stench ripped through her singed nostrils and clawed at her throat. Uncertain of what lay ahead, she kept her head down as the unit trudged forward. She heaved and squirmed as the caustic sludge splattered her eyes and plastered her face. In the darkest reaches of the tunnel, there was no end in sight. The searing heat had been exchanged for a lack of air.

Her underpowered lungs heaved desperately to grasp what little oxygen remained in the tunnel. Without warning, her unrehearsed escape plan collapsed. Like an overworked pit pony, the unit carrying her to safety kicked out, faltered, collapsed, and died underneath her. Unable to shift forwards or backwards Charlie lay, drowning in burning sewage. Her radio, along with her hopes were gone, yet still she screamed. "I'm alive! Help!" Smoke leaked across her vocal cords, choking her dying words.

Behind her, the fire began to seep into the darkened tunnel. The flames crept up and along the tunnel walls. She felt the soles of her boots starting to melt. Her pitiful dance kicked out at the pain as her feet blistered. The surrounding smoke choked her eyes. She couldn't breathe.

A chain of explosions tore up the warehouse, sending shards and flares everywhere. The resulting firestorm ripped down the tunnel, scorching everything in its path. The furious flames burst past Charlie, setting her fatigues and hair alight. Section by section, the tunnel behind collapsed in on itself. In the flashing gloom, she swatted the flames from her blistering face. The inferno burst over her legs, making it impossible for her to reach for her Glock. In her rancid funeral pyre, she agonizingly writhed and raged at the inhumanity of her death.

The pain enveloped her.

All was lost.

CHAPTER 31

With a shuddering bang, the cable for the train snapped tight. The unit careered off, smashing through the flames. Charlie desperately clung to its edges. Every surface of her body shrieked and yelled as the tunnel took turns scratching, slicing, and biting chunks out of flesh as she skidded down the tunnel. Raw sewage crammed into her mouth and spat its way out of her nose and eyes—yet still, she held on. To let go would mean death. Another massive explosion brought an even greater back draft of fire and brick hurtling behind her. The wake spewed blazing shards and splinters into her body, yet still, she held on.

Relentless flames ripped across the slushy damp of the duct, torching her clothing. A blast of light hit her, but before she could react, her face cracked into the bricks of an open manhole. Blood, boots, wheels, and wires flew as the flashing flames chased their way in, around, and out of the torched crucible. With the flames turning to embers, Charlie grabbed at the open air. Through the heady confusion, a hand clamped her wrist. She looked up to find Rashad looming overhead in the backlit flashlight filling the backdrop. Leaning down like an angel from the heavens, he dragged Charlie's crumpled and blazing torso from the fire pit. He flailed sand all over her scorched and shattered torso.

His smothering hug enveloped her as life drained from her charred body.

CHAPTER 32

In the distance, an encouraging siren rang out, beckoning the child within her back to life.

"Charlie? Charlie?"

She floated back, peeled open her charred eyelids, and leered. The unmistakable odor of disinfectant climbed up her blistered nostrils and coated her swollen tongue. The room eventually settled into a hazy focus. Peering out of singed and swollen eyelids, a fat balding man who looked like Bassam after a shave gawked back at her. A crisp white collared shirt added to his disguise. His beaming face was as recognizable as it was undeniable. Against all customs and norms, he held her hand. In his eagerness, his grip tightened past the point of support and into the realms of discomfort. The unintentional pain helped drag her back into the room.

"Hello, my friend." Bassam was too busy squeezing her hand to produce any other form of response.

"Where am I? What happened?"

An ecstatic Bassam kissed her hand and opened the taps, full flow. "You are in the Balad Military Hospital, north of Baghdad. You were evacuated here from the warehouse fire." Spurred on by a cocktail of relief and joy, he answered every unasked question that he could imagine. "Rashad pulled you from the flames. We thought you were dead. You're safe. It's over."

Her body told her that things certainly didn't feel over. Her bandages wept and her body screeched. Chunks of charred skin creaked and cracked with every movement. She knew it would hurt if she laughed, but thankfully that time seemed a long way off.

"How did I get out?"

Bassam blushed. "I tied the train to the truck and drove off."

"You dragged me out?"

"I am sorry. I nearly killed you."

"It feels like you did. But I am alive. Thank you." It was Charlie's turn to squeeze too tightly. "How long have I been here?"

"This is your third day."

Panic ripped through her battered frame when her thoughts turned to Pop. "I gotta get to a phone."

"That's why I woke you." As Bassam spoke, he pulled out a large brown telephone that looked as if it would only receive calls from the 1970s. He gestured towards the large wall clock. "You have a call coming at six."

Bruised and confused, Charlie checked the clock. *Two minutes past six.*

Suddenly, the phone burst into life. The volume of the ring from the bell inside was only beaten by the length of its unfeasibly long receiver wire. Bassam retrieved the time machine from the other side of the room as Charlie painfully crackled and creased her protesting body into a sitting position. Excitedly, Bassam pushed the receiver hard against her blistered ear. When she winced at the pain, she watched him mouth one word as he cringed apologetically: *Sorry*. She forgave him in an instant.

"Hello?"

"Hello, girlie."

Charlie wept at the sound of her father's voice. "Pop. How are you? Are you okay? Where are you?"

"I am fine. Are you?"

"Never better," she lied.

As she croaked on, Bassam mimed his goodbyes. "Hang on, Pop, please." Charlie set him on temporary hold. Placing her hand over the mouthpiece she whispered, "Thank you." When he exited the metal door to the private room, a gracious Bassam made a big show of presenting the guard of honor. The friendly face and uniform of one of Rashad's rented policemen stood tall outside. The door had been delicately replaced into its frame.

"Sorry Pop. Where are you?"

"I am at the gas station down the mountain from the cabin. I called every day but couldn't get through. Yesterday they took the call and let me know you were okay."

"Who took the call?"

"I can't remember, I was just elated to heard you were okay. I was getting worried. I was worried sick. They left a message at the gas station for me to call this number at this time. I can't believe it—"

The tailing off of his sentence and the silence that followed showed that for the first time in Charlie's life, Pop was losing control.

"Are you all right, Pop?"

"Yes. I was just getting more coins for the phone. This thing is eating them." It sounded like it was Pop's turn to lie.

Charlie answered the unasked question. "I'm fine, Pop. Don't worry. I'm fine."

"Were you in danger?"

"Far from it. I had a blast."

"Then why are you in a military hospital?"

"Exhaustion."

"Burning a candle at both ends. Remember? I will give you all the details when we meet up."

"You do that. I was worried sick."

"I take it you left town when I called you."

"I had no choice. You were convincing. I came back here as quickly as I could. I went all *Home Alone* crazy and left traps all over the place. I slept in the chair most nights with my gun jammed at my side."

"What? You slept in your chair?"

"Every night, with my old Colt 1911 for company."

"Oh, I'm so sorry for putting you through this."

"It's nothing compared to what I imagine you've been though."

The lies flew like bullets. "Honestly, I have a few bruises and scratches. No big deal."

Pop still had concerns. "So, I'm safe?"

"Oh that? Oh, sorry. Yes. Yes. Forget it. That was my paranoia getting the better of me. You were always safe. I was just being a drama queen."

"You're never that." The line beeped. "Sorry, girlie, this thing is eating my money. I need to go. Same time tomorrow? I will bring a bag of quarters!" The panic in his voice told her that time was indeed running out.

"Okay, Pop. Same time tomorrow. Bring more cash! I love you."

"I lo—"

Not for the first time, a call with her father was cut short by fate and circumstance. The emotion this time around warmed her heart. The heavy handset fell by her side, as the pain she had hidden through the phone call reappeared from the shadows. There were truths to be told, but they would have to wait.

Struggling back into the least agonizing position, she sought any form of gentle distraction. Her imagination carried her off to the riverbank below Pop's cabin. In her mind, she lay out her fishing gear, checked the lighting and selected her favorite fly, the Bloody Butcher. Motioning the rod back and forth in her mind, she leaned in for a strike. Before the fly had time to kiss the river, she was asleep.

CHAPTER 33

The scent of jasmine blossoms carried in underneath the hastily fashioned awning, taking the strain away from the scorching overhead sun. A quiet section of the museum gardens had been commandeered to house the small ceremony designed to under-celebrate the return of the looted artifacts. The dimly lit abandoned undertones of the building's interior had been discounted as a suitable venue for the early morning event. Although early, the sun was already taking its toll on proceedings.

Front and center, two small rows of perspiring, overdressed dignitaries squirmed in hope of the event's early completion. A small selection of museum staff had been press-ganged onto the left flank. On the right sat a small table of finds, watched over by a posse of disinterested police. On the far side of the compound, Rashad's two deputies from the heist stood apart, proud yet uninvited. The boastful glows on the faces from the Central Bank added nothing to the lackluster event. They exchanged hastily printed certificates and fast fading smiles in front of a solitary photographer. Beside him, a passive reporter scribbled down the story he was told to report.

Across in the far shade, Charlie hid within the confines of her wheelchair, arm in a sling, ball cap covering her shaved and scalded head. Bassam and Rashad functioned as outriggers, keeping her upright and centered. The speeches wore on. Her patience wore out. There was no mention of the gold and no admission of guilt. Street looters were blamed, and the uninvolved Iraqi police were thanked. With the utterance of each insincere syllable, a sense of annoyance crept further over the trio. Rashad placed his bony hand tenderly on her shoulder. "I am sorry they did not do more."

Charlie bore no ill. "At least you're here. Uncle Sam is too busy winning hearts and minds to bother to even show up."

"We didn't do it for the medals," Bassam chipped in. Charlie freed the brakes on her chair.

"Take me for a spin around the museum. I have seen enough of today. Show me yesterday."

Her two-man entourage went to work. Rashad set her chair in motion as Bassam straightened the blanket over her knees. Why she needed a blanket in the ninety-five-degree heat was beyond Charlie, but she appreciated the gesture, nonetheless. Bassam eagerly held the doors open as, together, they left the scene of yet another crime. As they wandered the hallowed and haunted walls of the museum, each soul silently reflected on the recent events. They relived histories and retold tales. Gratitude flowed and dangers ebbed as they drifted through the halls.

Charlie turned to a smiling Bassam. "Were you with me every day at the hospital?"

"Mostly. They set aside a bed for me too. Don't tell my wife, but I enjoyed it. Rashad was there too."

A tear escaped over her cut and swollen cheek. "Did we get all of it?"

Bassam beamed and gently clasped her charred hand. "The gold? Yes."

Charlie melted at the realization she had made a difference. "Did we get the Chalice?"

Her savior dropped his head and his grip. "It is still missing."

"It was there. I held it."

"After the firefighters left, the looters came in. Everything was stripped. The place didn't officially exist, so they couldn't spare guards. Whatever survived has been taken. Everything is gone. But we have the gold and other precious artifacts."

For Charlie, everything hurt a little more. Her caregiver's words did not match his supportive nodding. "They are not saying how much was recovered. They are not saying anything was recovered. Technically, nothing was missing."

"A cover-up?"

"We can't hand back what they should not have lost."

"Who are *they*?"

"The Central Bank. Before the invasion, our most precious treasures were held there in secret vaults. The new donation will be handed over and taken back to the bank for safe keeping, for the people of Iraq."

"A public ceremony? The shipment will be jacked before it gets to the river."

"No. The gold is not part of the ceremony. This is only about the artifacts. I think you Americans call it low-key. It never happened."

The aches, pains, scratches, and burns told her a different story. "From where I am lying, it certainly feels like it happened."

Bassam tried his hardest to conceal their joint disappointment. "We know it did, and that's what's important."

To Charlie, a lifetime had passed since she first walked through the museum gates. So many memories. Such pointless loss.

They stopped at the section that once showcased the golden treasures from the Royal Cemetery at Ur. The glass on the cases was long gone, as were the contents. On the wall, a sign bore the only clues to the existence of the elusive Golden Chalice. Bassam brushed the layer of dust from the notice as Rashad pushed Charlie in for a closer look. She read the notice with heavy eyes. Bassam quivered with unconvincing hope. "We will find it one day."

Rashad took a darker stance. "Whoever in time to come lays hand on my jewelry with evil intent, may the great gods of the underworld impose on his corpse and spirit restlessness for all eternity."

"What is that?" inquired Charlie.

"The curse of Queen Yaba. It was carved into the entrance of her tomb. The tomb that housed the golden treasure."

"Gods of the underworld. I'll settle for that."

They shared stories and memories for what little time they had left together. When the time and transport came for her to leave, she was forced to stand. They parted poignantly under the damaged archway at the entrance of the Iraq Museum. She embraced a blubbering Bassam, incapable of speech. His entire energy was concentrated on squeezing the lifeblood from her body. Charlie welcomed the pain that accompanied the bear hug.

"Thank you, my friend. I owe you my life."

Rashad stretched to a lengthy handshake. "Thank you for everything you have done, Agent Glass. I am sorry for the bullets and the bang on the head."

Charlie stayed in the moment. "They led us to this place, my friend. And for that, I will always be grateful."

Rashad turned to face the future as they approached the waiting Humvee. "So, tomorrow you will see Abbas bin Firnas." Charlie's face showed she didn't recognize the name. "The statue outside the airport. The winged man. He will send you on your way."

A sallow, despondent sigh escaped the corner of her mouth. "Indeed, he will."

As she climbed into the back of the waiting Humvee, she did all she could to lift the edges of her quivering mouth. Her friends waved as the vehicle roared into life and bumped and barged its way into the passing traffic. Waving back, she hoped that they could both see her through the tiny, dusty, darkened window. Only when the museum disappeared from sight did she stop waving.

As the Humvee bundled its way through the traffic, the thought of leaving Iraq after such a short and torrid time, weighed heavily. It had been a truly ruinous affair that she had been incapable of ending it. Yet, despite all the murder and mendacity, this majestic country and its peoples had bewitched her. She looked forward to seeing the winged man again the next day. That would mean she was heading home.

CHAPTER 34

Rural Virginia, two months later

Sunbeams streaked between the ancient oaks that joined hands across the meandering river. Ripples glistened as they burst across the rocky outcrops outlining the edges of a shaded pool beneath Pop's isolated cabin. In the cool afternoon sun, the competition between Pop and Charlie was heating up. Whoever caught dinner would not need to prepare it.

Old Roger the big brown trout had yet to make an appearance.

Charlie had spent the first few days stateside in debriefings in downtown D.C. She had reserved her nights for report writing and recuperation. She caught up with paperwork not people. The interest shown by seniors to her reports and briefings fluctuated somewhere between minimal to zero. Mac was an outsider, a Brit, so he was first to hit the cutting room floor. The Bureau's need to distance themselves from scandals with foreign powers ensured that Kirk was designated as MIA. Dempsey had died in a fall, and Wayne, the dark web orchestrator, had mysteriously never even existed. The revelation that Hank was missing, presumed dead after a heroic firefight with arms smugglers, was particularly galling to Charlie.

In the solitude, Pop opened up. "Why didn't you go?"

Where?

"Hancock's posthumous medal ceremony."

"It's not my scene."

"Not your scene? Some might look upon it as disrespectful."

Charlie, like Old Roger, didn't bite.

"Your no-show must have raised eyebrows. There's something you're not telling me."

There's a lot I'm not telling you.

"The daughter I raised is not that disrespectful."

"Your point is?"

"He was part of it, wasn't he?"

"Part of what?"

"That Serpent organization."

"What makes you think that?"

"Under any other circumstance, you'd have been at that ceremony."

Charlie couldn't argue with the logic. "All that's behind us now. Officially, the project had been closed. We secured the return of a few looted artifacts by some guilt-ridden thieves."

"Hardly the win you were looking for. No medals, no commendations, and no awards."

"Thanks for reminding me."

"I don't mean to pry, but you risked it all for them, and what did you get in return?"

"My record lists attendance with the project team in Iraq."

In her heart she knew the detail was a worthless accolade, like the kind dished out at those crappy sports days where every kid gets a prize. Having her father point it out to her didn't really help.

"I'm reminded of something my friend Bassam said to me back in Iraq: 'We didn't do it for the medals.'"

"I don't mean to cast a cloud on your achievements—I am so proud of you. I just wish the world could know the part you played. Heck, I'd like to know the part you played. Those are battle scars, not paper cuts."

"One day I might tell you, Pop, but for now, you just need to know this..." She placed her palm on his arm. "Throughout the ordeal I was more worried about you than I was for myself."

Charlie looked away to avoid teary eye contact. Reflecting at the edge of the meandering pool, she knew, deep down, that one day she would be fine. For now, all she wanted to do was hook a juicy trout. Her fly flicked and dipped as the lazy afternoon clung to the horizon. As the fly drifted off, she settled down for a snooze. Suddenly, a juicy fish splashed and dashed, as if taunting her. Old Roger was back.

In a panic to win the day, a last-minute switch of flies was executed, to her father's amusement. Before her new secret weapon could be launched, another battle seemed lost. With a yelp of delight, Pop struck. His rod hit hard and buckled as he lifted the tip high above his head. Amazingly, a juicy trout flipped into sight in an overarching bid for freedom.

"Wow. It's old Roger! It's Old Roger!"

"Don't reel. Keep your rod up."

Overcome by excitement, Pop's yelling hit fever pitch. "I told you the *bloody butcher* would do the trick didn't I?" Charlie sped for the landing net just to get away from Pop's running commentary. "Ten-pound line, dry fly, gentle mending, and the perfect strike angle. I'll teach you it some day! That's if what I have is even teachable."

Old Roger leapt for freedom. "Woah!"

Charlie leapt too. "Just concentrate!"

"Pan fried!"

"What?"

"I'll have him pan fried, just a little butter."

Old Roger's next leap brought an even bigger yelp of delight for Pop. "Maybe use some of that wild rosemary growing out back."

As the old trout flailed and floundered his way into the landing net, Pop was enjoying his win. Tired and defeated, Old Roger eventually slithered into Charlie's waiting net.

"He's a beauty. The biggest I've seen pulled from this river."

"Must be the biggest fish in the county." Pop reached for the camera and turned just in time to find Charlie sliding Old Roger back into the river.

"What the hell?"

With a grateful flip of the tail, the trout darted back into the dark river depths.

"We'll have fish tomorrow, Pop. I've seen enough killing."

Her father was flustered by her vanishing fish act, but he understood. "I'm sorry, girlie, I never thought."

"You've finally gotten the better of him; surely that's all that truly matters."

Pop pulled her close. "I've got you home. That's all that truly matters."

When the pair held each other, Charlie's memories flooded back. "Remember the last time we hugged here?"

"Sure! We found Grant's button."

Charlie's laughter filtered through the leaves. "We?"

"It was quite the find. I see you're still wearing it."

"Sure am."

"It has served you well."

For Charlie, some stories were better left untold. "You can say that again."

Pop's oversized arms cosseted his daughter's fragile form. Despite his tender touch, the pain was intense. The scars had not yet healed—not that she let it show. All too soon for Charlie's liking, Pop let her go. "Okay, well get over there with that net. I at least need evidence of your crime."

"My crime?"

"Stealing my fish!"

Charlie chuckled. "Grand theft aqua."

Pop took a snap, unaware of Charlie's attempted humor. A gruff humph drowned the sound of the old shutter before he called it a day. "Let's get back. No point in being out here if we're not going to catch our dinner."

The pair trudged forward, tender hand in old hand. "So, whiskey tonight, Pop?"

Her father was restrained. "I've been advised by the doc to cut back."

"Sorry. I forgot. So, whiskey tonight, Pop?"

He yielded. "Sure!"

Under a blanket of laughter, they meandered, glad to be home and glad to be together. After the short lumber uphill, they took turns cleaning the mud from their boots on the scraper at the bottom of the cabin steps. In modern parlance, the cabin was off the grid. It needed an upgrade to fall into the "rustic" category. A late sun shot a gentle heat wave across their faces as they stomped up onto the veranda. With the rods placed in the rack and their baskets set aside, the pair took time to hold each other as tightly as her injuries would allow.

"Come on. Let's see what we can muster up from that larder."

Pop led her through the cabin door. Suddenly, a bulky figure lurched from behind the door, slamming it shut with an almighty crash. The cabin and its inhabitants shook. Pop charged in front of Charlie in a vain attempt to shield her from the intruder. The pair stammered, awestruck in the presence of the hulk looming over them. Dressed head to toe in white plastic overalls, he brandished an automatic pistol. Charlie glowered at her would-be assassin. Despite his most valiant efforts, Pop was reeling.

Charlie stepped to the fore. "Who are you? What do you want?"

The attacker pushed his cowering victims back into the room. "You know who I am, and you can guess what I want."

His voice and the face only rang alarm bells. "I don't know you."

The gunman sneered. "Think again."

Charlie glowered vacantly until a wave of realization knocked her sideways. "The Ritz?"

"'For one so forward, you are quite backward.' Wasn't that what you said?"

Railing against her inner terrors, she searched for clues and ideas. His ice-cold chiseled gaze hammered her soul. "Miroslav?" Her attacker seemed taller than before. The trouser legs of his plastic suit had been tucked inside his rubber boots. Latex gloves closed off the professional hitman look. He stood too far away to lunge at but was close enough that he couldn't miss if he fired.

She needed time. "Why? Why are you doing this?"

His accent thickened as his words darkened. "Simple. You stole my gold, and I am here to kill you."

Pop imploded at the realization of the inevitable. Floundering herself, Charlie couldn't support him. He fell backwards, scattering the side table and lamp onto the wooden floorboards. The bulb smashed into pieces across the floor. As he staggered back to his feet, Pop slashed his hand on the shards of broken glass. Blood spewed, yet he clung on. Charlie helped her father up into his fireside chair and turned on her attacker.

"He had nothing to do with this. Leave him alone."

"He brought you into this life. That's enough."

Charlie faltered. "I was only doing my job."

"And how well you did. Much better than we had planned."

"Planned?"

"Of course." Miroslav seemed to take perverse pleasure in the impending executions. "We were being threatened with a shutdown, just as our biggest haul was in the chamber. We needed a dumb patsy to relay positive news."

"I was a plant?"

"When I followed you to the Ritz, I thought you were the one. A stuck-up bimbo that needed an old button to help make decisions. Perfect for the job in hand."

"The job?"

"Fill out forms saying everything was fine. We even planted evidence, but you were too dumb to find it."

As Pop's bloody wound leached, he allowed Charlie to press hard on it. "I was smart enough to wreck your mission."

"And that's why I'm here. You cost me fourteen million dollars."

"They reported twelve million."

Miroslav scoffed at the irony. "You can trust no one."

Charlie clung on. "So, you're the Serpent?"

Miroslav loomed closer. "You really know nothing." He lifted the elastic forearm on his CSI-unfriendly suit and exposed a tattoo. At its heart, a snake wrestled with an Eagle for superiority. "*We* are the Serpent. French Foreign Legion. First Regiment. The best of the worst."

He spat venom as he brought a Beretta into her line of sight. "And I am here to prove that, to the pair of you." Whimpering and powerless, Pop bent himself double.

"You did well Agent Glass, but your race is run."

Charlie leapt forward in one last desperate bid for survival. "Please no!

Bang! Bang!

Charlie reeled. Blood gushed and splashed as Miroslav swayed and stumbled backwards. His torso ripped open further as Pop lurched through a haze of gun smoke, blazing away with an old Colt. Every bullet hit its mark. Miroslav lay gargling as a backdrop of black blood oozed across the timber floor. Unsteadily, Pop swayed over the grotesquely disfigured writhing body. He squinted down the barrel of the gun at the blood-splattered intruder. Before Charlie could react, Pop yanked the old Colt's trigger one more time, sending his last bullet smashing through Miroslav's right eye, smattering brain matter all over the scene.

Pop stared down in terror at the bloody aftermath, never losing contact with the one-eyed corpse.

Charlie clung to the floor, stupefied, unable to understand the terrorizing turn of events. Pop caught his breath and pointed his pistol across to his old chair. "I told you; I slept here with my old Colt."

"So, tipping over the table?"

"I needed to something to get to my gun."

The pair collapsed into each other's arms, numbed by events.

The old pistol clattered to the floor.

Gun smoke swirled.

CHAPTER 35

Paris, six months later

Charlie sat alone on her rooftop balcony, enduring a bituminous espresso. The tiny space was just big enough to house a withered pot plant, a small bistro table, and a solitary folding chair. Her oversized housecoat warded off the late afternoon chill, skirting the Paris skyline. As she swept her bangs to one side, the fading sunlight warmed the panels of her soul. She had been in a contemplative mood since her return from the US as she struggled to understand recent events. The D.C. cover-up that followed her ordeals had erased everything except her memories. To eradicate any traceable links, the FBI had recorded Miroslav's death as a justifiable shooting of a nameless drifter committing a home invasion. Nothing made the press. Nothing made sense. She fought to fathom the circumstances and her responses. The authorities could make everything disappear except her remembrances. The betrayals still hurt, but like her scars, she knew they would heal. She set down the miniature coffee cup in favor of a photograph. Under the Babylonian archway of the Iraq Museum stood her team. Lost faces from a past too recent to haunt her. Tariq, Hank, Dempsey, Mac, Kirk. Her friends. Her enemies. All gone.

She had traveled to Iraq, clueless and next to useless. Whilst she had not returned fearless, she was proud that she had stood tall when it had mattered most. Despite the fears, the losses, the deeds done, and pains endured, she had loved the mission, the danger, and the intrigue. Her naivety had been replaced by skepticism, but that could help keep her alive in the treacherous times to come. She had tasted adventure. There was no turning back.

With the sun disappearing behind a cold unlined cloud, Charlie eased her way back inside. Across at her little dresser, the lopsided lid of her old cigar box was pulled open. The Iraq Museum photograph was placed inside. The lid stayed open for one more minute. She took a moment to retrieve the small cuneiform tablet she had brought back from Iraq. Misplaced in her combat trousers was the excuse she gave herself. She marveled at the artistry within and the antiquity around the little clay treasure. She was now part of its history, and it was now part of hers. One day she would return the piece to the Iraq Museum, but that day was not today. For now, it was set for safe keeping back in her memory box. With great ceremony, she pulled her talisman over her head and studied it, as if for the first time. She adored every angle before sending it off into the battered old box with a gentle kiss and a "Thank you." Setting the amulet center stage, she flipped closed then centered the buckled lid.

Standing to stretch her back, she turned to stare longingly out over the Parisian rooftops.

The solitude was broken when her BlackBerry buzzed and flashed a message.

A smile broke across her face as she read the text.

AFTERWORD

Between April 10-13, 2003, over 15,000 objects were stolen from the Iraq Museum.

More than 8,000 precious artifacts remain unaccounted for.

***

Since the end of the Cold War, there have been over fifty armed conflicts worldwide. The black-market trafficking of small arms remains a one billion-dollar-a-year global business. Around five hundred thousand people are killed each year by the six hundred million small arms in circulation.

***

The Golden Chalice of Ur remains lost.

***

NOTE OF THANKS

Thank you very much for taking the time to read my debut novel. I hope you loved reading it as much as I enjoyed writing it. If you loved the book, I'd be keen to hear your thoughts. Quality reviews are an author's lifeblood. They have the power to make or break careers. I'd be delighted if you would take a moment to leave a positive book review on your preferred book purchasing site. - Many Thanks

KEEPING IN TOUCH

To keep pace with Charlie's adventures, learn more about the issues uncovered, receive updates, advance viewings, offers, freebies, and much more please visit jj-carson.com.

This book is a work of fiction. All incidents, dialogue, and all characters, are products of the author's imagination and are not to be construed as real. Where real-life locales, articles, or incidents may appear, the situations, events, and dialogues concerning those entities are entirely fictional and are not intended to depict actual events or to change the entirely fictional nature of the work. In all other respects, any resemblance to actual persons, living or dead, events, or locales is entirely coincidental.

For more information, or to book an event, please contact the author at www.jj-carson.com.

Book and Cover Design by JJ Carson

ISBN - Paperback: 978-1-7393956-0-5

ISBN - Hardcover: 978-1-7393956-1-2

BISAC Codes

FIC050000 FICTION / Crime

FIC031010 FICTION / Thrillers / Crime

FIC022080 FICTION / Mystery & Detective / International Crime & Mystery

First Edition: August 2023

Printed in Great Britain
by Amazon

27917621R00214